Circle of Deception

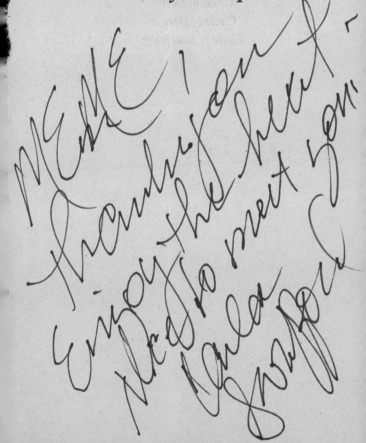

By Carla Swafford

Circle of Desire
Circle of Danger
Circle of Deception

Circle of Deception

CARLA SWAFFORD

AVON

An Imprint of HarperCollinsPublishers

Excerpt from *Circle of Desire* copyright © 2011 by Carla Swafford.

Excerpt from *Circle of Danger* copyright © 2012 by Carla Swafford.

Excerpt from *Nights of Steel* copyright © 2012 by Nico Rosso.

Excerpt from *Alice's Wonderland* copyright © 2012 by Allison Dobell.

Excerpt from *One Fine Fireman* copyright © 2012 by Jennifer Bernard.

Excerpt from *There's Something About Lady Mary* copyright © 2012 by Sophie Barnes.

Excerpt from *The Secret Life of Lady Lucinda* copyright © 2012 by Sophie Barnes.

EPub Edition JANUARY 2013 ISBN: 9780062225337

Print Edition ISBN: 9780062225344

10 9 8 7 6 5 4 3 2 1

To my sister and brother

Acknowledgments

I'M FORTUNATE TO be a Romance Writers of America member in three Alabama chapters: Southern Magic, Gulf Coast, and Heart of Dixie. They are filled with some of the most talented and giving authors imaginable. Thank you for being so good to me.

Chapter One

THE NAKED MAN swayed back and forth, his ankles bound by duct tape and rope to a massive hook suspended from the ceiling. A bare light bulb at the end of a long wire swung in the opposite direction, casting drunken shadows across every inch of his sweat-coated skin.

Abby Rodriguez's gaze followed the movement of Rex Drago's body as if watching a tennis match in slow motion.

"Enjoying the view?" His bored and resigned tone barely hid his sarcasm. Even upside down, his eyes taunted her.

"Yeah. Actually, I am." She sat cross-legged a few feet away on the warehouse floor, her favorite Sig in one hand, resting on her knee. "You've been working on your abs. Got them looking good. Almost an eight-pack. Maybe you could get a job modeling for romance novels." With his big arms tied behind his back, she admired how the muscles expanded each time he struggled with the tape. A sparse swirl of hair rested between his pecs and trailed to a thin line over his abs toward his groin.

"Funny. Real funny." He cleared his throat. "Get me down."

"Having a problem with your sinuses? I guess hanging like that"—she waved in his direction—"bottom up, could cause a problem. Kind of chilly in here too."

"Where's Jack and Nic?" His coal-black hair, cut high and tight, almost brushed the floor with each pass. She missed his long hair but the military style gave him a more deadly look. Heaven and Hell knew he already intimidated enough people with his six-foot-five height.

"Nic is monitoring the silent alarm, making sure it's off and no backup wired in. Jack's somewhere nearby, probably taking out the guard we spotted in the back that Savalas left behind."

Tilting her head, she looked a little harder at the tattoos running across his biceps on each arm. She never remembered seeing them on him before. Motivated less from curiosity than from her attempt to avoid staring at what dangled from his groin. Oh, yeah, that appendage had always been worth admiring, but the man already had an ego the size of . . . well, of his cock, and he needed no one stroking— For goodness' sake, her mind refused to stay on the problem at hand. Hand? Her gaze darted to his gorgeous penis and then away.

She sighed. Every time she worked with Rex, her libido revved up at the most inappropriate times. The man oozed sex appeal. With cheekbones to die for and eyes of a clear gray ringed by darker gray, Rex had looks that were saved from being too perfect by the scar that ran across his nose and near the corner of his lip to a point on his left cheek. Then again, the scar only added to his aura of danger.

He growled. "Are you planning on cutting me down anytime soon?"

She grinned big, knowing how much he hated depending on anyone's help. "Well—"

"Abby, dammit! Quit playing around." His body began swinging harder as he fought the ties.

"Is that any way to talk to a friend?"

"Some freaking friend," he muttered.

"What did you say?" She looked a little harder at one of the tattoos. Tiny writing around a delicate Valentine heart appeared to move as he flexed his bicep. Was it for a current girlfriend? Weird, he'd never been into visual displays of love. Even when he'd asked her to marry him years ago, it had been during a private moment and more of a statement than a proposal. Things changed. People changed.

Gunfire echoed through the large warehouse. What trouble had Jack stumbled across? Time for her to quit teasing the big baby swinging frantically in front of her and let him go.

"If I ever get down from here, I'm going to spank that sweet ass of yours red."

"Ha! That's no way to talk to the person who's saving you." She almost flinched when his glare turned to ice. Those beautiful eyes used to be filled with love when he looked at her, but no longer. Years ago, she'd made sure of that.

The jingle of a gun strap caught her attention. In a smooth move, she twisted, aiming her gun at the person behind her.

"What the fuck!" Jack Drago, Rex's brother, jumped out of her Sig's sight, clutching an M4 rifle across his torso. "Quit being a pain in the ass and cut him down. Savalas has more men coming and we don't have time for you two to reminisce." He glanced over his shoulder, checking the perimeter.

"I don't need help, especially *hers*." Rex continued to glower at Abby.

She wanted to laugh, but at the same time, the thought of Rex being killed scared her more than she wanted to admit. No way would she ever let him know that. She'd broken his heart once and he'd done the same to hers. She planned to never let it happen again.

"Fine, then! I'll put you out of your misery." She raised her gun and pointed it at Rex.

"Wait! Hold on! Abby, dammit!" He twisted and struggled with the binding around his wrists, causing his body to flop around like a hooked trophy fish.

The shot reverberated in the large warehouse and cut off Rex's shouting as he fell to the floor. She'd always been an excellent shot, and the little bit of duct tape and rope never had a chance.

"For Pete's sake, what the hell's going on here? Rex?" Nic ran to the big guy moaning on the floor. Her ball cap flew off, releasing a short ebony braid. "Oh my gosh, oh my gosh! Did she shoot you? Tell me where you're bleeding."

"Abby, dammit! You could make a preacher cuss. What if he'd cracked open his skull? We don't need to be slowed down dragging his big ass out of here." Jack nudged Abby to the side and stood over his brother while Nic cut the rope and tape off his wrists and ankles.

"My last name is Rodriguez," Abby said, arms folded over her chest. She secured the Sig in her shoulder holster. Frustration stiffened her back and lifted her chin. She refused to let the men browbeat her.

"What?" Jack squinted at her in confusion.

"You and Rex obviously think my last name is *dammit.*" She concentrated on staring back at Jack while Nic rattled on about Rex's cuts and bruises. She hated seeing the other woman fussing over him. For some inane reason, she wanted to be the one to do it.

Rex stood, drawing her reluctant attention as he rubbed the marks left behind by the bindings. He towered over Nic. Abby wanted to push her out of the way and run her hands over his hard body, checking for broken bones, making sure he was okay.

"You're crazy," he said, glaring at her.

That snapped her out of the mushy feelings. One eyebrow lifted, she said, "Yes, I am. And don't you forget it." With a flip of her hair, she sauntered off.

REX WATCHED THE come-hither sway of her hips as she strolled away. One day her smart mouth would push him too far. Then he'd pull her over his knee and give that nice round bottom the spanking it deserved. Only thing was, his hands would want to roam into darker, moister, hotter areas of her body.

He dragged his gaze to the woman standing next to him.

"Out in the van, I got you a new cell phone with all the fancy gadgets on it that you like. Plus, the prettiest Glock .357 with a buttload of magazines. Should be enough ammo to make mincemeat out of anyone who tries to take you again," she said. Nic Savage was the OS Sector's chief security officer. Though her job normally confined her to headquarters, she'd somehow convinced Jack to let her tag along on the rescue mission.

The OS, the Onyx Scepter, had recently reunited with its parent organization, The Circle, becoming one of the many sectors under its umbrella. The overall purpose of The Circle as a hired gun of the world had evolved over the years until it had nearly imploded when one of its founders decided to kill his former operatives. Now under a saner—though by how much was still up for debate—leader, Arthur Ryker, The Circle was in the midst of redefining its role in the dangerous world of protection. While the OS, possessing the elite of the deadly operatives, continued to run the riskier missions, The Circle worked on recruitment, training, logistics, and other less-risky operations.

Certain aspects and agendas of the organization Rex would most likely never understand or know, no matter the position he held, but basically The Circle, with the

OS doing the dangerous work, was on the right track, no longer killing for killing's sake.

"You don't have anything that will fit me in that bag of tricks of yours, do ya?" He nodded to the backpack Nic carried over her shoulder.

"Yeah. Abby gave me a heads-up when she spotted you." She tossed a bundle his way.

He caught the clothes and pulled on black jeans, sans his normal boxer briefs—none were in the pile—and a T-shirt. Instead of turning away and watching for trouble, Nic soaked in his every move. Her face flushed and dark eyes heated in admiration.

Rex sighed. He appreciated her helping out, like with the clothes and weapons, but he really wished she'd show a little more restraint during the mission. She was kind-hearted and had a crush on him the size of Stone Mountain. When he'd been in a low spot in his life, he'd let her crawl into his bed. She'd been a soft willing body, the warmth he needed to get through the nights after he'd lost his fiancée. He'd given in to Nic a few more times over the years, but he thought he'd been clear. They would never be more than friends. They had merely scratched an itch.

Then a little over nine months ago, he'd tried to explain they wouldn't be getting together again. How could he? He'd found out the woman he loved was still alive.

Abby.

One day they were in love, planning to get married, and then the next, while on assignment in Peru, he'd received the news she'd been captured by The Circle. At the time, a psycho named Theo Palmer controlled the reins of The Circle, and a lot of operatives were dying. The horror of the following weeks blurred together. Then it all came to a screeching halt when the pictures of her burned body turned up on the Internet.

Nausea bubbled in his stomach. He fought the sick feeling that always returned when he remembered the pictures. Rubbing his eyes, he shook off the memory. That had been a bleak period in his life.

For five years he'd believed she was dead. Then she'd helped a friend escape The Circle last year and returned safely to the OS. She was different. Colder, more dangerous than that gun she carried with her at all times. He'd heard she'd called herself A. J. during the time she worked for the evil son of a bitch Palmer. He had a hard time wrapping his mind around the thought of her accepting that way of life. The Circle under Palmer invoked nightmares many would never overcome. The ex-commander had claimed others had attacked Abby, but evidence uncovered so far pointed to Palmer being the one who had ordered her beaten before she was brought into their fold. Who knew his reasoning? But the man rarely did anything without an ulterior motive.

Over and over again, he'd tried to get her to talk to him about her time there, to explain to him how she'd been alive and working for the organization they'd considered the enemy, and why she hadn't returned to the OS years earlier. He was so freaking tired of trying to piece everything together.

Instead, she treated him like a mongrel in the midst

of a purebred kennel. She danced away from him every time he came near, snapping and taking nips from his hide with her smart-ass comments. Yet he still had more pain to endure.

The whispers began. He wished he could close his eyes and tell them they lied, but too many facts pointed to one person. His bastard of a brother loved taking other men's women to bed and Abby's name topped the list.

His brother had left the OS years before to work for The Circle. At that time, the rumors spread between the organizations that Jack had been in love with Theo's mistress and later had a fling with another operative's wife. No woman in a relationship appeared to be safe from his brother's attention.

Though it had been years since they were lovers, Jack and Abby were still chummy. So Rex watched his ex-fiancée and his brother tease each other and pretend to be comrades in arms and nothing else. But he knew. The *hell* he knew. They still shared a connection, probably friends with benefits, and he had no idea how to change it.

"Rex?"

How many times had Nic called his name? He pulled his gaze from the direction his traitorous brother and Abby had gone.

"What?" He bent down to slip on his socks and tie his boots. When he straightened, he squeezed his eyes shut for a couple seconds as the room shifted and spun.

"Are you coming?" Nic tilted her head toward the exit. "I've got the van running outside the door."

He blinked and rubbed his eyes again to clear the fuzz outlining her silhouette in the dim warehouse. Hanging upside down for a few hours would affect anyone's equilibrium. After a deep breath, he shifted his chin, hoping to make his ears pop and clear his head.

One lesson he learned that day was to never turn his back on the likes of Mikolas Savalas.

All he'd had to do was pick up a sample of the new ammo hitting the black market, ammo that several local terrorist groups were dying to get their hands on. The briefcase filled with money was a simple thank-you to Savalas.

When Rex walked into the warehouse near Atlanta, he'd been greeted by some of Savalas's men and several others he hadn't recognized. In seconds, and with no ammo in sight, guns were pointed at his head and the money was gone. Why had Savalas double-crossed him? What happened to honor among thieves? One thing was for sure—he couldn't wait to get his hands around that fat bastard's neck. Maybe he'd string him up naked and see how he liked it. Until then, he needed to get back to the OS Sector and track down the shipment.

From what Rex had heard about the ammo, it had to be a bunch of bullshit. It wouldn't be the first rumor about a high-tech bullet. No way could it be as dangerous as what they said, but he wanted that shipment, regardless of what was inside.

Feeling sure of his balance now, he nodded at Nic and started toward the door. After no more than ten steps, he became light-headed and stumbled. Hell, being dropped on his hard skull hadn't helped. He reached out to a nearby stack of crates and misjudged the distance, causing them to wobble. The top one crashed to the floor, barely missing his feet, and spilled its contents.

The first thing he noticed was the shoebox-sized plastic green boxes. They appeared to be the normal dry storage types for stowing several rounds of ammo. He slowed to a stop. One of the boxes had popped open. Something looked strange inside. Instead of the usual fifty-round cardboard cases, individual cartridges sat in their own small bubble-wrapped pockets. A long silver cartridge, jarred out of its slot, rested on top of the others. Grooves ran from the tip to the base of the silver cartridges. Rex had seen photos of them; yet seeing the real deal sent a chill sliding down his spine and filled his gut with apprehension.

When he'd arranged to meet with Savalas, he'd been working a lead on a large ammo shipment for the Inferno, an organization that believed the only way to bring in a new world order was to see the old one burn. The Savalas family was known to dabble in anything illegal but normally stayed away from the more exotic, hazardous merchandise.

He picked up the cartridge on top. Its design wasn't the only thing different. The Circle had heard the ammo was more dangerous than an armor-piercing type. A microchip the size of a period in a sentence placed at the tip of the bullet turned it into a miniature guidance missile. The design helped it to go through buildings and find the warm bodies inside. The little piece of metal could even seek out people within several yards of its maximum trajectory. That meant it could change course on its own. The sniper didn't have to be an excellent shot.

And that wasn't all it could do. A special chemical coated the bullet, so whoever it hit would explode into flames on contact. That was why the Inferno wanted it and started calling it Hell's Purifier. The space-age deadliness of the ammo scared the bejesus out of him. He only hoped the rumors were full of shit.

"Nic." Without looking, he knew she was nearby. When was she not? "Go get Jack. And fast," he said in a low, even tone. No need to frighten her.

"What's that?"

"Remember me telling you about the ammo the Inferno claimed they would use to take over the world?"

"Yes."

"This is Hell's Purifier."

"Holy moly!"

Normally he would laugh at her old-fashioned expletive, but he couldn't find it in him as he stared at the shiny cartridge.

Her hasty footsteps diminished as she raced toward the van and Jack. In no time, Jack stood next to him, and Rex wasn't surprised when Abby showed up a second later. Wherever one went, the other followed.

And he didn't like it one damn bit.

Chapter Two

ABBY'S HEARTBEAT SPED up when she spotted the cartridge between Rex's forefinger and thumb. Instead of holding the full length, casing to tip, he held only the casing end. They'd seen drawings and pictures but never thought they would actually find the shipment so quickly. Or maybe she'd hoped they'd discover it to be a big joke. The ammunition was the equivalent of napalm in a bullet.

"Fuck!" Jack reached down and picked up another green box. When he lifted the lid, silver glinted beneath the warehouse lighting.

"Yep, we will be if we don't get them loaded into the van, quick." Rex slipped the cartridge back into its pocket and eased the box into the crate.

"True that." Jack nodded. "Let's get to work and get out of here. Savalas won't be happy when he finds out his people let us walk out with them. A mil and a half for"—he counted—"three crates. Bloody hell, he's going to be pissed."

"His *dead* people aren't quite letting us do anything, but I know what you mean. What did he say when he strung you up?" Abby nodded toward Rex.

"He wasn't here. I recognized a few of his men, but the bastard wasn't with them, at least not where I could see him." He stood and rubbed the back of his neck. "I don't think we need to worry about Savalas. He knew when he screwed me over that he forfeited anything I found. He'll blame his own people and hope I don't sic The Circle on him later."

Abby pulled out her satellite phone and called the backup that waited down the street. Ten minutes later, with the crates loaded in the van, they were traveling up Fulton Industrial Boulevard toward the OS Sector.

Nic sat in the front passenger seat, one leg bent to the side so she could watch Rex drive the van. The woman acted like a teenager with a big crush. Some people never grew up.

Abby shook her head and then leaned across the cargo bay, elbows on knees, and softly said to Jack, "You know that with us stealing the crates, it won't slow Savalas or the Inferno for long. They're getting them from somewhere and someone, and all they have to do is produce more. We need to find the source."

Hairs standing straight up on the back of her neck brought her head around, and her gaze met light gray eyes in the rearview mirror. She imagined that with her and Jack leaning toward each other and whispering, it looked as if they were planning a rendezvous later.

Nic poked Rex's shoulder with a finger. "Watch the road." She glared at Abby as if it was her fault.

What was the woman's deal? Unable to resist taunting her, Abby lifted her eyebrows and pursed her lips as if in a kiss. The look she received warned her she better not ask Nic for a new weapon anytime soon, as firearm acquisitions fell under her jurisdiction. The small woman could easily turn the gun on her.

"Quit irritating Nic." Jack shook his head.

Abby chuckled. "Okay, bossman." She probably should be more respectful, but Jack never relied on a strict code of conduct. Even after Ryker appointed him as the OS Sector commander, Jack treated his operatives almost like partners. But everyone knew if they failed at their assignments, he wouldn't have a problem kicking their asses. In the back of everyone's mind was the memory that, only a year ago, to disobey orders within The Circle would've meant death. How the new and improved Circle would react was still up for debate, and no one wanted to be first to find out.

"Are you having a problem separating your feelings for Rex from your job?" Jack's steady gaze said more. That he wouldn't put up with her bullshit. "I can find someone else to take your place."

Abby's throat closed up for a split second. Why was she getting all choked up? He probably knew her better than anyone, including Rex. They'd gone through a lot, and although he had a right to be concerned, she didn't really like his question or her reaction. What was in the past was past.

Who was she fooling? Every time Nic whispered to, touched, or looked at Rex, Abby wanted to point her Sig at the woman and pull the trigger. Abby cringed. Jack had a point. Time to let it go.

She looked him in the eye and said, "I'll do whatever we need to do to stop these guys."

He nodded. That was one of the many things she liked about him. He never treated her like she needed a caretaker, and when she said she'd do something, in no way did he doubt it.

She couldn't resist another glance at Rex. The big guy stared straight ahead, but his rigid shoulders alerted her to the fact that he listened to every word.

Jack leaned toward her, placing his hands on her knees. "When we return to the OS Sector, I'll have the tech guys look over the crates. Chances are good they'll find some clue as to where they came from and who sold them. If we do that, then finding out the inventor and stopping him should be a piece of cake."

She scooted back a little, breaking contact. Crazy as it seemed, Jack acted as if he was coming on to her again. Why, after so much time had passed? Or was he only trying to push his brother? Those two had issues, and she wanted to be nowhere around when it heated up.

"Are there really that many arms dealers who would handle such a volatile weapon?"

"They don't care. They want the money. What's it to them if innocent people get hurt in the end?" Jack slid back, resting his shoulders against the van's wall.

"When are you going to let us lower beings know what you have planned?"

He chuckled. "One step at a time. We'll examine the

crates, try to find who invented it, and then we'll see if we can stop the manufacturer and distributor."

The van turned into an alleyway that appeared to be a dead end. Before they could go any farther, the wall slid into itself and the road shifted down as they drove into an underground garage. One of the OS's sentries had spotted the van through the camera and pressed a switch to open the secret door. Abby loved that about the new OS Sector. She always looked around for James Bond or guys in tights and capes.

The other OS Sector vehicle pulled in behind them. Then with metal doors slamming and everyone talking at once, they headed into the lower levels of the building while personnel unloaded the ammo with extreme caution to take to the labs.

If not for being stopped in the hallway by Charlie, the new mechanic for the OS—she could fix anything with just a hairpin and duct tape—Abby could've avoided being alone with Nic. The small woman had the female version of the Napoleon complex.

"I'm glad we have a few minutes to ourselves. A little girl-to-girl conversation, A. J." Nic gave her a tiny grin.

Sure the woman was petite, possibly five-two, and Abby felt like a giant next to her—being five-six wasn't really that tall, just barely above average height for a woman in the United States—but Nic gave her the creeps.

"Call me Abby. What can I do for you?" She handed over her backpack filled with extra ammo, the OS-owned satellite phone, and laptop. Her time as A. J. had been spent as another person in another life best forgotten.

"We're grown women, Abby."

"Some more than others," she muttered.

"What?" Nic placed her hands on her hips.

She waved her hand. "Nothing. Just thinking of other grown women."

Eyeing her with suspicion, the smaller woman said, "I know you and Rex have a past, but you really need to let it go. He's with me now. You're Jack's little friend—"

"Little friend?" Abby shook her head to check for anything loose that could have caused her to hear it all wrong.

"His favorite—"

"Favorite?" Amazed by the idiocy coming out of the woman's mouth, she could only stand there with her mouth hanging open. What did she think she was to Jack, his favorite slave? And to call her little was like calling a wolf a lamb. Since the age of thirteen, and being five-six at that point, she'd never been called little.

"Quit being so sensitive." Nic's dark, round eyes widened. "I'm only offering you some advice so you don't embarrass yourself and Rex. And, for that matter, me and Jack. It would be best for everyone if you left Rex alone."

Abby took one step toward Nic before she even realized it. The woman's face washed of all color, and she turned her head away, raising a hand as if in protection from a blow.

What the hell? Abby's fists still hung by her hips.

"Abby, dammit!" Rex moved between her and Nic. "What do you think you're doing? If you hit her, Jack will string you up. You know how he feels about fighting among operatives." He shook his finger as if he were a parent berating a wayward teenager. "You're bigger than her. I never thought you were a bully. I knew you'd changed, but not that much."

"What's going on?" Jack walked in, his forehead creased and eyes narrowed. "Dammit, Abby! What have you done *now*?"

Her chest ached as if they had stabbed her in the heart. That was it. The final straw.

"You got that backward," she said through gritted teeth.

"You're saying Nic started something?" The questioning look on Jack's face said he didn't believe her.

The air in the room disappeared. Her heart pumped hard, trying to take care of oxygen-starved lungs. She inhaled deeply, trying to recover from the one-two blows delivered by the men she cared for and had always thought of as being fair and good, no matter their pasts.

She finally regained her voice. "I was talking about Abby Dammit. Remember?" Everyone stared at her with different degrees of confusion. She could almost hear a trombone go *wa-wa-wa-waaa*. "Well, you all can go fuck yourselves." Then she headed toward the door and her apartment.

"I didn't know she was so touchy." Nic's sugary-sweet voice followed her down the hallway. "Maybe she's having her period."

Abby hesitated in her march down the hallway. Did that little twit actually say that? She shook her head. Christ! The ignoramus set women's rights back thirty years with that statement.

Taking solid, long strides, she continued walking, turning at the entrance to the appropriate hallways without thought.

That woman wrote the book on passive aggression. No. She was only a follower of the big kahuna, though most likely she had never met Abby's mother. The one person who lived and breathed passive aggression. No other person in the world had it down to such an art. Yeah, Mrs. Leigh Ann Rodriguez was a typical Southern belle through and through and the original author of *How Can I Be Nice and Make You Feel Horrible?*. But Nic didn't have a blood relationship to protect her, and she had no idea how close she came to turning up black and blue.

Of course, with Rex and Jack fooled by her act, that left Abby on her own in dealing with her. Not that she could really do anything. No matter how catty the woman acted, she was protected by the fact that if Abby responded with open hostility, she would appear to be a spurned lover. Or like what Nic had said: "So sensitive."

After years of her mom's jabs, Abby was savvy enough to catch the underlying meanings, and her *sensitivity* had saved her life more than once against all of the bad men and women out there. Of course, men referred to their sensitivity as a *gut feeling* and were admired for it.

"How did it go?" Liam Kelly stood next to the elevator, leaning his shoulders against the wall, long legs crossed at the ankles. A fine-looking Irishman with ebony hair and a brush of gray at the temples that looked sexy only on men, and he was off-limits. Everyone knew that Charlie, the new mechanic, was in love with him—that was, everyone but Liam.

Why they didn't get together was beyond her and wasn't a problem she had time to worry about. Did everyone know how she felt about Rex? She hoped to hell not. And if they did, everyone should forget about them getting together. Not going to happen.

Liam shoved off the wall and pressed the UP button. Unlike the old OS building, where all the operatives lived underground, the new site was set up for all the floors to be used. Part of the more open and, should she believe, legal Circle organization.

"We got the shipment but we need to cut off the source before they release more." She eyed Liam from half-closed lids as they stepped into the elevator and he punched in the floor number beneath the penthouse. Every floor but the top one was broken into four apartments. Barracks for the single operatives were in the building next door. The OS's penthouse belonged to the commander of The Circle, Arthur Ryker, for whenever he visited.

"What's going on?" she asked.

Since being suspended and demoted last year, Liam normally stayed out of mission business. She guessed that was better than being eliminated. From what she'd heard, he'd come close.

"I may have you a lead on the inventor."

"Then tell Jack."

"I thought it best that the info came from you."

Stepping off the elevator into an oval-shaped foyer with four doors, Abby stopped outside the far right one.

She turned. Liam remained in the elevator, his hands braced on each side, holding the door open. She'd forgotten that he wasn't authorized to enter the executive area of the OS. It had to be hard on him. For a short time, he'd been the head of security for The Circle, taking over after she'd returned to the OS.

"Why do I have a feeling I don't want to know where you got the info?" She walked back to the foyer. His stare was intense, never wavering to check her out like most men. Maybe she should be insulted by the lack of attraction, as he was known to be a player, but she'd always felt comfortable around the smooth-talking Irishman.

"I got it from Ice. He knows a lot of people who Jack wouldn't approve of. Word got to him about the new ammo, but before he had a chance to track it down, Rex was investigating. So we thought that was the end of it. Then it all went bugger."

"Got it from Ice Takahashi, huh?"

A few months ago when Collin Ryker turned over the OS to his brother, rejoining it to The Circle, one of their more deadly operatives, Ice, went AWOL. And only last week had he shown up again. From what she'd heard, Arthur Ryker hadn't disciplined him and had ordered Jack to back off. So she suspected the leader of The Circle knew all the facts about his disappearance. No one had ever heard of an operative leaving without permission and doing whatever he wanted without disciplinary action. Maybe that was why everything concerning Ice caused Jack to hit the roof. How could Ryker expect Jack to control the OS Sector if he couldn't reprimand his people?

"Yeah."

"Then why doesn't he tell Jack?"

"Sure. Two operatives he'd love to see take a nose-dive off the Bank of America Plaza tell him that the arms dealer he's looking for is in his backyard?" Liam shook his head.

"Ouch." The Plaza was known as the tallest building in the Southeast, so that would be one heck of a long dive. "Is he here in Georgia?"

"No. In Alabama. Ice learned Brody Walker sold the goods to Inferno for a large chunk of change."

"If you call a million and a half dollars a chunk," she said. Brody Walker? Damn. That was a name from her past she never expected to hear again. But why was she surprised? Considering how self-involved he'd been in high school, she imagined he decided to deal in weapons instead of drugs because it sounded classier and still kept him in the lifestyle his family provided him while he was growing up. He wasn't much of a straight arrow back in the day. From what she remembered, when he got caught selling stolen goods in high school, he'd used his all-American title to his advantage. Why would a rich boy from a good neighborhood do such a thing? Someone set him up. Yeah, right.

"You heard of Brody?"

"Yeah." She blinked several times to clear her mind. Had her expression given something away? She watched as he shifted to another foot. "Do you think Ice is right?"

"He's certain. Though Jack might doubt it."

She promised Liam to tell Jack immediately, and in

the little time it took her to walk into her apartment and punch in the number on her cell phone, she reported to Jack what she'd been told.

"I'd hoped it wasn't him. His security is set up so that he'll see us coming from a mile away. We'll have a hard time reaching him before he escapes." By the tone of Jack's voice, she knew his blue eyes sparkled with excitement.

"He's that big?"

"Yeah. You probably know him. He came from your hometown."

"I do. Though I haven't heard from or seen him since he graduated from high school."

"That will be helpful in our plans. He'll make no connection between you and The Circle."

"I had no idea he'd become involved in such a dangerous line of work." When he didn't say anything more, she asked, "So can you tell me your plans now?"

"Tomorrow. Be in my office at seven hundred hours and be sure to read the file I just e-mailed you."

Whatever he had planned, she could tell she wouldn't like it. He was too happy.

Chapter Three

AFTER A SHOWER and before calling it a night, she picked up her cell phone and punched in a number she knew by heart.

"Hey, Mom. How you doing?" Abby curled up on her sofa as she stared out the window.

"Darling, I was beginning to think you'd forgotten my phone number."

She'd told her mom many times that her job carried her out of the country and into areas without phone service. But the woman continued to make it sound as if she intentionally waited so long to call. Maybe she was right. Abby dreaded calling since she always felt guilty about something, no matter if it was her fault or not.

"I'm calling now. How's your arm?" The last time they'd talked, her mom had cut it on her favorite rosebush. She'd complained about how deep it was and how she'd gotten blood on her favorite pants.

"It's okay, I guess. The scab will take forever to disappear." The whiny tone grated on Abby's nerves, but she closed her eyes and concentrated on saying the right things.

"Be sure to keep putting the antibacterial cream on it that the doctor gave you."

"I'm not a child," she huffed, and then said, "When are you coming home?"

"It wasn't that long ago when I visited." Her mom had moved south of Birmingham, Alabama, to the small town of Sand City, the county seat of Sand County, to be closer to her son after he'd been elected county sheriff. Abby's half brother was six years older and looked nothing like her. Edward and his wife had a little boy who was as cute as a fat puppy. He'd probably grown several inches since she'd last visited.

Traveling three hours each way on her rare off days wasn't something she looked forward to. Anyway, the mileage wasn't the problem so much as the depressed funk that came over her when she visited.

"That was before Christmas when we met in Birmingham for lunch. It's March. I think it's time for you to come see your brother too. You really need to work on organizing your life. Tell your boss you need more time off. Go to a lawyer and tell him you're being overworked."

"It's not that easy."

"Excuses. Your brother works long hours but he still finds time to visit every other Sunday for dinner and he calls me several times a week."

Geez! Her mom hadn't taken long. Usually she waited

at least five minutes into the conversation before telling her how her brother was better. From the moment she was born, they'd been compared to each other. He was near perfection in their mom's eyes.

Abby's shoulders drooped. Considering her mom was right didn't help the matter. Despite being arrogant and a male chauvinist, he was a kind son, a good husband, and a great dad.

And she'd be wasting her breath pointing out that Eddie lived only three miles away and in the same state and city as her mom.

When she almost died at the hands of The Circle, she'd contacted her mom and half brother. The reunion had been stiff. That was when she realized why she'd been so rebellious growing up. Being a round peg in a square hole caused a lot of damage to both parties. Since then she called her once a week but quickly learned the older woman hadn't quite forgiven her for acting and looking different.

Unlike Abby, her mom was petite and willowy. With deep green eyes, clear rosy skin, and soft brown hair lightened to near blond perfection—concealing her age from all her close friends—Leigh Ann Sanders-Wentworth-Rodriguez was old-school Southern and quite proud of it.

Abby looked a lot like her father, Dr. Roberto Rodriguez, with her dark hair and olive skin. When she was sixteen, she remembered feeling for the first time out of place beside her light-skinned mother and blond brother as they lowered her father's casket into the ground.

"I'll see what I can do." Abby rubbed her temple,

hoping the on-coming headache wouldn't get worse. "Mom, do you remember Brody Walker?"

"Mitzy Walker's son? Yes. He's doing really well. They say he made a killing in California before the housing boom went bust. He retired at thirty and owns a beautiful farm off I-Sixty-Five. Why do you ask?"

"Nothing. I heard his name come up and remembered he lived near there."

"Listen. I have to go. Eddie and them are coming over to take me out for dinner."

"That's nice. Tell Edward hi and hug Suzie and Tommy for me."

"Very well. I guess that means I won't be seeing you for my birthday."

Damn! She'd forgotten her birthday was in a couple days. That would explain why her brother was forking over some money when her mom usually fed his family each Sunday.

"I'm sorry. I have to work. But that's part of why I was calling . . . to wish you a happy birthday."

She huffed again. "Thank you."

Abby rolled her eyes. The woman was a drama queen. She loved being the center of attention, especially men's. Abby had learned how to deal with it when she was younger—just step into the background and blend.

"I'll talk to you soon."

"Bye." Then her mom hung up. No "I love you" or "be careful." At least Abby had done her duty and had a confirmation on Brody's whereabouts.

One thing Abby had learned over the years, the world

was a mighty small place. Like her, Brody had grown up in Vestavia, an old-money Birmingham neighborhood. Though Abby had never run with his crowd, she'd heard a lot about him. Quarterback of the high school football team, sweetheart of all the teachers, and mischievous rich boy whose parents always bought him out of any trouble he created. After being transferred around to several different in-state universities, he finally graduated from the University of Alabama at Birmingham. At least, the last part was what she'd read in his file earlier.

She rubbed her eyes. Goodness, every bone in her body ached. She picked up her cell phone and texted Jack that she'd done her part and confirmed what they knew so far. Hard to believe how much one person could change in ten years. How could the golden boy turn out to be an infamous arms dealer? She'd probably never know, and she sure didn't want to know up close and personally.

ABBY JUMPED STRAIGHT up in her seat when a door slammed. Her neck burned like a day-old sunburn, as she'd fallen asleep on the sofa with her chin resting against her chest.

Stiff and bent over, she struggled to walk into her bedroom. The years in The Circle had taken their toll on her body. Broken bones, gunshot wounds, and deep lacerations that left ugly scars on several areas of her skin attested to the dangerous life she'd chosen.

Rumbling coming through the walls reminded her that Jack had given the suite between theirs to Rex. He was The Circle's second-in-command; she'd thought he'd use the penthouse when Ryker wasn't in residence. Then again, he'd never been known to expect much and had no problem bedding down in a field with the other grunts working for him.

Who was Rex talking to? She couldn't hear a second voice. He must be talking on his phone. The baritone voice stirred memories of hot nights in twisted sheets a lifetime ago.

For the last two weeks, her dreams had been filled with the man who slept only twenty steps away. She knew how many. The first night, she'd numbered each one until she stood outside his door with her fist raised, but she hadn't knocked. What would she say? *Hi, I fucked your brother, and oh yeah, during that time, I was pregnant with your baby.*

THE NEXT MORNING, Rex leaned back in his chair as his gaze followed his brother's pacing as he walked a path behind his massive desk and back to where everyone sat around an oblong mahogany table. The office took up one side of the second floor. Every square foot was utilized to allow several operatives to meet with the boss and, when needed, to break out into groups to plan mission strategies. An even dozen, counting Jack, were going over the events of the day before and what had gone wrong. The meeting was called to plan ways to find the ammo manufacturer and the fellow who invented it, while at the same time stopping Walker from selling any more of the ammo.

His brother stopped his pacing and rubbed his shaved head in deep thought. With the tattoos covering one arm and piercings in his brow and lip, Jack looked more like the leader of a motorcycle gang than a professional soldier.

The door opened and Abby slipped inside, squeezing in between Charlie and a male operative whose name Rex couldn't remember. All eyes turned to her and the room became quiet.

"Sorry." She grimaced. Abby picked up a Styrofoam cup from the stack and lifted the coffeepot, steam drifting up from the black liquid. "I forgot to set my alarm."

Although he knew better than to stare, his eyes refused to look away. Her hair stuck out every which way from the ponytail she'd pulled into a bright pink clip. So girly and unlike her. She wore her usual gray top and black jeans, and from where he sat, they appeared wrinkled. What had she been up to last night? As far as he knew, no one had visited. Not one sound had come from her suite, and he'd been listening after he'd hung up with Ryker. Lying in bed with a hard-on and staring at the ceiling, he'd wondered if she still slept in an oversized T-shirt and thick socks and nothing else. Those long legs, smooth and bare, stretched across the bed with her perky breasts pressing against the thin cotton. He remembered how soft she looked and felt in his bed.

His cock filled out, and with a furtive shift beneath the table, he adjusted his pants. Hell, he didn't need to think about her in bed while in a room filled with co-workers.

Jack spoke up. "Orders have been given to move forward in our efforts to obtain the information we need from Brody Walker to halt production. But Ryker has given us instructions that he's not to be eliminated or harmed in any way that interferes with the goal of this mission." Jack crossed his arms as he waited for the room to settle back down. Many of the operatives wanted Brody's head on a pike along with other body parts and complained about Ryker tying their hands.

They'd received news that morning about a shipment reaching Inferno's facility, and knowing Brody was responsible didn't encourage goodwill. For years, the radical organization had created havoc with The Circle. So anyone supplying them with weapons and ammo would be considered the enemy and deserved to die. Life in The Circle was kill or be killed.

"As you know from the files in front of you, his farm is protected with sophisticated equipment as well as several guards patrolling with dogs. I would like to hear what you think is the best way in."

Everyone started talking at once, giving suggestions on the best way to handle a high-security location and a man with the money and means to acquire weapons and men to protect him.

Rex watched Abby take a sip of her coffee, and then her tongue darted out as she licked her lips. The bottom one, full and plump, glistened. He remembered how she would bite her lip when he'd kiss his way down her body.

"No way!" She slammed her hands on the table and stood, glaring at Jack.

Startled out of his thoughts, Rex glanced from Abby to his brother. Shit! What had he missed?

"Do you have a problem with it?" Jack looked his way.

"Like I care what he thinks," she said before Rex could answer.

"Rex, ignore Abby's childish fit. This is the best plan."

He opened his mouth to ask what in the hell they were talking about when Abby pointed a finger at him.

"You. You convinced him, didn't you? This was your way to get back at me for letting you hang in the breeze at the warehouse." Her nostrils flared.

By God, she was beautiful when she was all revved up.

Several of the operatives chuckled, and some had the sense to cover it up with a cough or a hand.

"Abby, you're the only one who has a connection with Walker. Ryker sent Rex specifically to work this case. He's been working on his cover with several arms dealers for the last seven years. It makes sense that you go undercover with Rex to visit Walker. We don't need to scare him off. It could take days, weeks, before we catch up with him again. We need him relaxed and willing to talk. You've already received the invite to the charity function at the Wynfrey in Birmingham."

Rex glared at his brother. What was the asshole up to? The only time operatives of the opposite sex worked undercover together was either as siblings or lovers. And in no way could he treat Abby as a sister, even if they needed to create a sick scenario like that. Besides, Walker would know they weren't siblings.

Hell, no!

Did he say that out loud?

"Enough! It's settled." Jack's eyes narrowed. "You and Abby are going as a married couple. You'll make Walker believe it too. We need his trust."

Damn. He had blurted it out.

"Fine. Whatever you say, boss." He grinned and wondered if Jack remembered their last discussion about what *boss* spelled backward.

His brother gave him a one-fingered salute.

Yeah. He remembered, the double SOB.

Jack called the names of the leaders from each group, broken up by area of expertise, and passed around outlines of what he wanted answered before they left next week. They had only six days to get their shit together.

Rex glanced over at Abby on the opposite end of the table; she looked shell-shocked. He wanted to tell her she had nothing to worry about when it came to his behavior. That he knew how to be professional.

But he would be lying. Maybe *he* was an asshole.

He narrowed his eyes, studying her. She owed him some answers, and he planned to take advantage of their time together.

She glanced his way and frowned and then shifted in her seat, giving him her back.

With a swipe at his mouth, he erased the pleased grin from his face. He'd been waiting years for answers, and by God he'd get them. Or die trying.

Chapter Four

ABBY WATCHED THE door close behind Rex, leaving her alone with Jack.

"Okay. Let me have it." He folded his arms and leaned a hip against the conference table.

She wanted to cry but she refused to embarrass herself and Jack. Digging her fingers into the back of a chair as she stood, she concentrated on keeping her voice even. "I can't believe you did that." She raised her hand to stop him from interrupting. "You, better than anyone, understand why I can't work with him like that." The last word faded from lack of air. Her dry mouth emphasized how the news had bothered her.

He rubbed his eyes and then his chin. The silence stretched between them. Was he rethinking his plan?

"How much do you like working for The Circle?"

The question caused her to blink. She hadn't expected it.

No need for her to hide the truth. "You know over the last few years it has strangely kept me from falling apart. I can't imagine going anywhere else." She tilted her head. "Why? If I refuse, am I fired?"

"No. I won't kick your ass out like you deserve for giving me hell. But I can demote you. You and Liam can hang out together. Persona non grata. Do you want that?" His blue eyes cooled with each word.

He might as well have slapped her. She understood being the OS Sector's leader was a hard job. Their line of work required they possess the type of confidence that could be grating to those less sure of themselves. Keeping the strong personalities of a hundred or more people balanced while satisfying Ryker wasn't an easy task. But she'd never said no to Jack on any of her assignments.

Truth be told, she'd betrayed Theo, the psychotic former leader of The Circle, and helped a prisoner escape. Although Theo had been insane and the prisoner her best friend, betrayal was betrayal, no matter how she justified it. She and Liam did have that in common. But it wasn't her fear of being fired or demoted that had her fighting the assignment.

"I think you need to help me understand where you're coming from by asking me that question." She might as well give him a chance to lay out his reasons.

Jack pushed away from the table and looked away. "I'm explaining this only because I know what you went through when we thought Rex was dead." He cut his ice-cold eyes at her.

She didn't need reminding that The Circle had lied to

her back then, making her and Jack believe Rex had died. If two talented operatives had no one waiting for them elsewhere, they would most likely stay put.

And there was no need for him to say that; she better not expect an explanation again. Allowing an operative to balk at an assignment could lead to indecision in the field, practically ensuring the person would be found dead later and possibly get others killed.

"Thank you." She bit off each word and opened her eyes wide when he glared. She resented his attitude. He thought he was protecting her, but she didn't need or want it.

"We don't have months or even weeks to set up this operation. We need answers quickly. Who's Walker's source, and where are they manufacturing it? You're familiar with our target, and Rex has established an identity in the arms black market as a big player. You know this, and I know you're panicking because of your feelings for him. Those feelings are the perfect cover to get this job done without Walker being the wiser. We have other female operatives willing to go the distance, but they don't have the knowledge you possess without even having to pretend." He crossed his arms, looking at her from beneath his brows.

"Go the distance?"

"Yes." He watched her without blinking.

"You want me to sleep with him . . . with Rex?"

"If needed for your cover, yes."

Her face heated. A mixture of embarrassment and anger spread down her neck and torso. Her nipples beaded.

Embarrassment could do that. It had nothing to do with remembering his cock yesterday, reminding her of what she'd forgotten years ago. The man had more than enough to get the job done. Not only did he have the right equipment, but he was also so aware of a woman's body.

When they'd dated, goodness gracious, they fell into bed that first night, and after they became engaged, he always made sure she was ready for him and completely satisfied when they finished making love. He had a sixth sense for where to touch and what to whisper in her ear to set her off. The way he wielded his tongue in or on any part of her and was able to bring her to a screaming climax had amazed her. She'd loved draping her limp body over his massive, hard one and grinning as she listened to his speeding heartbeat slow.

A quick glance up and she caught Jack's gaze drifting back up from where her stiff nipples pushed at her blouse. She lifted her chin and crossed her arms. Tempted to chafe her arms as if she was chilled, she refused to lie to him and herself.

"I'm a professional. If needed, I'll do it, but you better be sure Rex understands that's all it is. A job and nothing more." She pushed back her chair and stood.

"I'll expect nothing less from you and Rex." He picked up a folder and tossed it to her. "Study this. There are a few facts you'll need to know about his cover as Rurik Volkov. And I included his personnel file too. You deserve to know everything."

Everything?

Abby looked at the folder in her hands. A sick feeling

came over her. What would she learn? Did she really want to know? When he'd prepared to go to Peru, she'd never asked any questions. She knew as an arms dealer, he had an assignment that was more dangerous than others.

The world of buying and selling arms was a small one, and it had taken Rex several years to establish his cover as a Russian American with no scruples when it came to making money. In fact, he'd been in Peru working on an arms deal at the time Abby had gone to New York to purchase a wedding dress. The Circle had set up her kidnapping and played on her belief, and later Jack's, that Rex had died in Peru. Then Theo had produced pictures of Rex's bullet-riddled body. At the time, she and Jack had no reason to mistrust The Circle. Not until a couple years later did the war start between the two covert organizations. She had no idea then she was fighting against the man she loved. The lies, so many lies. Not until later had they realized the OS had been innocent.

Jack left her alone as she opened the thick folder.

Clipped inside to the front flap was an old passport picture of Rex. At the time, his hair brushed his wide shoulders. With soft gray eyes narrowed and mouth straight, even grim, he appeared years younger, so exotic and yet a no-nonsense businessman. He looked nothing like the laid-back, sensual good ol' boy she remembered.

When she reached the year of her "death," several pages from the OS's psychoanalyst revealed Rex had been required to attend anger-management sessions. The order had come after he'd incapacitated three other operatives during a safety meeting. Most of the notes had sections blacked out, but one sentence had been missed:

Mr. Drago exhibits severe grief behavior due to the violent death of a loved one.

Tears welled as she blinked, fighting the urge to let them flow.

She understood what it meant. She'd been there, done that. Only someone who had gone through the loss of a loved one could fully understand. When she'd heard the news of Rex's death, she'd accused Jack of lying to her. For days, she'd told him he was wrong, but then the report came in. The Peruvian government had raided a terrorist camp. The same camp Rex had been visiting undercover as the arms dealer, Volkov. Everyone had been killed and the bodies dumped in a mass grave. The names released as evidence of their success. Rex's undercover name listed in black and white.

For months after she'd received the news that Rex had died, she moved from denial to anger to depression. Even after she moved on, the anniversary of that day haunted her. No matter how she fought it, as the day wore on, she would become pathetic, crying and drinking to forget the nightmare. But even in her worst moments, she'd never harmed another person. For Rex to feel such pain, to be so angry, how could she ever expect him to forgive her? Odd that, until she read it in his file, she'd never wondered what he'd gone through during that time. She selfishly had remembered only what she'd endured.

She slammed the folder shut. *Damn you, Jack!* What

was he up to letting her see his brother's whole file? With a sigh, she shoved away from the table.

It was time for her to truly move on and quit feeling sorry for herself. They were each alive but their relationship had been dead and buried years ago.

REX TACKLED HIS brother. They rolled on the floor, fists slamming into ribs and kidneys. The hollow thuds filled the exercise room.

"You bastard!" Though two inches taller, Rex still didn't have an advantage. Jack fought dirty and didn't make any bones about it.

"Ha! What does that make you?"

They rolled back and forth across the mat, not letting the other get an advantage. Jack broke free and jumped to his feet. Rex followed, lifting his closed hands, looking for another opening to slam his fist again into his brother's nose. Blood coated Rex's hands and Jack's face, with more streaming down Jack's chin onto his T-shirt.

Jack darted to the side and landed another blow to Rex's ribs, knocking the air out of his lungs. Rex bent down and inhaled deep as he looped an arm behind Jack's knees and brought him down. Before his brother could move, he thrust his elbow beneath his chin.

"I should end everyone's misery and put more pressure on your trachea, you manipulative asshole." It felt good seeing his brother's face turning blue beneath all the blood as he leaned a little harder, blocking off his air.

"Rex!"

"Stay out of it, Abby!" Rex grinned down at his brother. "Don't fuck around with my life, Jack." He lowered his voice as he ground out each word between clenched teeth. "You've already done it once and I let you live, but don't think for one minute I won't kill you if you do that to me again. I have my limits."

The blue eyes staring at him looked so much like his mom's, filled with pain and a little hopelessness, that he eased his hold. Jack took advantage of his lapse and brought his knee up. At the same time, he slammed his fist into the side of Rex's head.

"Enough!" Abby stepped between where he was curled up on the floor and his brother. With her hands on her hips, she faced Jack, daring him to go around her. "That's enough! What kind of example of leadership are you showing your people?"

Rex rolled onto his back and looked around. A large crowd surrounded the mats. He hated that Abby had come across them acting like hormonal teenagers.

"We were sparring." Jack lifted the end of his T-shirt to wipe off the blood.

ABBY EYED THE bruises and blood on the men. "Yeah. Right. Sparring."

Before she could say more, a gleam shone in Jack's eyes. "Be sure to tell your mom and brother about your newly acquired husband. Remember you have six days before becoming happily married to Rurik Volkov."

"Asshole," she muttered at Jack's retreating back. The

spectators returned to their training while others followed their leader and left the room.

"Your what?" Rex rolled over onto all fours and then stiffly rose to his feet.

A clammy feeling washed over her. She'd hoped to break the information to Rex slowly and in private. When they'd been lovers, she'd hid everything about her past and her family, never stopping to think how she could explain the truth after they were married. Being involved with a covert organization had been only part of it, as any operative knew how family could be used against them. Her lying started after her mom kicked her out at the age of eighteen. Telling everyone that her family was dead eased the hurt a little. Then later, she almost believed it was true.

A shadow fell across her face, drawing her back to the mess she'd started years ago. She looked up. Rex stood toe-to-toe with her, leaning over her with his huge tree-limb arms crossed over a broad chest. The sparks in his eyes reflected the intense anger he obviously held back.

"You have some explaining to do."

"Is that like, 'Hey, Lu-cy! You have some 'splaining to do'?" She really shouldn't tease an overgrown ape when he was so close and pissed. Letting a wisecrack loose during tense moments was a bad habit of hers.

He clasped her underneath her arms and lifted her until they were nose-to-nose. "I'm serious. We were going to be married. Had you started feeling guilty about lying? Is that why you never returned to the— Ugh!"

Her first kick grazed his knee. She pulled her leg back to take better aim.

"Put me down." She dug her nails into the tender flesh near his wrists.

"Dammit! What did you do, sharpen your claws?" He didn't release his hold and neither did she. Then he began to shake her. "Stop it! I want answers!"

Her hands slid up and gripped his upper arms the best she could, but the muscles were wider than her palms. The firmness beneath her fingers and the way he lifted her without a grunt reminded her of how easily he could toss her around and arrange her in any position for lovemaking. All those years ago, his strength excited her, just as much as his gentleness took her breath away.

Memories heated the juncture of her thighs, causing tingles to race across her torso and up to her breasts. Her gaze dropped to his lips. One corner lifted in a permanent sneer from the scar on his face, giving him a lethal air. She found her lips only a breath away from his, and before the thought registered, her tongue darted out and traced the pale line of his scar.

He flung his head back. His face whitened with unseen pain. A second later, he released her.

Abby stumbled. She reached for his arm to regain her balance, but he jerked away as if he couldn't stand having her touch him. A knot twisted in her chest. All romantic feelings dissipated as she tried to find her voice. She'd forgotten how he'd always ignored her questions about the scar. She guessed she wasn't the only one with secrets.

"Why did you lie to me about your family?" His gruffness softened with each word.

"Can you say for certain that in our line of business

operatives' families are safe?" She rubbed her upper arms. "My father died when I was a teenager, but I still have my mom and brother. Edward is married with a little boy. I don't want to see them dead."

"Using a lot of caution, it's possible to keep them safe. People getting married should be able to trust each other, tell each other everything."

"Like you told me about when you and Jack were kids and how you got that scar?" His attitude was justified, but she didn't care for his tone. He'd always brushed off any questions about his life before working for the OS. She'd let it slide to stop him from asking the same of her.

"I told you, my childhood was nothing to brag about." He pressed his lips together as if trying to hide the scar. "This isn't about me."

"Ha! It's more about you than you obviously believe." A glance over her shoulder showed an empty room. Someone had closed the double doors. "We knew each other a total of six weeks when we decided to get married."

"Time isn't important when a man and woman are in love."

"Love? You mean lust," she said in a soft tone.

Mary and Joseph! It hurt to say that to his face. She had a hard enough time trying to convince herself. Though she was tired of lying, the need to move on and quit hurting each other required her to say it. If Nic wasn't the woman for him, he needed to find someone else. Only it couldn't be her. She would hurt him again. That was a fact.

He opened his mouth and closed it as his face

darkened. Earlier he'd been angry, but that was nothing compared to the fury building in his eyes. His fists balled into massive white knuckles.

"Enough about the past." She raised her hand. He growled, grinding his teeth. A tremor started in her belly and traveled down her legs until her knees felt like jelly. If she didn't know him the way she did, she'd be afraid for her life. The flames of hell shot from those beautiful eyes. Doing her best to show him that he couldn't intimidate her, she gave him her back and sauntered toward the doors. "We need to concentrate on the mission to stop this asshole from selling any more heat-seeking bullets."

He grabbed her arm, pulled her around, and leaned so far down that she could feel his breath against her face. "Fine. We'll be all about the job. But I won't forget you told my brother what you refused to tell me." His lips came closer to hers. "Remember, that lust you mentioned will come in handy the next few weeks. I expect a great performance for your mother and the rest of your family. You never know who may report to Brody. We can't take a chance of being exposed."

She refused to move back or drop her gaze. He wanted to upset her with the promise of intimacy. Pushing down the desire to cover that mouth so close to her own, she lifted one eyebrow and cupped his groin. The semihard cock surprised her but she managed to keep her composure.

"I believe you need to worry about yourself and your performance." She squeezed.

He groaned and shoved her away. "You think this is a game?" His chest rose and fell.

"No." She dragged her gaze from below his waist. "No. I'm dead serious. And I don't want my family to turn up that way—you know, dead. It's only because of my connection with Brody that I'm involved in this mission, and everything we do can endanger my family. I'm willing to chance it, this time. Brody Walker and whoever created and manufactured those bullets need to be stopped."

He moved around her and opened one of the doors. "That's right. When I'm pumping into you, be sure to close your eyes and remember you're doing it for God and country." The door closed behind him with a solid bang.

Abby shut her eyes and breathed deep. A shudder escaped as she lowered her head. Why did she feel like karma had decided to bite her on the ass?

Pulling in another lungful of air, she lifted her head and straightened her shoulders. She needed a drink and a sympathetic ear.

Chapter Five

"WELL, LOOK AT what the cat dragged in." Olivia Ryker stepped out onto the patio of her country home.

After nearly five days of training and working with Rex, Abby needed a break. Her nerves were wound up tighter than a miser staring at the offering plate on Sunday morning.

Smiling until it hurt her face, she and Olivia hugged. There were few people she felt comfortable enough to hug, and strangely, the dangerous woman squeezing her tight was one of them.

Laughter spilled out of the open doorway.

Abby looked up and spotted Marie Ryker, Olivia's sister-in-law, and Charlie standing inside talking. Disappointment weighed down her shoulders; she'd desperately wanted some one-on-one girl talk with Olivia. She shifted to high alert when she realized what Marie's presence meant. She never left The Circle headquarters without her husband on her heels. If The Circle had royalty, Marie would be the queen and her husband, Arthur Ryker, king.

"Come on. I'll fix you a margarita too." Olivia led the way through a bank of French doors into a sizable family room. "We were about to stir up a batch. The men are downstairs talking shop."

"How's it going, Marie?" Abby asked, nodding at Charlie at the same time.

"Fine. Good job on saving Rex the other day." To Abby, Marie looked like a miniature adult, and standing next to Charlie, who was a foot taller, she appeared even smaller. No matter the woman's size, Olivia had told her she had guts. Being married to a man like Ryker, a woman would need to be strong-willed or he would run all over her.

"Thanks. I wasn't alone. Rex went into a dangerous situation and despite the odds came out with what we were looking for." She turned to catch Olivia staring at her. "What?"

The glint in her eye worried Abby. "I've got an idea. We'll have margaritas in a little while. Everyone come with me. There's something you have to see." Olivia walked past her and unlocked a door. Hanging on one wall were around twenty rifles and shotguns and a couple of machine guns. On the opposite wall were shelves with cases of ammo. From her prior visits, Abby knew there were more closets like it throughout the house. All set up as small armories in case of an attack, the rooms also had steel walls behind the drywall and could serve as panic rooms.

"Take these." She yanked off lightweight jackets from hooks, tossing them to her, Charlie, and Marie. Then she pulled a huge bag from the top shelf with a grunt. "I think I need to exercise a little more."

Curious as to what Olivia had planned, Abby followed her with a shrug. Charlie raised her eyebrows and stepped in line, tagging along behind Marie. When they reached a large SUV in a garage holding about fifteen automobiles that ranged from an old '66 silver Caddy to a new, just-off-the-line Jaguar XKR-S in Ultimate Black Metallic, Abby came to a standstill.

"My goodness, girl. How do you decide on what to drive?"

"Those are Collin's babies. My baby is right here." She patted the bag.

Abby had a feeling something deadly was inside the olive-green duffel bag. The woman had an unnatural proclivity for weapons, sniper rifles in particular, and the bag was long enough to hold one.

After a crazy quick ride out of the garage in a SUV and down the long drive, Olivia cut to the left and drove teeth-rattlingly fast over a field until all of the lights from surrounding houses disappeared. If Abby had a guilty conscience where Olivia was concerned, she'd be getting nervous at that moment.

"What are you up to?" She held on to the dashboard as they came to a stop.

"I bought myself a new rifle and haven't tried it out yet. Collin thought maybe you would like to help me break it in."

Abby had been right. The bag's contents were deadly, from-a-distance deadly, as in the sniper variety. "Well, I had hoped to share a drink with you." She opened the door and nearly fell out onto the damp ground, her knees shaking from the jarring ride.

The four women ambled over to a long table set up several hundred yards from a tall mound. They were at the Rykers's private firing range. The upper beam of the headlights from the SUV lit up the area.

Olivia unrolled what looked like a thin mattress and placed it on the ground.

"I can't stand for the creepy-crawly things to get on me."

As Abby handed each part of the rifle to Olivia to assemble, she recognized it. Similar to Olivia's favorite rifle, the only difference was a missing microcomputer on top.

"Where did you get this?"

"A guy I know builds them special and doesn't mind having a woman tell him how to design it." She picked up a plastic box and flipped open the lid. When she pulled out the same kind of silver bullet Rex had found, Abby stumbled back.

"Damn it, Olivia. Where did you get those?"

"Rex sent over a box for Collin to examine and test."

"Is that a Hell's Purifier?" Marie craned her neck to get a better look.

Charlie muttered, "Shit," and looked around as if she was trying to figure out a safe place to hide.

"Hell's Purifier." Abby shook her head. "I hate it when people call inanimate objects names like that.

It romanticizes it. Where do people come up with that crap?"

"There's nothing romantic about the Inferno. I'm guessing they expect this to cleanse the world for them." Marie's frown changed in a blink to a full-blown smile. She slapped Charlie on the shoulder and pointed a thumb toward two large black SUVs pulling up.

Rex and Arthur Ryker stepped out of the nearest SUV as a couple guards exited the other one. Hanging back, Abby watched the scarred and intimating leader of The Circle give his wife a crooked smile. He appeared human.

"Be careful, Olivia. We don't need to be playing with them." Collin walked out of the shadows and kneeled next to his wife.

Where did he come from? The man was creepy good at showing up where he wasn't expected. He'd proven that a couple times in the past.

Abby heard a click and looked over to her friend.

Olivia had set up the rifle on the mat and stretched out behind it. "I never play around with my weapons—you know that, sugar pop."

Collin growled in warning, "Olivia."

She grinned as she looked through the scope. "Watch this." She took a deep breath, waited a second, and then squeezed the trigger.

A ten-foot section of the twenty-six-foot dirt-filled mound exploded into the air, leaving a hole the size of a bowling ball, spewing fire, in the concrete wall behind it.

"Jesus H. Christ! That's some ammo!" Charlie raised her arms and folded them over the top of her head, eyes wide.

Abby's hands trembled as she stuck them in her pockets. She'd understood what Rex and Jack had told her about the bullets, but seeing them at work confirmed how dangerous they were to civilians and military personnel alike.

"Everything all right with you?" Rex stopped next to her.

"We've got to stop this guy." She swallowed, trying to calm down.

"Just think if we had the microcomputer set up on this rifle with the software to program the microdot, the bullet could've turned and hit Charlie." Olivia looked over her shoulder at the other woman.

"Jesus, Jesus, Jesus." Shaking her head, Charlie dropped her arms to her sides. "If you'll excuse me, I'll be in the SUV."

Collin shook his finger at Olivia, obviously holding back a smile, and walked over to talk with Rex and Ryker. Surviving deadly situations as often as they did, it was easy to develop a warped sense of humor that was hard for others to understand.

Abby waited until Marie followed Charlie into the SUV and closed the back passenger door. "Olivia, why do you do that? You should be ashamed of yourself. She admires you and you just scared the crap out of her." Sometimes she wondered what caused Olivia to act that way.

"Admires me?" Olivia's forehead wrinkled and she darted a look to where Charlie sat with her back to the side window, avoiding her view of the mound. Marie patted her friend's shoulder and listened intently to her.

"What's the real reason you brought me out here?"

Olivia looked over her shoulder at where the men stood before moving her attention back to Abby and softly saying, "I knew if we stayed in the house, you wouldn't feel comfortable talking about Rex. I hadn't planned for them to follow us out here."

"What makes you think I want to talk about him no matter where we're standing? I certainly don't want to when he's only a few feet away."

With delicate eyebrows lifted, Olivia dipped her chin. "Are you really trying to pull that on me? I know you. For the last few months now, you've pretended you like how things are between the two of you. Now that you're going undercover, it'll be different. You know, pretending to be a married couple, you'll be with him up close and personal every waking moment. This is your chance to see if what you two had was real."

"Hey, I already know it was lust and nothing else."

"If that was true, it wouldn't bug you so much to see him with Nic."

"It doesn't bug me." She turned away, hoping the shadows concealed her flushed face.

"Liar." Olivia grinned. "Just go with it and see what happens. If nothing else, you'll have him out of your system and show yourself to be an excellent operative willing to go the extra mile."

"Have you and Jack been talking?"

"Jack? Hell, no."

Seeing Olivia's reaction, Abby decided to ask, "Is it true that you and Jack hooked up for a short while before he came to work for The Circle?"

"Who told you that?"

She shrugged. "Just something I heard and figured you wouldn't mind me asking."

"You of all people should know you can't believe everything you hear."

Abby stared at her for a few more seconds. Olivia hadn't really answered her question. Not that it was important. She just liked to deal with the truth. Often it helped her understand people's reasoning for saying the things they did. A person's past influenced their every thought, including how they reacted to situations and their expectations of how others would react.

A pop followed by a whistling caught her attention. Then an explosion of light lit up the darkness nearby. The sharp smell of burned skin and hair filled the air as it rained thick blobs of something. In seconds, everyone ran low to the ground, straight for the shelter of the SUVs. Abby slid to a stop next to a wheel for extra protection. Rex bumped into her as he landed on his knees beside her. At the other end of the SUV, Ryker hunched over Marie, protecting her with his body.

Abby shook her head. Why had the woman gotten out of the vehicle? Marie would be so much safer back in the SUV—that was, if the person or persons shooting resisted firing on the vehicles. Then she heard Charlie cussing on the other side of the passenger door. A smart woman to drop to the floorboards, but they needed to find out who was shooting before someone was killed.

"Where's Olivia?" Panic raced through her body. She pulled out her Sig from the holster at the small of her back.

"She can take care of herself. Were you hit?" Rex eyed her with concern. Moisture on her face and arms warned she would need to take an extra-long shower that night.

"I'm fine. Where's Olivia?" *Oh, God.* She prayed the pieces of burning flesh hadn't been anyone she knew.

Rex jerked his head toward where they'd parked earlier.

Abby stretched her neck to peer over the bumper. Olivia and Collin crouched at opposite ends of another SUV. So far only one person had been hit. No sight of the guard who had been standing near the vehicles. She guessed it was him. Where was the second one?

Several more pops echoed in the air; then the ominous whistling sound zipped overhead and struck the second guard, who was kneeling behind an overturned firing range table. His body exploded and scattered chunks of flame over several yards. Abby heard choking near her. Marie threw up in the grass while Ryker held her hair from her face.

A sick feeling clutched her stomach.

"That whistling, is it what I think it is?" She kept her voice low, not sure if she did so to keep the enemy from hearing her or to listen for that horrible sound.

"Yeah. We heard a case reached Inferno. They're pissed and want the rest. They must have the software to program the chip."

"You're sure it's them?"

"We haven't heard of anyone else receiving one." At that moment, the revving of several engines broke the silence. "The cavalry is on the way."

"Help for us?" She hated the helpless feeling.

"Ryker called in support after the first shot." Rex thumbed her cheek and leaned forward.

Abby jumped back when more gunfire echoed around her. The difference was no whistling followed.

A motorcycle slid to a stop nearby. Jack cut the engine and let it fall to the ground. "After we fired back, the shooter disappeared. Anyone else get hit?"

A few other motorcycles pulled up, and Circle operatives scrambled to check over everyone while headlights flashed in the trees from the direction they believed the sniper had hidden.

"It appears they only got the two guards," Ryker spoke up.

Olivia headed over to where Abby stood.

"A bit of a coincidence, wouldn't you think?" Abby asked, not really expecting an answer. She suspected the sniper had killed only the guards on purpose. Maybe the Inferno hoped it would halt The Circle's efforts in stopping the sale and manufacture of the Hell's Purifier.

When Jack didn't answer, she noticed how his gaze remained on Olivia as if he wanted to see for himself that she was okay.

"They could've easily taken out one of us, and it would've certainly slowed down the investigation but never stopped it." Rex stepped in front of her.

Why block her view of his brother? Her attention on Jack was nothing more than curiosity. Olivia acted like Jack was nothing more than furniture, but he stared at Olivia as if she were a piece of spicy candy.

She had to admit that Rex's back was a better view. Wide shoulders and small hips with just enough of a curve down to his buttocks that her fingers itched to grab his cheeks.

A light touch on her arm brought her gaze to her friend's concerned face.

"Let's go back to your house and have that drink I promised you, Marie, and Charlie," Olivia said. "I believe we deserve it. Let the fellows figure out what the hell happened tonight. They like all the blood and gore. Besides, Marie looks a little pale. I think she could use one. Charlie looks no better."

Abby glanced over to Charlie sitting in the SUV with her hands over her face and Marie once again trying to comfort her friend. "You've got to apologize to her for what you said earlier, especially after all this."

Olivia shoved the ammo box next to the disassembled rifle inside the bag. "You're right. But you've got to admit she was funny. That expression on her face . . ." She chuckled, shaking her head as she sauntered to the vehicle.

"Shh, behave yourself. You're incorrigible." Abby fought a grin. Olivia wasn't really making light of the guards' deaths. She caught the desperation in her eyes, wanting to lighten the mood a little. Maybe there was even a little relief mixed in as once again they'd thwarted death. "Charlie is a sweetheart and reacted like normal people do. Our problem is that we're no longer normal. We've seen too much."

"You're right again. I'll apologize. I could use a normal friend in my life." When Abby faked a gasp, Olivia laughed and slapped her on the arm and then opened the door. "Hey, Charlie, how about I make that margarita extra strong?"

Abby didn't hear Charlie's response, but Olivia howled with laughter as she climbed in behind the wheel.

She grinned. Most likely it had been graphic and physically impossible to do. Enjoying her friend's warped sense of humor, and happy to be alive, she slid into the front seat. Unable to hold back, she glanced over toward Rex. His gaze remained on her as Olivia drove by, heading to the house. In that moment she realized she'd been lying to herself for some time.

She still loved Rex.

Chapter Six

"WAKE UP, SLEEPYHEAD."

Abby lifted achy and swollen eyelids. The deep, sexy voice matched the masculine face hovering above hers. Stretched out alongside her, propped up by one hand near her head, Jack grinned big. The loop on his bottom lip glinted.

She groaned and covered her eyes. "Please don't tell me I screwed up again." *Oh no, oh no, oh no . . .*

He chuckled and moved off the bed. She squinted at him from between her fingers. *Thank you, God! He's wearing clothes.*

"The only thing you screwed up was drinking too much before a mission." With a stretch, he twisted at the waist and then straightened his shirt. His khaki pants flowed over muscled thighs that pulled at the cloth in the right spots. What a beautifully toned man.

"I don't have a hangover. One margarita isn't too much."

She glanced at the clock on her nightstand. "Shit, Jack. I only got in bed two hours ago. That's why I feel like crap."

"That's your problem. Time to get up. Rex is downstairs and waiting."

Abby tossed the sheet to the side. The oversized T-shirt she'd worn to bed covered her well enough for a mad dash to the bathroom. The mirror confirmed she had dark circles beneath her eyes. Refusing to think about the horror they'd gone through the night before, she splashed cold water on her face and pulled on a bathrobe. When she returned, she glared at her boss and then noticed the clothes draped over her bed.

"What's this? I don't need you picking out something for me to wear." From the corner of her eye, she spied a couple of her suitcases next to the door. "What are you up to?" She lifted a suitcase, its weight telling a story. "You packed for me," she said.

"You sleep like the dead. I could've strangled you before you had a chance to defend yourself." Jack opened the door into the hallway as he grabbed the suitcase from her hand. "You and Rex have a party to go to after a brief meeting downstairs. You'll be newlyweds flying in early from Vegas and staying at the Wynfrey in Birmingham for the evening. To be all fresh and ready to meet your mommy dearest the next day." He added, "We had to move it up. Another shipment is scheduled in the next few weeks for Inferno. Brody will be at the party. A perfect opportunity for you two to meet and become fast friends. So don't give me a hard time. Wear what I left you. I'll meet you in my office." He quietly shut the door.

Men! They love giving orders. She sighed. Problem was she wanted to keep her job. She hurried through a quick shower and applied makeup. Then she dressed in the outfit Jack had left on the bed.

What in the world?

The dress was nothing like anything she'd ever owned. Cocktail length, the cream silk hugged her in all the right places, dipping low in the front and the back going high into a stand-up collar. The style was reminiscent of what a 1950s movie star would've worn. Beneath it she wore a lacy bra and garter along with a barely-there thong. The whisper-thin hose stopped at midthigh, and she slipped into matching high heels. She enjoyed feeling sexy. This was a new experience.

She looked through her jewelry for anything that would accentuate the clean neckline. Giving up on finding anything perfect, she settled for a thin gold chain and small pearl earrings.

At the last minute, before leaving the room, she pulled her hair back and used the fanciest hairclip she owned. The mother-of-pearl overlay gave it a sophisticated look.

With a finger hovering over the DOWN button next to the elevator, she hesitated. Jack never did anything without a purpose. Sure he said a party, but what else was he up to? And why dress for it so early? Her hand glided down the sleek material. No matter his plans, she loved wearing the dress. Shoulders back, head held high, she inhaled deeply, releasing all her tension and pressed the button. She could handle him. She could handle anything either brother threw at her. As the door slid closed behind her and the car began its descent, she shook her head. The best way to handle the niggling feeling was to quit worrying and go with whatever he had planned.

Obviously, Jack planned to throw her into the fire by letting the public see her and Rex as husband and wife at a fancy party. She'd read everything The Circle had on Brody and studied Rex's files. To delay it would only give the Inferno a chance to take possession of more ammo. Besides, if they waited any longer, problems would start creeping up, giving her and Rex time to get on each other's nerves.

The first thing she noticed as she walked off the elevator and headed to the office was the slight hum of a crowd. When she opened the door, she almost turned back around.

Rex and Jack stood near a huge bouquet of flowers. A sullen Nic whispered frantically to Liam, while Charlie and Olivia sat at the conference table with Collin. What the hell were Olivia and Collin there for? Had someone died?

A movement near the flowers brought her attention to the white bells and doves immersed in fringe-tipped curtains draped over one wall. Next to a podium stood a tall, well-built man dressed in rhinestones and sunglasses and wearing his coal-black hair in a pompadour.

What was an Elvis Presley impersonator doing here? Her gaze jumped to Rex and Jack. What were they trying to pull?

One of The Circle's IT guys, holding a small video camera, pointed it at her with the red light blinking.

"Surprise!" Jack stepped over to her and waved at Charlie. "What are you waiting for?"

Charlie shoved a small spray of flowers into her arms. "These belong to you. Congratulations."

Stunned, Abby grasped them to her chest and looked at Rex. The satisfied look on his face ignited her anger. She caught Jack's arm.

"What the hell are you doing?"

"Can't you tell? I've come to Vegas to give you away to my good buddy, Rurik. Unless you'd rather have Elvis walk you down the aisle." Jack grinned and clasped her arm, nearly forcing her to where Rex stood. "When you called, telling me that you two crazy kids couldn't wait a minute longer and wanted all your friends here, I got on the first plane out." As the IT guy aimed the camera at Rex, Jack leaned over. "Play along."

"Are you *crazy*?" she shot back under her breath.

"If I had told you before we did it, would you have done it without arguing?"

"Hell—"

"That's what I thought," he said, cutting her off before she could raise her voice and mess up the recording. "I'll explain more after we're finished."

When Elvis launched into "Love Me Tender," Abby followed Jack's lead and held on to his arm all the way to the podium as if in a dream. Or was that a nightmare? They stopped in front of Rex. He looked wonderful. Dressed in what appeared to be an expensive black suit, gray silk shirt, and tie, he grabbed her hand and lifted it. Feeling numb, she didn't even think to protest how tightly he squeezed her fingers.

When Elvis asked her to repeat the vows and she

merely stared at him, he covered his discomfort by making a quip about the bride needing a fried peanut butter sandwich for nourishment. Less than two minutes later, Rex/Rurik slipped two rings on her finger, and the preacher/Elvis pronounced them husband and wife and ordered them to kiss.

Rex's lips pressed hers for a second and then he stepped back. Nothing earth-shattering or romantic about it at all. How often over the years had she dreamed of this moment? What if she hadn't gone shopping that fateful day and been kidnapped by The Circle? What if they had really gotten married? The kiss would be different, deeper, richer, hotter. What had happened? Her head spun with all the best-forgotten memories racing through her mind. She wanted to scream, *Stop!*

With a shake of her head, she stumbled off the platform set up for the altar. Rex caught her elbow until she regained her footing, but he didn't pull her back into his arms. Then Elvis belted out "Viva Las Vegas" in perfect pitch.

She squinted and rubbed her forehead. When would she wake up? Talk about the kookiest dream ever. Through the strange haze, she looked at Rex playing Rurik and wondered if she was also two people. Surely all of this wasn't happening to her but to someone else.

Everyone shouted and threw flower petals as they walked toward the door. Thankfully the IT fellow stopped filming when they stepped away from the stage area that would fit perfectly in any Las Vegas wedding chapel. They stopped at the conference table, and Rex handed her a pen and pointed at a blank line near the bottom of an official-looking form. She paused and then studied his face. She remembered that look. Molten-gray eyes burned into hers. He wanted her.

She leaned down and signed her name, noting his signature of Rurik Volkov. Before she moved away, Jack lifted the sheet and pointed at another spot. She signed again next to where he placed his finger.

When she straightened, Olivia and Charlie looped their arms through hers and moved her to a chair. She stared off, not focusing on anything around her.

"Abby, are you okay?" Olivia hovered over her, awkwardly patting her shoulder.

"Olivia?"

"Yeah, hon?"

"Quit hovering. You're scaring me." The woman never hovered. Abby concentrated on breathing: deep inhale and long exhale.

"Sorry. Your eyes are open so wide, just like the scared raccoon Collin found in the garbage the other day. You've got me worried. And to tell you the truth, you need to avoid wearing cream. Beige might be okay, but cream sucks the life out of your skin tone."

Abby glared at her until Olivia moved away and sat on the other side of the table with her arms crossed, shaking her head, mumbling and shooting her evil looks. In the back of Abby's mind, she was amazed that Olivia had apologized but to ramble on about colors and skin tones . . . that was enough to scare her. Things must really be bad if a former cold-blooded assassin was rattled by everything going on.

Charlie pulled out a chair nearby, wedged her elbow onto the table, and propped up her head in one hand, smiling.

"So starting this morning, you can jump on that stallion and ride him all you want. But I better warn you not to turn your back on Nic. She's madder than a puppy in a wet sack." Charlie nodded to the other end of the room.

Abby glanced over at Nic. Rex was leaning down to let her whisper something in his ear. Judging from the way the woman's hand clasped his upper arm, nails digging into the material, Nic was upset and wanted Rex to understand how much. But all Abby could think about was how that thick muscled arm belonged to her and Nic needed to let go.

As soon as the thought crossed her mind, she was ashamed. The whole arrangement was part of a ruse to set up Brody Walker. None of it was real.

She covered her eyes and bowed her head until her forehead rested on the shiny table. A couple solid bumps would help her to think clearly. She stopped banging her head when Charlie snorted.

"How're you going to explain to your mama about the bruise on your noggin if you keep doing that?" Charlie shoved her on the shoulder.

She was right. Somehow she needed to find a way to explain her new husband, not counting any facial bruising. No need for Rex to be accused of wife beating. Knowing her mom, she'd call the police. Then again, what better way to get him out of her hair so she could do her job? No. His presence was needed to get closer to Brody.

Lord of Mercy, her head hurt.

ARMS CROSSED AND his jaw aching from holding back the need to throw an uppercut into Jack's smart-ass mouth, Rex halfway listened to Nic's complaints.

"Did you hear anything I said?" Her dark eyes flashed in irritation.

"Tell Jack how you feel about it. This is all his idea."

"He won't listen to me. But maybe if I insist on field time again, I can be helpful," Nic said with her usual furor. "You know, by speeding up the mission, there will be no need to be alone with her. I'll think of something." She patted his arm. "Thanks. Let me see what I can come up with." Before he could stop her, she pressed her lips to his cheek and flounced off.

He drew his attention back to Abby. She lowered her head to the table and slammed into it a few times. Charlie spoke to her and she stopped. Hell, that proved she hated how his brother had tricked them into going along with his harebrained scheme as much as he did.

But maybe it would work. They needed Brody to believe they were what they appeared: a newly married couple in love and the groom involved in similar illicit work. A perfect reason for him to stay near Abby and keep her safe, while using every minute they had together pulling answers out of her. She'd always been close-mouthed. Case in point was the family she'd never mentioned. Yet, he knew of several inventive ways to loosen her up and get her to talk.

Rolling his shoulders, he wanted out of this monkey suit his brother had insisted he wear, and more importantly, he wanted that infuriating woman alone.

His gaze remained on Abby as she listened to her friends. Her brief smile shot liquid fire from his heart to his groin.

She looked beautiful. If The Circle hadn't interfered all those years ago, they might've been parents by now, or at the very least enjoyed years of being in the same bed. All that smooth skin and dark hair spread out for him to taste and touch. He shifted and tugged at the end of his jacket, covering any visible evidence of how looking at her affected him.

A flash of metal on his hand caught his attention. He'd never worn a ring, and he'd expected to be annoyed by the feel, but he rather liked how it reminded him of Abby. When Jack had handed the rings over and she had slipped one on his finger, it had struck him that she'd be wearing a ring like his, a sign of ownership. He'd liked that. He'd liked it very much. Maybe too much.

He looked at Abby and the ring on her hand sparkled under the office lights. *Hell, yeah*. No matter what anyone said, she belonged to him.

ABBY SNEAKED A look at Rex. He towered over all the men in the room except Liam, but where Liam was whipcord lean, Rex's thick muscles and solid build gave him an appearance of a football player, a dangerous-looking one with a scar and military haircut.

Over the next thirty minutes, they stood in front of a beautiful white wedding cake and let the photographer do his job. When it came time for the bride and groom to feed each other, she narrowed her eyes in warning. He behaved and didn't smear the vanilla fluff into her face, but he did take advantage of her hand being close to his mouth. His tongue darted out and licked the center of her palm. She squeezed her thighs together. *Oh, that feels so good.*

She needed to get away from him, even if by a few feet. As soon as she could, she strode over to a chair and flopped into it. When Jack suggested taking pictures of her throwing the bouquet, she refused to budge. No more playacting. When the real deal came along, she didn't want to compare it to the pretend one. Truth be told, nothing could compare to having an Elvis-style wedding. Unable to resist, she lifted her gaze to Rex and corrected herself: nothing could compare to having an Elvis-style wedding, with a dangerously sexy man as the groom.

Jerking her thoughts to the mission ahead, she said, "That's enough. Even the president of the United States would believe we're married." She shook her head. "I don't understand why you think we need that many pictures. It's not like my mom will ask to see them. She's going to be pissed enough with me eloping." With one shoe off, she rubbed her foot. "Don't we need to head to Birmingham?" The plain brass nautical clock on Jack's desk showed it was after one p.m.

"You two go and change clothes. I'll meet you back here in thirty minutes." Jack waved them off as he talked into his cell phone.

ABBY EXAMINED THE ceiling of the elevator as she rode up with Rex. The temperature rose with each floor they passed.

"You're beautiful in that dress."

Pulled by his soft voice, she looked up and touched the back of her neck. She took a deep breath. Why didn't they ventilate these boxes? "Thanks." She forced her gaze to look at anything but him. The picture of him filling out the perfectly cut jacket was forever branded on her retinas.

"Abby—"

As soon as the steel panel opened, she hurried to her suite and shut the door behind her, blocking Rex and all thoughts of him. They never locked their doors in the OS Sector. Who would dare steal from them? She only hoped he wouldn't try to follow her. If he just gave her a few minutes to regroup.

In seconds, she stripped off the dress and carefully hung it in her closet. She decided to wear a simple flair skirt and wraparound top. The royal blue and bright white complemented her olive skin. What would Rex think of her dressing in two feminine outfits in one day?

She laughed. Why did it matter? They were playing a part and nothing more. As soon as he learned about the baby, he wouldn't have anything more to do with her. He'd deserved to know but it was so long ago. She shook her head. Standing there and debating the right and wrong of what had happened was hopeless.

Had she screwed up again?

Straightening her shoulders, she opened the door and headed back to Jack's office. Relieved not to run into Rex and deal with the mixed bag of emotions he invoked, she walked in and stared. Nothing remained of the wedding. Seeing everything back in place brought a weird feeling of desolation over her. Refusing to dwell on it, she looked at Jack and Rex.

"What?" Their sudden silence brought out her insecurities. "Did I interrupt your secrets?"

"Come and sit down. We don't have a lot of time. The party starts at eight. As usual, we'll have a few operatives on hand. If you have any trouble, just signal to one of us." Jack leaned back in his chair.

"We really don't need to go over the plan again." Rex stood. The white sport shirt and dark slacks showed off his broad shoulders and firm buttocks. She caught herself before sighing out loud.

"Humor me. We've ensured the news of your recent nuptials reached Brody, and he knows you both will be at the party. Play it safe. Get him interested in the two of you. That will be your ticket to one of his private parties at his farm. Then maybe you can find hints on who designed the ammo and where the facility is located." Jack handed a large brown envelope to Rex.

Abby knew inside the envelope was everything needed to don their new personas: Mr. and Mrs. Rurik Volkov.

A few short minutes later, they drove out of the underground garage, heading toward I-20 and Birmingham.

Abby appreciated well-built cars, and the Cadillac CTS provided by The Circle for their cover didn't disappoint. She leaned back, enjoying the luxury of the soft leather and new car smell. Her old Honda Accord didn't compare.

Rolling her head on the support to watch Rex, she decided the car suited him perfectly. Her gaze dropped and returned to his profile. He oozed sex and danger.

"Do I have cake on my face?" he asked.

"Was this your idea?"

He glanced her way and then returned his attention to the interstate. "No."

"When did Jack tell you?"

"This morning when he woke me up."

"I wish he'd warned me."

She was married. Yet not really. But they were expected to act married. Her fingers curled into her skirt. The freedom of knowing she could touch him and pretend it was part of the job had her aching to feel his warm skin beneath her fingertips, to taste the curve of his neck, and to inhale the manly scent only Rex possessed. Her nipples tingled with the thought of rubbing her naked breasts against his chest.

"That's one of the things I've always liked about you."

"What?" That she dreamed of being naked and sated in his bed again? Face flushed, she turned away, hoping he hadn't noticed.

"You're quiet. Not filling in the silence with chatter."

"I'm not much for talking to talk." Her dad had been soft-spoken and said only what was needed. She figured she took after him.

Who did Rex take after? As much as Rex loved to talk, he never mentioned his dad. A couple times he mentioned his mom, but she had no idea if either of his parents lived.

She coughed to clear her throat. "Are both of your parents living?"

"They're dead."

"I'm sorry." From the unusual two-word answer, she guessed he'd rather not talk about them. "Do you have any other siblings besides Jack?"

"Nope. Just me and Jack." He glanced her way before returning his attention to the road. "Why the sudden interest?"

"I guess since you're about to meet my family, it feels strange not to know anything really about yours." She felt so exposed while his life remained closed to her.

"Jack and I were teenagers when our parents died. There isn't really much to tell. My dad beat my mom to death and then he turned up dead the next day. The police said it was suicide."

His voice sounded flat as if repeating a story that had happened to someone else.

Unable to think of anything to say, she patted his thigh. He placed his hand over hers before she could move it away.

Frustrated with her body's reaction to his touch, she slipped her hand out from under his and crossed her arms, staring out the passenger window.

How sad to lose both parents so close together and in such a horrific way. She wondered if an aunt or uncle had been there for a gangly young Rex; the image was too heartbreaking to think about.

The clacking of tires running across the interstate filled the car. Her eyelids drifted down and then flipped back open. With so few hours of sleep, she fought to stay awake, but knowing a good driver controlled the wheel and that her body needed to rest, within minutes her body relaxed and she slept.

REX CHECKED ON Abby. A quick look confirmed what he suspected. She was sound asleep.

He preferred her hair down and not in the ponytail she often wore when she worked, but the pretty clip allowed a few strands to escape, giving her a soft look. The dark brown appeared rich as mink. During those weeks, so long ago, when they had been lovers, her hair fell to her waist, and he often woke with his hands wrapped in it.

She inhaled deeply and shifted in her seat. The top of her blouse gaped. He tried to keep his eyes on the road, but his gaze returned to look every couple minutes. Her breasts rested in a bra that barely covered the tips. A faint tan line caught his interest. The swimming suit she owned must be too small, as the paler skin formed what looked like the point of a two-inch triangle. Damn. She better not try wearing anything like that around him. Hell, around anyone.

A rough patch on the pavement shook the car. He checked the road and then Abby. The way her breasts swayed and jiggled shot blood and heat into his groin. He swallowed a whimper.

He forced his gaze to move away. What was he? A sixteen-year-old pervert staring at a sleeping woman's boobs?

With a subtle adjustment of his cock, he glued his eyes to the road but his thoughts refused to stay off Abby and their *fake* marriage.

Jack and his big fucking ideas. Arranging the wedding as part of the cover-up was so like him. Jack always loved interfering in his life and acted as if he lacked walking-around sense.

What did he think Rex was doing during those years when his big brother worked for The Circle? While Jack was screwing everyone's daughters, girlfriends, and wives, Rex survived, just barely, especially after receiving the news that Abby had died. For the first year, he hadn't cared if he lived or died. When Jack left for the other side, Rex regarded him as dead. To work for an organization that hunted and killed OS operatives . . . no pussy was that good. The rumor was that Jack had left the OS to be with Olivia. She'd been The Circle's lead eliminator.

Rex didn't see it. The woman was a coldhearted bitch.

What Abby had in common with the woman, he had no idea. One thing for certain, The Circle had changed Abby. Guarded to the point of caginess, she avoided any mention of her time there.

He skimmed a hand across the top of his head.

All of it was a mystery, and in the next few days, he'd learn the truth.

Chapter Seven

"OH MY GOD! This place is beautiful." Abby stared at the grand stairway that led to the second-floor master bedroom.

They had arrived at the Wynfrey Hotel moments ago and were immediately brought to the presidential suite on the top two floors. The spacious living area had an actual working fireplace and floor-to-ceiling windows overlooking a suburb of Birmingham.

In all the undercover missions she'd been assigned to by the OS and The Circle, she'd never experienced such luxury. She skimmed her fingers over the Chippendale table, loving how everything looked so Old World. Yes. She could get used to living in such richness.

"We have a couple hours before we're needed down-stairs for the party. If you want to finish your nap, the master bedroom is upstairs." Rex stood in the middle of the living room with his feet set apart and arms crossed as if he were on the bow of a ship ordering his men to fire the cannons. "There's another large bedroom through those doors." He pointed to double doors on the opposite end of the living room.

So two bedrooms. Good. He could sleep downstairs and she'd take the other one. Not only on another floor, but also preferably in another suite. She knew that wasn't about to happen. With a glance at Rex, she bit back a sigh.

The short sleeves of his sport shirt tightened around his biceps and the fine hairs on his forearms emphasized his strength and masculinity. Though sexy, that wasn't what caught her attention. His eyes. Those light gray eyes were filled with concern and a touch of male interest and drew her to him.

She placed her hands behind her back and chewed on her bottom lip. *Do not touch. You're too vulnerable to him at this moment.* Her fingers actually tingled. His skin looked warm, deliciously hot to the touch.

"I've slept enough on the way here." With a side step, she headed toward the front door. With her back to him, she waved a hand over her shoulder. "I think I'll do a little shopping." Where had that yellow streak down her back come from?

"Shopping now?"

She shrugged. "Why not? The hotel is attached to the shopping mall. I should be safe. Besides, it'll give me a chance to work off the extra energy and stretch my legs." With a hand on the knob, she couldn't resist looking back. If she stayed, she would want to touch him, feel that warm skin, so taut and alive, run her hands over every inch.

His heated expression warned her before he said, "I'll come with you."

"No need. You probably need some rest. Driving in that crazy traffic from Atlanta would wear anyone out."

He studied her for a couple seconds. "It'll be best if I stick with you and let everyone see us together."

"Really. You don't need to."

"You might as well get over it. We're newlyweds and must act the part." He picked up his cell phone and shoved it into a pocket. "I'll be with you every step of the way."

Frustrated in more ways than one, she shook her head in resignation. "Fine," she huffed, and marched out of the suite with Rex on her heels.

In the elevator, Abby tried her best to ignore Rex's presence. Heated tension radiated from his body in waves. He smelled good.

He leaned down and said into her ear, "I like that color on you." His deep voice seduced her senses as his breath caressed her ear and neck. Without trying to be obvious, she folded her arms. Being so near him and the way he stared at her—possessive and aware of his effect on her—made her nipples ache from being tight and hard for so long.

She turned to comment and her nose hit his chest. Refusing to be intimidated by him, she tilted her head back and glared.

"Why do you really want to go with me?" She shoved at his abs. He didn't move an inch. "And why are you so in my space?"

One blunt-tipped finger traced her ear. "*Dusha my-ah.*" She swiped at his hand. "What's gotten into you?"

A brief sneer that passed for a smile crossed his face. "Practicing my Russian for tonight."

"Well, save it for later."

He chuckled and moved to the other side of the elevator.

Heaven help her, she needed to chill and quit letting him bother her. But every time he leaned in close or brushed his hand against hers, she forgot how to breathe. What made it all difficult to resist was that she remembered his talented mouth. The man knew where to kiss, lick, and suck a woman until she screamed in surrender. Was it any wonder her body stayed on ready whenever he was around? And when he spoke Russian to her, her legs almost melted out from beneath her, and she had no idea what he'd said. The steel doors opened and she'd never been happier to reach the lobby level.

"Do you have a particular store in mind, or you planning to wander around until the party?"

"Don't be a smart-ass," came out weak, even to her ears. Desperate to get a break from his sexual pull, she looked around for a store he'd hate to be seen in. Maybe he'd even go back to their suite and leave her alone for a few minutes. Then she noticed a familiar sign. "I'm going there." She pointed to a pink and white sign.

"Damn," he murmured beneath his breath.

Grinning big, she bounced through the open door of Victoria's Secret.

REX DIDN'T CARE that she enjoyed seeing him uncomfortable in such a feminine environment. Since her return to the OS, he'd rarely seen her laugh, and certainly not so carefree. The Circle had changed her, made her solemn. She used to laugh at the smallest things. She'd always had a smart mouth but it had become acidic. Since her return to the OS, he still caught glimpses of the old Abby, but the new, more deadly one fascinated him. So he stood off to the side watching her. Plus he needed to keep an eye on her, in case word had gotten out that Rurik had arrived early. His presence was known to stir up trouble. The people he dealt with were not known for trusting others and would be suspicious of his presence in their territory. And of course, the usual trouble could show up as his height made people nervous, a strange phenomenon that happened to him often enough but usually where alcohol was served. Drunks lacked a filter or sense of consequence, and his head being a foot above everyone else's guaranteed a target on the back of his skull. He had a feeling a woman's lingerie store wouldn't be much different. At least, he hoped they hadn't started serving liquor.

Speaking of trouble, Abby picked up a skimpy red bra with matching thong. He groaned. As she pulled out a few more matching sets of lingerie, he moved behind a rack to adjust his cock. He was so hard he hurt.

"I'm going into the dressing room for a minute."

Certain he would burst and not caring, he absorbed her movements. The way she rolled her hips with each step and how the edge of her skirt flipped and turned, showing off her long legs. He wanted to run his hands over her silky skin and work his way up to the heat he remembered so well. Would his touch still excite her as it had once long ago? Would he find her creamy and swollen?

He followed a step behind her. He wanted answers to those questions.

"Sir. Sir! You can't go in there. That's for ladies only." A saleswoman moved between him and the room Abby entered.

Knowing an overprotective husband wouldn't be excuse enough, he said, "I'm her bodyguard. She's not allowed out of my sight." He pulled out a wad of bills, peeled off two hundreds, and grabbed the woman's hand, folding her fingers around the paper.

The woman's penned-on brows rose as she nodded, staring at the money. "I'll give you twenty minutes and then you must come out."

"That will be long enough." He grinned, but her nervous look warned that he'd failed to assure her of his honesty.

A short hallway led to three changing rooms with only one door closed. He jerked it open. Abby gasped as she twirled around to face him.

She'd taken off her blouse, leaving on the skirt that fascinated him. Her bra matched the cream-colored wedding dress she'd worn earlier and pushed her breasts to delightful mounds that begged to be touched.

"What are you doing back here? You're going to get us in trouble." She turned her back, but with the mirrors he could still see everything. "The last thing we need is to draw attention."

Seeing all of that smooth skin, his fingers burned to touch her. He ran his palms down her bare arms.

"Then you need to be very quiet." He turned her around and pressed her back against a mirror. His mouth covered the pulse on her neck. She smelled of flowers and sweetness. The softest skin Rex ever touched heated beneath his tongue and fingers. As he tasted her special flavor, his leg separated her thighs, and he thrust his erection along silk-covered moistness. He didn't care if she darkened his trousers. Hell, he probably helped her.

"Rex. Please," she moaned.

At first, he expected her to shove him off, but instead she hooked her fingernails into his shoulders and held on as he licked and sucked his way down her neck to her breasts.

Satisfied that she wouldn't fight him, he ordered in a low rumble, "Do not move your hands away from the mirror."

"Why?" She gasped as he yanked her bra down and cupped her breasts, nipples tight with need against his palms.

"Time for you to learn not to run from me, from this. You know better. I'll find you and bring you down." His tongue swirled around the end of a taut coral tip. He loved how they were pebble hard. He bit at the tender flesh and sucked hard.

She gasped his name.

His hand slid between their bodies and her legs. "Is your clit as stiff as your nipples?"

She whimpered and tossed her head back and forth as his finger slipped beneath the piece of silky material and pressed into her moistness.

"Oh, yeah. Hard as a pebble." He dropped to his knees, slipping her thong down her long legs. She didn't resist as his hands spread her legs apart. Her well-trimmed mons, swollen and wet, was petal soft. His thumbs opened the folds to allow his tongue to dip inside. One swipe and he grinned and looked up. "See, your body remembers me. Spread your legs a little wider, sweetheart."

In the throes of sexual need, her eyes half closed, she arched her back and moaned, rhythmically pressing her groin against his hand. He tongued the hard knot, keeping his gaze on her. She moaned and used her fingers to twist and pull at her nipples.

He stopped to press his cheek to her thigh for a second as he rubbed her clit with a thumb. "I love watching you. Later you can put on a show for me." That was a sight any man would pay good money to see. His cock pulsed. Damn, she was so hot. Her obvious immersion in what he did to her body almost caused him to lose control.

His mouth returned to licking and sucking her responsive clit. He thrust a finger into her hot depths and she whimpered. A second finger pumped into her brought a hissing *yes*. His other hand squeezed a cheek to hold her in place.

Another long hiss released between her teeth matched the length of time her flesh throbbed beneath his tongue. He continued to flick and draw on the bundle of nerves until the last tremble faded.

He licked her slit from back to front. "That's a good girl." Then he kissed her thigh, followed by her stomach, as he slowly stood. The mixture of embarrassment and satisfaction on her face brought a grin to his. No matter how she acted, she still wanted him. His hand cupped her mound and squeezed before he stepped back. Her hips thrust forward, wanting more.

The dazed look on her face was assurance he could move away without her kicking or harming him. If she hadn't enjoyed his touch, she could easily have used her deadly skills to retaliate by hurting him bad. Considering how his cock ached like a son of a bitch, it would've been agony.

ABBY LEANED AGAINST Rex as she tried to regain strength in her legs. The moment shattered her, and it was more than just the best climax she'd had in years. For her to look down and see the man of her dreams servicing her, obviously enjoying what he was doing and knowing just the places to touch, pushed her over the edge. The vibration shook her from spinning head to curling toes.

Hiding her face in his chest, uncaring that her makeup smudged his shirt, she fought the tears welling in her eyes. His hair tickled her palms as she ran her hands over the nape of his neck and up the back of his head. Oh, God, he felt so good in her arms. She missed him.

"Shh, it'll be okay," he whispered.

Her eyes burned. Hell, the last thing she needed to do was cry or feel anything. It was all wrong. She couldn't do it again. She'd never be the woman Rex fell in love with all those years ago.

Without warning, she slammed her heel on top his foot.

"Shit!"

He stumbled back, holding his foot in one hand, and crashed into the door.

"What's going on in there?" The saleswoman's voice sounded worried.

"Get out," Abby said beneath her breath to Rex. "Tell her I'll be out in a minute."

His gray eyes glowed with future retribution.

She turned her back. A couple seconds passed before she heard the door open and close. Rex's deep voice soothing the woman's complaints faded as he led her away.

Not wanting to waste time, Abby quickly drew up her thong and adjusted her bra. When she straightened, a pale face with two large dark circles surrounding darker eyes reflected back at her. Why had she let him get to her? He did know ways to make a woman happy. He'd proven it once again and in a dressing room no less.

In automaton mode, she wiped away the smeared mascara and pinched her cheeks, hoping to bring some life back into her face. Finger-combing her hair, she stuck out her tongue at herself and then finished dressing.

Within five minutes, she exited the dressing room. She bought all of the underwear, partly because they were beautiful but also to make up for putting the saleswoman in such an awkward position. People who worked in retail were mistreated enough, and Abby didn't want to add to it. When Rex whipped out his billfold, she cut her eyes toward him and gave him the evil eye.

"Okay. Okay." He walked away. "Stubborn woman."

The saleswoman rang up the purchase, and while

Abby punched in her code to pay by debit, she felt the woman's stare.

"Excuse me, miss, but I have to tell you that you're one lucky woman," the saleswoman said in a stage whisper.

"Pardon?"

"A man built like him and with his voice, I get goose bumps just thinking . . . uh, you're a very lucky woman." The woman then stared over Abby's shoulder. "Yeah. A lucky, lucky woman."

Abby snatched her receipt and bag from the woman and turned. Rex stood a few feet away and probably heard every word. Talk about blowing his ego out of proportion—geez, she really dreaded dealing with him after he proved he could have her any time, any place. She hated the helpless feeling that came over her whenever he touched her.

A little tender between her legs—he needed to shave— and all wound up from the whole embarrassing situation, she slapped the bag into his chest. He clasped it in reflex. She continued walking and headed for their suite and the final preparations for the cocktail party. The last thing she felt like doing was partying, undercover or not.

When he stood to one side of the elevator, facing her, and smiled his crooked, charming smile, she corrected her earlier thought: The last thing she felt like doing was saying no to that infuriating, dipped-in-testosterone male.

Chapter Eight

ABBY HELD THE champagne glass to her lips and tilted it without taking a sip. First, she had never liked the taste of any liquor or wine. Second, when she dared to drink, she either cried like the world had come to an end or she acted like the fool by telling everyone around her that she loved them. Thus, she pretended to drink to fit in with the crowd as part of her cover. People also make comments whenever someone doesn't drink. Who said adults didn't cave into peer pressure?

When Rex led her into the party, the dim room filled with a hundred-plus people talking all at once nearly sent her running. Most of her work with The Circle had been surveillance and elimination and rarely undercover work. She hated pretending to be what she wasn't. Maybe it was all tied in with lying about her family for so long. But she'd thought she could handle this situation—her playing like she was married.

She looked up at Rex.

Make that a woman married to a Russian arms dealer attending a charity cocktail party and waiting for another arms dealer to show up. Then they would simply make nice and wait for an invite to one of his infamous weekend parties at his farm. Their big hope was finding or hearing something there about the facility making the ammo.

Rex socialized rather well as the dangerous but charming Rurik. Women followed him with their eyes, taking in how the dark gray jacket stretched across his broad shoulders, and whenever he placed a hand into his pants pocket, his jacket lifted up in the back, showing off his tight butt.

She knew what they imagined when they admired his long legs and size 12 shoes. Yet they had no idea what she knew. True, in his case, big feet equaled a big cock, but just as important, the man had a wickedly talented mouth.

The champagne splashed out of her glass. She looked down at her shaking hand and reined in her reaction to the memories. She brushed at the little black dress she had found in her suitcase. Jack had great taste. Thankfully the time they'd spent in the suite repairing the damage done to her makeup and changing clothes had left little room for more than a couple of speculative glances before riding the elevator down to the ballroom level.

He hadn't touched her again, but he stared hard. With his arms folded over his chest and ankles crossed, he'd leaned back against the elevator door, his gaze leisurely drifting over her as if weighing the different methods to make her climax again. By the time they'd reached the party, she'd been wound up.

A quick shake of her head brought her back to the present.

"What's going on, babe?"

The accent sounded so strange coming out of Rex's mouth. It was a mix of Russian and a crispness of someone who'd learned English in the Northeast.

He rested his arm over her shoulders and squeezed her to his side. Though she reminded herself it was part of the act, she wanted to kick him in the shins. Rex. No. Rurik. She needed to remember to prevent slipping up later.

"My head's getting a little fuzzy from the champagne." She raised her glass.

One dark brow lifted.

"Okay, okay. The smell is causing my head to spin." Barely restraining the desire to stick her tongue out at him, she looked away.

Just then she spotted Brody walking in. He looked as gorgeous as he had back when he'd been an all-American quarterback in high school. At six feet, he moved with the grace of an athlete who hadn't allowed himself to grow out as he grew up. And as further testimony to his active lifestyle, his sun-kissed hair matched his tanned skin, and neither appeared to be artificial.

And speaking of things artificial, a tall blonde with too many hair extensions and dressed in a slinky red number looked broodingly at the crowd as she clutched his arm. She said something that Abby couldn't hear, but she easily read the profanity on the woman's scarlet lips. Brody laughed and then kissed her, showing several glimpses of tongue. His hand squeezed a breast so large and perfectly round there was no need to guess if they were real or not.

Yeah, that was the old Brody. He loved to be the center of attention no matter if it was good or bad. Maybe Abby was a little disappointed that he wasn't fat and balding. Something about a person who had everything going for him in high school and then continued to be as blessed later on seemed unfair. That sounded shallow, but she had her reasons. Besides, he probably didn't even remember her.

"It's showtime," she said as she rose on her tiptoes and kissed Rex's cheek to ensure he heard.

"So that's him." Rex dropped his arm to her waist. "Introduce me."

"Give me a minute." When he looked puzzled, she added, "We went to school together but it wasn't like we were friends. He was a couple years ahead of me and spoke to me only once."

"You had a crush on him." Another time, the surprise on his face would've been funny.

"Shh! I'm trying to think of the best way to approach him without sounding too obvious. Remember Jack said to wing it." She nibbled at the corner of her lip as her gaze followed Brody making his way around the room. "Like I know what in the world I'm doing. You distracting me isn't helping," she murmured.

"You need to quit distracting *me*," Rex grumbled.

"Huh?" She blinked up at him. He stared at her mouth. She released her lip and shook her head. "Behave."

Before he could say anything more, a husky voice she remembered once upon a time came from behind Rex.

"Why, I do believe that this here is the infamous Rurik Volkov I've heard so much about."

Rex turned with his hand still on Abby's waist. "I know you?" His Eastern European accent became as heavy as Brody's good ol' boy drawl.

"No, no, no. I've never had the pleasure, sir." Brody held out his hand, his big smile appearing more predatory than friendly. One top tooth slightly overlapped another, giving him a cute little boy look. His little imperfection brought back memories of her huge crush in high school—that was, her and about every other girl at Vestavia High.

"I'm Brody Walker of Walker Industries. A mutual friend told me you'd flown in today from Vegas."

Rex shook his hand and stared hard. "Mr. Walker. I've heard of you. And who is this mutual friend who likes to keep track of me?"

What arms dealer liked the thought of someone following them?

"I'm honored that you've heard of me. I'm nowhere near the caliber of entrepreneur as you are." Brody held his smile. "And let's say the friend is someone who is highly paid to keep up with my competition and possible business partners. Anyway, presently we are in the same line of work."

"And what line of work is that?" Rex dropped the man's hand and shifted as if he planned to protect Abby.

"Why, we're philanthropists. We have the desire to improve our fellow man's life by making him feel secure." Brody chuckled at his own joke.

"I never heard it put in such a way." The deep guffaw from Rex startled her, so unlike his usual sexy chuckle. His hand tightened on her waist, keeping her from moving away.

Abby understood he needed to project the image of a man who lived cautiously but was still approachable. If Brody found them interesting enough, they would be invited to his farm.

Without introducing his companion, Brody looked over at Abby. "This must be the new wife." Hard for her to believe, but his smile widened. He lifted her hand and placed his other hand on top. "How're you doing, darling?"

"Fine. And yourself, Mr. Walker?" She allowed a small grin to show.

"Now, is that a Southern drawl I heard from that sweet mouth?"

She eased her hand from between his. "Yes. In fact, I went to Vestavia High with you."

His hazel eyes sparkled. Damn! The man was good-looking. One major problem: He knew it.

"What was your family name?" Brody asked.

"Rodriguez. Abigail Rodriguez."

"Yes! Ed's little sister. I remember. I broke all of his records in football at Vestavia." He looked her over again.

People who knew her brother often did that. Edward was green-eyed and blond; though the older he became, the darker his hair had gotten until it was more of a light brown. "You're nothing like him."

Her brother was the sheriff of Sand County, so of course the local bad guy would know him. Edward hated being called Ed and only tolerated family calling him Eddie. Professionally, he preferred Edward or Sheriff Wentworth. Once she'd moved out of the house, he'd been Edward to her.

"Different dads."

"Let's move over to a corner and catch up on old acquaintances." He reached for Abby's arm, ignoring the huff of the blonde next to him.

The hand at her waist held tight. "No. No way will I allow my wife to sit in a corner with a strange man." Rex's voice sounded friendly enough, but he spoke between clenched teeth.

Going along with his pretend show of jealousy but remembering their goal of being part of Brody's crowd, Abby pouted. "Aw, Rurik. What can he do in front of this crowd?" She lowered her eyelashes and looked up from underneath at the men.

Before Rex could answer, Brody said, "Ah, but, darling, he's right. There are many things a man can do in public that could cause a husband to protest." He leaned over to the blonde and slipped his hand inside the top of her dress and cupped a breast. "Isn't that right, sugar?" The slinky material outlined his hand. The blonde gasped and closed her eyes in sensual bliss when his thumb and forefinger pinched her tight nipple. Instead of pulling away, she moved closer and raised her knee to rub her body against his.

Abby's eyes widened. She'd seen high and intoxicated couples become too frisky in crowds before, but Brody and the woman appeared straight and sober. When Brody cut his eyes over to her and Rex, she knew then. He enjoyed shocking people.

"Excuse us. We get a little carried away at times," Brody said to Rex as he unwound the woman, but his hand remained in her clothing. "We need to talk and I would dearly love to get to know your wife a little better."

"I cannot imagine what we would say to each other." Rex eyed the blonde, the smirk on his face saying to Brody and Abby that he found the display interesting. Was it part of the act? Then he dragged his gaze away. "Maybe if you explained."

Brody chuckled. "You and I could find it to be beneficial. Most profitable, in fact." The man obviously loved testing boundaries, for his gaze traveled to Abby's cleavage. "But this is not the time or place."

He might be handsome, but she in no way felt the same for him as she did years ago. His hungry look almost brought her dinner up.

Abby jumped when Rex placed his arm over her shoulders. His hand massaged her shoulder. The touch didn't do anything to calm her nerves. She'd had others come on to her before and it never bothered her, but being aware of Rex watching the interplay with Brody made her nervous. She didn't like his show of interest.

And why was that? It was supposed to be a simple operation: one arms dealer meeting another, possibly negotiating a business deal. When did it become two men eyeing each other's woman? If Rex thought she was about to trade places for the good of the operation, he was sorely mistaken.

"Our suite is upstairs. Nice place. Plenty of room to relax." Rex lowered his voice.

"Ah, but I'm meeting with a couple friends. And, anyway, this hotel has too many people milling around. No control. Not safe at all. And I like being in control." Brody shot a look at her. "How about I send someone to pick up you and your little lady, and y'all come and stay the weekend at my farm? Then we all can get to know each other."

"Sorry, but we have somewhere to be tomorrow," Abby said.

What was she thinking refusing his offer? They wanted a way into his place, and the invitation provided a simple solution to get around the freaking farm's security. Surrounded by guards patrolling on ATVs, cameras, and motion sensors, the only way into the house without drawing too much attention was by walking through the front door.

Then again, for her to jump up and accept the offer would appear strange. Brody could be testing them. And she wasn't ready for whatever Rex and Brody were planning with their contemplations directed at her and the blonde. She looked up into Rex's face. Or was she putting off the inevitable? That thought froze her up tight. Once they entered the house as a couple, she would have to sleep with Rex—and possibly Brody—to maintain their cover. Whatever it took to stop the ammo from being manufactured and shipped to Inferno, she would do it. It didn't mean she would like it.

Lifting her chin, she straightened her spine and smiled. Whatever it took to get the job done.

Rex's hand slid down her side, his fingers resting on the soft edge of her breast. His thumb swept up over the lower half. She inhaled sharply. Every nerve ending had been on high alert since the orgasm in the dressing room, and his possessive attitude in holding her close made her think of sex and nothing else. No matter how often she reminded herself they were on a mission, she wanted Rex in and on her.

Oh, goodness, she wanted to see if Rex's technique had improved. The oral exam he'd provided earlier said he had.

Brody's gaze drifted to where Rex's hand rested. When his eyes and grin widened, her stomach twisted in a knot. Sleeping with a stranger, old crush notwithstanding, was not on her bucket list and was different from wanting to sleep with an old lover.

"That's just sad about this weekend." Brody's hand stayed in the blonde's dress, squeezing and pinching, as he spoke to Abby. "How about next weekend? To think of it, that would be better. I have two other couples staying with me. I say more the merrier. Give me your number, and I'll send you a text next week with the directions." His good ol' boy act didn't fool her for one minute, especially with him molesting his girlfriend in front of everyone. He had something planned and the way he stared at her was . . . disturbing.

"Much better," Rex said. "My sweet Abby must introduce me to her family." Rex spread his fingers as he recited his cell phone number to Brody. She felt his thumb brush over her nipple. The tip hardened as the heat shot down to her groin and moisture prepared her for something more.

She held her breath. Would Rex try it again? The naughtiness excited her more than she would ever admit to him. When his hand moved away, she exhaled.

Out of the corner of her eye, she spotted Nic serving hors d'oeuvres. Jack worked the bar as several women stood at one end flirting outrageously with him. If she looked around instead of concentrating on Rex, she would see another Circle operative or two.

"Would you like a snack?" Nic nearly dumped the whole tray on Abby. "Oops. Sorry." The last was said in a sneer. Jealousy showing its ugly face.

"No, thank you." Out of pure spite, Abby leaned into Rex and rubbed her breasts along his side. "I'm worn out, Rurik. Let's go to bed."

Rex continued to share small talk with Brody, and once Nic showed up, his body tensed. When Abby's body rubbed his, he tightened even further and she wondered if he'd shatter into a thousand pieces.

Yet she wasn't sure if what he did next was an accident or a lesson for playing with fire. As he turned to step away, his hard groin grazed her hand. Her fingers tingled with a need to cup him, but she refused to play further. Ashamed of letting Nic get to her, she ducked her head and pulled out of Rex's embrace.

"Please excuse us," Rex murmured to the couple as he grabbed her arm and led her toward the exit.

"Slow down. I've got long legs but I can't keep up," she said.

He didn't look like he cared if she kept up or not. As they rushed out the room, Abby caught a glimpse of Jack's face across the room. Why in the hell was he laughing?

Chapter Nine

"WHAT THE HELL do you think you were doing down there?" Rex stood over Abby with his hands on his hips, daring her to move off the couch that he'd thrown her onto.

Uncertain if he wanted to choke or kiss her, at the moment he leaned toward choking. With her dark hair mussed and face flushed, she appeared turned on and pissed. Damn, she was hot. Maybe kissing her would be better.

"I don't know!" For most women, that would be the beginning of an apology but not for Abby. She looked as if she was just getting wound up. "First, I get only two hours' sleep, then I show up at a crazy Elvis-officiated wedding, then you get me off in a freaking public dressing room, and then an hour later I watch two people feeling each other up and getting turned on and not caring. Then you manhandle me in front of them." She shot an evil glare at him. "This has been the most fucked up day of my life." She shoved his chest as she stood, and he stepped back, giving her room. "No. Make that third most fucked up day. The first was the day I was told you were dead. The second was when I was kidnapped. No. Wait! First was when I found out you were alive! Crap! Maybe my whole life was fucked up because that's a whole lot of fucked up days."

Rex watched her as she paced back and forth. Her hands waving in the air, she added a couple stomps on the floor for emphasis as she worked herself to a fevered pitch. Despite being horny, he couldn't help but start laughing.

She faced him, her chest heaving, and pointed a finger. "You! You and Jack. You're both fucking jackasses. That makes sense! Jack's certainly the biggest. The wedding was his idea alone, wasn't it? Don't answer that, because if I find out it was all your idea, I'll kill you and don't think I can't." A few short steps brought her close enough to stab him in the chest with her fingertip as she spit out each word. "Quit laughing. Quit! What's so funny?"

"I've never heard you scream so many curses in such a short length of time. I do believe it's one of your many hidden talents." They needed to talk about her serious screwup downstairs, but she looked so good flustered and confused. He liked knowing he had a part in doing that to her.

"Humph!" She turned her back and headed for the couch again. "I still don't see what is so funny. You really need to take this operation more seriously." She flopped onto the cushion at one end, crossing her arms again. Her bottom lip stuck out a little.

He sure wanted to suck on that plump piece of flesh. Hot damn, she looked so good.

"Quit looking at me like that." Her gaze dropped from his face to his groin. He knew what she'd noticed. The reaction couldn't be helped. Whenever he was around her, he was semihard, but when she acted like a spoiled brat who needed a spanking, he became a tree trunk.

"Stop acting like a brat or I'll have to take you over my knee." His hands at his sides fisted to keep him from reaching for her.

"You and—" She stopped midsentence when he took one step toward her. "You want me to dare you. That would give you a good excuse for beating my butt." With a gracefulness brought from hours of martial training, she moved off the couch and walked around him. "I'm going to bed. I'm tired and I need my beauty sleep before visiting with my mom tomorrow."

Another long step and he stood in front of her, almost nose-to-nose. "We'll talk in the morning about how you almost threw this mission off track."

"That's what you say." She lifted her chin.

"What I say counts." He wouldn't back down. Not when they were so close to getting inside an operation that could mean an end to several months' worth of investigation and, more importantly, could save lives.

"You're not my boss. Jack is."

Before Rex even realized he'd done it, he'd grabbed her upper arms and pulled her off her feet to look into her wide eyes. "I might not be your direct boss, but I'm second-in-command of The Circle and that technically makes me Jack's boss and yours. I agreed to be only lead operative here to keep confusion down. You've been at this long enough to know we do whatever it takes to be successful. Failure is not an option. Ryker was lenient when he first took over, allowing others time to adjust to the new command. Since then he's decided that in our line of work, fear works best. Firing is only one solution to a disobedient operative. If you screw up big enough, he'll have you killed and won't think twice about it."

"Jack won't let him."

The smug look on her face infuriated him. Bad enough she played with her life like that, but she dared to throw his brother in his face?

He shoved her away. She stumbled but caught herself on one of the chairs.

"Fuck Jack! So I was right. You and Jack were lovers. Do you really think he'll willingly risk his life to save yours? I know him better than you ever will. Jack looks after Jack. He fucks a woman only if she's unavailable. Were you two fucking when we were engaged? I would imagine that as soon as the news came in that I was dead, he dropped you like a hot cartridge."

"You don't know shit! That you even think that of me and Jack, that we would be together while you and I were engaged, my God! It shows how stupid you really are."

Rex's whole body tensed up. As a kid, his father used to beat him when he brought home bad grades. With him growing so fast and large, people always expected him to be smarter than expected for his age and would tease by calling him T-Rex, for the large dinosaur with a small brain. Everyone knew Jack was the smart one in the family.

He wasn't a helpless kid anymore. He might not be smart, but he refused to be treated like an idiot. A dead coldness came over him.

"Go to bed, Abby. You're tired." He started walking toward the door.

"Where are you going?"

"It's really none of your business." He quietly closed the door behind him. He needed a good stiff drink.

OH, CRAP. ABBY hung up her clothes. Numb and tired, she washed her face and brushed out her hair. Looking in the mirror, she didn't like what she saw. When had she become a total bitch? If she'd been anyone else, she would've walked out too.

How could she call him stupid? Though Rex never talked about it, Jack had told her a few things about their childhood. Mainly that their father was crazy, and he beat the two of them often, especially Rex. The old man had thought Rex was lazy and stupid.

She really needed to apologize. What had come over her? She'd gone without sleep before while on assignment and never acted like that. Between being nervous about seeing her mom and lying to her as part of their cover, and seeing someone who had played a major role in her teenage fantasies, it was no wonder she had overreacted tonight.

Yeah. That was it. She'd wait up and tell him how sorry she was about her behavior and explain a little.

Feeling a little better, she pulled on her Tweety Bird pajama pants and *Dark-Hunter* T-shirt. She turned on the bedside lamp and stretched out on top of the covers to read the latest Sherrilyn Kenyon book.

HER EYES OPENED. Where was she? Oh, yeah, the hotel in Birmingham on assignment. She rubbed her eyes and sat up. Her hand caught the book before it fell off her chest. Without wasting time, she tossed the book to the side and tiptoed across the room to the stairs. A noise had woken her up. The living room was dark except for a light that shone from beneath the double doors leading into the second bedroom. Rex's bedroom.

She padded softly down the steps. The sound of a news announcer chattering about the stock market echoed through the door. Then someone began to talk as if whispering to another. Seconds later, she heard a thumping sound—of flesh slapping wet flesh.

Rex better not have brought Nic to the suite. Was he nuts? He could blow their cover. All the work put into the mission so far would be wasted.

She ignored how her heart ached with the thought of Rex naked on top of—

No. Why think about it until she knew for sure? She wasn't a coward. Turning the knob, she opened the door and halted midstride.

Rex was alone. The sheets and comforter at his feet

with legs sprawled out and his hand wrapped around his cock. Pumping. With his eyes closed and forehead creased, he concentrated so hard that he missed her entrance.

He continued to pump as she blinked to clear her vision and watched. No way could she move. Where she stood, the foot of the bed faced her, giving a clear view, leaving nothing to the imagination. One broad hand slid up and down, while the other massaged his balls, tight and high between his legs. He stopped.

Her gaze shot to his face. His eyes remained squeezed shut. She looked back down. His thumb rubbed across the plump tip; moisture glistened on the head. When he began to pump again, she let her gaze drift up his taut abdomen as it jerked with each downward stroke. His small beaded nipples begged to be licked and bitten. He groaned.

Again she looked to see if he was aware of her. A line of dark lashes stayed lowered, not revealing the light gray eyes beneath. Her gaze caressed his powerful chest until he thrust his hips to pound harder and faster. His biceps released and bulged with the power he asserted on his long, magnificent cock. His thighs trembled each time his heels dug into the mattress.

All that force and masculinity working toward one goal was so beautiful, so incredibly animalistic, she yearned to be part of it, wanted him thrusting into her with the same force and single-minded concentration. But she didn't want him to stop from attaining his own satisfaction. She wanted to see him come. See his face as he climaxed. She could spend her entire life watching him like that.

That was a lie. A part of her craved to touch the throbbing ache between her legs and stroke with the same rhythm and vigor.

Afraid to move, almost afraid to breathe, she watched and waited. His cock darkened and his hand sped up as he tightened his hold. His breathing became deeper as she inhaled and exhaled with him. Mouth open, head slung back, he took in an endless gulp of air as his whole body arched. He thrust two more times and then climaxed as he released one guttural word:

"Abby."

She lifted her gaze to his. Molten-gray eyes watched her from beneath dark lashes.

Excitedly disturbed but mortified, she numbly exited the room. Not until she was halfway up the stairs did she stop. She crumbled onto a step and leaned against the cool railing. Her skin felt hot and tight on her face and arms. Panting as if the air in the room had thinned, she swallowed and worked on regaining her senses.

She wanted Rex with all her being. Jack, Olivia, and even Rex had told her there was no reason for her not to take advantage of the setup and enjoy the benefits. Why fight it any longer? Not until that moment had she realized she'd been denying herself the one thing she wanted so badly. She thought she'd come to terms with every gritty part of her job. So what was her problem? What held her back?

She was scared. Spitless.

Chapter Ten

THANK GOODNESS FOR Nic and Jack, and she never imagined being thankful about that. But when she walked into the living room the next morning, filled with dread about facing Rex and trying to figure out what to say, there they sat on the sofa looking at a map on a laptop with Rex staring over their shoulders.

Nic gave her a smirk. Abby wanted to hug the little twit, even when she said, "Well, look at who the cat dragged in. You want an aspirin? You really need to lay off the alcohol, especially when you're on duty."

Too tired from tossing and turning all morning, she shot Nic the bird and shuffled over to the counter with the coffeepot. When the woman gasped, she felt kind of bad about her gesture, considering Nic was so clueless. Everyone at The Circle loved the small woman; it wasn't Nic's fault that everything she said grated on her nerves.

She poured a cup and carefully took a few sips of the evil brew. Rex always loved the stuff extra strong.

Eyeing the group, she liked how Rex, standing in his usual pose, arms crossed and feet well planted, filled out black jeans and a gray shirt like they were tailored for him. They probably were, if she had to bet. Even when they'd first started dating and he'd favored leather everything, the gothic-looking clothes had been tailored especially for his tall frame. And his hair had hung between his shoulders, though he'd often pulled it back tight and braided it. Was Nic the reason for the more mainstream clothing and haircut? Abby had been partial to the long hair. It had given him a sexy rock-god look.

"Now that Abby's decided to join us, let's go over the statistics." Jack clicked on the keyboard. "The farm Brody mentioned last night is about four hundred acres, a sizeable spread in Alabama. He has six workers who keep it productive, with the main crop being peanuts." He shook his head. "An arms dealer growing peanuts. Takes all kinds."

"I see electric fencing but no brick walls. Does he use guards and dogs?" Rex squinted at the screen.

"Yeah." Jack nodded. "We'd been told he had more until I sent Liam to investigate. From what we found, that's all he has. Maybe he's so arrogant he believes no one would be dumb enough to break in." Abby rolled her eyes. Was there any doubt? Ignoring her, he continued. "We haven't come across a building with an unknown purpose. But we still believe his manufacturing facility is somewhere on the property. The trucks, coming and going with supplies and shipments of peanuts, could easily include items to produce or ship ammo."

"What about the designer? Has there been word yet of what he looks like?" Abby said as she stopped next to Rex and looked at the farm layout. Rex shifted from one leg to another and his hip bumped into her. She glanced up, and he gave her an innocent look. Her arm tingled and face warmed from the small contact.

Flashes of memory shot across her mind's eye, showing glimpses of his hand stroking and fondling hard, thick flesh. Heat like what had engulfed her last night brightened her face further.

What was her problem? She wasn't a naïve preteen. Concentrate. Nothing was more important than the mission at hand.

Another brief vision of a hand squeezing and pumping caused her to inhale too sharp and she coughed. Rex, Jack, and Nic looked at her for a second. She shook her head and waved at them to continue.

Christ! Rex and her libido were driving her crazy.

She barely caught what Rex said as she regained control of her brain.

"Let's not forget it could easily be a woman. We screwed the pooch when it came to chasing down the designer for the Blossom Flower drug." Rex referred to their last mission where Jack and Ryker almost lost their lives searching for the person producing a drug that caused women to crave sex so they could be sold to sex traffickers.

"Only one woman has been in the house more than any of his current flavors." When Jack glanced over at her, she knew she wouldn't like the answer. "Your mom, Abby."

She groaned. What could she be doing at an arms dealer's house? Farm or not, the man was young enough to be her son. No matter how gorgeous her mom was, she was fifty-eight years old.

"There has to be an explanation," Abby said hopefully.

Nic released a giggle and quickly covered her mouth. Ignoring Nic's enjoyment in how uncomfortable the whole conversation was becoming for her, Abby tilted her head and widened her eyes, letting Jack know he better answer fast.

"Actually there is. She's the head of the Save Sand City Museum campaign, and Brody appears to be the largest contributor. What better way to stay on the good side of a small town community and keep an eye on the local police department?"

"Mom is very proud of my brother, and considering how she loves bragging about him, Brody probably hears about every investigation that's going on in all of Sand County."

Abby glanced toward the bathroom. By the way she was feeling, she wasn't sure how much longer she would last before getting sick. Especially if Jack told her that her mother was having a fling with Brody. Maybe she kept his books. She'd worked in Abby's dad's practice as the office manager and bookkeeper when he was alive. Yeah, that had to be it.

"Maybe. But your brother was elected sheriff only six months ago, and your mom's been visiting with Brody for at least a year." Jack sat back, one hand holding his elbow as his other rubbed his chin. He stared hard at the report on his screen as his tongue played with the loop piercing his bottom lip. Was he as confused as she was by her mom's actions?

A niggling feeling at the back of her mind warned that she'd just missed something important.

"When are Charlie and Liam showing up?" Rex's voice, deep and gruff, caused her to blush.

She remembered the rough groans escaping his lips last night, of how he arched his back in pleasure with each thrust of his fist. Heat flooded her body again as she replayed each sensual moment. Considering the different types of missions she'd been through over the last few years, she should be unaffected by such a display, but she couldn't get it out of her mind. Watching Rex masturbate last night had excited her more than she ever wanted to admit. It had been natural and beautiful. After what he'd done to her earlier that day, she understood he needed some type of outlet. It wasn't like she had offered to pay him back for his generosity.

Oh, goodness, the man's tongue needed to be registered as a lethal weapon. Really. How had she not had a heart attack?

When Jack picked up his cup and moved over to the coffee machine, she once again pushed herself to pay attention.

"They're going to see if they can get hired on as day laborers," Jack said in answer to Rex's earlier question. "Word's out that the farm needs help preparing the fields for peanuts. By having them nearby, they can keep an eye on the comings and goings and report back. As a bonus, if you and Rex need help, they'll be nearby."

"With Alabama's strict immigration laws, farmers are begging for help. Should be easy for them to get picked," Nic chimed in.

"Nic and I'll be hanging out at a popular bar in Sand City and letting the locals know we're in the market for some land. It's amazing the info people will tell all in the name of being helpful." Taking a long sip of his coffee, Jack slowly looked from her to his brother and back to her.

Did he know about last night?

No. Otherwise, Jack would be giving her hell. He'd love nothing more than to have something to hold over her head and tease her with. If he did know, why wasn't he teasing her?

What was he up to?

When he glanced at her and sipped his coffee again, she went over their conversation so far. Then it hit her.

"Rex. Nic. If you two would excuse us for a few minutes, I need to talk with Jack." She stared straight at Rex. "Privately."

His eyes narrowed for a second and then he nodded. "Nic, come with me. We'll talk about how to set up the bugs you gave me."

The man had enough sense to not argue with her. Maybe he was glad he wasn't the one in trouble. This time.

Like a happy puppy, Nic followed Rex to his bedroom, chatting all the way. Bedroom? Why the bedroom? If she wasn't so angry with Jack, she would have a word or two with Rex about his choice of rooms. Then again, would her bedroom upstairs be any better? Yeah. It at least had a sitting area, and Nic wouldn't like coming on to the big hunk in the same room Abby slept in and, as far as she knew, regardless of Rex's mussed up bed, Rex had too.

When the door closed with a click, her fingernails dug into the back of the couch. Who was she to dictate where and with whom he could go? The marriage was a fake and no one outside the suite would know.

Well, crap. She had a problem for sure. Jealousy had no place on a mission.

REX WANTED TO stay, but he actually needed to ask Nic for an extra bug without Abby knowing. From the intel he'd received from Jack and their discussions leading up to the wedding, Abby's brother was an important key to finding some answers. Every time they'd mentioned bugging her brother, she'd claimed he was as straight and narrow as they come. One thing he'd learned over the years, even brothers could screw up.

"I hope she hasn't been mean to you." Nic's hand rubbed his upper arm and dropped to squeeze his hand.

"Abby? Nah." He stepped away and picked up a black bag with the bugs provided for use in Brody's home. The bag looked like any normal man's shaving kit. Inside, he stored his razor, shaving cream, comb, deodorant, and toothbrush with paste, but in the false bottom were six tiny listening devices. Even if someone emptied the bag and cut the bottom, the bugs and the foam they were encased in would stay hidden. Ingenious, if he said so himself. "Do you happen to have an extra bug I could take with me?"

"Did something happen to one of them? I told Sal to pack tight." She reached for the bag, but Rex held it above her head.

"No. Everything's okay. I want an extra in case something comes up." He set it in the bathroom and turned, bumping into Nic, who was on his heels. "Whoa." He held her arm until she regained her balance. "I also want it to have a single feed receiver." The other bugs' information was received by The Circle's big computer mainframe and accessed by phone. He wanted to be the only one to hear.

"I don't know. I could get in a lot of trouble if Jack or Ryker finds out." Nic scooted a little closer and ran her hand up his chest. Damn, they probably should've gone to the sitting room upstairs. The way Nic touched him and glanced at the rumpled bed, she clearly expected a reward for going against Circle rules.

He moved near the door and crossed his arms. "I don't want you to get in trouble. If you can't, I'll understand."

"Rex." She followed and ran her hand over his chest again. "While Abby and Jack are occupied, we can do the same."

As soon as she looked into his face, her hand dropped to her side.

His brother might be an asshole who loved unavailable women, but Jack would never jeopardize a mission by fooling around while the husband was in the next room. And for the current job, Abby was his wife.

"You and I talked about this. We had a good time, but now we're friends and nothing more."

She stuck out her chin, pressing her lips together. After a few seconds, she said, "I know that's what you said, but anyone with eyes can tell Abby has a thing for Jack. I don't want you to get hurt. She's got you all tied up with this pretend wedding and meeting her family. You'll only get hurt again."

"That's for me to worry about." He pulled her into his arms and hugged her. "I appreciate your concern, but I'm a big boy and can take care of myself." With a light kiss on the top of her head, he released her and held out his hand. "Still friends?"

Her big eyes looked into his. "Sure. Friends." She shook his hand. "I think we can set up one of the bugs you already have for a single feed to your phone. Where's your laptop?"

Rex was relieved but unsurprised that Nic took his rejection so well. One of the things he liked about her was her easygoing nature. She was protective of those she liked and a pain in the ass to those she didn't. And Nic made no bones that she didn't care for Abby. He never asked why, as he expected Nic being Nic one day would change her mind once she knew more about Abby.

He listened for the couple in the next room. Besides, Nic was wrong about Abby and Jack. At least, she'd better be wrong.

JACK SIPPED FROM his coffee cup again while staring out the glass doors leading to the balcony.

Did he really think Abby believed his calm routine? He knew he'd screwed up, and it was time for him to pay the piper.

"How long have you been investigating my mom?"

He looked at her as if he wanted to lie but reconsidered. Obviously, he decided the truth would work best. How many times in the past had he not come to that decision with her? Before she could delve deeper into that horrible thought, he said, "For eighteen months."

Abby raised her hands in the air in frustration, and when she realized how crazy she looked, she dropped them to clasp the back of her head.

"A year and a half," she said in disbelief.

"We've been watching Brody for three years. When he moved to Sand City, your brother was already there. Once your mom moved in and she met Brody, we had to investigate."

"You set me up." She rubbed her temples.

Why was it that when people became powerful, they couldn't talk straight and tell people what they wanted them to do? Why manipulate them? Was The Circle's influence so tainted from the past that the leaders thought deception was the only way to control every situation?

She sighed and then asked, "Why the elaborate hoax?" Crap. He was looking at her again, measuring, trying to decide if he wanted to tell the truth or not. "You know I think you and I have been friends for too long. Every time you give me that how-little-can-I-get-away-with-telling-her look, I want to bop you on the head."

"You have to trust me on this."

"In other words, you don't want to argue anymore."

"Touché."

What was the use talking to the hardheaded man?

She rolled her eyes and headed toward Rex's bedroom. It was too quiet in there. Considering how much noise Rex usually made while *having fun*, she doubted Nic had convinced him to give her a ride. No. She refused to even think of them doing the nasty.

A loud knocking at the door had Abby turning on her heels and heading to the entryway.

"I thought you said Liam and Charlie weren't coming," she said to Jack in a low voice as she stopped a few feet from the door.

"I did."

"You didn't order room service either, right?" Abby backed up from the door, and Jack grabbed the gun in the holster at the small of his back.

"Right."

Rex came out of the bedroom with gun in hand, pointing slightly down, and Nic behind him, weaponless.

When Nic opened her mouth, Abby shook her head and placed her finger to her lips. She probably wanted to ask the question they all had: Who in the hell was it?

Thankfully, she'd checked out the best place to stash a weapon last night and settled on the buffet cabinet next to the door. She pulled out the Sig with attached suppressor from inside the drawer.

"Who is it?" Waiting to see if they overreacted, she

stood to the side. The door frame would slow a bullet but it wouldn't protect her.

"Room service."

"We didn't order anything," she said in an even tone.

"Ms. Nic Savage ordered lunch for four."

"I did. Sorry. I forgot," Nic said in a low voice as she looked up at Rex.

Jack waved Nic back when she headed toward the door. "You know better. No room service ever." Opening a secure location to an unknown asked for trouble. He signaled for Abby to open the door.

She hesitated. When she winkled her forehead and dipped her head at Jack, silently asking if he was sure, he nodded.

Not wanting to scare an innocent waiter, she placed her gun on top of the buffet and edged it behind a large fat-bottomed lamp, hoping it would escape notice. Then she swung the door open while standing to the side. The burgundy short jacket proclaimed he worked for the hotel, but the pistol with suppressor pointing at her told another story. He shot twice as she reached for her gun. One good thing about shooting at a moving target: most people missed. Luckily he had, though she was certain one grazed her hair.

The man landed face-first inside the suite.

Rex and Jack had their weapons out, smoke drifting from the barrels. The way the man's blood spread quickly on the carpet, their aim had been dead on target through the heart with only one exit wound from what she could see. Another bullet probably met bone and remained inside.

For a few seconds after the blasts of gunfire, everyone was quiet, waiting for shouting or screaming outside the suite. The *clack, clack, clack* sound of shots through a suppressor were loud enough to grab someone's attention. Thankfully, one of the pluses the concierge mentioned when they checked in the day before was how the suite was private and soundproof. She doubted he'd intended the noise to be firearm related.

With no alarm triggered, everyone began to move as if on the same string.

Jack called The Circle with a request for a cleanup crew, telling them their would-be killer was sprawled on the beautiful gold carpet and his body needed hauling off without drawing attention. Rex looked into the foyer toward the elevator and then closed the door.

Abby yanked out the tall garbage bag in the small kitchen. After using a steak knife to slice it open, she slipped it beneath his body before more blood soaked the rug. The wounds continued to seep.

"Get me a couple towels out of the bathroom quick," she said to Nic.

Faster than she expected, the woman returned, tossing them to her. Abby worked at staunching the blood to stop more from pooling on the plastic. Considering the mess they already had on the wall and beneath the body, they needed a miracle that the crew would be successful in cleaning it off everything it had sprayed on.

She turned to ask Rex for help in moving the body, as it weighed more than she'd expected, when she realized Nic had disappeared.

"Where did Nic go?" she asked Rex.

He jerked his head toward his bathroom. Then she heard retching.

"Is this the first time she's seen someone get killed?" Everyone thought they could handle the results until they experienced it. Abby had been sick for days after her first.

"No. The first one had his arms around her when he was shot. She hasn't gotten over it." That was rough. It was after Abby's fifth that numbness had set in, although she often wondered if anyone ever became blasé about taking a life. Her friend Olivia handled it better than anyone she knew, but even for her the stress became too much, and she'd had a nervous breakdown.

Hours dragged by as they double-checked the plan for the next day and helped the cleaning crew with the mess. All went smoothly with no more uninvited guests, no complaints lodged, and no local authorities showing up. They decided only the Inferno had a reason to kill Rex. The crazy organization believed his alter ego, Rurik, would interfere in their goal of obtaining all of the Hell's Purifier ammo. Killing the obvious competition would leave them as the only bidder.

Once Jack and Nic left with the others, she stepped onto the balcony for a few minutes of fresh air. Shivering, she tucked her hands under her arms. No way would she go back into that room smelling of cleanser and death. Would she always associate the two?

Another deep breath and a small amount of hope held her there. She wanted Rex to follow her. But at the same time, she needed to stop her body from wanting what would bring only heartache.

The scrape of a footstep warned her of Rex's presence. The warning proved he could be a kind man at times. For all his size and his attitude, he was light on his feet, and he only allowed his foot to drag a little to warn her of his approach.

She wanted to hate him. He'd broken her heart when she thought he'd died. Of course, it wasn't his fault that she'd lived with the sorrow for so many years, believing he'd left her by dying. Stupid logic, but it'd been a part of her for years.

"Why are you standing out here in the cold?" His gruff voice was a good distance from her on the long balcony. Each word as chilly as the weather.

Once the sun disappeared over the horizon, his temper had become shorter. She understood. Death always brought on a need to reaffirm life. With so many people around, they couldn't touch, sink into each other to forget. Besides, memories of what he'd done yesterday—his mouth on her and his hand on his cock—continued to threaten to bring down the wall she'd built against him.

A breeze picked up. The wind felt wonderful against her heated cheeks.

"The cleanser smell was getting to me," she said without turning around.

The sensation of a furnace near her back warned that Rex stood inches from her. Then his arms wrapped around her, pressing her shoulders to his chest. A noticeable ridge settled in the small of her back and jarred her for a second, though she loved knowing he hungered for her as she did him. She hadn't expected it after his broody attitude all day.

"I'll warm you."

There was no doubt they would be making love—no, having sex—before much longer. She needed to make something clear first.

"Rex."

"Hmm." His warm breath tickled the top of her head. He shifted and his hands slid over her breasts.

She closed her eyes and inhaled deeply. He groaned and squeezed the mounds, her nipples tightening against his palms.

"I understand this is just us playing a part and getting some mutual pleasure out of it," she said as she struggled to keep her mind on what she wanted to say.

He stopped. "Playing a part, huh?" The small thrust to her back warned he cared little for her remark. One broad hand dipped into her bra and cupped a bare breast. "And getting *some* pleasure?"

He lifted her breasts into the cold air. Before she complained of the chill, he rubbed his palms across the beaded tips. Heat infused her whole body.

"Jack might come back any minute." She closed her eyes.

"Did you do this with Jack each time you two went on assignment together?"

"No. The missions were more the straightforward type, no pretending to be husband and wife." Her eyes opened as her temper flared, but that didn't stop her body from responding to the way he pinched and pulled at the hard nubs.

"No mutual pleasure?" He tossed her words back at her.

"Jack and I don't feel that way for each other." She hoped he understood it was the truth.

"You know, I'm fucking tired of hearing his name on your lips."

He tightened his hold on her breasts, squeezing to the edge of pain as he kissed her neck, the warmth of his breath behind her ear.

"Hey, careful." She pulled on his wrists. He eased up slightly. His teeth nipped at her lobe, and she caught her breath when he jabbed several times with his hard cock against the small of her back.

"You want it."

He was right. She wanted him between her legs and pumping, but she had a little pride left. Was he doing this only to prove that he could have her anytime and anyplace?

"Rex. Stop. Please." Even to her ears, the words were weak.

"You love it. Look me in the eye and tell me you want me to stop. Even though I feel your body molding to mine even while you say stop." He was right. She couldn't stop her body from rubbing against his, her fingers reaching back, digging into his buttocks.

He released her breasts and turned her, pushing her shoulders against the wall next to the sliding glass doors. She refused to look him in the face, afraid that he would see her need. Then he'd know how much control he had over her. He only had to tell her to strip and she would.

"That's what I thought." His smugness was hard to fight. His voice, his touch, and even the heat from his body proved he was right. Another pump against her stomach reinforced how hard and big his cock had grown.

She craved him so badly. Weak. She was weak when it came to Rex.

No! She refused to be used. She wanted him but not yet. Not like he wanted her at the moment. He thought she loved Jack. How wrong could he be? She never wanted Jack. It had always been Rex, and she would never let him use her.

"Let me go, you son of a bitch." She hissed each word beneath her breath.

"You're beautiful when you're mad."

"I'm serious, Rex. Let me go now." She balled up a fist and hit him in the stomach. He grunted and then stared at her.

"Okay." He stepped back, his hands raised in surrender.

A SHUDDER ROLLED DOWN his body as he worked to control his desire to chase after her. He'd pushed her too hard. She needed time to realize what had almost happened was inevitable. Somehow he would make her understand he was the man for her and in the meanwhile wipe out every trace of his brother from her body.

He stepped into the suite, closing the balcony door behind him.

The distinct sound of the shower being turned on brought him to a stop outside his bedroom door. The hell with giving her time. As he climbed the stairs, he pulled off his shirt and flicked open his pants.

Maybe he needed to remind her what it was like to be his.

Chapter Eleven

ABBY WATCHED UNSEEING as the water heated up the shower.

Moments earlier when she'd stumbled into the living room and run up the staircase, she'd headed straight for the large bathroom. Sweaty and sticky and chilly all at once, she needed warm water flowing over her, quick. Now that she was away from his sensual pull, she wanted to go back and wrap his warm arms around her.

When Rex had stepped away from her on the balcony, she'd felt colder than she'd ever been in her life. She squeezed her eyes shut. Christ! They'd come close to having sex for the first time in years. But that wasn't what had blindsided her.

Looking at his face, angry and sullen, she'd realized they hadn't kissed one time since the wedding, and a simple brush of the lips didn't count.

She did remember the last time. He planned to leave

for Peru the next morning. They'd made love slowly, drawing out the pleasure to ensure it would hold them over until he returned a month later, mere days before they were to marry in a civil ceremony, nothing fancy. He'd kissed her hand and worked his way up her arm, lightly pressing his mouth across her chest and up her neck until with such tenderness, such love, he sipped at and lingered on her lips. He'd stopped and cupped the side of her face. Those eyes fascinated her. Only a glimmer of light gray showed beneath lids heavy with desire. After a press of his lips to each corner of her mouth, his gaze caressed her face as if he searched for an answer. When her breathing became shallow from fighting the need to feel his lips against her own, he'd covered her mouth, dipping and stroking. It had been the most romantic kiss. Most likely what Sleeping Beauty had experienced with her Prince Charming.

Tears streamed down her face. Unable to wait a second longer, she stepped under the water, partially clothed and uncaring. The steamy spray pounded her face and head. A shadow near the door shifted. She braced her hands on the tile wall, her back to the room as she tried to block out the man's presence. How long he'd been standing there, she had no idea and really didn't care.

A click warned her he'd opened the shower door. Then he gently turned her around and pulled her shirt over her head, slinging it into the corner. He leaned down and kissed her neck as his hands covered her breasts. Taut nipples greeted him, welcoming his warmth. She hummed her own welcome as his wet, bare chest met hers. His hands stripped off the rest of her clothes and they landed with a plop in the corner too.

Sparkling drops of water jagged his eyelashes as he looked down. Speechless, she stared up at the face she'd loved for so long. The face she knew would fill with disgust and hate one day if he found out the truth about her.

"Abby," he said, his tone filled with an emotion she didn't recognize.

When she opened her mouth to question him, he kissed her. No tongue. A sensation of masculine lips moving against hers took her breath away. He nipped at the lower one and licked the sting. She reached up and held him in place as her tongue searched for his, needing more from him. He leisurely stroked hers, refusing to join her frenzied response as he claimed her mouth.

Her nails dug into his shoulders, as she wanted to be closer. Strong hands lifted her buttocks as she wrapped her legs around his hips. His cock, hard and hot, slipped along her tender folds but not in. He held her too close and wouldn't let her pull away enough to sink down on him. Their tongues twined as their desire flamed without satisfying their burning need. He rocked against her, remaining outside, only bumping her clit.

She tried to move her mouth from his to beg him to take her, but he pushed her against the wall for support as one hand grabbed her hair, holding her head still. His mouth dominated hers, thrusting and retreating until she gave in, allowing him to show her what he wanted.

Never had she imagined that being controlled and kissed in such a way would turn her on, but she almost couldn't breathe. Ravenous desire drew the skin on her body tight; pure want ached in every bone.

When his mouth let her go, she cried out and struggled to pull him back.

"Abby, Abby." Wild with need, a moment passed before she could focus her eyes on his. "On your knees."

Confused by his command, she blinked and stared at him.

"Now. On your knees now." His gruff voice sent shivers of delicious yearning down her body.

With legs too wobbly to remain standing, her hunger to touch him overtook all her sense; she didn't argue but slid to his feet. She licked the thick cock, erect and hot, before her and tightened her grip and then released to tighten it again.

"Yeah. Squeeze me there."

She opened her mouth and drew him in with a hard suction while she wrapped one hand around the base. She then squeezed and pulled each time she moved her head back. His hips worked his cock in farther until her throat tightened around the head. His hands gripped her hair again, directing her movements.

"Harder, suck harder." His fingers tangled in the wet strands as he worked her back and forth. He tasted like she'd remembered, all male.

He moaned and then pulled her off him and lifted her face.

She licked her bottom lip, and his gaze followed her tongue as if he wanted a taste too.

"Fuck." He shook his head and then grabbed her

around the waist and stepped out of the shower. Without a care for the sheets, he dumped her in the middle of the bed. "It's time we did this proper."

She opened her arms and spread her legs, knees bent. *Please love me.*

All the breath left her body when he plunged into her. Each thrust produced the friction she craved. Consumed by more than basic desire, she reached out and pulled his face to hers.

"Kiss me again."

He nipped at her bottom lip. "This? Or this?" His tongue filled her mouth.

Unable to resist the burning desire to make him lose control, she sucked on his tongue with the same rhythm he rammed into her. His hand cupped her buttocks as he lifted her hips. Her body clinched. She cried out as each wave released over and over again. He continued to pump. When he finally pressed his groin to hers with his cock still in her, his back bowed and he roared his satisfaction.

Resting on his elbows, he bent down and rubbed his nose against hers. The innocent gesture coupled with the half smile on his face melted all the walls she'd built over the years. She brushed the back of her hand over his scar. He snared her wrist and pressed his lips to her palm.

Her eyelids closed. Tingles swirled down her arm, across her breasts, and ended where he swelled once again. He caught her ankles, pushing her knees toward her ears until every fold was exposed. Lifting his body slightly as he clasped her forearms and pressed them to the mattress, he began moving again, pounding his body into hers. His cock stretched her tighter than before. Unable to move, she gasped for each breath as too many sensations shot in all directions at once.

He controlled her with his strength, but she felt safe, free to experience everything he had to give her.

"That's it. Let it go. I got you." He pulled back until the tip slid over her clit. Before she begged for his return, he thrust one more time into her heated depths, and she screamed his name while the pulsing between her legs faded.

REX SAT ON the edge of the bed as Abby slept. Her light breathing soothed his chaotic thoughts. No other woman aroused him more while sending him to the loony bin at the same time.

The things she did with her mouth.

He dug the heels of his hands into his eyes. Wherever she'd learned those moves, he tried to convince himself it wasn't important. He'd be damned before he asked. What would he do if he learned his brother was the teacher?

Shit.

Years before, during their time together, sex had been pretty good. Looking back, he would have to admit it had been more vanilla than chocolate swirl. Hell, last night had been a ton of nuts, sprinkles, and a load of passion fruit added in.

He shook his head at his crazy analogy. His stomach

growled. No wonder he was hungry for food. He glanced over his shoulder at Abby; he needed his energy to keep up.

Being careful not to wake her, he stepped into his briefs. An itch on his back reminded him of Abby's nails digging into his skin as he brought her to climax after they left the shower. Hearing his name on her lips as she came each time had pushed him over the edge.

His cock grew heavy. His need for nourishment warred with his need for Abby.

With another glance at Abby, Rex decided to let her rest. So he quietly jogged downstairs to the kitchen at the other end of the living room. The cold pizza squeezed in the small refrigerator with an icy beer at two in the morning never tasted better. He leaned on the counter and looked out at the balcony.

What had gotten into him? He loved how she responded to his commands, the way she wanted him, willing to follow each instruction without objection. For a strong, deadly woman, she sweetly showed a side of her nature he'd never known. He shifted one leg to give his cock extra room. All it took was thinking about what they had done in the shower and he became as hard as a telephone pole.

After taking the last swallow from the bottle, he chucked it into the garbage with the others. He looked up at the landing that led into the master bedroom and to the woman sleeping within.

Abby was going to be pissed when he walked away after the mission was done.

He straightened his cock. In the meantime, she'd find out what it meant to belong to him.

"WHERE DID YOU GO?"

Abby turned on her side and soaked up his predatory walk across the room to the bed. Not many men his size moved as gracefully; they normally appeared cumbersome and unsure of where to place their foot next. She envied him. All her life she'd felt uncomfortable in her own skin. She never knew where to rest her hands or hold her shoulders. Clumsy and oversized compared to her mom, she felt like a hockey player on a balancing beam. How could she not with a mom who was no taller than five-two and weighed in around a hundred and five? At five-six and a weight she tried not to think about but worked out constantly to maintain, Abby towered over her petite, über-feminine mom.

"Thirsty," he answered.

"Ah, I need to talk to you about tomorrow." She sighed when his big arm came around her and pulled her chest to his. His breath ruffled the hair at her temple.

"Hmm." His hands lightly rubbed up and down her back.

"My mom can be brutally honest about her feelings in regards to whatever is going on around her. Just be patient and don't take anything she says personally. It's her way of coping with change." Like coming to terms with how her daughter left her father's funeral and didn't show up again for years.

"Everything will be okay. Don't worry." He kissed her forehead. "We have a few more hours before we have to leave. Let's get some rest."

He tossed a leg over hers. His stiff cock pressed against her thigh. Without a word or added movement, he acted as if he wanted to be a nice guy and let her sleep. How did he expect her to ignore that?

"Don't you believe sleeping is overrated?" She bit her bottom lip to stop from smiling.

He pushed her shoulders back and looked down into her face. "I thought you would never ask." And then he kissed her.

Chapter Twelve

ABBY WIGGLED HER butt in the passenger seat. She had no idea the sheriff of Sand County was paid enough to own a house like the one in front of her.

The two-story colonial-style home with brown brick and white shutters wasn't exactly what she imagined her brother living in, but he'd always claimed he wanted a big family one day. So she imagined space would be essential, and a good thing considering their mother had volunteered his home for their stay. When Abby had called the day before to inform her of the elopement and their visit, her mother had insisted her twenty-two-hundred-square-foot *cottage* was too small. Geez, the woman would go stir-crazy in Abby's three-room suite at the OS sector.

A gray Mercedes-Benz sat in the drive. Her mom was waiting for them. They pulled their Cadillac behind her car. She truly hoped her mom stayed on her best behavior.

"Well, *milaiyah my-ah*, are you ready for the next act?" Rex asked.

"Quit." She stepped out of the car and tugged at her dark pink blouse and wiped her hand down the side of her black pants. Simple but classic-looking.

"What?" He opened the trunk and lifted out two pieces of luggage.

"I don't understand Russian, and it will only make my family uncomfortable." She hated how narrow-minded it sounded and bitchy, but she refused to admit he made her nervous. The words sounded like endearments, and the not knowing drove her crazy, but certainly not crazy enough to ask. Maybe deep inside she was afraid of what it could mean. Could it be that they were falling back in love? If that was true, she'd need to tell him everything. But not today. Not when he was about to meet her family, the same one she'd never told him about. She covered her mouth for a second. Just as she hadn't mentioned another important member. Obviously there was a pattern to her lies. Or could she call them omissions?

She really had a problem. First things, first. They needed to deal with her mother and give into her bias against people speaking languages other than English for now. She'd learned long ago to pick her battles.

"Sorry. Just take my word for it. My mom's a little opinionated." She expected lightning to hit the ground nearby when she said that. The few times she'd spoken her father's native language, Spanish, her mom had thrown a tantrum of massive proportions.

When Rex didn't comment, she looked his way. He was staring straight ahead and not smiling.

She followed his gaze and her stomach flipped.

"Edward, put the gun down," she said with her hands on her hips. Her brother stood on the long front porch with a shotgun pressed to his shoulder, aiming it at Rex. She waited for him to lower the barrel. When he didn't, she asked, "Have you gone crazy?"

"Abigail?"

"Don't you remember the uncomfortable reunion last year, brother dearest? It's me, and I still prefer Abby." Though she'd seen her mom a few days before Christmas, she hadn't seen her brother since their reunion last fall. Rex wasn't the only one who'd believed her dead.

Rex said beneath his breath, "Abigail?"

"Don't act surprised." She slapped his arm. "You know that." She stomped past her brother and nudged the barrel toward the ground before opening the front door. "Crazy testosterone-saturated idiots."

"I resemble that remark!" Edward laughed at the old joke he'd been making since they were kids and held out his hand to Rex. "Sorry about that. Being the sheriff, I have to be careful with strange cars coming up my drive. I'm so happy that my sister got married. We thought . . . never mind what we thought."

Leaving the door open, she left them to get acquainted as she went in search of the others. Her mom and sister-in-law were in the kitchen, sitting at the table talking. A familiar sight from when she was a kid. The adults normally congregated around the table, eating and gossiping, and at times, playing cards. The kitchen was always the hub of the house. The men stayed in the den, watching whatever sport was in season or standing outside smoking and complaining or bragging about everything.

Then she spotted her nephew at a small yellow picnic table playing with a miniature car track set up on top. He was such a beautiful, sweet child, with plump cheeks and big round brown eyes.

"It's about time you arrived."

Her mom was as beautiful as ever. Not a hair out of place and wearing a short-sleeve sweater set and brown slacks, Leigh Ann Sanders-Wentworth-Rodriguez would never leave her bedroom without makeup and the right clothes.

"Good to see you, Mom." She hugged her and received a halfhearted one in returned. Abby straightened and turned to the other woman. "Thank you, Suzie, for inviting us to stay."

Suzie Wentworth's smile was relaxed and sincere. "I've been so excited about getting to know you better and meeting this mysterious man who swept you off your feet. So romantic. I would never have the guts to run off to Las Vegas to elope, but it must've been so much fun. Certainly something to tell your kids about."

Abby stiffened. Practiced in ignoring the unknowing sting had her pulling herself together. She never deserved children but she played along.

"Suzie, you're embarrassing my sister. Give them a little time to get used to marriage. They have plenty of time." Edward came into the kitchen, carrying one of the suitcases. "We're giving you the guest room upstairs in the opposite corner from Tommy's. That should give you a little privacy." He hugged her and whispered in her ear, "Don't you worry. It took a while for me and Suzie, but one miracle child will be enough."

The sorrow he hid behind that statement surprised her. She had no idea his dreams of a large family had ended with Tommy. No matter that they'd never been close, she felt bad for him.

"Well, are you going to introduce me to this new husband of yours?" Abby's mom hated to be ignored and she was right. It was rude of her not to introduce him. "Mom, this is Rurik Volkov. Rurik, this is my mother, Leigh Ann Rodriguez."

"How are you doing, Mr. Volkov?"

"I'm fine, ma'am."

"You speak English very well."

"Mom!"

"Well, he does."

"You're right. My parents migrated to the States during the seventies with their parents. At home, we were allowed to speak only Russian, but we spoke English everywhere else."

"What area in the States did you grow up in?"

"Actually, Huntsville, Alabama."

"Mom." Trying her best to draw her attention away from interrogating Rex, Abby asked, "I heard you personally saved the Sand City Museum."

Her mom's piercing gaze warned her she understood what Abby was up to and didn't appreciate her interruption.

"Abigail, what have I told you about exaggeration? People will begin to disbelieve anything you tell them."

Had her mom just called her a liar?

"Your mom has done so much. She's a powerhouse," Suzie piped up. Obviously she worked at being a peacemaker. How long would she do it before proclaiming it a lost cause? Abby remembered being ten at the time she gave up.

"You're sweet to say that, my dear. I saw a need and was happy to pitch in." Her mom patted Suzie's hand and smiled.

A stabbing pain shot through Abby's chest. Why was she jealous of her sister-in-law? The woman was a saint for having her mother-in-law living so close, not counting being married to Abby's arrogant brother.

"Mr. Volkov—"

Rex interrupted her. "Please excuse me, but I'd love for you to call me by my given name, Rurik." He picked up her hand and lightly kissed it. The pleased look on her face confirmed he'd passed the first test. She loved old-fashioned manners.

"Rurik. I'm surprised Abby found such a gentleman. A switch from the hoodlums she used to date." Her laugh caused Abby to raise an eyebrow. Maybe she should feel embarrassed, but the mom flirting and insulting her daughter in the same breath was the one she knew so well. Leigh Ann loved a man's attention and obviously it included her son-in-law's.

"Once I had her in my sights, I refused to accept defeat." He grinned back at her, and his usual mocking smile looked mischievous.

Abby looked from her mom to Rex and back. What was going on with them?

"Ah, a real man." She turned to Abby. "Finally, something of me shows up in you. Your taste in men has improved." Looking back at Rex, she asked, "The scar. How did you come to have such a sexy one?"

"Mom!" She'd gone too far.

"No, no, I don't mind." He fingered the scar. "When I was a kid, my brother and I played too rough."

He'd always ignored her questions. Could it be so simple? If that was true, why hide how he'd gotten it from her? He chuckled but it sounded hollow to Abby's ears. There was more to the story.

Tired of hearing the teasing and flirting between the two most frustrating people in her life, she decided it'd be a good time to talk with her brother. Alone. And speaking of frustrating people, her brother should certainly be included with the other two.

"Edward, how about helping me by taking the luggage upstairs while those two get to know each other?"

"Sure." He followed, picking up Rex's case and a large garment bag. "Hell, what do you have in this, a body?" He tossed the bag over his shoulder and grunted.

"Or maybe you're getting soft since you're an old married man with a kid." She lifted her two cases and headed up the stairwell her brother indicated with a nod.

"You better be careful. You're an old married woman yourself." They reached the upstairs hallway. "I don't remember Mom mentioning where you two met."

"Through a friend at work." Since reconnecting with her family, she'd claimed to work for an international construction company. It was amazing how few people delved further into what she did for a living. Just in case, The

Circle had layered information on the Internet and created dummy corporations to protect her and Rex's cover.

"For some reason he seems familiar." Edward dropped the suitcase on the floor and spread the garment bag across the bed.

Watching him check the towels in the private bath, she opened her mouth to ask what he meant, but stopped. No need to light up his curiosity by being defensive. They sure didn't need her brother to start nosing around Rex's past, especially as Rurik Volkov. No way would a small county sheriff recognize an international arms dealer. Sand County wasn't a hotbed of crime, especially not the global type. Otherwise, he'd already be on alert about Brody.

"Tell me again about the shotgun you met us with. That seemed a little extreme to meet a car in the driveway, just because you didn't recognize it." Though they were never close growing up, he'd never mistreated her as a kid, and more often than not, just ignored her. She'd been no threat to the attention their mom paid him. He received it all.

An even six feet tall, he looked athletic and healthy with his sun-kissed brown hair, broad shoulders, and flat stomach. As a teenager, she'd wished she'd inherited her mom's looks like he had so others wouldn't ask if she was adopted. She'd loved her dad but he worked so much, he was rarely around. Her last name being Rodriguez had helped only a little.

"Being in law enforcement as long as I have, you put away a lot of crazy people. It always pays to be cautious." He placed his hands on his hips and tilted his head. "Are you sure this guy is right for you?"

She covered her mouth more to hide the smile. He hated it whenever she teased or laughed at the things he said or did. But she loved having a family member worried about her. Her heart ached with the new experience.

"There is no other guy for her." Rex stood in the doorway with his chest out and chin up. Ready for battle, he stared hard at her brother, daring him to denounce his claim on Abby.

That was how it appeared to her.

Hoping to bring down the tension level in the room, she slipped her arms around Rex's waist and looked up admiringly at him. "I have eyes for no one else, stud muffin."

Edward choked. "Stud muffin?"

Maybe she'd layered it on too thick, but it had done the trick. The tension had dissipated.

Rex looked down at her and growled, "Your mother wants your help."

She glanced over at her brother and back to Rex. Well, hell. Were they going to pull it out and measure?

"Okay. You two behave," Abby said, pinching Rex's arm in warning. "I'll be back. She probably wants me to set the table. Everyone knows not to let me touch the food or I'll burn it." Neither man laughed. She'd tried. Abby slowly walked out of the room, looking back a couple times, shaking her head. Hopefully she'd return before they hurt each other.

REX CROSSED HIS arms. Their few minutes on the front porch earlier had told him a lot about Abby's brother. He loved his family and that included his wayward sister, and his job was more than a position and badge. It was close to a religious calling.

Edward's face hardened. "I don't know you, and if I ever hear of you hurting my sister, I won't care that you live in another county and state. I'll track you down and hurt you ten times worse than any suffering you'd caused. Do we understand each other?"

Suddenly Rex knew Abby's brother was going to be trouble. Not that he worried about the threat—he'd never intentionally hurt Abby—but to Edward any unknown element marrying his little sister needed to be investigated. By looking into every aspect of the man's life, he would be assured of her safety and happiness.

Rex did his best to shrug off the worry. Any information the sheriff uncovered would be what The Circle wanted him to find. For now, Rex would tell him as much of the truth that he could. Maybe it would keep him satisfied for a while.

"I would stab myself in the eye before I hurt her or let anyone harm her." No half-truth there. "Anyone who got between me and Abby would severely regret it." The warning hung in the air.

Edward stared hard. Without flinching or looking away, Rex waited for the man's next move.

"It's like that, huh?" Edward snorted and then walked out of the room.

Damn. Did the man see too much? Both siblings were going to be the bane of his existence.

Chapter Thirteen

"ABBY, DAMMIT!"

"What did I tell you about that?" she warned as she scrambled into the bushes and stooped behind a thick azalea.

After a tension-filled dinner, they had told Edward and Suzie that they wanted to stretch their legs along the short path to the lake. Even fighting mass amounts of mosquitoes was worth escaping the house and her mom's sudden interest in their personal life. Plus the stroll would give her a chance to ask Rex what her brother had to say.

They had reached the pier's ramp when a pop echoed over the water and the railing next to her splintered. They ran for cover near the shore. She'd prayed they would make it before another shot zipped by her head. Rex had grabbed the back of her shirt and tossed her to the ground,

"Get down!" Then he'd dove in behind her.

So there they were, waiting to see what happened next.

Everything was quiet. The sun setting above the trees on the other side of the lake glowed on the mirrorlike surface. Hard to imagine someone out there trying to kill them.

"I told you we needed to stay armed." Rex shoved his way in front of her.

Refusing to give ground, she scooted to the side and peeked around pink blooms.

"We had no reason to believe the Inferno would send someone new already." She hoped the shooter didn't plan to spray the bush with gunfire. The thin branches were no protection. He was right. Dammit. Leaving her Sig in the bedroom hadn't felt right, but she worried about her family seeing it.

"I have a gut feeling it isn't the Inferno," he said.

"Do you think it's Brody?"

"Bad for business."

"I agree." Abby knew that Brody would want Rurik alive in an effort to capitalize on his contacts. "If it's not the Inferno or Brody, I think we need to talk to my brother again. He's holding back on us. With him meeting us at the door with a gun and questioning you, really, he's never been the protective brother. We'll have to be careful of how we handle it. By nature and profession, he's cynical to say the least, and we don't want him asking us questions in return."

"Hell, yes, he's holding something back." Rex leaned over and brushed at her shoulder. "Spider."

She twisted to look for more creatures on both shoulders and various areas of her body and landed on her butt. "Did you get them all?" Her skin crawled from the thought. Slapping at specks of dirt or whatever, a shower would be next as soon as she got back into the house.

He chuckled and returned his attention to another stand of trees off to the side of the small cove. "Just one and it was only a granddaddy longlegs."

A shiver ran down her spine. Though they weren't poisonous, she couldn't stand them. All spiders gave her the creeps. They were almost as bad as snipers.

Had the sniper left? Most would leave as soon as they hit their target, except the fellow had missed. Checking the area, she weighed their options: run for it and hope the sniper missed again or wait until dark and hope no one came looking for them and walk into gunfire.

The high-pitched sound of a keypad being pressed reached her ears. She looked over at Rex. He had a cell phone to his ear.

"Yeah. Did you hear it?" Even from a couple feet away, she could tell it was Jack talking on the other end, though she couldn't make out what was being said. "Good." Rex squinted at nothing in particular. "Are you sure?"

Abby heard Jack shout a string of curses at his brother.

Then Rex said, "Fuck you too," and hung up as he stood.

"I take it the sniper got away." She straightened and slapped at her jeans for assurance against any more creepy-crawlies.

"They're trying to track him down. But for now we're okay."

Before Rex could say anything more, his cell phone vibrated. "Yeah?"

He headed up the path toward the house, listening intently. "I'm okay. It didn't get near me. No. It would be hard to hide a rifle on me." He darted a look at her and lowered his voice as his long legs ate up the ground. "Behave. Yeah. Thanks anyway. Sure. Me too."

Me too?

The voice had been a panicking woman's, high pitched and talking rapidly. Nic? Were the last two words in answer to "I love you"?

She knew how guys worked. They could have sex without caring for the woman. It was only a bodily function to most of them. A need fulfilled by any woman who was handy. Their time together last night and early in the morning had been a fluke and possibly a part of the plan to get her cooperation in treating him like a real husband. And she would admit she enjoyed it and wanted to do it again. But was his heart tied up with Nic? Circle operatives were trained to do whatever it took to get the job done. Was she only a job? One that he also enjoyed? He'd hardened enough times to prove that.

She rubbed the back of her neck, staring wide-eyed at the trees and bushes leaning over the path, the air thick and heavy in the early spring heat.

Though she hated to admit it, she dreaded bedtime. All the zinging of her nerve endings whenever she touched Rex did little good considering his feelings appeared to be centered on Nic.

And no way would they have sex while her brother, sister-in-law, and nephew remained under the same roof.

She squeezed her eyes shut for a second. But then again, when it came to Rex, she had no self-control.

"LET ME HANDLE it," Rex said, pushing Abby toward the stairs. "Go. You can have the shower first."

Her brown eyes studied him. Was she remembering their last shower? His cock lengthened at the thought. He kept his gaze steady.

Or did her indecision stem from concern about the method he intended to use in questioning her brother about the shooter? His first inclination was to beat the shit out of Edward for placing her in danger.

From the info Nic had given him, the sniper had nothing to do with Brody. The good sheriff had broken up a moonshine operation last week and the cousins of the fellow in jail had taken exception to it. Though the sniper had gotten away, one of the cousins had been caught trying to steal a Circle SUV. The operative had been assigned to keep an eye on the house and had parked in a wooded area across the water. Bad luck for the cousin. Good luck for the Circle operative. The cousin had confessed everything like a sinner in a confessional.

Later, Rex might regret not telling Abby what he found out, but earlier he'd enjoyed watching the jealousy steaming from her ears. He could've easily turned down the volume on the phone but he would have missed seeing her face flush with anger.

But her brother still had some explaining to do. Allowing his sister to walk into a precarious situation blind like that, there was no excuse.

"Have a nice walk to the water?" A shadow moved from the dining room.

Speak of the devil. The cocky asshole.

Rex grabbed the front of Edward's shirt and lifted him to his toes, slamming him against the wall. The man brought his arms up to break his hold, but Rex shifted and placed both hands at his throat without crushing it.

"You should've warned me that Rod Davison's cousins were after you. One of them almost shot Abby." Nose-to-nose, he bit off each word.

Edward stopped struggling. "Is she okay?"

"Yes. She has enough sense to keep calm, and that's the only reason she's still alive. If she'd been like most and gone running up the path, she'd be lying in the dirt with a bullet wound in the back."

"There's no way the Davison cousins mistook her for me."

"They were going to take out your whole family." Nearly pressing his nose to Edward's, Rex said, "And your sister would've been the first one."

"How do you know this? Who in the hell are you?"

"Someone you don't want to cross."

"FBI? DEA?"

"Who I am is none of your fucking business."

"The hell it is!"

Edward threw a hard right into Rex's ribs. The lights from the kitchen dimmed for a second as he tried to regain his breath. His hold on Abby's brother loosened. He stepped back, chest rising and falling fast.

"Everything that happens in Sand County is my fucking business."

Being careful to take small gulps of air, Rex rubbed his abdomen. "Not this time. Stay out of my business and I'll stay out of yours." He towered over the shorter man. There were a few advantages to being so freaking tall. Intimidation was one of them. "Don't ever put Abby's life in jeopardy like that again."

"Are they in jail? Who's holding them?"

Either the man was too stupid to realize the danger he was in or too brave for his own good. Possibly, a little of both.

"Yeah. Call your jail. They should have the fellow by now. There's a good chance his cohort might show up too." Rex glared and then turned away. The man had a wicked punch but he better count himself fortunate that Rex hadn't hit back. It was only the thought of explaining to Abby why he called an ambulance for her brother that stopped him from drawing blood.

Rex stomped up the stairs to the bedroom. Furious with her damned self-centered brother, he'd completely forgotten about another danger.

He shouldered the door open, his attention on rubbing his stomach. The sweet smell of clean woman hit him first. Lifting his gaze, he drank in the soft, damp-haired beauty sitting on the corner of the bed, towel-drying her hair. Nothing smelled as good as a woman.

Without turning around, he kicked the door closed. Her head jerked up.

"Well? What did you learn?" she asked.

He knew in his lust-filled head she was asking about her brother, but he had to bite the side of his mouth to keep from saying, *That I love tasting you, especially when your legs are spread, and you're coming against my tongue.*

"R-Rurik?" She stumbled over his name. Though they were alone, they couldn't take a chance of someone over-hearing them.

Three long strides, and he crossed the room, tearing off his shirt and reaching for her before she could escape. Every thought in his head centered on his need to touch, taste, fuck her.

Palms out, she tried to stop him. "Tommy's down the hall. My brother and his wife are downstairs," she said, every word light and airy as if she had a problem breathing.

Swatting at her hands, he reached into the terry-cloth robe to cup and massage her breasts. Silky and warm, her skin felt wonderful.

Oh, hell, he wanted her so much. He groaned as his cock pressed against the zipper of his pants. Even with cotton separating him from the metal, the teeth surely would leave an imprint. He didn't care. He wanted to touch more of her.

"Damn you, Rex," she whispered near his ear. Then her tongue licked the pulse at his throat as she unzipped and shoved off his pants and boxer briefs. "Damn you."

"From the moment I was born." He held her as she tried to lean back and look in his face. He didn't want to explain. She was right. Making love to Abby was a noisy affair when done right, and he never could be quiet about it and preferred to do it correctly and thoroughly. It would kill him, but he would hold off. "Shh. We need some rest." She whimpered. "I know. That asshole better confirm his invite soon. When he sends the directions, we're out of here. We won't need to be quiet there."

"We don't? How's that?"

He shook his head and stretched out beside her, clasping her tight, letting his groin press to her hip for a moment in a mild form of self-torture. "Later. I'll tell you later. For now, let's get some sleep." With a sigh, he rolled onto his back and hauled her halfway on top of him. Glad she couldn't see his bruised rib cage from the altercation with her brother, he concentrated on relaxing.

"For a man who can't shut up while having sex, you're sure closemouthed when it really counts."

Her head bounced on his chest as he chuckled. Only Abby made laughter in bed sexy. He shifted his hard cock. It was going to be a long night.

Chapter Fourteen

"WHY DIDN'T YOU tell me that you saw Brody at the charity cocktail party?" Abby's mom stared accusingly while wrapping an arm around Brody's elbow.

Where did the nice morning go to, and why couldn't the afternoon be as nice? Abby had helped Suzie prepare breakfast, scrambling up some fluffy omelets and cinnamon toast—that was, she'd handed Suzie the ingredients. Anyway, mornings like that brought an ache to be normal with a husband and children.

Some people enjoyed spoiling a good thing.

She looked at the tall, good-looking guy smiling with the largest self-satisfied grin she'd ever seen on a person's face.

"Don't give her a hard time, Leigh Ann. She's in love and you remember how that is. No one else exists." His bleached white teeth sparkled.

"Hello, Walker." Rex's deadly tone ratcheted up the tension in the room.

"Volkov."

While Brody was all flash and smooth charm, Rex was mystery and lethal sex appeal. Of the two, she'd place all her money on Rex. But during her time with The Circle, she'd learned to never underestimate an opponent. Looks could be misleading.

"Suzie, look who's come to visit." The older woman still held on tight to Brody as if he were a beau come to court her.

How wrapped up was she in his sale of illegal firearms and ammo?

"Hey, Brody. Eddie's at work but would you like a glass of tea?"

"No. I'm fine. I'm actually here to see Rurik. As I mentioned the other night, I'm having a small weekend party at my farm and wanted to invite Abby and Rurik. You know, extend our Southern hospitality to our newlyweds."

"That sounds wonderful and so generous." Abby's mom beamed at her. "If only I didn't already have plans, I would join in."

Abby's heart traveled to her throat thinking of her mom in the middle of the mission. Well, more than she was already involved.

"Sure. Another time." Brody kissed her mom on the cheek. "Excuse me while I talk with Rurik."

"Very well. I love your dinner parties. Your weekend parties must be marvelous," the older woman simpered.

Rex followed Brody into Edward's study. As soon as the door closed, her mom turned. "What business would your husband have with Brody? You better not be planning to cheat him out of his money. He acts all laid back but he's a sharp businessman and eats people like you for dinner."

Stunned, Abby blinked a few times, giving herself time to recover. She knew her mom had a low opinion of her, but each time she lobbed a sneak attack, she caught her off guard.

"Okaaay. I'm going to pretend you said that to protect me from Brody and not the other way around."

Her mom wrinkled her forehead. "Whatever are you talking about? You come here with a husband who wears thousand-dollar suits and no visible means of income. And you say he trades commodities but he doesn't act like a broker. I don't trust those Russians. Capitalism is new to them and all that freedom has made them pushy."

"More pushy than Americans? Besides, how should a broker act?" Ah, hell, why did she allow her mom to push her buttons? She closed her eyes as she shook her head, holding up both hands. "No. Never mind." Looking her in the eye, she did her best to soothe her worries. "We don't plan to hurt Brody, and I'm sure Rurik can handle himself."

Rather proud of how she remembered to call Rex Rurik, she almost missed the way her mom's neck stretched and chin popped up before she asked, "*We* don't plan?"

Abby hung her head and sighed. The best way to handle the mess was to redirect her mom's attention. "Mom, let's not argue in front of Tommy." She nodded to where her nephew watched a cartoon. Turning to her sister-in-law, Abby widened her eyes, pleading for help. "Did I hear you say that Tommy was taking karate?"

"Yes. He loved that DVD you got him, and he begged to take lessons. We're so lucky to have a dojo in Sand City. It's amazing how much he's learned." Suzie smiled big with pride.

Abby had sent him a copy of *Kung Fu Panda* for his birthday last month.

"He's smart like his daddy," her mom said, and started on all the fine qualities of her grandson.

Abby rolled her eyes, and Suzie giggled. Obviously, her sister-in-law knew the secret to cutting her mom off from creating more drama.

Thinking of drama, she wondered what Rex and Brody were talking about in private.

"GO FUCK YOURSELF." Brody Walker's good ol' boy persona slipped a little.

"I thought it was a reasonable offer." Rex leaned back on the desk, ankles and arms crossed, giving off the appearance of someone who didn't give a damn while he centered all his attention on the angry man pacing in front of him.

A wall full of pictures of Abby's brother receiving medals for his work with the community dominated the study, while trophies lined up on shelves from former high school and college glory days stood sentinel. How would he feel to hear an illegal arms deal was being negotiated in his study?

"I need twice that figure to consider the deal." Brody broke into his thoughts.

"Hey, you came to me with your cash-flow problem." He lifted one eyebrow when the man's face turned red. Though he hated to admit it, his brother's plan to squeeze Brody by continuing to confiscate his shipments worked. They'd hoped eventually he would need money to cover production for the same order of ammo over and over again. Inferno wouldn't understand Brody's bad luck and no way would they provide more funds. Rex doubted they'd even been told what had happened. To tell them that someone was stealing their orders would reveal Brody's group had been compromised or that their security work was shoddy. Besides, the only reason the Inferno hadn't killed Brody was that they received one shipment. From what The Circle had learned, it was a small one.

"I told you after I fill this order, hell, any orders we receive—and there will be hundreds of them—I'll make sure to double the price and you'll have your money tripled in six months or less. But I can't take you to the shop."

Rex had hinged the deal on being able to inspect a shipment of goods as they were manufactured. Whether or not Brody sensed a trap, he wasn't sure. He knew if he pressed too hard, he'd cause him to cut and run or worse. He and Jack had promised Abby that they'd protect her family by not placing them in greater danger than they were already.

"You want me to hand over a bundle of cash and not inspect your production line? I'd be a poor businessman if I didn't. How do I know you're telling the truth?"

"And I wouldn't have gone to you if you'd been a poor businessman. I find it refreshing dealing with blunt people. Let's say you'll have to learn to trust me." Like a switch flipped on, Brody's face lightened up. "Enough of business. Tomorrow I'll send a car over to pick up you and your wife. She's so delightful. It will be nice to become reacquainted." Rex didn't care for how that sounded, like he would allow him to touch Abby. "I bet she has some stories to tell. Did she ever tell you that she ran away from home, and it wasn't until last year that her mother even knew she was still alive?"

He wasn't about to admit he knew nothing about Abby. He'd thought he knew everything he would ever need to know when they planned to marry years ago, but each day he realized he knew nothing. So he worked at maintaining a bored expression and pressed his lips together.

"I agree with her mother. Abby's a closemouthed one. Unlike most women who yak on and on about every little thing until a man wants to put a muzzle on the bitch." Brody smirked and added, "Some of them look better with one on, if you know what I mean."

"Good thing I don't have to worry about that." Rex curled his fingers. Tingles shot up his arms as he squeezed, trying his best not to hit him.

"You're so right." Brody chuckled. "I bet she's a screamer, though. Those quiet ones you have to watch out for. Take for instance the slut I was with the other night. She talks all the time but never says a word when I fuck her. Though with all that flapping of gums, she's worked up some muscles, and that big mouth of hers is talented. Lordy, Lordy, she can suck a cock like a man." With his back to Rex, he leaned over to look closer at a picture on the wall.

Rex's vision narrowed. So, what, the bastard swung both ways? And more importantly, why did he believe he could talk about Abby like that? How could any person talk about a man's wife with so little respect and not get hurt? No less talk about any woman in that way. Hell, if not for the mission, he'd be nailing his ass up on the wall next to the photographs.

"Will five o'clock be okay for the car to be here?" Brody turned around and grinned. "We'll have a couple days to relax and enjoy each other's company. We may even learn to trust each other."

"I'll drive my own car."

Brody chuckled. "See? We don't trust. Partners must trust each other." He slapped Rex on the back as he headed toward the door.

"Partners are allowed to inspect the goods as they're made. That would be a good way to show your trust." He rolled his shoulders. Why did it feel as if he'd been stabbed in the back? He desperately wanted to gut the man. For now, he looked away to keep from revealing the hatred in his eyes.

"You're a single-minded man." Brody opened the study door. "Yes. This weekend will be good for us. We'll have to see if we can come to an understanding first."

With one eyebrow raised, Rex cut his eyes over to Brody.

That was progress. For the man to even hint of possibly giving in to Rex's terms was a good sign. Then again, once they arrived on the farm, they would be on his turf, in his control. The guards and dogs holding off outsiders also held people in. He owned a lot of acreage, perfect for hiding a factory and burying curious visitors.

"WHAT WAS THAT all about?" Abby closed the bedroom door behind her. She'd been frustrated with how her mom and sister-in-law had stuck to her side all afternoon. Without being rude, she couldn't find a way to get Rex off alone until a couple hours before dinner.

Rex tossed a switchblade onto the bed as he placed a foot in a nearby overstuffed chair to rip the Velcro apart on his ankle holster.

"He wanted to borrow some money." His satisfied grin said a lot, but for the last several hours his body had vibrated with suppressed rage. Twice she'd caught him staring out the window with his hands fisted and knuckles white.

"So the plan is working. He's hurting for funds, and we're invited to his farm for the weekend. Before you came out, I got a text message from Jack. They hired Liam but not Charlie. We're fortunate one got hired. Nic and the crew are about a mile down a public side road and have part of the road dug up for maintenance," she said, making quote marks in the air for the last word, "and are setting up the receiver in the van. Once we place the bugs, we should be able to work fast from there."

"If nothing goes wrong." He shucked his pants and picked up a pair of gray sweats from the dresser.

"Where are you going?" She tried her best not to stare at the way his ass filled out his boxer briefs, perfect to cover with her hands and squeeze. Why was she always in sexual overdrive whenever he was around?

He stripped off his shirt and pulled a sleeveless jersey on. "I'm going for a jog."

"Give me a minute and I'll come with you."

"I'll go by myself. Need to clear my mind."

"Okaaay." Her forehead wrinkled as she watched him leave. What was that all about? If anyone had problems dealing with the mission, she'd expected it to be her. She was the one endangering her family and not confessing everything to Rex.

REX HATED LYING to Abby. A couple things needed to be seen to without her around. He slipped into Edward's study and picked up a picture frame. The day before, he'd stuck a bug on the back beneath the stand. When he was in the room with Brody earlier, he'd noticed the picture frame was in a new spot across the room. He wanted the mic closer to the desk. A better chance he would catch anything Abby's brother would say.

He turned the frame over. The mic was gone. Dammit. Sweeping the area with his gaze, he searched the desk and floor, even kneeling to reach beneath the furniture in case it had rolled off. Nothing.

Dammit. Not that anyone would track it back to him,

as the mic was self-sufficient. The tiny internal memory chip was activated only by voice vibrations and recorded conversations up to eight hours. He just didn't need anyone hearing what he and Brody had discussed.

No use getting bent out of shape by it. He had other matters on his mind. For now, he needed to talk with his brother. They had a couple things to iron out. Only two years separated them, but he and Jack had never been close, even while working the same type of job.

The disconnection came about years before both joined the OS. Their dad was a hard man who wanted to ensure his sons grew up to be real men. One day when Rex was ten, he'd been gathering apples from a small orchard they owned; his mom had promised to bake an apple cobbler if he brought in enough. Earlier, she'd forced him to take a bath, even putting some of the soft powder on his torso that reminded him of her. So to keep from needing another bath, he'd been careful not to get dirty.

When he entered the kitchen with arms loaded and his cheeks pink in anticipation of helping his mom mix the cobbler, he was surprised to see his dad and brother cramming their mouths full of the cold apple tarts his mom had baked the day before. He'd enjoyed hanging around his mom without his older brother's and dad's interference. They had gone into the mountains so his dad could teach Jack how to track wild animals. Dad was a big believer in knowing how to hunt, especially with the ever-present promise of the apocalypse coming. The man was one brick short of a full load. In other words, bat-shit crazy.

"Well, well, well, lookee at what the cat drug in. What

you got there, boy!" Mike Drago stood only a head taller than twelve-year-old Jack. At the time, his father appeared to be a giant, but all of that would change soon since Rex already stood at the same height as his older brother and had never heard of short man syndrome. So his dad resented Rex's height and in two more years that resentment would turn to hate.

"Apples for Mommy." He cringed, knowing what was coming.

"A big boy like you don't need to be calling your mother 'Mommy.' You're no baby. Hell, you 'bout tore her apart coming out."

Rex tried not to cringe again when his dad pointed to the counter. "Go and put those apples down before you bruise them up."

He passed within inches of his dad.

"Woo-ee! What's that smell? Are you a girl now?"

Rex hurried to place the apples next to the sink. He should've never let his mom put sweet-smelling powder on him.

"Hey, Jack. I do believe a strange little girl has entered our house." His dad crossed his arms and looked down on him. "I'm a real man and real men have boys. Not whiny, stinky girls."

His brother stood next to their dad. "I think you're right. What's that stinky girl doing here?"

Afraid to speak, he faced them as he backed into the corner and sat, pulling up his knees and wrapping his arms around them, hoping they would quickly tire of the game.

"I bet she's Miss Margie's." His dad sneered. "Little girl, you need to go home before Miss Margie comes looking for you. Would hate for you to get a whupping."

"Yeah, the old witch. You belong to her." Jack's sneer mirrored their dad's.

Miss Margie was a neighbor who hated kids, yelling at them if they walked across her lawn, eyeing them with mistrust when they rode their bikes near her house. The mean old woman kept to herself but even stranger was how she lived with her brother. No one, as old as they were, lived with a sibling. Something wasn't right. All the kids called her a witch and worse, and none of them ever wanted to belong to her. She might eat them like the old woman in *Hansel and Gretel*.

Unable to hold back any longer and frightened they would send him to live with old Miss Margie, Rex shouted, "I'm not a little girl and I don't belong to Old Margie."

"You smell like a girl. Boys don't smell like flowers." His dad glanced at Jack. "Go call Margie and tell her to come and get her little girl."

"No!" Terror of that strange woman gripped at Rex's chest.

"Yes, sir. We don't want Margie's kid here." Jack's obvious enjoyment in baiting his little brother and being on his dad's side was evident by the wide grin.

Rex knew with certainty that his dad would send him to live with Margie, especially when tears rolled down his cheeks. Only babies and girls cried.

"Look at the little girl cry." Jack pointed and laughed.

A disgusted look came over his dad's face. "He's as

dumb as he looks. That's enough." His dad's lips thinned. "I believe Rex understands he needs to stay out of his mom's powder. We don't want any fucking fairies in our family." He took a step away and then looked over his shoulder at Rex. "You should be ashamed of yourself. Get up from there, dry your face, and act like a man."

He'd learned a couple lessons that day: Never fully trust his brother to have his back, and his size attracted negative attention.

No, Rex had never felt close to his brother. They'd always been competitive in everything they did, spurred on by their dad. Now he wondered if Jack was playing some new game.

"What the hell are you doing here?"

Rex ignored his brother's rude greeting and slid the van door closed with a loud clack behind him. One of The Circle operatives jumped up from a chair and scooted around him to reach the passenger seat up front.

"I need to talk with you," he said, and then glanced at the other operative on the opposite side of Jack. She didn't look their way, and with the large earphones on, it was unlikely she could hear. He still wasn't satisfied. "Alone."

A couple seconds passed as Jack rubbed his shaved head and grimaced. Dark crescent shadows beneath his light blue eyes gave them an eerie glow. He'd probably been awake checking the tapes from the bugs Liam had planted since being hired on at the farm. Rex would plant more inside the house. "Okay. Let's step outside and walk a few yards beyond the tree line."

They moved far enough into the shadows of the greenery to not be seen from the road. Only the swaying limbs revealed and hid the side of the white van with each gust of wind.

Jack crossed his arms as he turned to face Rex. "What's crawled up your ass and died?"

"I want Abby pulled from the mission."

"Really." Jack spread his feet apart as if prepared to fight.

"Brody expects me to hand her over, and I'm not about to let that happen."

"Except for his little problem of being an exhibitionist, he's never demanded another man's woman. Nothing points to that being one of his hang-ups."

"You would know."

"What the hell do you mean by that?" Jack dropped his arm. The loops piercing his eyebrow and lip glittered in the waning light.

"You know what I'm talking about."

"Do you want to talk about that now? In the middle of a mission?"

"It's as good a time as any." His brother was right, but no matter how hard he told himself to leave it alone, he had enough of pussyfooting around and wanted answers.

"We thought you were dead," his brother said as he stared straight into Rex's eyes.

"So you hear I'm dead and you two fall into bed." Bitterness filled his mouth.

"It wasn't like that."

Rex concentrated on breathing and remaining calm so his brother would continue his explanation. "Quit beating around the bush."

"I fell in love with Olivia."

"Shit." Rex suspected that happened but had wanted it to be rumor only. "What does that have to do with you being with Abby?"

"I know you hate Olivia, but she had a rough life."

"I don't hate her anymore, especially now that we know she wasn't involved in Abby's disappearance. Not that I care for her, but she's Abby's best friend and my best friend's wife. We've come to terms."

"She's a lot different when she's not on the job. We had fun together. She'd picked me up for a one-night stand after an assignment. She had no idea I was an OS operative by then. I wrangled some information from her before she left me that first night and was able to track her down. I worked it out where we met up a couple more times. That's when I learned love will make a fool of you." He shook his head and squeezed his eyes shut for a moment. After a deep breath, he continued. "So when Abby disappeared, I contacted Olivia to see if she could help. Before I knew it, I was in The Circle and Abby was in their clinic. She'd been beaten by some street gang, they said, and then news came in that you had died. By then I realized that my fling with Olivia had ended before it even got started. She stayed on the road, and The Circle is so huge, we didn't see each other again for years."

He looked around, never resting his gaze on Rex's face

as he said, "Hell, she didn't even recognize me later. I guess with my shaved head and piercings, I'd changed. Fuck! She didn't remember my name." He rubbed his bare scalp and then cleared his throat. "Anyway, after Abby got out of the clinic, she was having problems coping with your death. We had become friends and I was comforting her. One thing led to another—"

Rex held up a hand. "I don't need to hear how you fucked her."

"I wouldn't—"

Crossing his arms, Rex tilted his head and lifted an eyebrow.

"Don't look at me like that. What I was going to say was that one thing led to another, but the next day we agreed it was a mistake. It never happened again. The woman mourned you for all these years. She still loves you."

"She has a strange way of showing it." Did his brother even know how to tell the truth?

"What about you and Nic? What do you think she makes of that? Everyone at the OS knows that you two had hooked up." Jack scratched his chest and waited for a comment.

What could Rex say to that? He hadn't been open with Abby about his relationship with Nic.

"You understand?" His brother held out his hand and waited.

The cawing of a crow nearby broke the silence.

Rex wanted to argue and hang on to the old wounds, but what good would come of it?

He grabbed the offered hand and pulled his brother

close. "If you ever touch her again or betray me again, brother or not, I'll kill you and spit on your cold, lifeless body."

Jack returned his solemn stare. "I wouldn't expect anything less."

Chapter Fifteen

ABBY TAPPED HER foot and stared out the living room window as she waited for Rex to return from his run. Yeah, run his ass. Most likely meeting with Jack and leaving her out of the plans. If he thought she would stand idly by while they decided how to bring Brody down, he was kidding himself.

"What's got you wound up tighter than a five-dollar watch?" Edward walked in wearing his dark brown uniform shirt and tan pants. With a badge on his chest and holstered gun at his side, he looked ready for business. Seeing him in his uniform reminded her how she needed to be careful with what she said and did or their cover would be blown. The job The Circle did wasn't sanctioned by the government and leaned heavily toward vigilantism.

"Rurik went for a run and he's unfamiliar with the area. Hate for him to be lying in a ditch somewhere."

"He appears to be smart enough to watch for erratic drivers." He stopped next to her and lightly touched her shoulder. "I know we've never been close, but something has been bothering me that I want to ask."

Her eyes met his. The compassion in his eyes helped her relax. She needed a distraction.

"Do you love him?"

She hadn't expected that.

Before she could answer, he continued. "I know it's not really my business. You're a grown woman who's lived on her own for years, but something has come up and I'm concerned about you."

That wasn't good.

"The other night at dinner, Rurik mentioned some of the countries he'd been to with his company. Some are very volatile areas, and from what I can tell, there are no direct flights into their cities."

"You had him checked out." She'd been afraid he'd do that.

"What had you expected? You never mentioned dating anyone when you came to visit last year and suddenly you show up with a husband. Then within hours of arriving in town, he's thick with Brody."

"Mom's thick with Brody too. Does that mean she's up to no good?"

"I didn't say he was up to no good." A glint in his eyes warned she had taken his bait.

"Quit beating around the bush and tell me what you want to know."

"Is he DEA?"

"What?" She never expected that. If he'd dug deep enough, he would find information about Rurik being a suspect in several illegal weapon sales. That couldn't be helped, considering it was the same information they wanted Brody to find. But she never expected her brother to think Rurik might be involved in anything to do with law enforcement.

"CIA? NSA?"

"What the hell are you talking about?"

"He didn't tell you that we had a heated discussion about the shooters last night?" Edward moved to a chair and sat back. When she remained quiet, he said, "Two fellows were found tied up and left at a substation's steps."

"What makes you think he had anything to do with it?"

He leaned forward, his elbows on his knees and with his hands clasped. "Abby, I'm not stupid. I have eyes in my head and you two don't act like newlyweds. Suzie and I never could keep our hands off each other, especially the first few months, and you two have been married only a couple days. And what newlywed with money would be interested in spending the night with her brother's family so soon?"

"Maybe not everyone is like you and Suzie. We're older and have been around the block a few times. We don't need wine and roses to realize how we feel about each other." Well, crap. A by-product of abstaining from sex during their stay, they avoided touching each other too. She wished she could say her mind stayed on the job, but she'd be lying.

He nodded, looking down at the floor. "Okay. Just understand I might be able to help you. Brody has been a concern of my department's since he bought that farm and placed armed guards on it. We haven't caught anyone hauling drugs out of or onto his land, but we feel certain something is going on."

"Don't be that way. He's just a good ol' boy who likes to party. Like what Mom said, he made all his money before the market dropped and he came back home to enjoy life as a young retiree."

Until now she never understood how much she loved her brother. He tried to be a good man, and she didn't want him involved. From the moment she met Brody, she had a creepy feeling that he would be bad news. A nagging in the back of her mind had warned her not to involve her family in the undercover operation, and for some reason she'd ignored it and she knew better than to do that.

He slapped his hands on his knees and stood. "Suzie's waiting for me and tomorrow will be another long day. Some of us have to work for a living."

There. That was her brother. Poking at her, trying to get her riled up and admitting more than she should.

She stopped him as he reached the door. "Edward."

"Yeah."

"I love you, big brother."

He smiled, like he used to for the camera while playing ball as a teenager. "Love you too, little sis."

She knew that she would do everything she could to protect him and his family. With certainty, he would dig deeper and that placed them in danger. What did a small county sheriff know about international arms dealers?

A COUPLE HOURS later, Abby listened to Rex's footsteps coming up the stairs. The house was built solid and normally Rex was pretty light on his feet, but tonight he either didn't care or was too tired to worry.

The lights were off, but the full moon brightened up the room. She watched his solid shadow as he crossed the floor and entered the bathroom, closing the door behind him before turning on the light. Lying there waiting for him was more intimate than having sex. Strange, but she always associated waiting for someone to come to bed as what lovers and wives did. When he returned, she watched his silhouette pull his shirt over his head and kick off his sweatpants.

The bed shook as he crawled in behind her. "Abby."

"Yeah."

"Nic and I are no longer lovers."

"No? What brought that up?" Did their time together during the last few days have something to do with it?

"I saw Jack while I was out."

"And?" Her whole body ached from tension. Thoughts of circling Jack's throat with her hands zipped through her mind. The dirty SOB better not have told him about what happened with the baby so many years ago.

"We talked about you."

Jesus H. Christ! Was he trying to drive her crazy? She wanted to yell, *Spit it out!* But pure fear held her back.

"I know about you and Jack."

"And?" Hadn't he already known? They hadn't lied or hid it. They had a one-night stand. Nothing more. Besides, her marriage to Rex wasn't real. So no need for confessions.

"It was the same for me and Nic. When you get bad news, it can make you do things you regret later."

"Yeah." She waited for him to touch her. He didn't move. "Listen, that was a long time ago."

"You don't have feelings for him, do ya?"

She never remembered him acting so tender and uncertain, wanting to talk—that was, besides giving orders.

"No more than as a friend."

He sighed. He actually sighed. Then it hit her. He'd been drinking. Another first, in a line of firsts with him.

When she heard snoring, she relaxed. Jack had kept his promise. He hadn't told Rex her secret. How much longer could she go without telling him about their child?

Chapter Sixteen

"I thought you said the security was low-key." Abby looked around as they pulled in front of the large ranch-style house.

Though an average four-foot fence lined the property near the main road, a decorative ten-foot gate stood at the entrance of the half-mile-long driveway. Once they'd given their names to the man standing next to a parked ATV, the guards patted them down for weapons and searched the Cadillac.

Expecting the search, Abby and Rex went along without protest. They'd hidden a few weapons in the car, hoping some would go undetected, and they would later sneak one or two into the house. The guards found two out of five. The guards had glared but said nothing as they were thrown in the back of the ATV, and they renewed their search for more until they were satisfied they'd found them all.

When the guards waved them on, a large Titan pickup

truck and black SUV had appeared out of nowhere and surrounded them as Rex drove onto Brody's property.

In front of the house, every man she spotted carried an AR-15 or AR-47 semiautomatic rifle. Scary crazy to say the least.

"Think of where Collin and Olivia live. They have ten-foot-high walls with broken glass on top. If Olivia had her way, they'd have a moat, but Collin was afraid it would scare the kids." He snorted.

She laughed, covering her mouth. What normal person, finding herself surrounded by armed guards, would be making jokes and laughing? No need to make the guards nervous.

"Well, yeah, you got me there."

The front door swung open and Brody jogged toward them. Faded jeans molded to his slim hips and runner thighs. With his pale yellow polo shirt showing off his tan, he stood out among his guards who dressed in black and looked ready to burglarize the house. Keeping an eye on Brody, she said, "We better get out before they think we're about to run over their boss."

Rex turned off the engine and the locks clicked. Before Abby could pull on the lever, Brody lifted the handle and held the door for her to get out.

"Welcome to Eagles Landing." The magazine-quality smile stretched across his face.

"Eagles Landing? Are there eagles around here?" She had noticed the design in the gate of two birds with wings spread.

"A couple nests. Most are found in northern Alabama."

"Interesting." She really was interested—she'd always thought the magnificent birds lived only out west. Avoiding Brody as he reached for her hand, she stood. She'd never been a touchy-feely type of person and never would be with him. A strong arm came around her waist and pressed her to a tall, hard body. She looked up into Rex's grim face. Scratch that—she'd never been a touchy-feely type until she met Rex.

"I'm so glad you're here and just in time. The other guests are waiting. Usually I have around ten couples, but I thought you might appreciate a more exclusive gathering. Four couples. Should make everything more fascinating." He waved them through into the foyer. "Your bags will be taken to your room. Don't worry."

Make everything more fascinating? What did he mean by that? The man made her nervous enough, but he continued to creep her out.

"Here" Brody indicated a servant holding a tray with several glasses of white and red wines. "Take one. I requested several bottles from the winery I own in Napa Valley."

Abby picked up a red and Rex chose white. The taste was bittersweet. Not bad, but she needed to keep her senses clear. Being an easy drunk wouldn't be a good thing in this situation. The glass shook a little as she raised it to her lips, pretending to sip.

Trying to shake off her uncharacteristic nerves, she concentrated on the beautiful house. So different than what she'd thought outside. Despite being one level, it was open and airy inside. The stained glass surrounding the front door brightened the large, elevated living area.

Two leather sectional sofas faced each other across a massive coffee table. The dark wood floor was broken up by thick white shag rugs. In the far right corner was a kitchen with a marble-topped bar overlooking the living room. The large table on the right as they stepped off the foyer could easily seat twelve without elbowing each other.

An archway to the left appeared to lead to a corridor, probably the bedrooms. When she looked beyond the sofas and a few conversational groupings of overstuffed chairs with small accent tables, she caught her breath. A long glass wall revealed a scene of what she could only call Eden. Palm trees, bamboo, ferns, and every color in the rainbow of orchids and lilies provided the perfect backdrop for boulders of different sizes with water flowing into a small pool. Everything looked natural and soothing.

"You like the courtyard?" Brody whispered in her ear.

She lowered her glass. "Oh yes. It's beautiful." She wanted to take off her shoes and dip her toes in the coolness.

"Later. You can try it out." He stepped away from her as Rex moved between them. "For now, I would like to introduce you to the others."

The glass pane slid open, allowing people to enter the room from the courtyard. The servant stood to the side to let each person pick out their glass of wine.

The first person to enter was the tall blonde with manufactured boobs Brody had brought to the cocktail party.

"You remember Greta. She was kind enough to play hostess for me tonight." Brody pulled her into his arms and kissed her. No light peck on the lips for them; instead tongues thrust and parried into each other's mouths, visible in flashes while Brody's hand covered and squeezed a full breast.

Feeling a little uncomfortable with the reenactment from the other night, Abby glanced up at Rex. With a smirk on his face, he watched with interest. She jabbed him in the side. His grunt brought his attention to her. She jerked her head at the display and lifted her shoulders.

"Such a sweet candy cane. Always in season." Brody chuckled as he pulled away. He then slapped her butt as she walked by, barely acknowledging them with a nod as she lifted a glass of white and slunk over to the sectional.

Next, a beautiful man and woman glided in. They looked so much alike they could've been related. Their long blond, almost white hair ended at the small of their backs. Abby had never seen a man with hair that long and silky and smooth. The desire to touch it had her clutching her glass a little tighter. Their eyes were the lightest gray and like the color of snow at night with a full moon. The only difference between the two was what they wore. His pale blue jeans were topped with a regular white button-up shirt, while the woman dressed in an ankle-length white cotton dress that was so thin, Abby could see her small dark nipples underneath.

Okay. Talk about getting creepier by the minute.

"I would like to introduce the supreme artists of photography, Leif and Spring Erickson. Their pictures have been shown in the renowned Museum of Modern Art in New York City and in so many galleries, they're too numerous to count." Brody leaned over and air-kissed their cheeks. "These are my dear friends, Rurik Volkov and his wife, Abby."

"So nice to meet you." The man had a slight lisp and the woman stared at Rex as if she wanted to eat him where he stood. What surprised Abby was how the man looked at Rex the same way. Uh-oh. The couple finally moved away with glasses of white wine—figured—over to the sofa to sit across from Greta.

The last couple to walk in looked like the average redneck and his barely clothed wife. His Dale Earnhardt Junior ball cap had sweat stains around the brim, and his wife's visible stomach sported a red eighty-eight dangling from a loop in her belly button.

"So you two are Brody's new friends." He reached out his hand to Rex and started pumping. "I'm Bubba Hagley and this here is my wife, Kristy."

Abby tilted her head as the men shook hands. The dark-headed man looked familiar to her for some reason. She'd never met a Bubba before and certainly not the one standing in front of her, but his dark eyes and the way he held himself reminded her of someone.

"So nice to meet you, sweet thang, and I hope to get to know you much better over the weekend." Bubba's grin warned he meant exactly what he was saying. Though he was handsome and a little thinner than she liked, his sable-brown eyes pulled her in, encouraging her to trust him.

"Now, sugar, don't let him frighten you. He's a teddy bear and loves all women. He gets carried away at times." His wife slapped his hand. That was when she realized he'd grabbed hers and held it tight.

"He doesn't frighten me." She tugged at her hand, and he continued to grin at her.

"Bubba, I'm Rurik. Her husband." Rex pulled on her wrist.

Were they going to have a tug-of-war, with her as the rope? Thankfully Bubba had the sense to let go.

With a crooked grin that Abby found interesting, Bubba chuckled as he released her and placed his arm over his wife's bare shoulders and joined the others. They had passed up the wine.

"Come over here and have a seat," Brody said as he moved onto the sofa with Greta. "We're about to be served dinner. We'll relax tonight, and tomorrow we'll go on a tour of my farm."

Abby looked over at Rex and grinned. Though she doubted Brody would point at a building and say, "And that's where we make the world's deadliest bullets," at least they would have a better idea of where it could be located.

"Who's he?" She watched the redneck lean over and whisper something into his wife's ear. The woman's eyes widened as she giggled. When she took a furtive glance over at her and Rex, Abby wondered what she thought was so funny.

"I have no idea." He downed the last of the wine and then leaned over to answer without the others hearing. "The photographers are actually the twentieth richest couple in the world, so they must be his backers. No matter how much money he made in real estate, he doesn't have the funds needed."

"Do you think he's the inventor?" She nodded toward the redneck. "I hate being presumptuous, but I don't think he's that smart," she said softly.

Rex wrapped an arm around her shoulders and pulled her closer. If the others wondered about their delay in joining them, they would simply appear like many new-lyweds, becoming immersed in each other.

"Looks can be deceiving but I agree. We've learned that lesson a few times. What about Greta?"

"Give me a break. She's too interested in impressing Brody with her body. Her mind would be the last thing she'd use."

"Do I hear the hissing of jealousy?" he teased, and then said, "And by the way, she's doing a great job." The grin on his face showed how much he appreciated it too.

Abby looked at the woman. She reached across Brody toward a bowl of fruit placed on an end table. Her breasts swung free of her gaping blouse, giving everyone a clear view. Brody took advantage and tweaked a nipple. With a squeal, she shot up straight to her knees and clasped his hand, not letting him move it away.

"Maybe I need to do the same to you," Greta teased.

He lifted his shirt, showing off a toned broad chest, and she twisted a tiny male nipple. Brody moaned and, from the slack expression on his face, enjoyed it.

The redneck wife howled with laughter and reached over to her husband, appearing to try the same move. In-stead, Bubba grabbed her and started tickling her sides. The two albinos, as Abby thought of them, smiled and watched the risqué roughhousing.

"Obviously, he has the inventor stashed away somewhere. Maybe we'll get lucky and have the information we need by the end of tomorrow."

When Rex stayed quiet, she looked up. His eyelids heavy, he gazed into her eyes and then looked down at her lips. Unable to stop herself, she licked her bottom lip. The pupils in his eyes widened until the gray disappeared into the black rim of his iris. She'd never seen him react so fully to her like that before. Was all the sexual horseplay exciting him?

"Hey, you two. Quit being antisocial and come over here and have a seat." Brody laughed as his hand shot between Greta's legs and underneath her skirt. She squealed—goodness she could hit high notes—and cupped his groin.

"Mr. Walker, dinner has been served in the courtyard as you instructed," a servant announced with all the fanfare of one who lived in a castle.

Abby expected horns to blow next.

"Let's go back outside. We're eating Roman-style today." Brody lifted Greta as she screeched in excitement.

"Save my ears now." Abby never understood a woman needing to sound like a banshee.

Face flushed, Rex snatched her glass and placed it on a table nearby. Before she could ask why he'd done that, he picked her up. She inhaled deeply, but thankfully no high-pitched sound escaped.

Hand pushing against his back and arms straight as she remained upright, she looked over at the last two couples. The redneck tossed his wife over his shoulder; the giggles emerging from his back indicated she thought it was a hoot. But the albinos softly spoke to each other and followed behind the group into the courtyard.

Next to the waterfall, a large red rug held a long, low table and dozens of cushions in every color of the rainbow. The crystal and silverware glistened from the candles arranged on the rocks and around the water. The early evening temperature was perfect to relax in and eat. Abby hated to admit it but she loved Brody's house, especially the courtyard.

With a smooth move, Rex placed her back on her feet next to the table.

Brody and Greta sat at one end with the albinos at the other. The redneck and his wife took the area on the left of Brody, leaving the pillows on the right for her and Rex.

At first, Abby tried sitting up but quickly realized the table would be too far away, so she followed the other couples' lead and rested on one elbow with Rex stretched out behind her. She could tell he was enjoying himself as he pulled her to his body, buttocks to groin. Oh, yeah, the hedonistic life had its perks.

"Let's toast to a wonderful weekend of discovery." With a glass raised high, Brody stared at Rex and then Abby.

What the hell did he mean by that? The glint of lust in his eyes wasn't good. Then again, she'd been an operative long enough to use it to her advantage. But how would Rex react to it?

Chapter Seventeen

REX SHOOK HIS head. The wine tasted good. He was more of a beer guy, but he'd learned over the years that he could hold his liquor pretty well. Mostly he would get a little maudlin but he would relax and sleep hard.

He noticed Abby's drink stayed about the same level; then he remembered her saying something about being an easy drunk. He wondered if she became more open. Sure would be nice for her to become a little chatty. He'd never known a woman to be so close mouthed.

Her butt moved as she reached for a slice of watermelon. He groaned. Hard as a bowling pin, he wanted to grind against her. She was so close that he could smell the flowery shampoo she'd used.

Before he could stop himself, his nose was buried in her hair, his hands holding her head in place. Fuck, he wanted her and bad. Though they'd only spent two nights at her brother's, it felt like it'd been five years since he'd been in her. From the first time he'd ever touched her, she'd always felt right. Like no other woman was as soft or he would never tire of her. How the heat of her body was perfect for his aching cock. Ah, hell, he hurt so badly. He thrust against her buttocks.

"Rurik?" Abby's voice, filled with concern, brought him back.

He kissed the top of her head and released her. Uncomfortable with his uncharacteristic public display of affection—hell, lust—he looked straight toward Brody. The man stared back, grinning.

Bastard, what was he up to?

For the next hour, they ate and Rex worked at keeping his hands to himself. Brody knew no restraint, and a few times, he expected the man to spread Greta open and have at her in front of everyone. Jack had warned him that Brody enjoyed having sex with an audience, but he guessed he hadn't really expected it.

Rex lifted his glass of wine. "Brody, this is good. I wonder if I could purchase a bottle or two from you." Maybe he could talk Abby into drinking in their room later. He still had questions for her, and lately he was beginning to feel a little desperate for answers. Though his brother had provided a lot, there were still more.

He rubbed his eyes. Dammit, he needed to keep his mind on the mission.

"I'll be happy to send you a couple. You couldn't buy it anyway, as it's my own private stock." Brody withdrew his hands from beneath the blonde's clothing. "Let's all call it a night. A servant will show you to your rooms.

Tomorrow, be sure to dress casually for the tour. We'll be riding ATVs, plus I thought we would get some hunting done. I have a surplus of wild pigs we need to cull on my land. Nothing like a smoked pig for dinner."

Brody was a mixed bag, one moment talking about private wine and the next planning a hunt for their dinner. He was certainly a new age redneck.

Stretching his legs, Rex grabbed Abby by the waist and followed the servant to the front of the house and the archway they had seen earlier. When they walked into the large bedroom suite, he grinned. The mattress was large enough for his height. There had been numerous missions where his feet hung off the end; even the hotel's bed caused him to curl up a bit to keep from hanging off. French doors lined one wall. He opened one set and moved out to what he thought was a private patio. Instead it was the same courtyard they'd been in earlier. Looking back, he noticed all of the bedrooms lined one side of the courtyard.

Across the way were more French doors with no curtains, but that bedroom was larger and had to be the master. Brody hadn't wasted time. He had all the lights on, putting on a show as he pounded into the blonde from the rear. Bent over the bed, arms straight, her breasts swayed with each thrust.

Having seen more than he ever wanted to of a man he didn't trust, he turned to walk back into his bedroom when he noticed the tall redneck and his wife staring out from their bedroom, but instead of watching Brody, they looked straight at him.

Rex nodded and returned to Abby, closing and locking the doors behind him.

GRABBING HER SMALL suitcase, Abby rushed into the bathroom to wash up and change into her favorite oversized nightshirt and gym shorts. She stared in the mirror. The woman peering back at her had large dark eyes that looked wide and frightened. Why? In less than a week, she'd gone from sure-footed operative to a confused and sex-starved maniac. Sex-starved? Was that the right adjective for a woman who'd gotten plenty from Rex only a few nights ago? What was wrong with her? She needed to pull her act together and keep her mind on the mission.

She wished she could blame all the crazy thoughts and feelings on Brody. Why couldn't the man keep his hands to himself? His beautiful muscular body and his masculine fingers pinching and probing the blonde in front of everyone—she'd never thought of herself as a voyeur, but wow! It was ten times better than Cinemax After Dark.

One last look in the mirror and she caught the flush on her cheeks. She wanted Rex. Would they take a chance that Brody had cameras hidden in the bedroom? Between the glass in the French doors and the mood lighting in the courtyard, could others see inside the bedroom?

She covered her eyes and shook her head. Talk about crazy missions. How much crazier could it get than watching Brody feel up his girlfriend and then talk about killing pigs? Never a big advocate of hunting animals—humans could at least defend themselves—she refused to shoot a wild pig.

Swinging from sensual overload to surreal violence and back to the promise of another night with the sexiest man alive, she expected to fall off the edge of sanity.

Peeking between her fingers, the man likely to push her into madness stood behind her. His warm gaze caressed her backside as she watched his reflection in the mirror.

"Are you about finished in here?" His deep, rumbling voice rolled down her spine and heated her groin. Oh, yeah, she loved the sound of his voice, and with the accent he used to maintain his cover, she melted further until she locked her knees.

"Uh, yes."

She moved sideways to slip by him. He shifted until her back was pressed to the door frame.

"Get in bed and strip." He leaned in and the old Rex whispered in her ear, "I want you ready for me. No cameras in the room, but there is a listening device and I don't give a fuck what they hear." His big hands clasped the back of her head as his thumbs rested beneath her jaw. He lifted her face to his. "Don't argue with me. Don't push me. Not tonight, Abby."

Then his mouth covered hers. Each forceful thrust of his tongue caused her to moisten with need. She wanted to tell him to go fuck himself, but being honest, his domineering attitude turned her on even more.

She'd never gotten into the dominant/submissive game some people enjoyed, but that wasn't what Rex was trying to pull. If there was anything Abby had learned in those first few weeks together, it was that Rex knew what he wanted in bed and from a lover and he didn't mind expressing it. His forceful, authoritarian tone turned her on like nothing had in a long, long time.

Abby walked into the bedroom, surprised to see a large cloth shade had been lowered from a recessed area in the ceiling. Nice. The delicate crystal accent lamp on the nightstand gave off a soft glow, enough light for her to strip and crawl into the huge bed.

When Rex closed the bathroom door behind him, he was naked and hard. She liked how his cock swayed with each step he took to the bed. There was something sensual and dangerous about his movement that caused her heartbeat to pick up. He looked like a king entering his harem and expecting satisfaction. He tossed back the cover from where she'd covered herself, chilled by the air conditioner working overtime.

His grunt of approval brought a half-grin to her face. He was playing the part perfectly. Lord and master approving his slave girl's obedience. Who was she to make him stop when she enjoyed the new sensations?

She opened her arms.

"That's right. Open up to me." His hands scooped her body to his as his mouth covered a taut nipple. Her head fell back, mouth open in a silent scream of pleasure as he feasted on the other breast. "So sweet."

His hands clasped her waist and maneuvered her until she spread out on the bed with his knees next to her head. He leaned across her torso, one hand clamped over her mound. "You're so hot and moist." His finger split the swollen lips and rubbed the hard knot.

She arched, pressing her groin to that talented digit.

"Please, please." She bit the inside of her mouth as she came close to saying *Rex* instead of *Rurik*. Touching his hip, she stroked his warm skin, loving how hard and masculine he felt beneath her fingers.

He widened his knees, straddling her head so his cock dangled above her mouth. With her attention centered on reaching what fascinated her, she jumped when his mouth covered her clit.

His mouth moved from her and she lifted her hips. "No. Take me into your mouth and then I'll give you more," he said.

One slow thrust of his hips and his cock entered her mouth. She gripped the base of his cock to stop him from choking her as her other hand caressed his ass and tenderly stroked his tight scrotum. As she sucked, he began to carefully fuck her face while his tongue lapped at her excitement.

"So responsive." He licked and sucked on her inner lips. He nibbled at her clit, and each time his teeth grazed the tip, she arched and his cock muffled her scream. "That's it. You're so good." He tried to move away but she held tight and pulled harder with her mouth. She wanted him to come. In response, he took another long lick from her clit to her anus and she screamed again.

When she finally released him, she looked over to where he was stretched out on his back, loose limbed and satisfied, swiping his arm across his mouth.

He cupped one hand over her mons and used the other to pull her closer until his cheek rested on her stomach. "I want you again."

She glanced down. Okay, no sleep tonight.

Chapter Eighteen

ABBY YAWNED AGAIN and choked. Spitting and coughing, she thumped Rex's back in anger.

"Shit! If I swallow another bug, I swear I'll scream." Each word shook out of her mouth as the ATV traveled at breakneck speed, keeping up with the others. With her arms wrapped tight around his chest, she felt his chuckle. No need for him to say, even if she could hear him, that he was thinking of the last time she'd screamed and the last unusual thing she swallowed. "Shut up!"

He howled with laughter.

She ducked her head, and unable to resist, she bit his shoulder.

The ATV sprayed rocks and grass as he slid to a stop.

"If you don't be careful, I'll pull you over my knee and spank that bottom." Rex eyed her with interest and then squeezed hard on the gas, kicking out dirt and more as he caught back up with the group.

Eyebrows lifted, she grinned. Why did the idea turn her on? What was going on with her? She acted as if she couldn't get enough of Rex. She'd never been so obsessed with a man like she was with him.

Brody waved them over to one of five long metal buildings. By the time the dust settled, they were gathered in front of a door marked OFFICE. They already knew the routine, as they had made two other stops since starting out.

When the men had gotten up before the crack of dawn to hunt wild pig, she'd thought about protesting the chauvinistic division but opted instead for the facials and manicures Brody offered. Lot of good they'd done with all the crap flying in her face and hair now.

So after a light lunch, the fellows had picked them up on ATVs and went on a tour of the grounds. One peanut field followed a hundred more with an equal amount of cornfields. The first building had been near a couple silos and the next building was a large barn for milk cows. The handsome playboy had milk cows? Abby had a hard time wrapping her mind around that.

The smell and sound warned Abby she wouldn't be interested in going inside. Then someone caught her attention off to the side.

"You coming in, Abby?" Rex asked.

"Nah, you go ahead. I have no interest in seeing buildings jam-packed with chickens. I'll stay out here and stretch my legs."

As soon as the crowd closed the door behind them, she walked around the corner. She ran her hand along the back of her jeans, ensuring the knife remained in its holster. Only two weapons survived detection from Brody's guards: a switchblade and a Beretta pistol. Rex had the gun. "How's it going, Liam?"

Dressed like a hunched over old man, Liam eyed Abby and looked around. "This is one mission I'm not enjoying at all. You have any idea at all how filthy chickens are? They eat their own poop. I don't believe I'll ever eat another one of those feathered beasties in my life." He straightened and rolled his shoulders.

"Have you found anything that looks like an ammo facility?" She swatted at the gnats hovering in front of her face.

"There's only one area so far they've limited all employees from going into, and that's at the far northeast corner of the property. It's an overgrown mountain filled with limestone caves. They claim it's dangerous because sinkholes are everywhere. So far that's the most logical place to build a secret manufacturing plant. The consistent temperature inside a cave would be helpful." Liam continued to scan the area. "I would check out the area, but I can't get away for longer than fifteen minutes, too little time." He quickly stooped over. "Got to go." Then he scurried around the corner.

She turned to see everyone filing out of the building.

"You missed seeing where all that chicken you like to eat comes from." Bubba stopped next to her and looked off in the direction Liam had disappeared.

"Who says I like chicken?" She noticed he'd torn off the sleeves from a plaid cotton shirt, revealing sinewy arms. Though on the thin side, he was still strong, and the cold way he looked at Brody when he thought no one was paying attention would give anyone a chill.

"All women love chicken."

"I haven't met a man who didn't." She thought of what Liam said and mentally corrected herself.

"Ha! I guess you just did. My family had a farm when I was a kid, and they're some of the meanest creatures on earth."

So two men.

"Those little bitty things?" She looked up and down his tall lanky frame. "Aren't you rather big to be frightened of little birds?"

"I haven't always been this big, honey." His look stroked her as sure as if his hand slid down her body.

She backed up a couple steps and crossed her arms. She didn't like that at all. Who was he? One fact for sure was she would need to watch him carefully.

"Hey, sugar, you're not scaring the woman, are you? Her old man looks as if he could snap you like a twig." Kristy wrapped her arm through his and pulled him away.

"What did he say?" Rex walked up and glared at the redneck's back.

"Nothing really. Talking about chickens." They headed toward the ATVs. "Where to next?" She wanted a shower so bad. The heat, bugs, and dust were about to do her in. When she was younger, all of that wouldn't have bothered her, but the older she became, the more she enjoyed her creature comforts.

When a couple of the ATVs cranked up, muting anyone overhearing, Rex leaned over and said, "We're to go around the edge of the fields and reach the house by sunset. Maybe tonight we'll hear something that'll give us a lead. I'm all for taking Brody to Sector and beating the shit out of him until he tells us where it is." He handed Abby her helmet.

"I've wondered about that. Ryker has been holding back." Before he started the engine and the noise drowned out their voices, she said, "I spoke to Liam." His gaze drilled into hers. Knowing time was short, he kept quiet. "He said the northeast area of the farm is off-limits." Then she quickly added the information about caves and sinkholes.

"Makes sense." He straddled the seat and scooted up to make room for her. "We better go before they turn around and check on us."

Over an hour later, as they took the last curve on the dirt road, Abby spotted a Sand County sheriff sedan parked near the long, detached garage.

"What the hell is he doing here?" Abby said after they stopped a few feet away.

"You're asking me?" He gave her a look that said *He's your brother, not mine.*

"Yeah, yeah. I know."

Rex pulled off his helmet, and what little hair he hadn't cut off stuck out every which way. She imagined hers looked the same. Before he stood, she slicked his hair down, silky and thick. She wondered what it would take to talk him into growing it long again.

She quickly turned around before he could see her face. Like lightning in a storm, the reminder of what she kept from him struck. No way would he be around her after the mission. She'd already decided he deserved to know the truth, but not until they stopped the manufacture and sale of Hell's Purifier. One problem at a time.

First up was to find out what in the hell her brother was doing at Brody's.

"There she is now." Edward touched the brim of his cap and dipped his head toward Greta and Brody. "Hey, Sis, I need to talk with you."

That was it. Next time she saw Jack, he'd get an earful about mixing family and business, especially when the family was in law enforcement and she was in the business of killing people. The two didn't mix at all.

"Sure. Let's go around back. I'll show you the pool." She turned toward Brody. "That okay?" Manners had her asking, though she had no doubt he wouldn't care.

She shook her head at Rex when he reached for her. The way Edward was frowning, he better stay back.

"Sure." Brody turned to Edward. "Come and visit sometime and bring the whole family. We can barbeque and have a good time."

Edward nodded again but didn't say anything as he followed her around the garage and through a fence to the pool. She'd found the path that morning as she'd been given the facial next to the pool.

"What's so important for you to interrupt my weekend? And it better not be about Rurik."

His face flushed and he looked away.

Well, crap. She'd never believe her brother could get embarrassed unless she saw it with her own eyes. She could scratch that off her list.

"Sorry, Abigail—"

"Abby. You're only adding fuel to the fire." Her jaw hurt from gritting her teeth.

He took a deep breath. "I had your husband investigated some more. Sis, he's a dangerous man. You need to go home with me and I'll tell you all about it."

She stood there, unable to say anything. Where had this protective brother been when she'd been younger and needed someone looking after her? She wanted to be appreciative, but she'd seen and done too much.

"I know."

His head swung back to look at her. "What do you mean you know?"

"I know everything about him."

"You know that he deals with illegal firearms and ammunition?" He clasped her arm. "Do you understand that means he's an arms dealer? That he'll sell arms to someone who'd want to harm you and your country? I have a contact that checked him out. It's not a cover for any government branch. If you stay with him, you'll be as guilty as he is." His green eyes begged her to listen.

"I think you need to leave and never come back. You may never understand this, but I'll be okay. You need to stay out of it or you'll get hurt." She pulled out the invisible shield she'd used around Theo, the old commander of The Circle. The man had always looked for a reason to hurt a person, and out of self-defense, she'd learned how to shut down her emotions so they wouldn't show on her face.

"What does he have on you?" Her brother clasped both arms and shook her.

Before he had a chance to say another word, she broke his hold and held her knife to his throat.

"Edward, as I said, you need to stay out of it. Go home and stay there." Two of her fingers pressed the side of his neck to keep the blade from going in. The edge was so sharp that if he moved a little before she could catch herself, she'd slice his throat.

He raised his hands.

"Abby, what's going on?" Rex came around the corner, the Beretta in one hand pointed at Edward.

She slowly backed off.

Edward touched his neck and looked at his fingers. No blood. She'd been careful.

"Okay. Have it your way. Just be ready to suffer the consequences." He stepped back and glanced at Rurik and his gun. "You have to understand that as the sheriff, I have an obligation."

Then he walked toward the path and back to his car.

Chapter Nineteen

REX WATCHED ABBY as she smoothed on her makeup. Back against the headboard, ankles crossed, he enjoyed watching her fix herself up. Like any man seeing his woman do those little feminine things to get ready, he wanted to tell her not to worry about makeup. She was pretty enough without it, but he remembered his mom saying that it made a woman feel special. Of course, in his eyes, Abby was special enough.

He squeezed his eyes shut. Sure his brother claimed that he and Abby had had only a one-night stand while she was grieving losing him, but how did Abby feel about it all? He needed to talk to her about it but not here where Brody could listen in. For two days, he had avoided the issue. So what were a few more days? Mission first, personal business second. He'd continue to enjoy the benefits of pretending to have a relationship with Abby, and when the mission was over, they would talk about the past, get everything out of the way. Though he had feelings for her, he wasn't sure if he could ever trust her. He knew it didn't make sense. She'd thought he was dead, but why his brother? Anyone but his brother.

"Are you ready or asleep?"

He opened his eyes. Dressed in a simple black dress with a slight flare just an inch or so above her knees, a thin strand of pearls, and matching earrings, and all that glorious neck to run his tongue up to where her hair was pinned in place, Abby took his breath away.

"Your eyes are open but I don't think you're here." She snapped her fingers in front of his face.

He grabbed her hand and pulled her on top of him. "I was thinking how I would like to lick every inch of you." His hand skimmed up the back of her leg until he cupped a bare buttock. "Damn, just thinking of you only wearing a thong under this dress is going to kill my concentration."

"Who said I was wearing a thong?" Her crooked grin shot iron through his cock until he ached.

"You're an evil woman, Abigail Rodriguez." How was he going to think tonight?

"Volkov. Abby Volkov. Remember?"

Though he knew it was all an act, it bothered him to think she had another man's name, even a fake one that he used. Logic had nothing to do with how he felt about her. He wanted her to have the Drago name.

"True. Newlyweds." He slapped the soft round globe. Her eyes flared. No doubt about it, he needed to investigate how he could get those dark eyes of hers to flare up more. "It's time for us to meet them in the dining room."

She backed off him and the bed, yanking at the hem of her dress. It was conservative even with the slight flair, but he wanted to pull on it, too, bringing it below her knee. He didn't want anyone seeing more than they should of her.

"Not the courtyard?"

"What we know of Brody so far, we'll probably end up there, spread-eagle and naked."

ABBY STEPPED INTO the large living area and stopped. The glass panels had been pushed to the sides, opening the room to the courtyard. A lit dance floor had been erected where they had eaten Roman-style the night before and was surrounded on three sides by the waterfall and a small pool. The dining room table had been moved to the middle of the living room so everyone could get a good view of the courtyard.

The albinos were already sipping wine and stood next to where their name cards waited for them.

"Ah, there you are." Brody handed her and Rex a glass of wine. No choice of red and white. "Tonight, we will toast a successful hunt. So the devil's wine for all. This is a special blend champagne I think you'll enjoy."

At that moment, Bubba and his wife entered the room behind them.

"Whoo-ee! That's some kind of setup." He grabbed his wife's hand and pulled her over to the dance floor. "Where's the music? I'm ready to dance."

Disgruntled, Brody squared his shoulders. "We'll

dance after we eat. Come and have some champagne with us. We're about to toast our successful day."

Something was up. Abby wasn't sure what and hated waiting to see if he would at least give enough hints for them to figure it out themselves.

Brody held up his glass. "To a successful kill. A nice big fat pig for us to eat tonight." Two servants came in carried the largest tray she'd ever seen, and in the middle was a complete pig. She had to admit it smelled good, but seeing it all together, ears to curly tail, her stomach bubbled at the thought of eating it. "With one shot, Bubba brought him down. Cheers!"

She sipped on the wine in the hope her stomach would relax. *Whoa!* She looked at her glass. Talk about good. She sipped a few more times. She looked around. Everyone was nodding and holding out their glasses for more.

Rex leaned down. "You have to hand it to the man. He has good taste in wine. I don't think I've ever tasted champagne like this."

"I'm glad everyone is enjoying the blend. Drink as much as you want. I brought in several cases, and we have the night to finish them off." He laughed and everyone chimed in.

With the help of the servants, the plates were filled with pork and plenty of other side dishes. Abby pushed the meat to the side and ate the vegetables. By the time dessert arrived, she couldn't eat another bite, even though she was a big fan of apple pie and ice cream. Her wine-glass remained full—not because she was avoiding it like she had last night, but because every time she took a sip, a servant refilled it.

Rex laughed at something Bubba said. Even the albinos were smiling and giggling. Abby jumped when Brody clapped his hands.

"Tonight's entertainment as you probably already guessed is dancing, but not any old dancing. Dirty dancing. And to encourage everyone to participate, I have a special surprise." He nodded to a servant, who handed him a long box. "To the most inventive and sexy couple goes"—he flipped open the lid—"gold and silver plated dueling pistols."

She didn't know much about antique weapons, but they were beautiful. Every inch of the guns was engraved with designs. But to her they weren't worth dancing like that in front of everyone.

Brody nodded to a servant and music flowed into the room. Greta squealed and jumped onto the floor, shaking her hips to "Love Is Strange."

Bubba followed with Kristy singing along to the music and dancing around him. The albinos joined them but held each other at arm's length and moved like two robots. No rhythm at all.

Abby pulled on Rex's sleeve when he started toward the dance floor. "Tell them I had to go to the bathroom. This would be the perfect time for me to check out the alb . . . uh . . . Ericksons' and Roberts' rooms."

"I should go."

"You're being watched a lot closer than me. I can plant the bugs too." Even as they talked a servant off to the side glanced their way. "It won't take me but a few minutes." She downed the last of her champagne and moved toward the bedrooms.

The music pounded all the way to the first bedroom she came to after theirs. It belonged to the albinos. She shook her head. She needed to quit calling them that before she embarrassed herself and said it to their faces.

The room looked like a storm had hit it with clothes and jewelry strewn everywhere. She stood back and let her gaze decide on the areas that looked out of place. Disorganized people unconsciously organized the things they wanted hidden. Inside an open closet, she noticed a zipped up suitcase. Behind it in the wall was a safe, the type hotels used, where people make up numbers to lock it. Most people used simple codes, which they should never do. She tried one through six. It didn't open. Then she tried the number one six times. It clicked open.

Inside was a briefcase filled with documents. She was able to piece together two things: one was that Rex was right—they financially supported Brody's venture in new age weaponry. The second was even more terrifying: Leif and Spring weren't husband and wife but brother and sister. She glanced over to the mussed king-sized bed. Sick.

Nothing else indicated the inventor of Hell's Purifier.

She placed everything back, set the safe to the un-imaginative code, and placed a bug near the closet. Then she peeked through the curtains to make sure everyone was still dancing. Greta and Brody bumped and ground as the albinos stiffly shimmied against each other's backs.

Yuck. Bubba tossed and twirled Kristy in several well-thought-out moves. Obviously he had a lot of practice. Rex stood to the side, sipping on the champagne.

Wasting no more time, she raced into the next bedroom. This one looked a lot like hers and Rex's: neat, with all of the luggage locked. The safe's door was open. She walked over to the window to check on the others again when the corner of some material sticking out of a bureau caught her eye. She opened the drawer, and inside was a blanket and pillow, stuffed there as if someone had been in a hurry to hide it. She glanced at the bed, checking the covers. None of the servants had been ordered to clean the rooms as they would in a hotel, thus the reason the albinos' room was so messy.

There were several pillows on the bed but only two on one side were wrinkled. The others were neatly pressed and arranged like they would be before someone slept in the bed. The Roberts weren't sleeping together.

The music stopped.

Crap. She better get back before they came looking for her. Without wasting time, she placed a bug behind the bureau.

When she returned, everyone was off the dance floor, drinking and snacking on finger food. Dancing was hungry business it appeared.

Brody stepped in front of her and offered her a small plate filled with slices of various cheeses and wafers and a glass of champagne. "Here, Abby, eat some cheese and crackers. It'll settle your stomach."

So Rex had claimed she had an upset stomach.

When she reached out, he pulled back. "Unless you're sick from something else besides food. Are you already expecting, Mrs. Volkov? Maybe you should stay away from the champagne."

She paled. Brody's eyebrows rose. Recovering as quickly as possible, she said, "No. I would love some champagne. I believe the heat and dust got to me a little bit, but I feel so much better now." To prove it, she downed the glass.

"Wonderful! More music. Now everyone get up there and show us how it's done!" Brody hooked an arm around Greta's waist and swung her around. The woman's thong was visible as her dress flew up in the back.

The thumping beat of "Be My Baby" started up.

She looked up at Rex. "You ready?"

"I'm not much of a dancer."

"From what I can tell, I don't think it matters." They glanced over at the dance floor. Brody and Greta ground their hips against each other while the others danced their own version. Abby moved with Rex to the dance floor.

"Move your hips like this and I'll dance around you." Hands on each side of his waist, she hesitated.

Compared to his height and wide shoulders, his hips were small but solidly padded by muscles. Her gaze dropped a little farther and the visible bulge to one side of his zipper caught her attention. Avoiding the almost irresistible urge to cup him, she rotated his hips and watched the bulge grow bigger and longer. Somehow she remembered to move in the opposite direction in front of him and tried to keep a rhythm of sorts. Every time his groin brushed her body, she gasped as if she'd been burned, and with the small dance floor it became unbearable. Finally Abby and Rex called it quits and sat on the floor to watch the other couples.

Brody continued to pour more of his special champagne. Blurry eyed, Abby shook her head, turning down the glass, while Rex downed another.

She'd hoped to regain her senses when they sat down, but he'd pulled her onto his lap and the hard length beneath her warned the champagne and dancing affected him in the same way.

Moments before the lights had dimmed for the slower song, the albinos disappeared. Bubba and Kristy held on to each other, talking softly, but no hip action to speak of. They laughed and stepped away, sitting at the table, drinking another glass of champagne.

Alone on the dance floor, Brody and Greta humped each other from the chest down. He dipped down and brought his hands underneath Greta's dress and lifted it until everyone could see him breaking the sides of her thong. Then his hand slid to the apex of her legs and his fingers jabbed into her. She tossed her head back and thrust her hips. His other hand rubbed up and down the front of his pants.

Tingles traveled over Abby's body, concentrating on her groin and nipples. As if he sensed her dilemma, Rex pulled her back closer to his chest, her butt rubbing up the length of his cock. His hands cupped her breasts and he pressed his fingers against her hard nubs and rubbed through the cloth. Her whole body felt on fire. She couldn't take her eyes off the lecherous scene in front of her, uncaring if the shadows hid her and Rex or not.

Normally she'd turn away, a little embarrassed by the public display, but all her inhibitions disappeared like each piece of clothing taken from the woman on the dance floor. She'd never felt so free and turned on.

The couple continued to move to the music. Brody yanked on Greta's dress, tearing it off until she was naked, moving her body in waves. He leaned over and sucked on a nipple, pulling with his teeth. It looked painful but the look on her face said otherwise. With a smooth turn, his back was to the audience and he picked her up. Her legs opened and wrapped around his waist. Then he turned. His hands cupped her softly rounded buttocks, and from the floor, Abby could see his cock entering and partially leaving her, glistening from her moistness.

Fire infused every inch of her body. She clenched and released her thighs, enjoying how Rex groaned with each movement. When Rex's fingers slid up her leg and thrust into her heat, she arched her back. His thick fingers filled her but not to the extent she wanted, needed. Then he hesitated. She smiled. He hadn't expected her to be truly bare.

"Fuck, Abby. No thong. If I had known you were telling the truth about being naked underneath that dress, I would've been hard all night."

"Then I wish I had insisted on proving it to you earlier. Thinking of you wanting me all that time would've been so damn sexy."

"You're a cruel woman. It's difficult enough keeping my mind on business." He shifted, pulled his fingers away, and spread her legs to rest alongside his. A few seconds passed as his hand moved between them. Was he unzipping his pants? Before she moved to help, he pushed her a little forward, parted her slick folds, and entered her, thrusting up, filling her. With Brody and Greta fucking on the stage and Bubba and Kristy whispering and watching the show, Abby and Rex were in the shadows, no one the wiser.

He wrapped his arms around her and pulled her back until her head rested beneath his chin. She swayed with the music, enjoying the feel of his body inside of her. Her dress covered his lap. They looked like they were rubbing against each other and nothing more. Knowing no one could really tell what was happening turned her on even more.

After a couple minutes, Bubba and Kristy stumbled out of the room.

"Want another sip?" Abby reached for her glass and offered it to Rex.

His masculine lips pressed to the edge and she carefully tipped it. When he had enough, she placed her lips at the same spot and finished the drink.

She glanced over at the dance floor. Brody didn't appear to be slowing down. She had to admire his stamina.

The room blurred and shifted. Without protest, she felt Rex cup and massage her breasts, his thumbs circling over the stiff tips. As if it had a will of its own, her body arched into his touch.

"Oh, you feel so good." The words sounded more like a purr.

"I've never been so horny. I can't get enough of you." Rex gripped her to move faster. "Harder. I need more." He lifted her higher and thrust into her fully.

She leaned forward and he followed, pounding into her. There was no hiding the fact he was fucking her. Animalistic and brutal but she reveled in his strength and stamina. Rough fingers helped pull her dress over her head. Feeling liberated, she soaked in the sensation of air caressing her skin.

Despite being immersed in Rex taking her, she looked toward the stage. Brody and Greta mimicked the same position but with a difference. His fists held her hair as if they were reins, pulling her head back, arching her back, and the angle of thrusts entered her body in a more narrow and painful way. From Greta's expression, she loved the pain.

"That's hot," Rex breathed in her ear.

She nodded, watching Brody hammer into the woman.

Rex cupped her breasts and squeezed as he pushed into her hard and lifted with his legs. The ground moved out from beneath her and she clasped his wrists, holding on.

"Hook your feet behind my thighs and hold on."

Not sure what he planned, she did take pleasure in how tightly his groin pressed into her. When he started walking toward the bedrooms, each jarring step shot the most exquisite sensations between her legs.

"What are you doing?" she asked Rex.

"I found some lube in the bedroom earlier tonight. We're going to try it out without an audience."

His hand slipped over her mound and rolled her clit. She screeched, arching her back as Rex held her tight.

Maniacal laughter followed them down the hallway.

Chapter Twenty

"WELL, MY, ARE we two little rabbits or what? I've never seen two people get it on for so long. Quite an imagination, by the way." Brody's voice sounded as if he was next to his ear. "You're the man!"

Rex turned over and caught Brody staring at Abby's bare ass and slender back. With one hand, he snapped the sheet over her.

"What the fuck do you want?" Blocking Brody's view as much as he could, Rex sat up, tossing a corner of the sheet over his groin. An uneasy feeling came over him. The man liked to stare too much.

Brody chuckled. "The servants reported that you two were finally sleeping, but I wanted to see for myself. It's a quarter to one."

Rex's gaze shot over to the windows. Sun lit up every inch of the courtyard. He blinked and rubbed his face, cutting his eyes back to Brody. "That champagne had a kick to it." He never remembered having a drink affect him like that.

"Yeah, I guess you could say that." Brody quickly added, "You're welcome to stay and sleep it off. I'm going into Birmingham to take care of some business."

"Your other guests?" He shifted, and stabbing pain raced down his back to his balls. *What the hell?*

"They left this morning." The smirk on Brody's face needed to be wiped off, but at this point Rex needed to do some damage control, and that had nothing to do with the mission.

"Give us a few minutes and we'll be out of your hair." He shook Abby. She groaned and rolled over, tangling her long legs in the sheet. He adjusted the material again to cover one taut nipple.

"Like I said, no hurry." Brody tilted his head as his grin widened. "Take your time. Sleep it off."

"Thanks, but her mother's expecting us to stop by her brother's to say good-bye." As far as he knew, Leigh Ann couldn't care less, but it sounded like a reasonable explanation. Their mission had failed miserably, and it was his fault. He dreaded telling Jack that alcohol and whatever Brody put in the champagne had interfered with his sanity.

"Leigh Ann, huh?" His skeptical look said it all. Obviously everyone knew she wasn't really the hovering mother type. "Sure. No need to tell me that you enjoyed the weekend. I could tell. So I'll be in touch soon for us to talk about our possible business venture." He nodded and glanced one more time in Abby's direction before closing the door.

Maybe there was a way to save the mission, but at that point he wasn't sure how.

"WHAT THE HELL got into you two? Do you want to be the one to tell Ryker that we fucked it up?" Jack paced back and forth in front of where they stood with their heads hanging low.

Abby rubbed her eyes and bit the side of her mouth. It wasn't the time to make a smart-ass comment about Jack's turn of phrase. How could she even let such a thought cross her mind? She'd never been so embarrassed in her whole life.

When Rex had shaken her awake and rushed her to dress, she'd been shocked to find out that the morning had long gone, and they had missed their last chance at drawing information out of Brody. Then again, he'd told Rex he would be in touch.

"We won't mess up next time." Even to her ears that sounded so lame.

"What about the information we gave you about the caves?" Rex lifted his head and squared his shoulders.

"Next time I'll send in Liam alone. He knows how to act like a professional." Folding his arms, Jack glared at Rex.

He was right, but Rex wasn't alone in the blame.

"Listen. Brody was never alone, and with so many people crawling through that house, we rarely had a moment alone either. From the second we arrived until we left, he never talked business. The guy is strange and so hung up on wanting everyone to see his junk." She coughed. Her face flushed.

Damn. She and Rex had sex for days and couldn't get enough of it, but there was a world of difference between doing it and talking about it, especially to Jack.

"Oh, I know all about it." His eyes chilled as he looked at his younger brother.

Rex stepped toward Jack. "You know what?" The menace in his voice warned Jack to tread lightly.

"Exactly what you think." Fists balled, he leaned into Rex. Though a few inches shorter, Jack was equal in bulk.

"You asshole. Liam had no way of knowing. Who did you have spying on us? And why did you believe we couldn't be trusted?" Rex shoved at Jack's shoulder.

Before Abby could stop what was coming, Jack shoved back and said, "I knew you couldn't keep your dick in your pants. You talk about me disrespecting Abby, but how do you think she feels being fucked in front of an audience?" Jack pushed again.

"Whoa! I'm right here, fellas! You two need to chill." She moved to separate them, but before she got close enough, Rex swung, slamming a fist into his brother's face.

Then the fight was on. No way could she break it up. So she stepped out of the van and hoped the equipment wouldn't get smashed. When two men are determined to fight it out, the best route was to duck and run. A person could get hurt sticking their nose between two warring brothers.

Abby stood outside with two other operatives, watching

the van rock back and forth as crashes and the sickening sound of flesh hitting flesh resounded inside. The fighting would stop for a second, but that was only for them to take a deep breath and verbally abuse each other, and then the fighting began all over.

Tired of the total pointlessness of the argument and certainly tired of the brawl, she'd started to slide open the door when a black SUV drove up. Nic.

Ah, hell. That was all they needed. No matter what Rex believed, the woman would freak once she heard about Abby and Rex having sex. Not to mention how many times.

Abby eyed the dark-headed woman. Nic slammed the door and glared at her.

Okay. Someone had a big mouth at the OS Sector.

"You had to throw yourself at him, didn't you?" Nic's head bobbed in her fury.

Before Abby could defend herself, Nic picked up a rock and flung it at her.

"What the hell?" Were they in second grade?

"In the olden days, they stoned sluts." Again, she snatched up a handful of rocks, wound up her arm, and pitched them hard.

The operatives stepped back and laughed. No help there. They clearly wanted to stay out of it.

"Slut? You're crazy! Stop!" Several more rocks pelted her. Abby didn't want to hurt her, but Nic wasn't acting like she'd stop, especially when she bent down to reload.

She charged the smaller woman and a rock grazed her cheek. The stinging warned her she'd been cut and a warm tickling flowed down to her jaw. For a split second she thought about breaking the woman's arms, but instead she grabbed Nic in a bear hug. Restraining her arms, keeping her from throwing two more handfuls, Abby could see as they struggled that blood was sprinkling over Nic's face. So she guessed there was quite a bit on hers.

Nic released an earsplitting scream of frustration.

In self-defense mode, Abby shoved her away and covered an aching ear, certain that she'd busted the drum. Nic fell to the ground and screamed again. Heaven save her from the crazy woman.

"For goodness' sake, Nic, what is wrong with you?" She leaned over to help her up.

"Get away from her!" Jack rammed his shoulder into hers to move her away.

"What—"

"How did she get all bloody?" Rex walked past Abby and helped Jack lift Nic from the ground. One brother wiped at her face with the corner of his shirt while the other one slapped off the dirt from her clothes.

Abby looked down at her blood-spattered shirt and jeans that were peppered with dirt from the thrown rocks. Her cheek throbbed and matched the ache in her ear and shoulder. What was the matter with these two men? The hell with them. What was wrong with her? And why was Nic so important to them? Sure, the woman was pretty with her black hair and brown eyes and tiny at five-two, but geez! She was crazy!

With tears filling her big brown eyes, Nic said, "I had

to defend myself. I don't understand women like her. She's unnatural."

Rex looked up at Abby, his forehead all wrinkled. "What got into you? You're bigger and stronger. You could've really hurt her." One gray eye was hidden by a purple swelling, and the scar on his cheek had a long scratch alongside it.

She checked on Jack. His jaw was black and blue, and one lip had swollen to twice its size.

Abby looked around for the two operatives, hoping for some backup. She caught sight of the last one disappearing into the van. Cowards.

"You're taller and stronger than Jack and that didn't stop you." Using the back of her hand, she swiped at the seeping wound on her face. "I didn't throw rocks at myself and roll around in the dirt. She lost her mind and started acting like a lunatic." No way would she mention why Nic had gone psycho.

"I know he can defend himself." Rex stood over her, his hands on his hips.

She refused to move an inch. Nose-to-nose, she glared up at him. "She works for The Circle. Everyone who works for the organization has to take self-defense classes. Besides, I've seen her on the firing range. She's a damn good marksman. And she's got a good right arm."

"Hey!"

They turned their heads toward Jack and said at the same time, "What?"

"I'll take Nic back to the OS Sector and have her checked out. Abby, you and Rex need to go back to your brother's house and see if you can get Brody to contact you again. Liam and I will check out the caves."

"I'm going with you." Rex shook his head.

"Me too." She wanted to see if they were right at least about something.

"Fine. But you still need to keep your cover at your brother's. Meet me at the van on the corner of Maple at nine tonight, and we'll go in from there."

Abby headed toward the Caddy with Rex behind her. She didn't want to think about how Jack and Rex hurt her feelings by siding with Nic without asking for details. Business as usual. One thing she'd learned from working with men, they could beat the crap out of each other one day and act like long-lost friends the next. In the brothers' case, she didn't expect them to mend fences with a couple fights, but maybe they would get some issues out in the open. She'd learned a long time ago that it was up to her to protect herself. She wanted to be treated as an equal. *Be careful what you wish for.*

"Rex! You're not leaving me, are you? Jack can go with her and you can take me back to OS Sector," Nic said.

Was she a glutton for punishment? Otherwise, Abby wouldn't have turned around to see Nic with her sad-dog look and Rex turning back to her. Probably to comfort her and talk about how the big, bad Abby mistreated the itsy-bitsy Nicky.

She rubbed her arm across her eyes. Man, oh, man, she was tired of it all.

"Nic, you have a job to do, and we don't have time to take you back to OS. So I suggest you straighten up and start acting like an adult and a trained operative. This mission isn't finished." Rex then turned around and walked toward the car. "Close your mouth before you collect flies."

Her mouth closed with a click of her teeth. Blinking, unable to move, she jumped when he snapped, "Are you coming or not?"

"Yes, sir!"

She followed behind him, not sure what to say as she slipped into the passenger seat. The shocked expression on Nic's face would've normally had her laughing, but Abby was as confused as Nic about Rex. She kept taking short peeks at him all the way back to her brother's house. When did he decide to take her side?

Chapter Twenty-One

"WHAT DO YOU mean he never came home?"

Abby arrived at her brother's house with two marked and one unmarked Sand County cars parked out next to the road. Her mom's car and another car she didn't recognize were parked near the garage.

Her mother met her at the front door with the news. "His deputy reported that he called in and said he planned to talk with you over at Brody's. That was the last anyone heard from him. We're all worried sick. When the deputies went to Brody's place, they were told everyone was gone and only the employees were there. The groundskeeper let them search the house and came up empty-handed. Where did you go?"

Abby didn't take offense to her mom's preoccupation with her son's uncharacteristic disappearance. Truth be told, she rather not explain the cuts and bruises on her face. "Rurik had some business to take care of."

"Don't go blaming your husband for this. You're always passing the blame to someone else. You never take responsibility." Tears streamed down her cheeks, ruining her perfect makeup. Her hair stuck up in the back as if she'd gotten out of bed and never combed it. It was so unusual to see her mom anything less than flawlessly coiffed and primped.

"Okaaay. Mom, I'm not sure what you're saying, but we'll help in any way we can." Abby's eyes widened when her mom flung herself into her arms.

"If anything ever happens to him, I'll just die," her mom sobbed.

Abby closed her eyes and nodded. She never expected it to be any different. Her mom was more concerned with her brother.

Rex lightly touched her shoulder. "Abby, I'll talk with the investigator."

A brief smile crossed her face and she nodded. "Thank you, Rurik. I don't know what I would do without your help." Her mom released her and hugged Rex. "I'll go check on Suzie. She's upstairs keeping Tommy occupied. It helps her to not think about the horrendous turn of events."

Frustrated at her mom's overdramatization, Abby covered her mouth to stop herself from blurting out, *Why think the worst when he could walk through the door any minute with a logical explanation?* That would only start an argument, and they needed less stress, not more.

The next few hours dragged by. Her mom decided to stay overnight and Suzie convinced her not to sleep on the couch. Abby tried to be empathetic about her mother's concern with her missing son, but didn't she see how her overreaction affected Suzie? There had to be a logical answer to her brother's disappearance.

Abby helped Suzie clean up the kitchen while Rex and Tommy played a rousing game of monster trucks in the den. Her mom had decided to rest in the bedroom next to Tommy's.

"I'm so sorry that Mom is being such a pill to deal with." She scraped off a plate and handed it to her sister-in-law to place in the dishwasher.

"She's always worried about Eddie. You probably remember she never wanted him to go into law enforcement." Suzie placed a glass in the top rack.

"He's smart. Whatever is going on, he'll be okay." Abby had to think positive. If anything happened to him because of her bringing this mission to his backyard, she'd never forgive herself.

"You're right." Suzie stopped fidgeting with the plate in her hand and looked up at her. "Can you promise me you'll do everything you can to bring him back to me?"

Abby blinked. "Why do you think I can do anything?"

"You hold yourself the same way Eddie does. There's something about a person who knows violence and how to defend themselves. They square their shoulders and walk with a confidence most people don't understand. I saw it in you the first time you visited us last year. You haven't been working in an office for a construction company. Eddie leaves out paperwork and I see stuff. I disagree with what he's found investigating you and Rurik.

You two aren't into anything illegal. You don't give me those vibes."

That surprised Abby, but then again, she felt a little guilty for underestimating the intelligence of her sister-in-law.

"I appreciate the vote of confidence, but Rurik and I are no more than what we seem." Her whole body tensed. She hated lying to family, and she liked Suzie a lot.

"He loves you so much. It's really sweet to see how he can't take his eyes off you."

Abby shook her head. "Do you want me to rinse this off? The pasta is stuck to the sides." She lifted a pan from the stove.

They needed to change the subject; otherwise, Abby would start thinking Suzie saw something that she hadn't. Her sister-in-law misunderstood Rex's cynical distrust of her every move as love. He watched her because he thought she would betray him in some way. The man didn't trust anyone. Well, maybe he trusted her a little more than before. She still couldn't believe he'd taken her side over Nic's.

By the time Abby reached the bedroom upstairs and changed into dark clothes, she wanted the operation over with. Involving her family had been so wrong. Never again would she allow Rex or Jack to talk her into mixing family and business. She didn't care if her mom was selling nuclear weapons from her home through the mail; she would stay out of it. Another operative could handle it. Or the government could take care of its own dirty business.

"Hey!"

She aimed her Sig at Rex.

"What the hell! Don't scare me like that. I could've hurt you." After she returned the gun to her drop rig, she stood and shook out her arms and legs. How long had she sat here waiting for the big doofus?

They'd been so busy trying to save the whole operation and their hides, the time to talk about what happened at the hotel and Brody's house had slipped by. Her face burned with the thought of how uninhibited they'd been while having wild monkey sex. There had been nothing romantic about it. If he didn't want to talk about it yet, neither did she.

"The way you were staring off, I could've taken you out before you blinked," Rex scolded without any true heat.

He grabbed the back of his shirt and pulled it off. With his pants riding low, she could see where his hips and groin met. Talk about sexy.

Looking down at the carpet while he changed into darker, hardier clothes for their nighttime raid, Abby concentrated on what they planned to do. Sneak onto the far side of Brody's property, meet up with Jack and a small number of other Circle operatives at the van, and then find a weak point in the security to enter the caves. She only hoped no exchange of fire would be necessary.

"What did the investigator really say?" She wanted Rex to tell her good news.

After all but one patrol car had left earlier, he'd told her mother that Edward's car hadn't been found.

Everyone hoped that was a good sign. Then again, the criminals—they all agreed it would take more than one person to stop Edward from returning home—could've dumped his body somewhere. They hadn't received a ransom demand or any type of note saying why he was taken. So they were waiting.

"They believe he's dead."

She gasped and then took a few seconds to gather her thoughts. "Why?"

"He'd received several death threats."

"But the moonshiner and his two cousins are in jail."

He shrugged his broad shoulders, which looked even broader in the black long-sleeve T-shirt. She was relieved to see he was dressed again. Her concentration needed to be centered on the mission at hand, but something felt off about her brother's disappearance. What a coincidence that it would happen at this time, and she'd never believed in coincidences.

"Could be he has more than two cousins." He buckled a thick belt with a gun on one side and a huge knife on the other. Similar looking to a police officer's duty belt, it had little cases with snaps lined up next to the knife along with a flashlight. The gear would be too heavy for her to wear, but on his tall frame, he looked ready to take down bad guys. "Let's go."

"Rex."

He looked at her. "Abby, are you calling me by another man's name, *milaiyah my-ah*?"

At least he looked at her. Not until that moment had she realized he'd barely glanced her way but a handful of times since returning. They had a lot of personal drama to talk about, but now wasn't the time.

"Rurik, I need to find my brother."

"Abby, we have people on it. Now you have a job to do. Time to concentrate."

She locked her jaw and nodded, refusing to let the tears fall. She was a grown woman and knew what she needed to do.

He opened the bedroom door and peeked into the hallway. "You first."

They left quietly though the back door. The officer in the patrol car out front was more for notifying everyone if Edward returned than for protecting the house, but they didn't want to explain their dark clothes, the late hour, or why they were armed.

A black van waited for them about a mile from the house with its headlights off. They split and carefully walked to the sides. There was no certainty that the people inside were who they expected. The window nearest Abby rolled down.

"About time you got here. We were about to leave without you." Behind the steering wheel, Jack leaned across the front seat and opened the passenger door. "Abby, up front with me."

"We had to wait for the house to settle down." There she goes explaining herself. She hated feeling like a wayward child after failing at Brody's. Tonight, they needed to be successful.

Jack jerked his head to the back. "Rex, have a seat and tell us what you've found out."

"The road in has six guards, with two of them in the trees, and cameras every ten yards. The electricity is underground and the box is located near where three of the guards stand sentry. We'll have to take them all out before they can alert the interior. I never could get close enough to the caves to see how many are inside. During the hour I watched, I spotted only two trucks going in and one out." One of the operatives sitting in the back handed him a map. "Here, here, and here are where we can find the caves. The entrance into the caves is in this area. Like I said, I couldn't get more information out of the guards, no matter how many drinks I bought." The paper crackled as he handed the map back.

So that was why he'd been gone so long on his jog that afternoon and returned with alcohol on his breath. Busy little bee. She tried to not let it bother her that he hadn't said anything to her. It was all a job, one that they'd become too immersed in for a short period of time.

The van started to rock and bounce along the dirt road Rex had pointed at earlier. They planned to go two miles or less before ditching the van in the underbrush and continuing in on foot.

Brody's people had no idea their lives were about to be cut short by a group of trained deadly operatives.

Abby stared straight ahead. The Circle was her life. She was good at killing and for a little while had forgotten that she wasn't normal with normal dreams.

Chapter Twenty-Two

"WHERE DID THEY GO?" Rex kicked out at a nearby crate. It landed against the stone wall, splintering one whole side and showing it was empty. Echoes of other crates being pried apart or bashed in vibrated throughout the cavern. Not a living soul had been in sight. "What the hell were those guards protecting?"

He turned to Nic as she wiped the sweat off her forehead with her arm.

"Some farm equipment and several rotten crates," she stated the obvious. The cavern was cool and the humidity tolerable but tugging and breaking open everything they came across worked up a sweat. "From the looks of it, this place hasn't been used in years. I can understand why no one would want to use this for storage anymore. The only cell tower is on the other side of the mountain. With no service, we're cut off from everything—even Jack's satellite phone can only work outside. By the way, Liam and

Charlie are here now. They checked the smaller caves, and they're empty too. I have a feeling Abby's screwed the pooch on this one."

At the mention of her name, Abby came in sight. Her hair was pulled back in a ponytail. She looked so feminine. He liked it. He wished it was as simple to decide what else he felt for her. He wanted her. That was easy for him to understand. He'd wanted her since she first joined the OS and had remained that way after she'd returned from the dead. That was it. He wanted her too much and for too long. Her scent, the taste of honey and salt on her skin, between her legs, the tender spot behind her ear, every soft inch of her pulled him in and brought a need to sink into her every waking moment.

When he woke up hard and aching for her after their night of wild sex, he understood how dangerous she'd become to him. The last time she'd disappeared, he'd gone insane, and when the news came that she'd died, all the light in his world had died with her. He never wanted to love someone like that again. To allow someone that much power over him was asking for trouble, and for it to be the same woman? They might as well strap a straitjacket on him and put him away.

A little distance was needed to clear his head. Whatever drug Brody had in that wine, he hoped to never come across it again.

"Rex!"

He rubbed his eyes and looked at Nic.

"Are you okay?" Her sweet face looked at him with such concern.

"Yeah." His gaze caught something shining in the wall near where the kicked crate had broken up. "What's going on here?" A missing chunk of the limestone wall exposed a hinge. "Hey, Jack! We've got something here."

He ran his hands over the wall and beneath a little lip was the latch. The wall moved smoothly, opening into another empty cavern. Except for the look of the floor, someone had moved a lot of full crates recently.

"Let's see where this cave goes. Everyone be careful and keep an eye out for traps. I wouldn't put it past the asshole." Jack aimed his flashlight along the floor and moved inside with Abby a step behind him.

Rex tensed. Why the surge of jealousy? He believed Jack had been telling the truth about the one-night affair. So what was up with the unreasonable fury?

For the moment, he needed to concentrate on tracking down Brody. The key to finding out who created the bullets and where they were being manufactured rested with him. And then they needed to beef up the search for Abby's brother. There was a good chance Brody had something to do with that, no matter how much Abby's mother denied it. What any woman saw in that bastard, he would never understand.

About ten minutes later, they reached the other opening. Damn. A one-lane dirt road wound through a thick stand of trees, the limbs arching over the road, hiding it from satellite pictures. They were less than three miles from I-65, an easy way to escape. Brody and his crew could be anywhere.

"About time you fellows showed up." Bubba stepped

out of the tree line. Dressed in camo with a rifle resting on his shoulder, he looked like any hunter walking through the woods in the south. Problem was, hunting season was several months off.

Rex pointed his gun at the man.

"I'll be damned. I thought you were dead," Jack said as he and Bubba slapped each other on the back. "Good Lord, man, you're skinny enough to be a skeleton."

"Others have tried, but I'm too mean." Bubba laughed. His accent was still Southern yet refined and less the good ol' boy with each word. "I heard that Collin's brother is running the show now. Is he any better than Theo?"

"Let's say Ryker likes grown women and he doesn't demand anyone call him master." Jack shook his head.

Rex crossed his arms and listened to the two men. He barely kept from tapping his foot.

"Who is that?" Nic asked in a whisper. The way she kept her eyes on the man and the way she asked the question, he could tell she was interested in more than just his identity.

"That's what I'd like to know too."

Rex looked over at Abby. He didn't like the glint in her eye at all.

"Jack, you might want to introduce me to your brother. I was working under an alias when we met in Brody's house."

"So you were involved in that clusterfuck." Jack referred to the failed mission, but the crooked grin Bubba gave said he remembered what Rex and Abby had done. The gasp next to him warned that Abby realized it too.

Rex's face tightened with Jack's unwitting remark. The man better keep his mouth shut.

"Clusterfuck, heh? I wouldn't say that exactly. I left in the middle of the night so I didn't see much." The man's gaze remained on Abby.

"We're wasting time. It'll be morning soon. Time to get back to our transportation and get out of here." Rex had had enough of the long-lost-buddy routine and wanted the man's eyes looking in a different direction.

"Hey, Rex. This is Ty Roman." Jack grinned from ear-to-ear.

He nodded toward the man formerly known as Bubba. He'd heard of the infamous bounty hunter. Rumor was he'd pissed off the Savalas family a few years ago and old man Mikolas called in a favor from Theo. Rex had figured one day they would come across his bones in a cell deep inside the basement of The Circle's old facility.

Ty nodded back. "Listen, Rex's right. They've already covered the entrance you came in. The asshole underestimated your ability to find the hidden passageway."

"How did you get involved with Brody?" Rex hadn't decided if he trusted the man, a wild card in his opinion. What was a bounty hunter doing working undercover?

"Paying an old debt," he said without adding more.

"You know another way around?" Jack asked.

"Nope."

"Where's your ride?" Abby piped in.

One side of his mouth lifted as he eyed her. "A few yards away, grazing."

"Grazing? You rode a horse?" Nic edged in a little closer.

What was it with these women ogling the guy? Tall and rawboned, he didn't look anything special; then again, Rex wasn't into men. So what did he know?

Feeling uncomfortable analyzing what the women were thinking, Rex pointedly looked at Jack and said, "If they've realized we found the passageway, then we don't have a lot of time here. They should be—"

A hissing sound passed his ear and a small limb near Rex's head shattered.

"Fuck! Down! Everyone down!" Jack hurtled into cave opening, dragging Nic with him. Several other operatives followed. The bounty hunter had disappeared.

Rex and Abby landed next to each other behind a thick stand of undergrowth.

"We've got to quit meeting like this," she said in her usual sarcastic tone. "It's hell on my manicure."

Rex looked at her nails and up at her face. She grinned. Christ! She could've been killed. Unable to tease back, he gritted his teeth.

"We're getting fired on and you're making jokes. Maybe you and Jack are made for each other." As soon as the words were out of his mouth, he wished them back. Her smile disappeared, and she looked away.

Each time gunfire zinged through leaves, thudding into the ground and tree trunks, a second later the crack of a rifle firing echoed around them. He couldn't tell how many were firing, though he pinpointed the general direction.

"Rex! Abby! Are you okay over there?" Jack stepped a little too close to the opening as the *zing* and *whack* of a bullet hit near his feet in warning. A second later the echo of the rifle fire reached their location.

"We're fine!" Rex wanted to squeeze Abby, wrap his body around her to protect her from the bullets zinging everywhere. "They want to pin us down until reinforcements show up."

"Yep, that's what I think too."

"We'll go farther into the trees." Rex jerked his head toward a steep cliff in the direction of the firing. When Jack nodded, he knew he understood that they were going to work their way around and try to come up behind the shooters.

"We need to split up." Abby looked up from where he still pressed her to the ground. He wanted to argue and keep her close and safe, but she was right. She hadn't gotten to her position in The Circle by hiding behind the men.

"Okay. No time to waste. Jack and the others should be safe enough but if we don't get the shooters before sunrise, I have a feeling we'll have more company than we can handle. You game?"

Abby nodded, her eyes round with anticipation. He felt the same. They were ready to kick butt.

"The usual? I come up one side and you on the other?"

She nodded again. "Sounds like a plan," she said.

He rolled off her and started belly crawling over the leaves and limbs scattered on the forest floor. A grin spread across his face when he heard her move off to the opposite direction.

After about twenty minutes he felt he should be safe

enough to gradually stand, keeping an old wide oak between him and the snipers. He heard the hiss of the bullet and as he grunted from the impact, he heard the shot. Damn, that burned like a son of a bitch. It wasn't the first time he'd been shot, but it was never easy to deal with. He wadded the tail of his shirt and pressed it to the wound on his hip. Of all places. If it had been his arms or side, he could deal with it better. But so close to a joint, every time he moved, blood spurted out and stung.

Hell, that hurt.

He squinted his eyes as he tried to figure the best way to climb the side of the mountain. Without wasting another second, he placed a foot on a rock and reached for a small sapling and worked his way above the caves. He slid once but caught himself before giving his position away.

When he stood several yards from a group of rocks overhanging the small valley below and the back entrance of the cave that Jack and the other operatives were stuck in, he waited. Abby should be in position soon. Then he heard the *chack* of a nighthawk. They were night birds but were rarely so far into the forest. It was the call signal they used before her capture. She was letting him know she was ready.

Thank goodness for the waning moon. Enough light to move around and see the darker movement of two snipers. He caught a third shadow moving a little closer. Abby. He would recognize that shape from miles away.

She fired. A blast of light from the muzzle of her gun gave away her location as she killed her target. When he caught the sniper closest to him aiming his rifle in her direction, he charged in, shooting. The fellow stood and turned. Rex unloaded the magazine into the guy. The sniper never got another round off; instead he stumbled and a scream cut through the night.

"Everything all right?" He looked toward where Abby had been last.

"I'm fine. How about yourself?" She was next to him. How had she snuck up on him?

"Fine. Let's get out of here before we really get stuck."

Chapter Twenty-Three

ABBY NOTICED THE limp Rex tried to hide as they made their way back to the cavern entrance. The sun's rays stabbed the night sky when they reached the entrance. Hard to believe it was morning.

She snagged his arm. "Have you been hit?"

He waved at Jack and looked down at her. Before he could say anything, the pounding of hoofbeats came down the dirt road. Ty Roman rode hunched over the horse's withers, looking like either an Old West rough rider or a Hollywood stunt double, whatever a person fancied as he pulled on the reins, causing the horse to rear. *Oh, come on. Was it all part of an act?*

"You got trouble coming and fast. They're on ATVs. I suggest you go back through and head out the other side. It's a smaller detail than what's coming." He held out his hand to her. "Come with me. I'll get you out of here." His devilish attitude didn't even tempt her.

When had she started lying to herself? Besides, what had she done to make the guy think she trusted him? Before she answered, Rex stepped in front of her.

"We don't run when others need our help."

"I can speak for myself." She nudged him with her hip. "Thanks, but I'm needed here."

Ty gave her his crooked grin that made her knees tremble. "I see." Then the roar of big engines coming closer filled the air. "I hope to see you again." He pulled the reins, leading the horse at a good clip toward the trees and disappearing down a footpath.

Abby turned to follow Rex into the cave when the zinging of bullets warned ATV riders had arrived. Several of the men shoved a couple large steel cabinets into the opening and then Nic drove a forklift into them, squeezing the metal into a tangled barricade.

"Jack, we're not going through that passageway back into the other cavern, are we? They'll pick us off like ducks at a carnival game." Abby checked her ammo and looked around.

She opened her mouth, about to remark how surprised she was they still had electricity, when the lights went out. Several of the operatives had their flashlights and quickly turned them on before Abby started to feel suffocated. She hated caves and especially the absence of light. The helpless feeling wasn't one she wanted to experience for longer than a second or two. It reminded her of the weeks she'd spent beneath The Circle when Theo had thrown her into a dark, damp cell. Never had she been so happy than the day that monster died.

The tension grew thick with worry and everyone tried to talk at once, giving suggestions to Jack as what to do next.

"Abby," Rex leaned down and whispered in her ear, "Do you feel that?"

It felt like a breeze. If the electricity was off, the air shouldn't be flowing. There had to be another way out.

"Yeah. Do you think it's another passageway?"

"Not quite. I was remembering how Olivia almost escaped from Collin one time. She told him about it, laughing about how she would've escaped if he hadn't been such a smart-ass and placed bars in the vents."

That sounded like Olivia.

Her gaze shot up to the walls. The flashlights Nic, Jack, and the other operatives held didn't go far enough to see if the darker spots on the stone walls were openings.

"As much as Brody used these caves, there's a good chance they're vented. Only how big?" Nic moved next to them and squinted, peering around stalactites.

"Can I borrow your light?" Abby asked the operative next to her. He handed it over. "Rex, let's get a little closer over there and then you can lift me up."

He grunted as he grabbed her hips and held her up.

"Don't you dare tease me about my weight." She stretched a little more and shone the light above a small overhang. "Bingo! The vent is huge."

"This should help." Nic leaned a ladder onto the protruding rock. "I found it in the corner behind some of the crates."

Abby reached out as Rex released her and she climbed up the ladder and onto the ledge. As she crawled into the opening, she moved the beam around, checking for anything that warned of booby traps or spiders.

"It's clear from what I can see." She moved about a yard. "Tell Jack I'll check it out and let you know what I find." On her knees, her head cleared the ceiling by several inches. "I think it's big enough for you too." No sooner had she said the last word than he was on his stomach, wiggling through the vent behind her.

"If you get my ass stuck, yours is going to be sore when we get out of here."

"Yeah, yeah, promises, promises. I don't remember asking you to come along." She tossed a grin over her shoulder and headed toward the other end of the air vent. "What did Jack say?"

"Nic's telling him now."

"All right. Just stay off my butt." Unseen by him, her smile widened. Deep inside, just knowing that he left Nic behind made her happy.

The flashlight clanked against the metal beneath her hand as she moved a little faster. Rex's hot breath on her rear end bothered her, even through the thick cotton material of her pants. She had to admit, everything about him bothered her, but not the way it should. She should be mad at him. He'd dismissed her as part of another assignment. And the way he smiled at Nic yet glared at her was so irritating. But no matter how he wanted to ignore her, the sex they had together had been special. Hell, spectacular! Drunk or not, she'd felt things with him she'd never felt with any other man. Not that she had a lot to compare it to since she didn't sleep around.

Olivia had teased her about being so picky. She said Charlie was a good example and that she should grab one of the single, good-looking operatives at OS Sector, keep his mouth busy, work him through his paces, and then move on. Then her stress would be cut in half. But when did she have time?

They'd gone about ten yards when a metal wall stopped her.

"Okaaay."

"What?" His hands clasped her hips, and she gasped. The sensation was too much like the time at Brody's. *Get a grip on yourself.* He was only looking over her shoulder at the wall.

"We have to decide left or right. It splits here." She looked down one dark shaft and then the other.

"Be still a moment and see which direction the air is coming from," Rex said.

"To the right," she said.

Then she heard the noise behind her, a mechanical twirl ending with a clank.

"What the hell?" Rex released her and backed up. "Damn it! They closed off the vent before anyone else could get in here. We better start moving in case we get trapped. They might have it set to close at the other end, too, wherever the hell that is." He pushed her butt to get moving.

"Okay, okay. I'm moving. Keep your hands to yourself."

"That's not what you said the other night."

"Oh, do you really think this is the time and place?" she snapped back.

He grunted but didn't say anything else as they crawled as fast as possible down the vent. Then they could see daylight. The sun was up. And there was a thick grille across the opening with a lock. Crap!

"What do we do now?" she asked. The huge steel lock meant business.

"Move over, flat against the wall. I need to get by you." Rex pushed on her to hurry. The width of the vent didn't equal the height.

"There's no way."

"Lie down. I'll have to go over you."

"Go over?" Did she hear him right? He wasn't smiling. She moved into position.

Stretched out on her stomach, she felt his big body slide over hers. His groin rubbed up her butt and then her upper shoulders before brushing her hair, and he reached the grille. Why would something so crazy send tingles scattering across her body? Definitely not the time or place.

At that moment, the metal beneath them began to shake.

She flung her arms over her head as the vent groaned and pinged. The sound of small rocks falling on the metal and welds as they broke filled the small space. Then a growing rumble rolled in.

"Oh hell! They've blown up the place." Rex covered her head with his body. The vent continued to shake as rocks fell for several minutes and then the smell of dirt billowed in. "Back up! Quick!"

She scooted away as soon as he moved. A glance in the

dark had her worried about going too far into the vent and mountain with possible aftershocks from the explosions. Numb with all of the possible ways to die, she lifted the neck of her shirt and covered her nose and mouth without losing sight of Rex. She wanted to see what he had planned. Deep inside she wanted to shout *Hurry,* but knew no matter what she said, he was moving as fast as he could.

On his back, Rex bent his knees and slammed both feet flat against the grille. It didn't move.

She crossed her fingers and began praying. It had been years, but she figured it wouldn't hurt.

The vent and surrounding rock began to shake again and lasted longer than before. The earth around them moved so much, she felt like popcorn in a skillet. Then what sounded like thunder rolled down the vent and brought a thick cloud of dirt with it.

"We need to get out of here. Try again." She coughed, blinking to clear her vision.

Rex kicked two more times, and the frame surrounding the grid creaked and bent. Several more hits and the metal piece holding the lock broke. The grate swung open with a loud screech.

"Come on!" Rex slid to the edge and looked down and then pushed off, his shadowy form disappearing.

Coughing, she crawled to the end. About four feet down, Rex, his face covered with a thin coat of dirt, stared up at her. With Rex being six-five, she guessed it was a drop of ten feet to the ledge that barely held him. Over his shoulder, she could make out a rocky slope tumbling down to a line of trees. She closed her eyes for a few seconds to regain control of her shaking legs. Now wasn't the time to have a breakdown. When she opened her eyes, she spotted, off in the distance, the road they'd arrived on; several SUVs and trucks blocked the road and cavern exits as smoke billowed over the people milling around. None were Circle operatives.

"Do you think it was Brody?" She looked down at Rex.

"He's not that stupid. The explosion will alert the locals. My money is on the Inferno. They don't care who gets hurt as long as they stop us from interfering with their shipments."

She looked behind her. The smoke surged steadily out of the vent. The bastards had used dynamite or C4 with all her people inside: Jack, Liam, Charlie, even Nic, and so many more. Christ!

"Abby, dammit! Jump!" he said urgently in a loud whisper.

She sat up and pushed off, feetfirst. He caught her around the waist and grunted as she slid down, rubbing all the hard places that she loved to admire naked.

His gray eyes darkened. She swiped at the dirt on his face. Being in the situation of nearly losing their lives, it forced a person to rethink what was so important. She leaned toward him.

He sighed and released her.

Sadness choked her for a moment. For him, for everyone. Maybe for herself. No time to get mushy. They needed to find a way out and a possibility of bringing back help. She ducked her head down and used the tail of her dirty shirt to clean some of the grit and tears from her face.

"Let's get moving," she said as she walked around him and picked her way through the bigger rocks and shrubs. A few seconds later, she heard him follow.

It took them close to an hour to work their way around and behind the vehicles. Everyone's attention was centered on the entrance. The face of the mountain was sunken in; smoke floated above boulders and tons of gravel.

"Keep an eye out and whistle if you see anyone coming." Rex bent low and scurried alongside a couple trucks until he reached one parked catty-corner to the others, the only vehicle that wouldn't need to be backed out, thus drawing less attention.

He opened the door and a buzzer went off.

No one made a move toward them as he jumped inside, cursing, and softly closed the door. She wasn't surprised that one of Inferno's men had left the keys in the ignition. While rushing in to participate, they must've believed everyone was trapped in the caverns.

The taillights came on. He slowed, shoving open the door for her to hop in. Once she was inside, he pressed the gas just enough to not sling dirt or draw undue attention.

"Well, what do you want to do next?" She turned to the side, a knee bent on the bench seat. "Rex?"

Deep lines etched around his mouth warned something was wrong. Big-time.

"We'll go over to the Lazy Inn on the outskirts of Sand

City and you can call Ryker." His voice sounded strained at the end.

"Where are you hurt?" When they had killed the snipers, she'd noticed his limp. "I asked you earlier and you ignored me, but I can tell something's wrong."

As if she hadn't said a word, he continued, "Then you'll need to call your family and tell them to leave town. They're not to tell anyone. Brody's going to be pissed and he might take it out of them. I'm not sure if Ryker will get here in time to protect them."

"What about the locals? We need to call and warn them. They have equipment to get the team out." Did she really believe they were still alive? She couldn't let any other thought cross her mind.

"Abby, honey. It's too late for them. If the cave-in didn't kill them, the lack of air will. Take care of your family and let Ryker handle . . . the rest." The last was said as if he was so sleepy he couldn't move his mouth any more.

He slumped to the side, and the truck swerved.

Chapter Twenty-Four

ABBY TOOK THE steering wheel and crawled onto Rex's lap, inserting a leg between his knees to press her foot to the brake pedal. She pulled the truck to the emergency lane, relieved that the road was deserted. When she got the truck in park, her attention turned to Rex.

Heart pounding, certain she would find no pulse, she checked his neck. A steady but slow beat alerted her she needed to act quickly. She then ran her hand over his head and neck. No swelling or bleeding. Frantically, she ran her hands over his arms and chest and found nothing wet with blood, even when she lifted his black shirt to double check the area. There were no new bruises or abrasions, so she continued to his back, sides, and hips. Her fingers came away wet. He'd been hit near his hip.

"Stupid, hardheaded asshole," she murmured. Seeing the big lug's face ash-gray and lax scared the bejesus out of her.

With shaking hands, she managed to crank the truck on the first try. She needed to get them to a safe spot and call Ryker. Then she'd see how bad he was hurt.

"Rex!" She shook him by the shoulders. The bright red blood on her fingers looked like gruesome paint. "Rex, I need to move you over so I can drive to the Lazy Inn. I saw it the other day and thought what a perfect place to hole up in." Almost in tears, she swallowed to calm the building hysteria. "Crazy, isn't it, how things like that can work out? Seeing something you might need and *boom*! Needing it." She laughed, the sound a little demented. "*Boom!* Explosions. Boom. Get it?" She really didn't expect him to answer and maybe that's when she realized she needed to regain control.

She managed to slide his body to the other side by exiting the truck and shoving her whole body against his. The smell of blood filled the air. Mumbling a few of Rex's favorite curses, she shifted the truck into drive and headed down the road.

Time dragged and every moment felt surreal as she stayed mindful of the speed limit. If the authorities stopped her, having the sheriff as a brother wouldn't help. Oh, Jesus H. Christ, her brother. In all of the horror with the cave-in, she'd forgotten they still didn't know what happened to him.

With her brother missing, they would definitely haul her ass in if she had a wounded man in the truck with her. Too many families had turned on each other in the past. Though thankful they hadn't found any sign of Edward in the caves, she prayed he was still alive. She'd heard other people say they could feel it if a loved one was dead or not. Why couldn't she feel it? She loved him in her own way.

She blinked, clearing the tears from her eyes. Not a good time to break down. Rex depended on her to get them to safety and contact Ryker.

The weathered Lazy Inn sign never looked so good. She pulled to the back of the low office building and hoped that if anyone spotted Rex, they would think he was taking a nap.

She reached for the door handle with blood-coated fingers and stopped. Closing her eyes for a few seconds as the desire to scream welled up, she breathed in deep to regain control and then wiped her fingers under her black shirt. What wasn't dried was sticky. She spotted a water hose off to the side of the inn as she exited the truck. A quick wash and she walked into the office. With her bruised face, dressed black on black, and coated in dirt and mud, she imagined she was a sight to be seen. But the clerk didn't pause as he accepted her money. When she returned to the truck, Rex hadn't moved. That frightened her so much. No matter how bad things had gotten between them, he'd always been full of energy and fire.

She needed him to wake.

She'd insisted on a room at the far corner of the property. He was too big and heavy for her to carry him, and no way could she ask for help. How would she explain all the blood?

"Rex, sweetheart, I need you to wake up." She shook him, begging and pleading. No response. Looking around, she spotted a maid's cart sitting outside a room and, a door down from it, an old ice machine. In seconds, she returned to the truck with a towel filled with ice. She needed Rex to wake up.

"Sorry, but you've got to wake up." She placed the cool towel to his face and moved it around, hoping it would revive him. A few seconds passed and nothing happened. She ran the towel down his neck. He groaned as the ice began to melt. He rolled back against the seat. She threw the wet cloth on the floorboard. "Rex, you have to help me. You need to get out of the truck and into the room."

He shivered. "It's cold."

Relief flooded her body. He finally spoke.

"I know, sweetheart. Sit up and help me walk you to the room. I'll get you under the covers and warm."

With her pushing and pulling, he sat up and stumbled out of the truck. By willpower and luck, she managed to get Rex into the room and sprawled across the bed.

He was out again, but asleep on a lumpy mattress had to be ten times better than the truck. She pulled a knife from under her pant leg and sliced off his shirt. Unfastening his pants, she carefully worked them down his legs, taking his briefs with them.

"Stupid man. You're not a superhero. You bleed and can die." She concentrated on reaching the wound and seeing the damage. Otherwise, she would throw herself on the floor to kick and scream in frustration.

Keeping her attention on the angry-looking hole near his hip, she felt around to see if the bullet had hit bone or anything major. His color still looked bad, maybe a little paler. He could be bleeding internally and she wouldn't know it until his body went into shock. From the way blood continued to seep and with no exit wound, she knew the bullet was still inside. With what little medical knowledge she had, there was no way she would go digging inside of him for the metal. That would only be asking for trouble. Nicking a major artery would cause the situation to become fatal.

Swiping her forehead with her arm, she walked into the bathroom and threw up. Refusing to look at her reflection, she splashed water on her face and jerked the towel off the rack and returned to Rex. She pressed it to the wound, hoping to stop the bleeding completely. Using his cut up shirt, she twisted it and slipped one end beneath him and brought it around to tie off. It didn't really place pressure on the wound, but more kept the towel in place. She covered him with the sheet and comforter.

Finally, she pulled out her cell phone to call Ryker and nothing but a blank screen greeted her. It was dead. Two days had passed since she last charged it.

She picked up Rex's pants and pulled out his cell. The busted screen said it all. Screw it!

Shaking her head, she looked around. There was always the old-fashioned way. She lifted the receiver from the phone next to the bed and called collect. After only one ring, one of the handlers at The Circle headquarters answered. She recited her code before they patched her through to Ryker. As one of The Circle's elite operatives, she had the freedom of not working with a handler as others did, but instead reported directly to Jack and thus

Ryker. With Jack possibly dead, Ryker was her immediate boss.

"What the fuck is going on there, Rodriguez?"

Abby held the phone away from her ear. The man had anger issues. How in the world did his wife, Marie, put up with him?

"Brody blew up the mountain and everyone was inside. I think only me and Rex escaped."

The other end was quiet for a moment. "Christ! Are they alive?"

"We're not sure of that, sir. But we need some help. Should I call in the locals?"

"What did Rex say?" Ryker's voice shot through the line.

"He didn't—that is, he told me to get my family to safety, but he's wounded and has lost a lot of blood. I've got him comfortable, though he's out cold." She quickly gave him the details of what happened and where they were staying.

"I see. Stay put. It'll take us a few hours to get there even by helicopter. I'll have someone talk with the locals, and we'll get a permit backdated. The report that goes out will say that a major construction project was going on at the cave, and explosives were used. We'll see if we can keep the federal boys out of it.

"Any explosions of that magnitude would bring in the locals without a tip before you even got away. For them to not be there already means someone is holding them back. We need to reach your mother or sister-in-law and get them to safety. You said your brother was taken?"

"We believe Brody took him. Knowing my brother, he didn't listen to me when I told him to stay out of my business. He probably questioned the wrong person and it got back to Brody."

"Most likely. Stay there. Take care of T-Rex. In the meanwhile, Brian from IT will call you with a credit card number to use. Then you can arrange to buy whatever you need to take care of you two until we get there." Then he hung up.

Abby leaned over Rex and caressed his face with shaking fingers. T-Rex? Men and their crazy nicknames for each other. Sitting on the edge of the bed, she ran her hand over his warm forehead and through the stiff ends of his hair. She wished he would let it grow back out. Why had he cut it?

She traced his scar, feeling a little guilty knowing how he didn't really like her touching it. She wanted to memorize every inch of his face. Her hand dropped to his chest and wide shoulders. A fingertip followed the design of a tattoo. They had been naked together so many times over the last several days, but not once had an opportunity come up for her to really look closely with proper lighting. When they were without clothes, they generally had better things to do than discuss body art.

She leaned in closer. The fine lines circling each arm's bicep appeared, at first glance, to be Celtic knots with a single word at the front and center inside a heart. The knots were words. She recognized the words on both arms. They were songs she'd loved at the time they were engaged. On his right arm was Leona Lewis's "Bleeding

Love." The single word was *love*. The other arm had the lyrics from Rihanna and Ne-Yo's song, "Hate That I Love You," with the word *hate*. The words in small print underlining *love* and *hate* were her name, the year of her birth, and the year she'd supposedly died.

She fell back in the chair next to the bed. Her hand covered her mouth. Tears streamed down her face. She didn't know what to make of all that. Her throat clogged with a suppressed scream of emotion. Rex had told her once that with all the scars he had, he'd never put ink under his skin. She leaned forward and softly caressed the nearest tattoo, confirming they were real.

"Now I'll have to get the suckers burned off." Rex's half-opened eyes stared at her.

Surprised that he'd answered her unspoken thoughts, she asked, "Why did you do it?"

"Because I loved you and I wanted to save the words from your favorite song. They made me think of you. And I hated . . . hated how you left me a broken man. Never again." He shifted on the bed and growled his frustration.

"Don't move. You'll start bleeding again."

He looked at her out of the corner of his eyes.

"Why are you looking at me like that?" She really didn't care. She was so happy he was alive.

"Wanted to be sure you weren't pulling my leg." His sad grin broke her heart.

"Huh?"

"I wasn't sure that you were really here or a hallucination."

"I'm here. You were shot and who knows how much

blood you lost with all the climbing through the vents and stealing a truck."

He sighed, nodding. Before she could stop him, he shifted. His already pale face whitened further. He took a deep, sharp breath. "I feel like milk left out in the sun."

"I swear. I thought you were dead. Jack and I were told you'd died in Peru," she said.

The pain he'd endured then was suddenly visible in his eyes, his face, and the way he held his body so stiff, not from this wound, but from the massive one he sustained years ago.

"We've gone over this. I believe you and Jack. This isn't the time or place." He stared up at the ceiling.

"When is it the right time and place? We're not going anywhere and I need to talk—" The telephone rang, interrupting her.

Was it a conspiracy to keep her from talking about what was hanging between the two of them? They needed to clear the air and she couldn't think of a better time. They were alone, and he couldn't leave without falling down on his face.

"Hello?" Abby said.

Without wasting any time, Brian gave her the information she needed to take care of Rex. The man was efficient.

Abby turned back to Rex. With his eyes shut and body relaxed, he appeared asleep. She knew better.

"You can play possum all you want, but you're going to listen to what I have to say." She crossed her arms and glared.

His eyes opened a crack. "Sure. Whatever makes *you* feel better."

The thought of placing her fingers around his neck and squeezing flitted through her mind. Smart-ass. Could he not tell when she was being serious? He'd come so close to dying. Even with help on the way, anything could happen: infection, the bullet moving and nicking an artery, and more that she refused to think about.

Still, he had a point. Was she confessing because she wanted to feel better about herself? How would the news help him? She could tell herself that he needed to know, but why not before? If he died after she told him, would it make a difference? There wasn't anything he could do at this juncture.

She'd never considered herself a coward and couldn't start now. Her chest heaved as she took a deep breath.

"I was pregnant with your child when I went to work for The Circle."

Chapter Twenty-Five

REX WATCHED ABBY'S lips move, but he'd gone deaf after she'd said *pregnant*. His child. She had his child and never told him.

"What the hell do you mean you were pregnant?" he shouted, though the words came out more like a screech. He'd never screeched in his life.

She flinched, closing her eyes as her mouth stretched into a grimace.

His mind raced. Why did she tell him now and not before? The woman was smart. By telling him as he lay unable to move, weak from the throbbing pain and loss of blood, she thought she was safe. Not that he'd hit her; perhaps he'd shake her for lying to him. Once again, she'd proven how little she knew him, how little she trusted him, to not tell him as soon as she found out. What about the last night they were together? The foremost question was, had she known before he left for Peru?

"When did you know?" he asked, keeping his voice low, waiting.

"Excuse me." She sprinted to the bathroom and slammed the door.

He closed his eyes. The sick sounds he heard told him the story. She'd known and kept it from him. His fingers dug into the sheets as his chest tightened. The need to cry welled up. His breath came in short bursts and his throat ached with silent screams.

For the woman he'd loved to hide their baby from him and not give him the opportunity to rejoice. What had he done to be punished in such a way? As a kid, he'd had his ass beaten for letting others take advantage of him. His dad had told him for years he was a dumb fuck and deserved whatever came his way.

He released the torn sheets and used the backs of his hands to wipe his face. Christ! He needed to act like a man. Staying on his back wasn't an option. If the bullet hadn't killed him yet, he could last a little longer.

Weak but determined to win, he sat up. The room spun as he tried to stand, and he fell back onto the bed, nearly missing it. Sweat poured off him and his body trembled as he worked to keep down whatever was left in stomach. He tried to pull the rest of his body onto the mattress, except his lower half wouldn't cooperate.

"What do you think you're doing?" Cool hands lifted his legs and shoved them back onto the bed.

Damn, he was naked.

He stared up at the stained ceiling. All he needed was to be a cripple too. For the moment, the numbness spreading from his wound to his toes was a relief. In seconds, the feeling came back in a rush of agonizing heat. He cupped the wound as if wishing he could make it better. Her gentle hand rested over his. He moved, causing hers to drop away.

She dragged a chair next to the bed and sat, watching him until she said, "I'm sorry."

He was unsure if he could look at her.

"Tell me. Boy or girl?" he asked softly, trying to control his temper.

"A little boy."

Jesus Christ. A son. He would be around five. Close to the same age as her nephew, Edward's son.

He caught his breath. His son?

"Tell me the truth for once in your life. Is Tommy our son?" That had to be it. He didn't look anything like his fair-haired parents. He and Abby were dark-headed, and with her brown eyes being a dominant trait, they would most likely pass on to their child.

Somehow he brought his gaze to hers. He doubted he'd ever forgive her.

"Tommy?" Her forehead wrinkled.

"Yeah. Your brother's son. He's five, isn't he?"

She vehemently shook her head. "No. No!"

"That's it, isn't it? That's why you acted so funny and hardly spoke with him. I've never seen a woman act like that around a kid." Maybe he wanted it to be the truth.

Tears streamed down her face. She continued to shake her head.

"You were afraid I'd figure it out. That you took our

child and gave it to your beloved brother. You've wanted your mother's approval for so many years, and this was your way of getting it. Make your perfect brother happy and your mother would finally love you." Pain pierced his chest and his hip hurt to the point every inch of his body ached. His head was about to explode. He wanted to stop talking but the pain of her betrayal was the final nail in the coffin.

"You're wrong. All wrong."

"I'll get my son back and there's nothing you can do to stop me. I know money produces results in custody hearings. So I can fight your family."

"Stop! Please stop." She landed on her knees next to the bed, her forehead pressed to the mattress near his arm. "You don't understand."

"What do I not understand? That you've proven once again how little you think of me? Why would I think you're any different than anyone else I cared for? Did Jack tell you how my dad beat me not only for being taller than him, but also for being dumb? His favorite nickname for me was 'dumbass.'" He laughed but the sound was mocking as he looked back at all of the past hurts. "In grade school, I was constantly called 'dummy.' The other kids thought I'd been held back and was only lying about my age. Teachers expected me to be smarter and more mature only because I was nearly twice the height of the other kids. Home wasn't any better. Dad would whip my ass for the same thing."

"Why didn't your mom stop him?" Abby's hoarse voice brought his attention back to the present. A stream of tears flowed down her face.

"And have his hatefulness turned on her? No. She stayed out of it. She said that men knew how to talk to their sons. Only my dad thought ridiculing us along with a few closed-fist hits were the way to straighten us out. The first time he broke my nose I was four." He'd never told a soul any of that.

"That's not right. She should've been there for you." Abby looked at him, pleading with her eyes for understanding. "You're wrong. I care about you more than you know."

"You cared enough to keep me away from my son?"

She covered her face and rocked back and forth.

"I swear, Abby, I'll be a good dad. I'd never treat any son or daughter of mine like my dad treated me." He hated the pleading in his voice, but the thought of a child of his growing up believing they weren't wanted wasn't going to happen.

When she looked out at him from red, swollen eyes, his gut tightened in fear. All those years of not being good enough, smart enough—

"Tommy's not ours. Never has been. Suzie went through labor . . . they have medical records to prove it. Nothing forged by The Circle's best, I swear."

"Then where's my kid?"

"You misunderstood." She sighed, the sound forlorn and tired. "They believed the depression and stress of losing you had weakened me, and the beating I received compounded it."

She wrapped her arms around herself and shivered. "I was four months along, just starting to show. But I had lost so much weight while I recovered from . . . then I started to bleed . . . The Circle handled the burial as . . . as I couldn't . . ." Her choked sobs filled the room.

"You miscarried." He threw an arm over his eyes and slammed a fist into the mattress. "Why did you think I shouldn't know this?" Using his arm, he rubbed off the tears and glared at her.

Most of her words were incoherent until the end as she said, "When I realized you weren't dead, I wanted to explain about Jack . . . I didn't know how without making you mad. I blamed myself. It happened the next day. We were told that you were dead in Peru, that they had thrown your body on a pile with others and burned your body and buried you. That night I didn't want to be alone. All day I cried believing you were dead and my baby wouldn't have a father, and then Jack showed up, angry, sad, crying too. We took comfort—"

He sliced his palm through the air. No way would he let her finish that sentence.

She nodded. Her gaze remained on the wall as she said, "Never would I do anything to harm our child. I had been so happy . . ." Her voice trailed off.

Seconds passed by and neither said a word as they mourned what they had lost.

Even if he wanted to examine his feelings about the whole mess, he wasn't sure if he could. The wound ached like a son of a bitch and interfered with his thinking. One thing was for certain: her distrust hurt. Until he thought she was dead, he'd believed she respected him.

Ah, hell. What was he doing? If his old man had been alive, he'd say feelings were for sissies.

Dammit, he wasn't an ignorant asshole like his dad. Men were human beings with desires and feelings; they only reacted differently from women and that was all.

A banging on the door made them jump.

Rex doubted Brody's people would knock before shooting, but it was better to be safe than sorry.

"Where's my gun?" He shifted on the bed, groaning as he jarred the wound.

"Under your pillow." Her voice muffled as she used the corner of his sheet to wipe her wet face.

He grabbed the gun and slipped it beneath the sheets next to his thigh, ready to shoot if needed.

She hurried over to the door and peeked out.

"It's Ryker."

She flipped the security bar to the side and unlocked the door, opening it wide.

Ryker filled the doorway. With his black eye patch in place and ugly scars alongside of his face, he'd scare the devil himself.

"Doc sent one of the nurses to take care of you. From what Abby told us about the position of the bullet, and how the bleeding stopped, you'll mend fine." The commander of a billion-dollar organization who hands out death like flu shots stepped into the room.

"I'm surprised to see you here," Rex said to Ryker as he nodded at the man who walked in behind him. The nurse spread out the contents of what looked like a fishing tackle box on the dresser. Most of the nurses working for The Circle were former medics and male.

Sitting in the chair near the small table, Ryker glanced at Abby with a worried look as he spoke to Rex. "I have a dozen people trapped in a cave. Ice is answering the local authorities' questions. This is where I needed to be for the moment. You are my second-in-command." Ice was the mystery man of The Circle. Some claimed he'd earned his name and his cold demeanor by killing his own father. Such a despicable act would take a cold-hearted man.

"Yeah. Second-in-command. Right." Rex slowly shook his head.

What was the real reason he was here? Ryker didn't trust anyone, with the exception of his wife. He'd already proven he wouldn't allow Rex to help in commanding The Circle. And no way would Rex continue to sit around with his thumb up his ass. That was part of the reason why he'd decided to help his brother track down the ammo.

When Ryker gave him an odd look, he figured he better say something.

"Ice is a good one to handle the situation. I never could— Damn, that hurt!" He frowned at the nurse. The needle the man was using to deaden the area looked to be two inches long. Returning his attention to Ryker, he said, "I never could read his face. The man could lie with the best of them."

"Is his hair still that neon blue?" Abby butted in.

Why did she want to know about the man's hair? Rex

remembered how Abby loved his long hair. That was why he cut it. He wanted nothing to remember how much she used to love to touch it.

When she shot him a funny look, he realized she was trying to get Ryker's mind off his smart-ass comment about being second-in-command.

Ryker grinned. "Yep. He's wearing a knit cap. He didn't want to but it was for the best."

"Warm weather for that," Abby murmured.

"You all right over there?" Rex asked.

"Just tired." She stood up. "I think I'll go outside for some air." She walked to the door. "Good seeing you, Ryker." With a glance toward Rex, she closed the door behind her.

"You got anyone watching outside?"

"Yep. She'll be fine," Ryker said.

"You need to be still now," the nurse said. "I'm going to take the bullet out and debride the wound before I stitch it up and give you an antibiotic. From what I can see, you should be right as rain in a few weeks." The nurse bent over his hip and began to work.

For the next thirty minutes, Ryker kept up a conversation until the nurse finished. Later, Rex wasn't sure when they left, although he remembered shouting for Abby until she returned and sat next to him.

The pain medicine he'd been given caused him to go in and out of consciousness. He remembered waking at one point and seeing Abby with a concerned look on her face. For a split second he'd been so happy to have her close enough to touch. She looked like an angel. Of course, the way his body floated above the pain helped. Then the memory of what she'd hidden for years brought him crashing back to earth.

His child. A son. Gone.

He wasn't sure what he planned to do about it, but one thing was for sure—he'd had enough of being the nice guy.

Chapter Twenty-Six

ABBY HELD THE binoculars to her eyes and followed the drama unfolding below her. The sixth body found in the rubble came out on a stretcher covered with blue plastic. Ice stopped The Circle EMTs to check the body's identity against a clipboard of missing operatives' pictures before waving them on.

Two hours earlier, she'd left Rex asleep with an operative standing guard outside the motel room door while she checked out the progress at the cave-in. The local news report had said stored explosives had detonated with no casualties. A simple mishap and a good cover-up.

The sheriff's department was thankful to be left alone to continue their search for Edward and hold off the media circus that would ensue if word got out about their sheriff missing. One of the benefits of being a small county, rules could be bent without many knowing. But she wasn't sure how much longer they would hold off before reporting him missing to the FBI. It had been two days since the explosion and three since her brother disappeared.

And one day since she'd unloaded the bomb of her miscarriage.

Rex had been in and out of consciousness while his body recovered from the barbershop-style surgery. During that time, she'd searched the Internet and contacted people, trying to find her brother while keeping her sister-in-law and mom up-to-date on . . . well, nothing. Brody and her brother had disappeared.

"Have they found Jack?"

She jerked around, dropping her binoculars as she aimed her gun at Rex. "You could've given me a heart attack or gotten shot again. How are you so quiet for such a big guy with a cane?"

He looked like hell, with his pale skin and deep grooves bracketing his mouth. A thin sheet of sweat covered his upper lip. His clothes even looked to be hanging off his body as if he'd lost weight in the last couple days. What was he doing? He should be in bed recovering.

He hobbled closer, keeping one leg straight to keep from pulling the stitches. The operative assigned to protect Rex stayed farther away. Smart man. She'd give him a piece of her mind later.

She lifted the binoculars from around her neck and handed them to Rex. "No sign of him yet. They've moved enough rock and dirt to fill in a stadium."

"What are you doing up here instead of down there in the middle of all that?" He hooked the cane on his arm and balanced on his good leg as he looked through the binoculars.

"I've been down there, but Ryker told me I was in the way. So here I am."

He stood so close that the heat of the day was nothing to the warmth radiating from him. Not from fever, but from his normal body temp. Those few nights they'd slept together, she'd enjoyed snuggling up to him, his internal heater thawing her body and heart. That had to be the reason men lost weight so easily. Their bodies generated so much heat that they burned calories by merely standing.

A flower petal caught in the breeze landed on his shoulder. She wanted to brush it off, but was afraid to touch him, afraid it wouldn't be enough. She missed running her fingers down his broad chest, following the sparse trail of hair to his navel and beyond. Like a well-fed woman who was starving, the hunger pains were twice as strong.

"Jack will be found. I've got a gut feeling," he said as he continued to watch the activity below.

"You really want him to be alive." The amazement squeezed through and pushed her voice up an octave. With all the fighting they did, she'd expected him to be indifferent.

He lowered his hands and looked at her. "Why wouldn't I?"

"From what I know, he hasn't always been a good brother."

"Don't think I'm being so noble. I want him alive so I

can kill him with my bare hands." The worry in his voice told her he had mixed feelings about that.

He handed her the binoculars and headed back down the small path to where his transport was parked. His stiff walk with the cane didn't mar the view from behind at all. The man had a fine-looking ass.

She shook her head in disgust. Time for her to move on and concentrate on finding her brother. She'd given the locals plenty of rope to hang themselves. Besides, Ryker didn't want her help digging out the bodies and tracking down Brody.

Then she heard a shout. Looking through the binoculars, her gaze followed Jack as he walked out of the yawning blackness with someone's limp body in his arms. With a thick coating of dirt over every inch of his body and clothing, he lowered the body stiffly onto a stretcher set up in front of him. EMTs surrounded Jack and the body. Several people slapped Jack on the back, sending clouds of dust into the air as they shouted their happiness. Behind them, several more operatives stumbled out of the darkness. She recognized Liam's tall frame leaning on Charlie's slightly shorter one. All of them covered with dirt. Emergency workers hurried over and helped by offering shoulders to those who stumbled out. Other personnel with stretchers waited a good distance from the caves in case the weak walls gave way.

Returning her attention to Jack and the stretcher, she caught an EMT leaning over it and examining the body. He placed a stethoscope to the person's chest and then shook his head.

Jack's shoulders hunched as he covered his eyes with an arm and his whole body shuddered. Another EMT said something to him and he straightened, lowering his arm to answer. No tears on his face, but in seconds the pain and sorrow aged him. He shook his head, causing dirt to fall in a cloud around his shoulders. The EMTs moved to help others, and finally Abby could see the face of the person on the stretcher.

She lowered the binoculars.

Nic. Nic was dead.

Closing her eyes, she said a little prayer. The woman was a psycho, but she'd never wished her dead. Rex and Jack thought a lot of her.

Brody needed to pay—not only for Nic's death but also for the six other operatives who had died during the operation. Every time they entered the field, the expectation was that it could be their last.

Oh, no. What about Rex? How much more could he go through? And what about Jack? She was grateful for Jack's survival, but she wondered at what price? She knew Jack praised his people when a mission was a success, but when things didn't turn out right, he blamed himself— even when it was out of his control. He believed he should be prepared for anything.

A quick glance behind her confirmed Rex had left. He hadn't heard the shouts. His brother was alive but his ex-lover, dead.

Between news of their baby and now Nic, what would he do? No one could continue to receive blows like these and not react.

She wasn't sure if she wanted to be around when it happened.

REX LEANED ON his cane and glared at his brother.

The crowd of workers came to a standstill. Birds chirped in the trees as generators hummed beside the cave's entrance. Everyone was quiet. Word had obviously spread about their fight a few days ago. They knew that even with his wound and Jack's severely bruised body, they were still dangerous to each other and anyone around them.

All of The Circle operatives were accounted for, dead or alive, and the forensics arm of the organization had stepped in. Jack pressed each one hard for answers. Not so much who was responsible—they knew Brody was the culprit, as he'd given the Inferno the info—but how had he found out about their raid?

Mere hours before they showed up, the charges were hidden in the cavern. The type of explosive used had been too unstable to leave for an unforeseen future need. They had taken precautions along with taking out the guards before they could give an alarm.

Could it be someone within The Circle who betrayed them? Since the upper ranks were the only ones to know about the raid in advance, who among the most trusted could have alerted Brody? He, Abby, and Ryker were the only ones of rank not inside the cavern.

At another time, Rex would have been worried about the answer to that dilemma, but he had a more pressing need. His brother had lied to him again, had sworn to his face that he had no more secrets when it came to Abby.

Jack turned around to see what everyone was staring at, and that was when Rex struck. With his wound affecting his balance, he knew he would have only one chance. His fist hit with a resounding smack. His swing shifted his weight to his left side and the stitched wound, and he nearly fell. A couple operatives grabbed his arms. He didn't fight their hold. He'd made his point.

"I'm sorry." Jack pressed the back of a hand to his cut cheek. "I tried to protect her."

"You lying asshole." Rex shook his head. "Some protection. You believe fucking them is protecting them?"

"Fucking? I haven't—" Then his eyes widened, and his mouth snapped closed.

"Oh, you're remembering now."

"Abby finally told you." His relief evident in his voice.

"Yeah." Rex leaned in, bunching his brother's shirt in a fist. "I've forgiven you for sleeping with her, but I'll never forget that you can't be trusted. Taking her to bed while knowing she was pregnant with my kid . . . that I'll never forgive."

"But—"

Rex jerked him closer. "Shut the fuck up. Then when you heard I was alive, you didn't even try to be a real man and contact me and tell me the truth. When I saw that you were alive, I was unbelievably fucking happy. Maybe I'm not as smart as you, but I know when I've been played." He pushed him away. "You're no longer my brother. You're dead to me. When this mission is over, I'll tell Ryker that I want to be reassigned to the West Coast division. The more distance between us, the better it is for The Circle and for your chances to live to an old age."

Rex and Jack stared at each other. No one spoke a word for several seconds.

"I'm really sorry about that and about Nic." Jack looked off to the side, avoiding Rex's angry glare.

"You slept with Nic too?" He shook his head, gritting his teeth. Hatred for his brother boiled over until he was certain he could kill him with his bare hands.

"No—"

"Don't lie to me again." For a moment, Rex felt a twinge of tightness in his throat. Too many times in the past he'd forgiven his brother for being inconsiderate and self-centered, but no longer. He'd reached his limit and needed to concentrate on what was best for him.

"For Christ's sake, Rex, that's not what I'm trying to tell you! I didn't sleep with Nic. Shut up long enough to listen to me! She's dead! Nic was killed in the cave-in. She pushed me out of the way and a rock hit her. Crazy thing was it would've missed me anyway, but she got in the way. They said she probably didn't even feel any pain. It was instant."

The men released his arms.

Rex stared at him. What game was his brother trying to play this time? He was tired. So tired of his manipulations. For years he'd gone along with it, believing his brother was smarter and knew what he was doing.

"I swear. You can see her if you want. The ambulance isn't back yet. There were too many wounded. They have her with the other bodies in one of the smaller caves so she'll be out of the heat until they can get here."

Seeing Nic lifeless wasn't an option. He shook his head. Another life gone. He clasped his hands behind his neck and shook his head. The silence continued. Rex looked at the people standing around, watching the drama between the brothers play out. Even the birds had hushed, though the generators still hummed steadily.

As if his acknowledgement of their presence was the release for others to talk, a brave soul asked another operative about checking the electrical hookup for the lights in the cave. That was everyone's signal to return to normal and avoid looking at the brothers.

Without a word, Rex turned and hobbled away. He ignored the tears on his face as he reached the waiting guard and his truck and got inside.

His feelings for Nic had always been mixed, but she deserved a long life. Why hadn't he insisted she come with them? By leaving her behind, had he ensured her death?

Her sweet face flashed behind his eyelids once he leaned back against the headrest. Another face moved in place of Nic's. Abby. He couldn't leave her alone to search for her brother. It was time for him to stop fooling around and make her understand how important she was to him.

Chapter Twenty-Seven

"SHIT, SHIT, SHIT." Abby ducked behind a Dumpster and counted to ten before peeking around the edge. The smell of rotten food almost overpowered her. She hoped it rained again soon.

The section of Birmingham she'd tracked her prey to would never be on any tourist map. Redbrick buildings coated by dust and hidden behind metal fences and topped with razor-wire lined the opposite side of the street. Hiding in an alley between an abandoned car dealership and a burned down restaurant, she waited for a certain person to exit the gate covered with sheet metal.

Normally she didn't do surveillance. Not long-term anyway. But after watching Rex and Jack argue, she'd rushed down to stop their intense face-off. Only she'd arrived too late and word had gotten to Ryker. He'd arrived an hour later, furious with everyone.

"What the fucking hell happened here?" Ryker's voice sounded like gravel in an oak barrel.

Jack straightened and lifted his chin. A defeated look pulled at his bruised and scratched face. "I underestimated the enemy, sir."

With a jerk of his head, Ryker directed Jack to follow him. They stopped not more than ten feet from where she stood. Grinding his teeth, Ryker looked like he could spit out pebbles as he listened to how the events unfolded and the number and names of the injured and dead.

"I take full reasonability for the clusterfuck," Jack said. His shaking hand slid across his shaved head.

"As well you should." Ryker crossed his arms and stared hard at Jack. "Finish up the mission. We have more intel for you to check out. You know what you have to do about Brody. When it's over, you and I will have a long talk about your future with The Circle."

Jack nodded and looked down at the paperwork Ryker handed him.

Abby had never envied Jack's position. One failed mission could find you demoted to grunt work, in a holding cell, or dead.

She didn't move fast enough before Jack caught her eavesdropping.

"Rodriguez! You're on surveillance duty. Get your shit together to watch the front and back entrance of this facility." He blasted out the orders, and she did her best to keep up as he headed to the impromptu control base. Her skills were wasted on surveillance.

"Whatcha looking at?"

The unexpected voice brought her crashing back to the present. In one fluid move, she kicked out and drew her gun.

Rex stumbled back; one hand slapped down her leg while the other held tight to his cane.

"Whoa! I guess you could say I deserved that. Put that away." He nodded to her Sig.

"You've got to stop it. I don't know how you do it, but you need to stop." Warmth flooded her face from embarrassment. She needed to be more alert. At the rate he continued to sneak up and scare the crap out of her, if she didn't die of a heart attack, someone else would take advantage and kill her.

"Who are you watching?" Rex looked over her head at the street beyond.

They had moved back to the hotel in Birmingham that afternoon, but they shared the suite with Ice and the operative assigned to keep an eye on them. Ryker claimed the man was there to ensure Rex stayed put and let his injury heal, but the big guy wasn't having any of it. And here he was in the middle of her assignment.

"What are you doing here? And where's what's his name? You know, your watchdog?" She turned her back on him to monitor the gate.

"Sal. Remember he had the tall Mohawk, skinny kid who worked in IS?" When she turned her head and frowned, he added, "He's gained some weight, works out, and now reports to Jack."

She looked toward the other end of the alley. Sal looked better without the foot-high Mohawk. The lanky fellow waved stiffly but remained several feet away. Rex had probably told him to wait at that spot, and few people dared to ignore his orders.

"Geez," she murmured, and turned her attention to the street. Jack probably arranged it so he could spy on Rex. She'd seen the second explosion, and that time it had been between the brothers. Obviously, their unresolved past had caught up with them. Nic's death surely didn't help matters. It was later when Charlie called with the details that Abby's name had been part of the blowup.

She wanted to tell him she was sorry about Nic's death, but the moment didn't feel right.

"Listen, you're not alone in trying to find your brother."

His warm breath tickled her neck. Every inch of her back soaked up the heat from his body. The drizzling rain had stopped a few minutes earlier, and she hadn't realized how chilled she'd become since then.

"I'm really not sure how Ryker managed it. He convinced them Edward was still alive, and the chief investigator has given us to the end of the week. If Edward doesn't show up by then, they're reporting it to the FBI. They haven't found anything to indicate foul play. The Davison cousins are still in jail; otherwise, we would have the feds all over us."

"Forty-eight more hours."

"Yeah."

A white SUV stopped in front of the metal gate. A guard came out and spoke with the driver, and with a wave of his hand, the SUV drove through the opening. The gate closed as soon the bumper made it inside.

"Who do you think that was?"

"I couldn't see the driver from here. That's the third vehicle to go into the facility."

"Brody's ammunitions plant?"

"We're not sure. I'm the third shift to watch from this side. Liam's on the other gate. During his time under-cover at Brody's farm, he overheard that Greta was obsessed with a Victoria's Secret store in a local shopping mall. Yesterday, Ryker sent one of the operatives to wait for her to show up. She did at lunchtime yesterday. They said she returned here and hasn't left."

"Jack assigned you?"

She hesitated. Since Rex was second-in-command of The Circle, technically higher rank than Jack, would he countermand the orders?

"Listen, I'm just surprised that he has you doing grunt work when your talents are better suited for more." He stepped back.

That helped. Her mind had become foggy with the need for his touch. She felt like it had been weeks from the last time *she'd* made love to *him*. There was no *they*. He enjoyed their time together but she refused to kid herself that he thought it was any more than a way to pass the time and maintain their cover.

"We're shorthanded." She stopped from saying more. They'd lost several operatives from The Circle's general population and the OS, including Nic. He acted like he was handling the loss.

He grimaced.

"Are you hurting?" she asked. What was he doing here? "Go back to the hotel and get some rest. If we hear anything, I'll be sure to let you know."

"How much longer are you going to be here?"

"Probably another hour. Charlie should be relieving me soon."

"I thought she was a mechanic."

Abby looked away and rolled her eyes. "Everyone is pitching in," she said without explaining the shortage again.

"I'll hang around until she gets here and then you can drive me back to the hotel."

"What's wrong with Sal?" She kept her gaze on the fence and the movement she could see between the sheets of metal.

"He can drive your car. We have some unfinished business."

That pulled her attention back to him. "What's that?"

"Not here. We'll talk about it at the hotel." He grinned and leaned back against the wall. The graffiti behind him rose and fell in black paint. The top portion of an *M* just visible above his head gave him horns.

She sniggered.

"What's so funny?" His dark eyebrows dropped into a vee and with the scar on his cheek, he certainly looked like a fiend from hell. Damn, he was a handsome devil.

She bit her lip to stop from laughing out loud. All she needed was to reveal her hiding spot to the people across the street.

"About time you got here," Rex said as Charlie walked up, and the rain started falling again.

"I'm not late. Hell, I'm early." Charlie was only a few inches shorter than Rex. So when she rose on her tiptoes and glared, she looked straight into Rex's eyes.

Abby grinned. "You're way early."

"If you don't mind, I'd like Abby to drive me back to the hotel," Rex said. The tone he used clearly said he would do whatever he wanted, that he only told her to waylay a fight.

"That's between you and Abby. I'm here now, so obviously I don't have a problem with it." Charlie raised her eyebrows and chuckled.

Abby looked at Rex and then back at Charlie. What did they understand that she wasn't getting? It didn't matter. She was ready to get out of the rain.

After they convinced Sal to take her sedan, they returned to the Birmingham hotel in the truck. Though Rex didn't like it, she drove. She couldn't put her finger on it, but he was acting strange. She wondered if he was popping pain pills. That would explain some of his behavior and was enough of a reason for her to insist on driving.

The suite was just as beautiful as she remembered.

"I expected Jack and Ice to be here," she said.

"Ice is handling the transport of the bodies, and Jack is setting the attack on the facility you were watching. They'll pick us up in the morning and fill us in then."

She had a feeling he'd set this all up for them to be alone together.

"You want a drink?" Rex limped over to the cabinet with the liquor lined up on top.

"I'll pass. Are you sure it's okay for you to drink?"

"Why not?"

"Well, pain pills and alcohol can be a deadly combination."

He poured a drink and watched her over the rim as his masculine throat moved up and down with each swallow. How could a man's throat be so sexy while doing something so simple?

"I'm not taking anything. Seen too many people become addicted. I take a couple strong ibuprofens every few hours."

Eyeing him with distrust—men do like to act tough—she pulled out the ponytail holder and fluffed out her hair in an attempt to dry it. She hated to think how bad she looked. Taking a deep breath, she reminded herself he was an adult and she wasn't responsible for his stupidity.

"Listen. I'm going to take a shower. If you could order me a hamburger, I would appreciate it." As soon as she said *shower* she regretted it. It brought back memories of the last time they had been alone in the suite together.

When she glanced his way, he was pouring another drink. She bit her lip, picked up her suitcase near the door, and trudged up the steps to the master suite. He held the glass in his hand and watched her walk up the staircase.

What had he wanted to talk about? Jerking her attention away, she hurried into the bathroom. On seeing the huge glass enclosure, the memories of her last shower there drove the breath out of her lungs. She locked the door. She needed to regain a little control, and besides, she needed that shower.

Then she caught sight of her reflection in the mirror. Whoa! Wet hair framed her face, highlighting her slightly pink, prominent cheekbones. Her lips appeared full and soft, and her skin glowed. That was a surprise. Not that she was beautiful, but she didn't look like the drowned rat she'd expected. Then she looked down at her T-shirt. The soaked thin cotton had become see-through and the dark outlines of her nipples were visible beneath a plain white bra. That all at least explained the heated looks Rex had given her.

She turned on the faucet and started the shower to allow the water to warm. Then she opened her suitcase. Nothing screamed sexy. Remembering the satin slip she'd worn underneath her wedding dress, she pulled it out of a side pocket. A little wrinkled, but maybe the steam from the shower would help.

Within thirty minutes she'd finished, leaving her hair partially dried. She felt so much better and more in control. After a light coating of makeup, she headed toward the stairs.

Chapter Twenty-Eight

EXCITED BEYOND BELIEF from the thought of having the evening alone with Rex, Abby had missed him so much that she didn't care whatever he had to say to her. She rushed down the stairs and came to a stop. A tray with a covered dish sat in the middle of the table, but no Rex. She checked the bedroom, carefully opening the door. No sign of him or his suitcase.

Tears welled in her eyes for a few seconds and then she shook her head. The last few days had been stressful and so uncertain. Maybe she needed a change in her life. Glancing over to the bedroom again, she narrowed her eyes. He'd never acted like a coward before, but for the moment she would enjoy her meal and relax. Being alone wasn't as exciting as making love to Rex, but she would enjoy her solitude.

She returned to the dining room and lifted the cover to find a hamburger with fries still steaming beneath it.

Within minutes she'd devoured every bite and decided a glass of wine would be a perfect ending. Then she snickered. Not exactly the ending she'd hoped for that evening.

The twinkling light beyond the balcony drew her attention and she decided to enjoy her glass there. Memories of how close they'd come to making love out there shot warmth through her body.

He didn't give her a warning, but she felt his presence and her heart picked up speed. The temperature on the balcony changed abruptly and a sensation of no longer being alone kicked her senses into high gear. The wind died down but her nipples remained hard as if they knew who stood behind her.

"A beautiful night. Unseasonably warm." She inhaled deeply and caught that special clean male scent of Rex.

"Hand me your glass." The deep tone brooked no argument. She turned and held out the glass. His eyes glimmered even in the darkness. A chill traveled down her spine. He looked stern, almost foreboding.

With slow precision, he slid the glass onto a small table and returned his attention to her.

"What are you wearing underneath that scrap of material?"

Looking forward to seeing his reaction, she said, "Nothing."

His snarl of a grin took her breath away. The Rex standing in front of her was the dangerous arms dealer Rurik, ready to take what he wanted.

Tingles shot straight to her clit.

"Face the city."

She hesitated. "What happened to us talking?" she teased.

"Now."

Was this what she wanted? Yes. The forceful, confident Rex excited her. She turned.

His heat covered her back and then strong hands rested on her hips, slid across the silky material, and stopped over her pelvis. Bunching the material, he lifted it until he slipped his fingers over her mons and farther.

"You're so slick and wet."

One thick finger divided her moist folds and stroked over the knot wanting his attention, but he continued until he thrust into her. Instead of withdrawing and thrusting again, he hooked his finger into her and lifted—placing tight pressure to the perfect spot needing his attention. His hand hauled her body up, lifting her feet off the floor, pressing her back against his clothed chest.

"I want in you. I want my cock in you with your body trembling, holding, squeezing." Every word he said caused her thighs to clench.

She gasped and held on to his arm with both hands. It was times like these that she realized how strong he was and how easily he could hurt a person. But the strange sensation of being a puppet in his hands didn't bother her. In fact, she liked the way he controlled his brute strength. Ripples of muscle moved wherever his body touched hers. A second finger hooked into her and his thumb rubbed and rolled her clit as his other hand matched the movements on a breast. She was his personal sex toy. And she liked it a lot.

"Yeah? You like that, don't you?"

She nodded, unable to make a coherent sound.

"Keep making those sweet sounds." His deep voice wove a spell around her.

The stone wall in front of her, protecting them from the edge of the balcony, stood waist-high to her. He leaned over her back, holding her tight. She released his arm and with palms flat braced her upper torso on the ledge. Her feet landed back on the balcony's floor. His hands grabbed the straps of the slip and jerked it down past her hips to pool around her ankles. Her ballet-style shoes remained on her feet.

"Don't move," he commanded.

If not for being so ready, she would've protested his tone, but instead she closed her eyes and sank into all of the sensations surrounding her. His warmth behind her, the light warm breeze caressing her skin, the distant sounds of automobiles and the world moving while she waited for what the man behind her did next.

He caressed her buttocks, and goose bumps popped over her skin from the anticipation. His warm hands clasped the inside of her thighs and spread her apart. The sound of a zipper being lowered and clothing moved caused her to shift with need.

A burning slap to her ass brought her straight up to glare over her shoulder. His face was in the shadows and with his dark shirt on, his belt still clasped, and his hard, thick cock in his hand, he looked scary sexy. She had to admit she liked knowing she was naked in front of him, ready for his instructions.

"Turn back around and don't move until I tell you."

Both hands gripped her hips, thumbs pulled her apart, and he eased into her up until the last couple inches. Then he thrust hard. Her body jerked forward and she barely caught herself from hitting the stone ledge. Facing forward, looking over the city beyond, she inhaled the fresh air as he began moving. She loved how full he made her feel. Though her knees were locked, the push and pull of his body rocked hers. Her naked breasts swayed and the tips brushed the sleek stone. The mixed sensations had her mouth open for extra air. Each pant matched his thrust.

She wiggled, loving how he stretched her and how the scratch of his pants fabric excited her more.

His broad hand slapped her ass again. "I told you not to move." Streaks of pain and pleasure raced directly to every highly charged sexual nerve.

Then he lifted her hips a little higher, and her feet no longer touched the floor. She moved quickly and caught the ledge before her chest slammed into it. That was when she realized he'd been taking her with his knees bent. At his full height and a better grip, he began to hammer into her. Her legs swung on each side of his. Her fingers gripped the stone warming beneath her chest.

Moist and needing to climax, she whimpered, wanting more. With the combination of the dangerous height and the lethal man fucking her, she needed to reach the pinnacle before her heart exploded. As if he realized what she wanted, his hand reached around and covered her mound to pinch her clit. She screamed. If anyone heard her that high off the ground and with the wind picking up speed, she didn't know or care. He pounded into her a few more times before he grunted and wrapped his arms around her waist, lifting her. Her back landed against his chest, his shirt warm, and she felt his heart beating hard and fast.

As if she were a doll, he turned her until he had an arm beneath her back and another at the bend of her knees. Then he carried her into the suite, his limp reminding her of his bullet wound.

"Your hip. Put me down before you pull the stitches out."

"Shh. Don't worry. I'm fine." To prove it, he took the steps two at a time with his long strides. When he paused beside the bed and looked down at her, his heated gaze studied every inch of her body. The way his eyes almost closed showed how much he enjoyed looking at her naked.

All thoughts of his wound were forgotten.

He released her legs and her body slid over his. For the first time in her life, she felt small, delicate, and feminine. His shoulders were so broad and chest so wide, she smoothed her hands across them until she clasped her hands behind his neck and pulled him down for another kiss. She licked and sucked, wanting more. Their tongues danced and twined together. His hands cupped her buttocks and lifted. She wrapped her legs around his waist. His cock, still out of his pants, was hard and ready. Open, wet, and needy, she lined up and thrust down. He groaned and arched into her as he threw back his head.

When she worked her hips up and down several more

times, she looked into his eyes. They glittered with a primitive satisfaction.

He grasped her hips. "Stop. Wait."

Then he peeled her off him and dropped her onto the bed. She sat up and before she could scramble back to touch every toned ripple of his body, his strong fingers dug into her knees and separated them. With her hands on the mattress behind her, and her legs spread out in a provocative position, she waited for his next move.

Once he stepped away, he double gripped the back of his shirt and jerked it over and off and then shucked his pants and briefs to finally crawl over her.

He slid into her heated depths with one fluid movement. Ankles crossed at the small of his back, she stared up at his face. Arms straight, he stared back.

REX WANTED TO explain to Abby what he felt for her. He never knew he was a coward. Saying *I love you* wasn't a common practice in the home he grew up in. He was more apt to get slapped around.

He cupped her dear face. If only he could stay inside her. She felt so good, smelled so good, looked so good. Heaven. The only time he ever felt he had a place in the world was in her arms and between her legs.

"Abby."

"Hmmm." With her half-mast eyes, she looked happy and satisfied.

"Let's start over."

Her bark of laughter caused her pelvis to shake and he almost lost control.

"I don't know if I can do it," she teased.

"No. Let's start over without the past." Did she understand what he was saying?

The smile on her face faded. Maybe she did.

"I would like that. A lot."

"Good. Hi, I'm Rex Drago." Unable to resist, he leaned down and sipped on a taut nipple.

"Agh! No fair!" She covered her breasts with her hands. "Nice to meet you. I'm Abby Rodriguez."

With his cock continuing to harden inside of her, he grinned and showed her how unfair he could be in bed. He withdrew to the tip and quickly plunged into her.

She arched into him, her hips reaching for more. Yeah. He liked that.

Unable to hold back anymore, he pumped hard and fast into her while keeping his gaze on hers. Then she screamed as she bowed her body and closed her eyes.

Before he could roll over, clapping near the doorway jerked him around. He pushed Abby behind him.

"A better show than the one you two put on in my home." Brody leaned against the door frame, while two of his thugs stood in the bedroom with MP5s aimed their way.

"Get the hell out of here!" Rex remembered to include Rurik's accent.

"You're not smart to have only one guard. The little fellow didn't put up much of a fight." Brody stepped out of the doorway and jerked his head toward the bed. Two more thugs walked into the room with handcuffs and rope.

Rex jumped the nearest man. His arm wrapped around the man's neck, keeping him in the line of fire.

"Don't shoot yet!" Brody shoved one of his own men against the wall.

A *crack* vibrated in the room. Out of the corner of his eye, he glimpsed Abby fighting the other man. A naked Amazon kicking butt. Beautiful. His attention divided between Brody and his gun-toting thugs, but he couldn't help admiring Abby's moves. With a twist in midair, one long leg kicked out and knocked the man out. Before she landed on her feet, another thug picked up a lamp and busted it over her head, and she crumbled to the floor.

Rex roared, slinging the man in his arms into Brody. In two strides he reached for the asshole who'd hurt Abby. The man slammed into him, jabbing his wound. Fury blinded him to the pain as he picked up the man and shook him. With his back turned, he didn't realize until the last minute that Brody had moved closer. A bright spray of stars blinded him and then he sank into darkness.

Chapter Twenty-Nine

ABBY SQUEEZED HER eyes shut several times, trying to adjust her vision to the blinking fluorescent bulbs on the ceiling. When it finally cleared up, déjà vu set in. The light wasn't going on and off. A naked man hung upside down from a hook, swinging back and forth, blocking and unblocking the light.

Ah, shit! Stretched out on her side and as naked as a redneck in a heat wave, she used an elbow to sit up and then lean back against the wall. Her wrists burned from rubbing against the rope. Looking around, she sighed. Raw cinder-block walls stood about ten feet tall around her, and only one steel door to escape through was across the room. What in the world happened?

"About fucking time you woke up," Rex said, his deep voice accented. That meant someone was listening at the door or he suspected the room to be bugged.

"What is up with you and getting hung upside down naked?"

"Ha-ha." He twisted his body. "Maybe the question should be why do people think it's necessary?"

He had a point.

He continued to make his body swing, causing the rope to jerk. Wouldn't it cause the rope to tighten on his ankles? Didn't it hurt?

"What the hell? Quit doing that. You're giving me a headache. The stupid light keeps blinking and that looks painful."

Then again, was there another man in the world who looked as good as Rex naked, hanging upside down from a hook? Checking all the parts she'd reacquainted herself with the past few weeks—she would need to be dead not to look—her gaze came to a stop. Instead of what she first thought were shadows, blood covered his side, dripping off one broad shoulder.

Terrified, she struggled with her own ties. "Stop moving. You're bleeding!"

"No shit, Sherlock!"

"Hey, no need to get snippy with me." She flinched when she looked down. The throbbing bump on the back of her head didn't help matters as she worked the rope around her wrists. It was a little loose. Probably Brody did it. He appeared to believe women were on the helpless side. Why do men underestimate women? The knot gave a micro inch. Thank God they did.

"What are you doing?" he asked.

"Shh!"

"Don't shush me!"

"Children, enough already. I could hear you two arguing down the hallway." Brody walked in all grins and golden looks. "Our kind hosts are getting a little antsy with all the yelling in here."

"Hosts?" Abby and Rex asked at the same time.

"You really thought I would have a munitions facility on my farm, didn't you?" Brody chuckled and placed his hands behind his back as he circled Rex. "No. The Inferno was kind enough to provide me with everything I needed to make all the bullets they desired since the . . . what? Is it now seven shipments that have gone astray?" He crouched in front of Rex, staring down into his eyes. "From what they've told me, I have you to thank for my troubles. I knew we were competitors, but I believed in honor among arms dealers. But you obviously do not." He dipped his finger into the wet blood dripping down Rex's side and rubbed it between his forefinger and thumb as if contemplating the thickness. Then with another swipe, he marked a gruesome X on Rex's naked chest. "You're a dead man. Even if I don't have you killed, my friends with the Inferno said they plan to take you out. Remember Leif and Spring Erickson?" He cleaned his finger in Rex's hair.

With a jerk of his head, Rex eyed the man with hatred. "I'm not surprised those two freaks are involved with a fucked-up group like Inferno."

Brody stood and slapped at his pant legs. Mere inches from Rex's groin, Brody chuckled.

"Damn, I never got a good look at it, what with the

way you kept sticking it in every orifice Abby possesses." He crossed his arms and tilted his head as he stared at Rex's cock.

"I don't play for the other team," Rex sneered.

"I do. Making the money that I do helps me indulge in all my fantasies. I bet if I was in the mood, you would find swinging both ways to be quite enjoyable."

Crappy crap. She never expected that. He'd always been such a man's man, even in high school. Sure he had guys hanging around him, but she'd guessed it had more to do with catching Brody's throwaway girlfriends than anything to do with personal pleasures. It gave a whole new flavor to friends with benefits.

"I've been told you've been feeding information to an organization called The Circle. They're a very interesting group. Rumor is they're trying to go mainstream, but someone high up in their ranks is fighting it. You never know when information like that can come in handy."

Rex's cold gray eyes remained on Brody. She could tell that even upside down, he struggled to keep his mouth shut. His jaw flexed as his teeth ground together.

With a shrug of his shoulders, Brody turned his attention toward her. She moved her knees closer to her breasts. Odd that the room's temperature dipped at that precise moment. With her ankles crossed and legs tight, she prayed he couldn't see any more than what he probably had already.

"And you. I'm sorry that you got mixed up with this bastard." His gaze swept over her as if he was unsure what to make of her. And despite tying her, he'd already proven he'd disregarded her as a threat. She still wasn't sure if she should feel insulted or relieved. Arrogance was many a man's downfall. "I'll see if I can find you something to wear and talk the nuts around here into letting you go."

Brody sauntered out of the room and gave a sardonic salute. "It's been nice knowing you, Rurik."

As the door closed behind him, Abby caught a glimpse of the guard and short hallway leading to another door.

"Well, that went nicely." Abby couldn't help the sarcasm.

"I'm looking forward to the day I smash in that pretty boy nose he loves so much." His voice lowered since Brody had mentioned the guard was able to hear them earlier. Rex grunted as he fought the tie around his wrists. "Come over here and help me untie my hands."

"Give me a minute." She worked harder at the knot. "When do you think Jack will get here?" Each tug stung like fire ants chowing down.

When he didn't answer, she looked over at Rex.

He glanced at her and then away. His face appeared to be made out of stone.

"What?" she hissed.

"He's not coming."

"Of course he is. He's my boss."

"Nope. Ryker suspended him."

"What the hell do you mean suspended?"

"They're investigating Nic's . . . the operatives' deaths."

His face became harder, more like cold stone. Why did he think he needed to shut off his feelings for Nic with her? Sure she'd been jealous of the woman, but she had also been there when he needed someone.

"That's the hazard of the job. When the enemy attacks, people can die." She hated sounding cold, but he needed to be reminded. Yet something was missing. What was Rex not telling her? Before she could ask, the shuffling of boots outside the door caught her attention.

Perfect timing, she dropped the rope she'd finally worked loose and darted behind the door.

"Untie me," Rex hissed.

She shook her head and waved a hand at him to be quiet. There wasn't enough time.

The guard walked in carrying a bundle of clothes. As soon as he noticed she wasn't on the floor, he dropped what he was carrying and reached for the pistol at his side. She closed the door, drawing his attention, and kicked his chin. He lifted off the ground and flipped backward as if he were a stuntman. Sprawled out cold, he didn't make a sound as she searched his pockets.

"Quit feeling him up and get me down from here."

She pushed him over to check his back pockets. "Give me a minute." Eureka! She found a knife strapped to his back in a sheath. The fellow had issues; the knife was as long as her forearm. When she lifted the blade, Rex eyed her with distrust.

"You're going to be careful with that, right? I don't need to come up missing any fingers."

"You won't miss one or two."

"You might." His lascivious grin looked even more

evil with the added pull of the scar and easily told what he was thinking.

She rolled her eyes and sliced through the rope, being careful not to damage his talented fingers. Handing off the knife to Rex, she stepped back.

As if he did it daily, he bent at the waist and caught the back of his leg with one hand while the other used the knife to cut the tied rope. His feet dropped but he caught the large hook with his free hand. His legs probably needed the circulation to return before he landed on his feet.

No way could she hold back the sigh. Right-side up, he was even more gorgeous. Muscles and tendons stretched and moved in ways that were nothing short of sensual.

Mouth dry, she turned away and swallowed. Seeing the clothes on the floor, she thought it best to cover up. No underwear. Go figure. But the black pants were soft and stretchy like the type worn to exercise in, and the plain gray T-shirt was a little small as it molded to her breasts and torso.

A thud next to her warned Rex had landed on his feet.

"Check his tag and see what size pants he wears."

"No way. I've touched him enough. Anyway, his clothes won't fit you."

Rex shoved her out of the way. "I can't go around naked."

"You won't hurt my feelings." She knew she had a mischievous grin.

With a sideways glance at her, he brought a blush to her face. She lost the grin. He actually embarrassed her with a look so hot she trembled. What was wrong with her? She hadn't gotten embarrassed last time he was naked and hanging from a hook. Of course, last time she'd had only faded memories. But now new vivid memories rose to the surface and heated her face. She bit the side of her mouth as she tried to regain control of her body.

He said, "Yeah. I can tell. Your nipples are hard. And if I stay naked any longer, I'll be in you, pumping."

Unable to resist any longer from the last time she looked—what, two minutes ago?—she realized he'd become . . . firmer. She quickly looked away. When had she become a wimp about looking at what interested her? She crossed her arms over her chest.

"Damn, quit." Abby shook her head.

He chuckled and stripped the poor guard of his black pants and shirt and then tossed the boots to the side. They were too small.

While Rex dressed, she picked up the boots and pulled out the laces, using the string to tie the man's hands and ankles—she knew better than to underestimate him. Taking the rope from the floor and one of his socks, she gagged him and slipped his watch off before checking outside the door.

The hallway, more like a small antechamber, had a table and chairs arranged to the side with the guard's cell phone vibrating on top.

"Are you about dressed? His cell phone is ringing." She looked down at the guard. The man was still out cold.

"He could be a little taller." Rex's disgust brought her head around. "And wider."

Snug around his hips, the black jeans teased the top of his ankles. She covered her mouth and bit her bottom lip to stop the giggles from escaping. He wouldn't appreciate the humor. But the memory of watching clips of Michael Jackson in the eighties with his white socks showing below high-water pants came to mind. Only MJ never filled out a pair of jeans like Rex. When he turned around, she barely caught the sigh released by the sight. The man was seriously taut in the cheek department.

"You ready?" Rex tore the guard's white T-shirt and pressed a swatch to the wound on his hip and then slipped into the shirt. The material pulled across his chest and shoulders, but the shirt fit a little better than the pants.

"Huh, yeah. From what I can tell, there are four doors. Two are open and show rooms like this one. So that leaves us to decide between the one straight on and one to the left."

"Go straight and I'll check the left one." Rex motioned to the door with the guard's Glock.

They padded over to the doors. The guard hadn't brought shoes, and the boots that were too little for Rex were too big for her, especially without laces.

As soon as she reached her door, Rex entered his. She eased it open and peeked inside. A man hung limply from chains bolted to a wall, his clothes shredded and bloody. His hair, dark with what appeared to be sweat and blood, fell over his eyes.

"Edward?"

Chapter Thirty

ABBY RUSHED OVER and lifted the man's head. Ty Roman. She tamped down the disappointment that he wasn't her brother.

"Ty." His eyes were closed and his mouth open, and blood dribbled from the corner of his lips. Time wasn't on their side, and she needed a way to break him out of the chains, quick.

She checked the locks and then swept the place with her gaze, hoping something would pop out that she could use. Nothing. "We'll come back for you. I don't have anything that'll unlock the chains. Sorry."

He groaned as he lifted his head and one brown eye stared at her. The other, swollen shut, matched the purple and black side of his face.

"Don't worry about me, darlin'. You just watch yourself. Nothing is what it appears to be." He grimaced and closed his eye, going limp.

"Abby?" Rex stood at the door. "We don't have time to help him."

"I know." She glanced at the man one last time before moving away. The vague warning Ty gave could mean so many things. Rex grabbed her hand and they darted through the other door Rex had checked out. Suddenly they were in a warehouse with stacks of boxes that stood above their heads to nearly the ceiling. Lights overhead lit their way every so many feet. As they ran, she realized how much space the warehouse covered.

A chuckle broke the silence along with the scrape of a boot moving across the cement floor.

Abby and Rex squeezed between a few crates. The man walked by with head down, looking at a cell phone as his thumbs traveled over the virtual toggle. Strapped across his chest was an M4, useless with his hands occupied.

Keeping it simple, Abby stuck her leg out, tripping the man as Rex slammed a fist into his face. Rex clasped the man's arms, stopping him from hitting the floor, while she swooped up the phone before the clatter alerted others.

They slipped behind another stack after they tied the guard and relieved him of the M4 and cell phone. For a few seconds they stood still, waiting to see if the shit hit the fan. How much longer before someone found the guard or missed the other one?

Listening for fast-approaching footsteps, she turned her back to Rex. Then she heard the sound of a zipper being raised. Or lowered. Had he lost his mind?

She looked over her shoulder as Rex pulled off the

pants from the taller guard. In seconds, he was tucking in his cock and carefully zipping up. A much better fit. He lined up a foot next to one of the man's boots, and in no time, his feet were covered with socks and leather as he yanked the ties into a double knot.

"Let's go." He led the way with the machine gun clasped in his hand and threw Abby the Glock he'd taken from the first guard.

The lit exit sign helped to point their way out, and Abby took a deep breath of fresh air as they ducked behind a huge white delivery truck. Security lights brightened the parking lot, glistening on the wet asphalt and the chain-link fence surrounding it.

"From what I could tell earlier, they have a guard walking the perimeter. We need to time him and see how long we'll have to climb that fence." Rex pointed ahead.

She looked at the razor wire and back at Rex.

"All we need to do is cut the hog rings." He lifted his brows as he looked into her face.

"If you say so."

"I got these when you were still in there." He nodded toward the warehouse as he lifted a dangerous-looking pair of clippers with long handles. "Bolt cutters. They were sitting on a crate outside the door. Lucky, huh? It'll cut the rings that hold the wire. A few snips and the fence will fall open like a Slinky."

"Whatever." She wiggled her toes. "You didn't see any shoes while you were looking for bolt cutters, did you?"

"No. You know, I've decided I hate fucking warehouses," Rex said under his breath as he watched for the guard.

"You do have a problem waking up naked."

"Don't go there again."

She grinned up at him as he stood behind her, looking down with that sexy sneer-for-a-smile look.

"You never told me the story about that scar." She wasn't sure why she asked, but maybe with all they'd been through recently, he would answer this time.

"It's important for you to know?" His fingers lightly touched her cheek as his thumb caressed her lips.

When she remained quiet, his smile eased.

"Okay. Jack and I were arguing over the last bag of chips and he hit me with a beer bottle."

"Beer bottle?" Not sure if she was astounded by the simple yet savage aspect of the story or that brothers could be so mean to each other, she traced the scar. He flinched but didn't move away as he always had before. "How old were you?"

"Thirteen." He looked away.

"Where did your brother get a beer bottle?" Sure they needed to stay alert and find a way out of the fence, but the chance to learn more was too tempting.

"Dad." His gaze flicked down to her face.

"What do you mean by 'Dad'?" From the way he grimaced, she knew she didn't want to hear. She pressed the palm of her hand to his chest, over his rapidly beating heart. "Never mind."

"No. You need to understand what's between me and my brother. Dad wanted us to fight. He constantly encouraged our fighting. That day he'd bought us a case of beer and told us to party. Jack was already upset about his football team losing. I smarted off about the chips, and in a flash we were rolling on the living room floor beating the shit out of each other. I got Jack pinned. Dad didn't like it. He tossed me off. I don't remember much after that, but Jack was pissed and he threw one of the bottles at me. The way it hit my face, it laid it open. I remember Mom screaming and Dad slapping her to shut her the fuck up. He refused to take me to the hospital. Child Services had already warned him if I showed up in the emergency room again that they would take me away. I never understood why he didn't let them. Maybe it was pride. To have someone take one of his sons away from him would've been hard."

Abby caught that he said "me" and not "us." Even as an adult, his certainty of being the one taken away, and not his brother, lingered. She understood so much of what he wasn't saying. An overgrown child with a soft heart had to learn to be tough or otherwise be thought of as less than a man, and in turn, he had a hard time accepting a brother's apology for sleeping with the woman he loved. And then to find out that woman had hidden the news of losing his child . . . it would top the long list of life giving him the finger.

"Rex, I—"

"Wait, someone's coming this way," he whispered, and lifted his chin in the direction of the gate.

Bent over and moving at a fast clip, two dark shapes worked their way toward where they hid behind the truck. Had the cavalry come to the rescue? No need for guards to move like that. Better safe than dead, Abby aimed the "borrowed" gun.

"Abby, dammit! Don't shoot!" Jack held up his hands while keeping low. Behind him was Liam.

"Where's Ryker?" Rex asked, squinting in the darkness beyond the fence.

"He's not coming." Jack eyed her. "I see you're still in one piece. Rex taking care of you?"

His comment surprised her. He'd always treated female operatives equally, expecting them to shake off the pain of wounds or broken bones and take care of themselves.

"I'm fine. Brody sure as hell didn't have anything to do with me being in one piece. The asshole has not only my brother but Ty too."

"Dammit, that man has the worst luck." Jack glanced back a couple times at Liam and Rex.

She wasn't sure if he meant her brother or Ty. Both appeared to be unlucky.

"What's going on? Why are you here without backup? And why isn't Ryker coming?" Rex crossed his arms. Fury deepened his voice.

Jack looked away, not meeting her eyes. "He said that he couldn't afford to lose any more operatives. Losing two more was nothing compared to the ten that it would take to get you out."

"That's a bald-faced lie. Ryker wouldn't do that," she snarled.

"Have you ever known me to lie to you?" One pierced eyebrow lifted.

She wanted to argue, but to what purpose? He was right.

"What about Collin and Olivia? What did they say?" she asked.

"We have no idea where they're at. Besides, what would it matter? Collin gave the OS to Ryker—he'd never interfere."

The sadness in Jack's eyes gave her pause. What else had he not told them?

REX WATCHED HIS brother. He looked different. Still the same tattooed, pierced psycho as before, but he appeared subdued, nowhere as animated.

"What are you doing here?" Rex asked.

"I have nothing to lose," was all he said as he walked toward the warehouse.

"Where're you going?"

"Taking care of business." Never looking back, Jack ducked inside the warehouse.

"What is going on, Liam?" He felt every drop of frustration boiling inside, wanting to blow. Abby obviously sensed it as she touched his arm, drawing his attention, and then she shook her head.

"Jack has it in his mind that he needs to save you and Rex," Liam said to Abby.

"We don't need his fucking help." When was the last time Jack ever thought of anyone but himself? His brother didn't care if he lived or died. Rex doubted he'd changed. There had to be something in it for Jack. "Why did you come with him?" Rex stared hard at the Irishman and former Circle security officer. The latter was enough of a reason to distrust him, but being around his brother added to his skepticism.

Liam leaned against the truck, unclipped the magazine in his gun, and shoved it back in. Then he looked up at Rex. "They can't suspend me, seeing as I'm already under suspension and I have no idea how much longer, maybe a week or ten years. And it's my nature to rebel. I've survived worse than Room 999, so they might as well eliminate me." He shrugged. "Of course, they know I be wanting death for some time now. And we be knowing they don't like giving us what we want."

Before The Circle bombed the OS, the splinter organization had an interrogation chamber called Room 999. Those who entered left in a body bag or hooked to tubes until they recovered, if they ever did.

"So you're saying you expect us to die?" Rex was sick and tired of people expecting him to fail.

"No. You misunderstand. I like it when the odds are against me. Makes the living more interesting, wouldn't you say? But the dying? That will be up to Sweet Mother Mary to decide." He flashed a grin.

Rex looked in the direction Jack and Liam had come from. No guard had shown up during the time they were talking. "Did you take out a guard?"

Liam nodded, all joking gone. He'd been with The Circle a long time. Had he forgotten they no longer took a life if it could be spared while getting the same results?

Rex hoped that wasn't the reason for the haunted look on the Irishman's face. "It won't be long before they discover the missing guards." He pressed his back to the side of the truck and looked around. "Where's Abby?"

"I saw her follow Jack into the warehouse." Liam flattened his body next to Rex's. How strange to look eye-to-eye with another person. He was used to being the tallest.

"Dammit! I know why she followed. She hadn't wanted to leave Jack's friend in the first place. He'd been chained and beaten badly. We didn't have time to look for a way to unchain him, and we still don't."

He trusted her with Jack. No matter what his brother would pull, Abby wouldn't fall for his line again.

Rex bumped the back of his head against the side of the truck in frustration. That didn't mean she wouldn't do stupid things in the name of doing right. He did worry about the woman.

"Fuck it! We might as well help too." Hell, he hated the thought of going back into that warehouse, but he wasn't leaving without Abby.

"Do you think that's wise? If he's hurt, he'll slow us down." Liam's eyes flashed with delight in what would most likely be another suicidal rescue.

"I don't give a fuck about Ty Roman. I'm after Abby. The woman has no sense at all when it comes to taking care of her own hide." He bent low and headed back to where he'd hoped not to return.

ABBY WATCHED THE hallway from outside the door as Jack worked the locks on the chains. Head down and arms stretched nearly out of the sockets, the infamous bounty hunter, Ty Roman, appeared to be dead, but Jack swore his heart still beat.

Rex was going to be so pissed. When she followed Jack, it had been more to talk to him about Nic, but when she realized what he was up to, she couldn't turn back. Though she didn't know Ty, no human deserved to be treated like that.

"Hot shit!" Jack said in triumph.

She turned to see Jack pulling the chains off the wall and from around Ty's torso and off his wrists and ankles. Luckily, Jack made it a habit to keep a few locksmith tools in his pockets. It appeared he wore cargo pants for more than style.

"We need to get out of here." She glanced at the watch she'd taken off the guard. They had been in there only for about eight minutes, but it felt like hours.

"I thought you had more sense than to stick around."

That voice sounded familiar. She turned and the bottom dropped out of her stomach.

Chapter Thirty-One

"EDWARD?" WHEN ABBY took a step toward him, he aimed an evil-looking sawed-off shotgun at her.

She raised her hands.

"Little sister, you better stand back. I'd hate to shoot you. If you'd done what we expected you to do and high-tailed it out of here, you wouldn't be in the spot you're in now. It's that son of a bitch Brody's fault. He has a soft spot for you. No matter how many times I've told him to fuck you and get it out of his system, he won't listen. For such a fucking genius, he has no common sense." Her brother swept his gun to the side, indicating for her to move over.

Brody? A genius?

Behind her brother were four guards, broad and mus-cled, their eyes glistening with the possibility of spilling blood, and she didn't want to think about what they had planned for her. One of them walked up and took the knife from her hand. Chances were one of those creepy-looking fellows had enjoyed beating Ty to a pulp.

She felt like everything was unfolding from the other side of a screen. No way would the person in front of her be the same big brother she had always looked up to. He was involved with illegal ammunitions? Threatening to kill her? What had happened to cause him to change?

"What's wrong with you? What about Suzie and Tommy?"

"You don't worry about them. They're reaping the benefits of my *night job*."

"Let her go. She's your sister for God's sake!" Jack lunged for Edward and at the same time, one of the guards stepped between them and took the blow with only a grunt. Two other guards grabbed his arms and held them. "You have no idea who you're messing with!" Jack threatened.

"Tell me about it?" Curiosity was written on his face. "I've tried to get Abby to tell me the truth about her husband. They don't act like newlyweds. How convenient for a world-class arms dealer to marry my sister."

She'd expected Jack to deny the marriage, but instead he didn't even glance her way. "They're really married."

He'd already threatened her brother and hinted at others being involved. Why keep up the lie? That wasn't important. If her brother understood the danger he was in, he'd let them go.

"Edward. Please. You don't understand. The people you're dealing with are crazy. The Inferno wants the world to burn so they can bring about a new world order.

You've always had a good head on your shoulders. Why be involved with a group who wants to destroy? You know they'll fail but in the meantime will kill a lot of innocent people. You were never like that. You weren't brought up that way."

Her brother threw back his head and laughed so hard, he wiped tears from his eyes. "I really don't give a fuck what you think. Money is a big motivator, and they're crazy enough to pay me big-time to help." He motioned for his men to take them. "Lock them up, but separately this time. Abby is a little more talented in self-defense than I had thought. Her husband should show up soon."

There was nothing left to do but tell her brother the truth.

"Remember the other day you wanted to know if Rurik worked for the government?"

He lifted his hand to stop his men. "Yes. And you swore to me he doesn't. So are you saying he does?"

"He works for an organization called The Circle. They're not part of the government, but you don't want to cross them. They've taken an interest in stopping the manufacture and shipment of the bullets you've invented." With Edward's involvement, he or the Ericksons had to be the inventor.

"The Circle? So what I suspected was right. I couldn't find much about them on the Internet, but Brody came across quite a bit. The man knows ways of digging up information that amazes me. He's an artist with a computer. I wish I had invented the guidance program for the bullets. But my partner was the genius who brought science fiction to reality. He understands he needs my help. While I have the marketing skills, I also had the connections."

"You're saying Brody was the one who invented Hell's Purifier? I don't believe you. It had to be the Ericksons. They're strange enough to be the type."

"What's the type?" He narrowed his eyes at her.

"Super smart and doesn't care for human life."

"Super smart. Yeah. I guess no one ever could call me super smart, but"—he nodded toward Jack—"why are you asking the questions instead of him?"

She shrugged and hoped she could get him talking again. Better chance of Rex and Liam realizing they hadn't returned yet. "You're my brother. I'm simply trying to get you to see reason and tell me the truth about Hell's Purifier." She wanted him to tell her who the inventor was. He made it sound as if the genius was Brody.

"Oh, I'm very reasonable if not pushed too far, and you're pushing. Where's your husband?"

"Please let us go." Her brother could always see through her.

He stepped back and tilted his head. "Are you part of The Circle?"

"No." Jack struggled with the men holding him.

"Yes," she said at the same time, glaring at Jack.

Edward pursed his lips and nodded. "That's what I thought. Explains your disappearance and how much you've changed. Sorry, Abby, but if you're going to play with the big boys, you have to pay the price."

"You're going to kill your own sister?" Jack finally

broke loose and slammed a fist into the man's nose before another jumped him and pulled Jack away.

A chill traveled down her spine. "If that's the case, then it won't hurt to let me know who the inventor is." She turned back to Edward.

"Even as a little kid you loved to ask questions. Drove me and Mom nuts when you never shut up. I can't tell you how often you embarrassed us. It was bad enough you looked like some little orphan we picked up in a country south of the border."

His insults didn't hurt as much as realizing her own brother hated her. They'd never been close, but she'd always admired him. The feeling obviously wasn't mutual.

"Hey, Brody, you going to hang out there or come in and tell Abby the truth? For some reason she won't believe me. I guess she thinks a dumb jock is always a dumb jock," Edward shouted.

From his tone, she could tell he had little respect for the man. Why was it so hard for her to believe? Brody had successfully hidden an ammunitions plant from the government and The Circle. So why not believe he was the inventor?

The doorway remained empty.

"You self-centered sick fuck! Get in here!" Edward's face flushed with anger as he edged over to the door, keeping his gun on Abby. He scrambled back when Brody walked in with Rex and Liam behind him, their guns aimed at his back.

"Tsk, tsk, tsk. How can you mistreat the man who

made you rich?" Rex jabbed the M4 into Brody's back, pushing him farther into the room.

Before she realized Edward had moved, he had an arm around her neck and his gun to her temple.

"If you want your wife to live, you'll put your gun down, Rurik. Or whatever your name is. Then again, I don't give a damn what you call yourself."

Rex's gaze shot to her and then to a point behind her, beyond Edward, in the opposite corner of where they held Jack. She heard Jack arguing with the men, and his voice remained in the same area of the room. Afraid to move and draw attention to whatever was going on, she kept her eyes on Rex. She needed to concentrate on talking her brother out of shooting her.

The bang in the small room caused her eardrums to go numb for several seconds. When her brother's hold became limp, she knew what had happened. Someone had shot him. She dropped to her knees next to Edward and touched the side of his neck with two fingers. Her hands shook so bad she wasn't sure if that was the reason she didn't feel a pulse.

She looked up. She'd forgotten about Ty. He held a gun—she had no idea where he got it—and pointed it at the men holding Jack. The men, realizing their leader was dead and no help would be coming from Brody, dropped their hold.

Jack kicked one fellow in the balls as he hit the other guy with a left hook. "You deserve it, assholes!"

Ignoring the chaos around her, Abby clutched Edward's shirt and pleaded, "Eddie, please hold on. We'll get you some help." She looked at the dear face she'd looked up to for so many years. His death would devastate her mom.

"SWEETHEART, LET HIM go. The cleanup crew is here."

She looked around, her eyes scratchy and dry. How long had she been holding her brother's head on her lap? She stood up and felt tears cooling on her face. The room began to swirl. Then she was in Rex's arms, being carried out of the room.

Weak and queasy, she cupped his cheek. "Put me down. You'll break your stitches."

"Shh. I'm okay. Let me take care of you. Close your eyes. You don't need to do anything. I got you."

"You don't need to do that. I can walk." Even to her ears, the protest was weak. She never remembered anyone saying they would take care of her. Sure, her mom cared enough to feed and clothe her, but her father had been the one who hugged her when she skinned her knee or celebrated with her when she brought home good grades. His office hours were too crazy for the day in, day out niceties and it wasn't until she was older that she had realized what she missed out on.

From what Rex had told her over the last few days, she wasn't the only one who missed out—but in a different way. Having a father who beat and degraded him at every turn and a mother who turned a blind eye to the cruelties, she was surprised how kind and gentle he treated her.

He kicked at the door leading out of the warehouse. Circle operatives scurried out of his way. She didn't care what anyone thought of Rex carrying her. She leaned her cheek on his shoulder and soaked in his warmth.

REX HUGGED HER closer. He never wanted to let her go. The thought of how close he'd come to losing her again terrified him.

"I thought Ryker wasn't going to help us," she said so low he barely caught it.

"It seems he decided to show up when he heard we'd gained control of the Inferno facility." He couldn't help a snort of derision. "We found the factory in the small building across from the warehouse. We got all the equipment, including the plans and specs."

Her arms wrapped around his neck and she closed her eyes. She appeared to be uninterested in hearing any more about ammunitions and The Circle. "Where are you taking me?" He liked how she trusted him enough to do that.

"Probably to bed for a week or more."

"That would be nice." She rubbed her cheek against him.

His chest swelled with a feeling so deep for this woman he was certain his heart would burst.

Minutes passed with several Circle operatives asking if they could help, and one was brave enough to offer to take her from him. He growled. Were they so stupid to think he would let her go after what they'd been through?

She'd squeezed tight, letting him know she wanted to stay with him. He liked that.

"Hey, Rex." Jack's voice brought him to a stop.

"You better stay away from me. You almost got Abby killed." When they had started working together, Rex had hoped they would be able to act like brothers. But when Jack once again led Abby into danger, he knew it was never meant to be.

"I know. I've really screwed up the last few days. I wouldn't listen to anyone and well . . . I'm giving up command of the OS Sector." Jack came around and stared at Abby. "She okay?"

"She's none of your business. And what I heard was Ryker suspended you."

"Well, that remains to be seen. He's set up a committee to investigate the mission. Someone leaked our whereabouts, especially the time we were in the cavern, and though we stopped most of the shipments, two got out. They'll need to track them down. The Inferno has them hidden somewhere. Brody should be helpful."

Rex shook his head. "I can't believe Ryker brought that sick asshole into The Circle."

"We were all surprised, but you have to admit the man must be a genius to design something so futuristic. He'd come in handy. His knowledge might be the only bright spot in that mission."

"Yeah, the assignment was royally fucked up. At least we stopped the manufacturing. I heard the Ericksons got away."

"Yeah. We found a tunnel beneath the warehouse that came out two streets over," Jack said.

Rex didn't give a damn about the rich bored couple who dabbled in ammunitions.

"When are they burying Nic?" He found it hard to wrap his mind around the knowledge he'd never talk with her again. She'd wanted him to love her so bad but he couldn't love her back. Not the way she wanted.

Abby wiggled in his arms. When he looked down at the compassion and kindness shining from her chocolate eyes, he wanted to strip her and kiss every inch of her soft, sweet body. They needed to hurry and get to the hotel. Others would have to trace the shipments and hunt the Ericksons down; he and Abby needed a break. A long one.

"Ryker had her cremated and her ashes flown to her grandmother in Kansas."

Damn. He didn't know she had any family left or where her hometown was. He needed to pay more attention to those he cared for. He glanced down at Abby again. And those who he loved. Yep, time for a change.

Rex started moving again.

"Where're you going?" Jack asked.

"Abby and I need to recuperate, and the best way is for us to fly out to Las Vegas and really get married."

Pushing back a little to look him in the eye, she raised her eyebrows. "We are?"

"Uh, about that . . . ," Jack started to answer.

No! Rex recognized that tone from his brother. Jack always acted so sorry whenever he screwed him over.

"You better not tell me that you two got married and never divorced. I swear, Jack, if you tell me that, I'll make sure Abby won't have to file for one, because you'll be dead." Red, he saw red. Maybe he was about to have an aneurysm.

"No, no, no. Actually, the papers you and Abby signed at the Elvis wedding, they were real."

"I signed my cover name. Signing as Rurik doesn't make it valid."

"You know the insurance papers I got you to sign before the wedding? Remember I was in a hurry and there were about ten sheets?"

"Yeah." His jaw hurt from clenching his teeth.

"The last sheet was a marriage certificate. I slipped that one in at the bottom of the stack when Abby signed."

Rex looked down at Abby. Her eyes were as wide and round as his. He liked the idea that they had actually been married for over a week. Only, he wanted a real honeymoon without dealing with a perverted high school crush of Abby's or her crazy family.

Turning his back to his brother, he asked Abby, "What do you think?"

"About us being married?"

He nodded. Words refused to come out. Would she say no? Would she want to divorce him? That didn't feel fair. He hadn't had a chance to be a real husband. But when had life been fair to him?

"It's all I ever wanted." Her hand cupped his cheek as her thumb caressed the scar. For once in his life, it didn't bother him. "What about you?"

"I've loved you for so long, Abby. You're my breath, my soul, my dream of all that's good about the world."

"You love *me*?" Her voice cracked.

How could the woman in his arms believe she was unlovable?

"Yeah, I do."

"I love you too." Tears streamed down her face.

He released her legs, pressed her against the side of a building, and kissed her. He didn't give a damn who saw them. The woman deserved so much better, but he wanted a soul-deep kiss. He grabbed her hand and pressed it to his cock, with only a layer of cotton material between them. "Let's get out of here before I take you against the wall."

"I wouldn't mind that, but I'm with you. I'd rather do that in privacy. Making love in front of everyone is a little more than I can handle." She stroked his cock through his pants. "And this is more than any woman can handle."

He chuckled and picked her up, heading to any vehicle he could commandeer, then to Birmingham and their hotel.

Chapter Thirty-Two

ABBY OPTED FOR a long champagne-colored lace gown. The little chapel in Las Vegas was what everyone expected, and it certainly delivered with lots of doves and white bows. It reminded her of her first wedding to Rex, but this time, they knew they were in love.

After a week of sensual bliss in the Birmingham hotel, Rex had insisted they go on to Las Vegas and make certain Jack couldn't come back later and claim once again that the wedding was a hoax and they really weren't married.

They were officially married thirty minutes ago. The only witnesses were Collin, Olivia, and Charlie.

Her husband chatted with Lewis Johnson, aka Elvis, the same man who officiated their first wedding. Apparently, he was a real ordained minister and associated with several churches in at least six different states, including Alabama and Nevada.

"Hello, beautiful." Rex leaned over and kissed her, thoroughly.

Her face heated up. "Mercy, you do know how to greet a gal." She'd gone to repair her hair after Rex had speared his fingers into it when they'd kissed at the altar.

The minister discreetly moved away.

"Are you sure you're okay with us moving to Seattle?"

She smiled, as she didn't care where they lived or what they did as long as they could remain together.

He'd decided to give up his position in The Circle. After Ryker refused to help save the two of them, he said he couldn't trust the man. She knew he also wanted to be as far away from Jack as possible. Collin and Olivia had started arranging adoptions for children from the Pacific countries and Far East. The Seattle office would need people to handle investigations and security for moving the children to the States. All done legally, of course.

She and Rex were as good as orphans themselves. Her mother refused to talk to her anymore. She blamed Abby for her brother's death. Others tried to explain she had nothing to do with it, but she refused to listen. To protect Suzie and Tommy's only source of income, the official report was that Edward had died in the line of duty. A hero's death. So her mother believed he died trying to pull her butt out of the fire.

And Rex refused to return Jack's calls. He claimed his older brother had used up all the chances he had to redeem the past.

"Olivia said Jack has been assigned to the Birmingham

Sector and is stationed in the little town of Sand City. Ironic, isn't it?" She suspected he asked for it, as he felt such guilt over Nic's death.

"I heard the suite we're booked in has a balcony. I want to see what it looks like at night too." The grin he gave her warned she would be holding on to the railing for dear life while he brought her to climax over and over again.

She accepted his abrupt change of subject to avoid talking about his brother.

"There is something romantic about balconies." The flare of heat in his eyes nearly satisfied her need to give as good as he dealt.

With a crook of her finger, she grinned as he leaned down for her to whisper in his ear, "I don't have any panties on."

He jerked his head back to look her in the eyes. "Damn, you don't play fair at all."

"Not when it comes to you. I want you hard and ready to go when we reach the hotel room."

His arms scooped her up and he threw her over his shoulder.

"What about our guests?"

"They'll understand."

As soon as the limousine door closed behind them, Rex said something to the driver in a low tone, and the driver closed the privacy window as he pulled away from the curb.

"What are you up to, Mr. Drago?"

"Well, Mrs. Drago, there's no way in hell I'm waiting

to reach that balcony. I've never made love in a limo before, and there's nothing like the present to see how it feels. Having you waiting for me all naked and ready for my touch . . . I may kill someone if they get in the way."

"Oh, Mr. Drago. You read my mind."

Can't get enough of Carla Swafford's
sexy, exhilarating Circle series?
Read on to find out how it all began with
a special excerpt from

CIRCLE OF DESIRE

and

CIRCLE OF DANGER

available now from Avon Books

An Excerpt from

CIRCLE OF DESIRE

OLIVIA ST. VINCENT typed the ammunition data into the keypad on the sniper rifle and then nestled her cheek against the stock's custom-fit pad. She waited for the information to be processed and her target to come into view.

Keeping her attention on the boardwalk outside the open window, she caressed the silencer attachment and sighed. Powerful and lightweight compared to others, the rifle was her favorite and the only one of its kind. She wasn't sure how The Circle got their hands on the prototype, and she knew better than to ask. She'd used it twice in the last eleven months and had no complaints.

She inhaled the fresh salt air coming in and watched the few early joggers trotting along the boardwalk next to Elliot Bay. Almost the whole length was visible from the empty fourth-story apartment. A strong wind picked up and splattered water off the windowsill onto her hands and the rifle, even though she sat a good three feet from the opening. She grabbed a soft cotton cloth and stroked off the liquid. It had rained for ten days straight since she'd arrived in Seattle, and only twenty minutes ago had it stopped. To the north, a break in the clouds showed deep blue sky. A miracle. Good grief, she couldn't wait to get back home to Atlanta.

One moment she was running her fingers across black metal, enjoying the bumpy finish. In the next, she was aiming at her target, taking a deep breath and then releasing it, relaxing, holding her trigger finger steady. He'd crossed the street and started down the boardwalk. Five foot eleven with a well-proportioned torso, he always wore the same dingy sneakers with orange Day-Glo stripes.

She squeezed her eyes shut for a few seconds and inhaled. Time to concentrate on the job. The Circle had given her orders to eliminate him, and she was programmed to follow. Later she'd hear he was a child molester or a killer like herself. Why she should care one way or the other, she wasn't sure. Maybe knowing helped her sleep at night. Not that it would matter otherwise; she was a killer and good at what she did. She never really had a choice.

She waited as he'd jogged a little past the half-mile mark. His feet pounded in a steady rhythm as the early morning light glistened on shifting muscles. Like clockwork every day, he hit the pavement at sunrise, jogging down the same area. Only thing about predictability, it could be deadly.

The area around him was clear, no one nearby. He turned down a short pier. Only a few feet more and he would be at the mark. She cleared her mind and inhaled, holding her breath for the fraction of a second. She squeezed the trigger. The jogger's body continued straight ahead, propelled by the bullet's trajectory, and then he toppled off the edge of the pier and splashed into the water as his god-awful shoes tumbled across the boardwalk. Perfect shot. That was why they sent her.

Once she pressed a couple buttons on the gun's microcomputer, she scooted away from the tripod and stretched with arms up, bending her back, getting the kinks out. Her back popped. After an hour in one position, it was no wonder her body protested, no matter how much she worked out. She shook her head when the image of the body landing in the water tried to resurface. Think of the good she carried out. Her job eliminated those who preyed on the weak. She performed as a tool for the greater good.

Yes. That was it. She was a tool.

Thinking of tools, she smirked at the gun. The usual brutal recoil dampened by the hydraulic system always surprised her. The rifle worked like it should with little firing signature, a thump of air and only a small amount of flash at the end of the barrel. The suppresser did its job. Unless someone stared directly at her open window and caught the small flare, nothing gave away her location.

Damn! If she'd been a man, she would have a hard-on now. She loved her gun. Objects she could control. People were a different factor.

As she closed the window, a warm breeze caressed the fine hairs on her arm. She shivered. Yeah, she was ready to relieve the pressure that had been building up inside. Playing the waiting game and finishing the job always sent her seeking the only outlet from all the tension. Others used alcohol or drugs to forget for a little while what they'd done. Sex with an anonymous handsome stranger was her drug of choice. Someone clueless about what she did for a living. Someone who held her as she used them for release.

She looked out the window at the crowd gathering at the end of the pier. She jerked her gaze away. Concentrate on anything but the finished job. Think of the gun she loved to control. Think of the power she held. Think about sex. A strong, hard, hot male body always helped. Think about getting away and planning the next job.

She reached out and caressed the two marks she'd made on the butt of the rifle. *Time for a third.* Her fingers shook; tears threatened her composure. Drawing her hand into a fist, she took a few deep breaths and then with well-practiced precision broke down the rifle and placed the sections into her luggage. Another tremor started at her hand and vibrated down her torso, before she knew it her whole body shook. Why couldn't her body cooperate? She'd done worse, been worse. Taking several more deep breaths, she closed her eyes and imagined a swing on a long porch, pushing against the wooden floor with a bare toe. Back and forth. Finally, the shaking stopped, and she swiped at her forehead, surprised by the sweat she found there.

She glanced at her watch. Time to get her act together and pick up speed. By the time the authorities responded to a passerby's 911 call, she needed to be on the road, heading to I-90 and Denver. Unless someone noticed the spray of blood before he landed in the water, they would be clueless that he'd been hit by a sniper until they dragged the body out of the water.

Inside ten minutes, she sauntered out of the fingerprint-cleaned apartment, pulling a rolling safari-chic suitcase behind her while clutching a large tote on her shoulder. The black linen pants, tailored black silk blouse, and auburn hair piled on top of her head shouted business trip.

The clouds in the blue sky had separated allowing the sun to peek between the breaks. Emergency vehicles zoomed by and their echoing sirens bounced off the buildings. They headed toward the boardwalk further down the street as a small crowd pointed at the water.

About the time she walked the block and half to the parking deck and threw the luggage into the trunk of her rental, her cell phone vibrated.

"Yes, sugar booger." She loved irritating the hell out of her handler.

Jason Kastler thought he was God's gift to women, and she took every opportunity to remind him his good looks were good only for one thing, to play a Romeo, an operative who seduced women for information. Whenever he walked into a room, women watched his every move as if he was a walking sex toy. He hated it when she reminded him that men stared too. With his sun-kissed blond hair, vivid blue eyes, and six-foot-six frame, he needed someone carving off his massive ego.

"Sugar booger? Christ, woman, can't you be the least bit respectful?" His growl revved her engine.

Good-looking *and* an orgasmic-inducing voice. It really was a shame. She could use him at the moment, though it would never happen. He liked to be the one in control. One thing about her, she always relished being the one on top.

"Respect is earned, doll. The job's done, and I'm heading to my next assignment's location. I already have a plan. Should take me a couple months to set up. I just need to scout the area," she said, ready to move on.

She tossed her purse to the passenger side and then slammed the driver's side door. Wasting no time, she had the cell phone plugged into the radio's speakers before cranking up the car. The state of Washington had a hands-free cell-phone law and ironically, considering her job, she followed all the traffic laws. The last thing she needed was to be pulled over for a minor infraction and be caught with the sniper rifle and numerous other weapons hidden on her person and in the rental.

"Change of plans . . . Theo wants you to return to the office. We have a ticket waiting for you at the airport." He was smiling. That light tone shouted his enjoyment in frustrating her.

She shut her eyes for a moment, anxiety curled in her stomach; he knew how much she hated flying. Not counting the up and down of the plane, the arranging for her arsenal to be shipped across country without her was a pain in the ass. The roar of the plane's engines didn't help the defenseless feeling.

Being ordered off an assignment by Theo was a bad sign. She avoided any face-to-face with him as much as possible. Hell, she'd worked hard for her freedom and for the last couple of years he rarely required her presence. So this meant something bad. Last time he'd made the demand, it had taken her a week to recover. He wasn't an easy man to please, and she no longer cared about satisfying his perversions. From the orphanage to the streets to Theo's control, there was always somebody waiting to use her, to take advantage of her. No more. She wouldn't go back to being that girl, begging for kindness and love. She squeezed her eyes closed, blocking out the images. No more. She dreaded being that needy little girl again. Tears welled up, threatening to spill.

Inhale. Exhale. Worrying wouldn't help. She struggled to regain her usual calm, steady façade. She took several more deep breaths, hoping it stopped the feeling of panic engulfing her. Pressure applied by her fingertips on the corner of her eyes pushed back the tears.

Olivia knew it was useless to argue. Operatives never won arguments against Circle handlers; disagreeing too much could be unhealthy. People had been known to disappear.

"Okay. Tell me which airline." She took another deep breath.

As he spit out the instructions, she turned the car toward a local UPS store and made her plans. Two hours later she boarded the plane, and all her weapons, including her gun, were on their way in several parts to her home in Georgia.

She settled into her first-class seat. After questioning the flight attendant, she learned the plane was full for the nonstop flight to Atlanta. She hated it when the seat next to her was used. No elbow room. Not that she was tall— a mere average height of five foot five—or big—roughly a hundred and twenty pounds. She didn't like strangers rubbing against her and often took the window seat, not for the view since she usually pulled down the shade, but so she could lean against the wall of the cabin, putting as much distance between her and the next seat. First-class seats were wide enough she could even pull her feet up beside her, but she always loved more room.

Pretending to stare out the window, she waited for the rest of the plane to load. One drawback to first class was having every man and woman file by, staring at those seated in the more expensive rows. Bloody hell, wouldn't they hurry up? She hated the closed-in feeling, the help-lessness, the sitting and waiting, the curious looks. Couldn't the freaking flight attendants help the tourists place their handhelds into the overhead compartment, so everyone would quit staring at her?

Closing her eyes for a few seconds, she mentally shook herself. What good was it to be short tempered, bitchy? Sure, crowds made her uncomfortable. Too many people pressing in, too many staring, guessing at what she did for a living. Was *murderer* written on her face, her clothes? She hated feeling like this. Add in her unexpected meet-ing with Theo, and she was certain she would go crazy.

When she was about to scream in frustration, the last person walked through. Whoever had the ticket for the seat next to hers hadn't arrived yet. Maybe she'd be lucky, and the seat would remain open. She rarely slept well the night before a hit, and it would be wonderful to stretch out.

The attendant pulled on the door and stopped when someone shouted from the walkway.

Olivia dug her nails into the armrests. Shouting always grated across her nerves. She always expected the worse. Had she screwed up and the local yokels or the big boys were after her? When she heard laughing, she realized whatever happened didn't involve the law. People rarely laughed when the authorities showed up.

"Sorry, my flight was late coming in. I almost didn't make it," a deep voice said.

She looked up. Oh, yes, this was what she needed. The man was a good six-one, possibly two, and the Armani suit showed off his wide shoulders perfectly.

He glanced toward the empty seat the attendant pointed to and then he looked at her. Those mysterious dark eyes punched the breath out of her. Set in an angular face with a small dimple in the chin, his eyes appeared almost amber, glowing with such a life force. His lips etched full but still masculine and begged to be licked. Oh, she liked the look of those lips. His nose was manly, not crooked from fighting but not a picture-perfect narrow one either.

Yeah, she liked the package in front of her. Now if she could remove the wrapping to see what lay underneath. Her body had been humming ever since she'd completed her mission. With those gorgeous eyes and his athletic body, she was more than willing to put him through his paces.

Maybe being stuck on a plane for five hours wouldn't

be so awful after all. This stranger she wouldn't mind touching or have him touching her. She reached out and introduced herself.

"Hi, I'm Olivia Roth."

"Joe Murphy." He held her hand for a second longer than necessary.

Her grin spread wider. Oh, yeah, this was going to be a whole lotta fun.

By the time the tires bounced and rolled on the tarmac at Hartsfield-Jackson Atlanta International Airport, Olivia already had Joe inviting her to dinner that evening. She felt primed and ready to give her new friend a good time. Since taking a stranger home with her was out of the question, she worked her wiles until he told her he was staying at the Marriott Marquis.

Then she remarked, "Isn't that a coincidence? I'm staying there too." She liked how his eyes glimmered when she said that. To him, she was a lone woman on a business trip, easy pickings for a one-night fling.

She ducked into the women's restroom at the airport and called reservations. The Marquis happened to be her favorite hotel, and they had room. When she stepped out, her gaze zeroed on Joe, leaning against the wall nearby; his eyes drank in every inch of her. Oh, yes, he was exactly what she needed.

They shared a cab, laughing and talking all the way to the hotel's check-in counter. As they walked toward the elevators, he mentioned wanting to visit one of the restaurants below street level. She smiled.

They would never make it. Though she detested

strangers brushing up against her, she didn't mind using one to release her tension, to forget what her job entailed. Her body using his throughout the night until he fell exhausted from her demands. And she had many demands.

Oh, yeah, a beautiful thing about being a phantom in the world of assassins, at the end of a mission she could enjoy a little downtime with a good-looking man. No one in the world knew what she did except her handler and Theo. She'd always been careful.

Leaning against the glass wall of the elevator, she stared as the lobby became smaller. A few more years and she'd kill Theo and disappear.

One corner of her mouth lifted as she looked from beneath her eyelashes at the man next to her. "I'll be waiting for you at seven-thirty." She felt like the spider waiting for the fly.

THE KNOCK CAME at seven-thirty on the dot. She liked how his amber eyes flared when she opened the door and waited with one hand on her hip. Her deep sigh brought that burning gaze to her breasts.

She'd dressed—better yet, undressed—specifically to push all thought of food from his mind. The lace-and-mesh deep ruby nightgown brought out the red highlights in her hair that flowed down her shoulders and made her skin appear a creamier white. Her full breasts tested the strength of the well-placed lace. Masterfully applied makeup emphasized the green of her eyes and the fullness of her dark red lips. Her bare toes peeked out beneath the edge of the gown and a fragile tinkle rang from her anklets, drawing his attention to her long, long legs as the slit at the side opened and closed with her every movement. She knew how to rein in a man's interest.

"I like a woman who knows her mind," he said in a low voice. His lips lifted, allowing only a flash of white teeth.

She stepped back and without hesitation he walked in.

"And I like a man who knows what he wants." She closed the door and leaned against it. With deft fingers, she locked it with a double click behind her.

"So no dinner." One dark eyebrow lifted.

"A man who picks up on the subtleties."

His body grazed hers as he moved closer and looked down, a grin flitted across his lips. "You look beautiful," he murmured. "Damn, you smell good." He inhaled, his eyes half closing as he brushed his thumb across her bottom lip. "You feel good too. Smooth, soft, hot."

Though she enjoyed being called beautiful, she knew better. Makeup and clothes could hide many defects and she was an expert at it. Yet she appreciated a man who would lie to get what he wanted, especially when she had done the same.

"For you. Hot for you." Her eyelids heavy, she leaned toward him.

He slid his hands down her arms. His gaze traveled a burning trail across her breasts. "Luscious."

"What a sweet talker." Her nimble fingers pulled at his tie and worked the knot loose until she had the silk material in her hand and tossed it over her shoulder. Then she started on his shirt.

His hand clasped her wrists before the second button made it through the hole.

"Wait," he said softly.

Her shoulders drooped. She wanted to forget about what she did today. Hell, to forget what she did for a living just for a few hours, to immerse all her thoughts in a hard male body. She took a deep sigh, causing her breasts to lift high enough to catch his attention again and remind him of what waited. Did he really want to chitchat? Patience wasn't one of her virtues.

She hoped to survive her nine a.m. meeting with Theo tomorrow and still go on assignment. And that could be anywhere, maybe Denver as she'd been originally scheduled, or even somewhere on the other side of the world, far, far away from Theo. What a lovely thought.

Anyway, the memories she made tonight would help her live through the time she spent with Theo or at the least make them bearable. She puckered her lips and looked up at him beneath her eyelashes, pretending to pout.

His heated look confirmed it worked.

"I have to taste you," he whispered, his lips brushed her cheek.

"Yes, sir," she teased. Before she could raise her face, he wrapped his arms around her and lifted her to his mouth. His tongue thrust against hers, tasting, stroking until her fingers dug into his back.

Whoa! The man knew how to kiss.

He lifted his head.

She liked how he tasted of whiskey and male heat. She wanted more. She tried to push him away but he grabbed her arms.

Who did he think he was? She preferred to be the one in control. Before she could show him how she felt about his manhandling, his lips fanned small bursts of hot air against hers as he said, "I couldn't resist a sample. I wanted to see if you're as spicy as you look."

Her skin heated and stretched so tight she thought she would burst from need. The man did have a way with words.

"And?" She rubbed her breasts against his hard chest.

"Another taste. Just once more." His mouth covered hers. He sucked in her bottom lip, and then his tongue dove into her mouth, taking what she offered, taking all he wanted. Whenever she tried to meet his tongue with her own, he thrust harder, opening her mouth wider, dominating the kiss and her response, showing her what he liked and giving her an idea of what else he expected from her. He decided on the rhythm of their kiss and she was surprised by how much she enjoyed letting him have the lead. Her body softened as he took her breath away.

His fingers gripped her butt and pressed his groin to hers. She leaned into him, letting him hold her weight, letting him have control. For a little bit.

Yet his kisses weren't enough. She wanted to see and touch every inch of him. Despite how wonderful his mouth felt against hers, she pinched his hard abdomen. Not enough to hurt. Just to draw his attention away from the kiss for a second.

"Bed?" she suggested with hope in her voice.

Her libido was on overdrive, and his kisses had been like gasoline on a smoking fire. That was her excuse for letting him get away with caveman tactics so far. She always liked being in control, but there was something about the way he held her, kissed her, touched her, made her want more. He dropped one wrist and held the other, leading her deeper into the room and toward the bed. She followed, taking in his broad shoulders and the way his hair met the back of his neck.

Happy that he was finally getting down to what she wanted, she purred.

She stepped in front of him and reached for his shirt. "Let's take some of your clothes off. You're overdressed in my opinion." She wanted to see what was hidden beneath his expensive suit.

Without a jacket, would his shoulders be as broad? Would he have defined muscles? Exotic tattoos? Scars? How far down did his tan go? How big and hard was he? She rubbed a hip against his groin. Oh, yes, he was hard. Men were easy to manipulate when sex was involved. And she was grateful.

He stopped in the middle of the room and looked at her. His face turned brooding as his eyes darkened and searched hers. The hot kisser from a few seconds ago had vanished. She wasn't sure what he was looking for, but she shivered in excitement. She liked being the center of his attention. The businessman had disappeared, and in his place was a dangerous and lethal man. Danger proved to be the strongest aphrodisiac. She knew that for a fact.

He looked ready to throw her on the floor and fuck her to death.

Death by sex? Now that would be the way to go. Lust slapped her libido into higher gear. She stepped back to recover her breath. At the same time, he clutched a handful of material at her shoulder and with a flick of his wrist tore the gown in two.

She gasped. "You son of a bitch!"

Chill bumps popped along her arms and across her chest. She wanted to believe the tingling was from the cool room. She knew better. She liked it rough, only that gown was her favorite and an original. With a fluid turn, she brought her leg up and he caught it, stopping her dead. Uncertain of what he was up to, she knew she needed to think fast, as only an expert in martial arts could stop her kick. Going with the momentum of her leg, she twisted her body midair and brought him down with her.

Instead of knocking him out or at least dazing him, he smoothly flipped her onto her back and seized her wrists, pulling them above her head. She kicked and bucked, trying to loosen his hold as he dragged her onto the bed. His knee jabbed her stomach, and she lost her breath. Before she could recover, something cold and hard clicked around her wrists. Handcuffs? He'd handcuffed her?

She blinked. "What the hell?"

"Shhh, Olivia. It will be over quick," he whispered in her ear.

With his knee still in her stomach, he held her cuffed wrists with one hand while the other unbuckled his belt.

"No you don't, asshole. There's no way I'll let that happen now," she said in a steady, angry voice. At the moment with her hands useless and his body pinning her down, her words were all hot air, but she wasn't about to give up.

He chuckled.

Heat flooded her cheeks. He actually thought she was funny. She bit the inside of her mouth. He may control her body, but she needed to rein in her emotions. She needed to think clearly about the situation and a way out.

"Uncuff me," she demanded.

He placed a finger on her lips and shook his head. "Don't raise your voice. I would hate it if you forced me to neutralize any unwelcome visitors."

She would never endanger an innocent, no matter what he thought. Too many variables could go wrong. First rule she learned in The Circle was You're on Your Own. Second rule, Protect the Innocent. She would handle this man and anything he dished out.

Wait. What did he say? Neutralize? Well, crap! No regular Joe off the streets talked like that. She needed out of this jam.

She peeked at the door.

And she would find a way to escape.

Whatever he did was nothing compared to what Theo could do to her.

Normally, she could protect herself as she had enough experience to keep the upper hand. But this guy was different from the others she'd picked up for sex. His toned body appeared to come from more than regular gym push-ups or daily runs. Few men could stop her like he had. Well, damn, she'd picked on the wrong one this time. Her recklessness had finally caught up with her, all because she wanted him so much. His soft voice and perfect manners had misled her.

She tilted her head and watched as he fastened the handcuffs to the bed frame with his belt. No hesitation. As if he did it every day. He shook her arms to test the hold. She was as good as stuck until he unlocked them or she found a way out. He acted as if she was merely a job. Was she?

"Who are you?" she asked.

He ignored her as his gaze traveled a heated path to her chest. He straddled her thighs, keeping her legs flat on the bed by using his weight. His hands rested on her collarbone for a second and then skimmed down, dipping and massaging areas as if he was searching or maybe testing for something. When his hands cupped her heaving breasts and squeezed, she groaned, hating how good his touch felt. Unable to resist, she arched her back, wanting more of his firm touch.

He dragged his callused palms over her sensitive nipples before slipping down her waist; taking his time as his eyes savored every inch of skin, his fingers continued with their examination.

He was examining her!

Was he looking for a locator maybe? Only another operative would think to look for one. The Circle embedded the device beneath the skin of those considered unpredictable. Luckily, she'd been deemed trustworthy, a small benefit from being Theo's former mistress. Then again, she never understood how they could use that as a gauge, considering how much she hated him.

An operative? Well, that explained a lot.

He lingered a moment at her hips, brushing his fingers across her shaved mons and then continued to her knees as he slid down and resting his weight on her feet. Her body bowed, trying to stay in contact with those strong, rough hands.

"Damn you. I don't have a locator on me."

Why not tell him the truth? He would realize it soon enough. But then again his hot gaze tempted her to lie and suggest a certain wet place to look.

She'd never been as turned on in her life. He moved onto the bed and jerked her legs apart, and she gasped. Open and wet, she throbbed in answer to his stare.

She kicked and he quickly clasped her ankles. His gaze returned to her mons. She wanted to tell him to go to hell, yet his hungry look sent heat skimming over her body. She liked his attention.

"And you would never lie to me," he quietly said.

She ignored his sarcasm. Deep inside her sex-hungry brain, his hands had slowed during the examination and wandered into areas less likely to hide a tracking device. The change told her he was rethinking his strategy. He wanted her despite his original intentions.

His fingers dipped and traced where she'd hoped he would venture. They retraced their path, returning to her breasts to pinch the tips. She gasped again. The electrifying tweak brought a flood of moistness between her legs. His fascination in her body was appreciated by her own.

She couldn't catch her breath, and she didn't want him to stop.

"Obviously you're a man who won't take my word for it." Unable to catch her breath, the words emerged nearly indistinguishable.

The handcuffs rattled and began to cut into her wrists. For heaven's sakes, they weren't even fur lined. He needed to learn no one treated her this way, even if it did turn her on. In the end, if she lived, he would learn not to mess with her in this way. She would stake *his* life on that fact.

She looked down and noticed the nice long bulge beneath his slacks. Good. She hated to believe he possessed more control over his body than she did.

Why wasn't he doing anything more? Tuned and ready, she wanted everything. He was pissing her off. What was he waiting for?

"Ah, come on. No need to play around," she said. Release one of her hands and he'd be waking up in the Chattahoochee River. "Let me go, and I promise you'll be surprised. I can take you places you've never been. . . ." She fell silent.

Stupidly she'd forgotten to arrange for a gun to be delivered to her room. For some reason she'd trusted him. See what she got for trusting a man?

If she'd been standing, she'd stomp her foot. Not a blink or look from him to indicate one word had registered. No longer did his hands probe and test but instead heated and rubbed to bring pleasure. His eyes followed every inch he touched. He mounded and then squeezed her breasts with the right pressure. She inhaled deeply.

Then panting, she groaned and arched into his touch again. Lord of Mercy, his hands felt so good. She wished she could control her reaction. The man wasn't human; not a drop of sweat touched his forehead, while she wanted . . . no . . . needed him badly. Her fingers dug into his belt as her body moved with each stroke. She hated feeling powerless.

He ignored her as his eyes remained on her heated body. Then he looked away for a second. When his gaze returned to her, she caught the conflict burning in their depths. He wasn't sure what to do next. Nice to know he was human after all.

Her own flaw of needing to be touched had brought her here. What about him? What did he really want?

Being angry and still aching for him drove her crazy. He thrilled her, excited her with the unexpected. Yet a part of her wanted to kill him.

He finally moved back. Seconds passed as his gaze remained on her. Like a bird caught in a cobra's stare, she stared back.

"Fuck it," he said in that deep, soft voice as he yanked off his jacket, tossing it to the other bed, and then rolled up his sleeves.

Her heartbeat picked up speed again. The sleek muscles on his arms showed how strong he was without being bulky. Just the way she liked it.

Then she noticed where his gaze lingered, radiating enough heat to scorch her, and she forgot everything. His stare centered on the vee of her legs. In a graceful move, he stretched out at the foot of the bed, and his arms wrapped around her legs before she realized what he intended. He pushed her heels almost to her buttocks, opening her wide, and then his mouth covered her.

Her back bowed off the mattress. His wicked tongue dove into her and licked the taut nub already throbbing for attention. His teeth scraped sensitive skin as he moaned with her. Two thick fingers jabbed into her wetness and worked in tandem with his tongue.

Each firm thrust of his fingers and tongue wound her body tighter. When he sucked on the knot of nerves, she gasped. There wasn't enough air in the room. She couldn't breathe. She'd never had a man go down on her like she was a honey jar, and he wanted every last drop. The sounds of his sucking and licking excited her as much as the act itself. Her hips rotated and thrust against his expert tongue and fingers. Her nipples hurt from being neglected, pointing high and stiff.

She squirmed, wishing she could free her hands to soothe the aching tips. As if he'd read her mind, a broad hand moved up and rolled and tugged one nipple and then the other, pushing her over the edge. She released a long high-pitched moan. Oh, hell, she'd never climaxed so fast or so hard. Limp, she opened her mouth and took gulps of air.

He moved up just enough to rest his cheek against her stomach, his stubble caused her muscles to flinch. His heartbeat throbbed against her thigh as his short breaths tickled her sensitive skin. Good. His treatment of her had pulled him in too.

She waited for him to take her. Though he'd done a

good job bringing her to the better side of satisfaction, she still felt a light humming in her body. She knew that meant she needed more.

Then his tongue glided from her belly button to her clit. Her hips reached for his mouth. Holy crap! It was as if she'd never climaxed. Her body hit second gear with the needle in the red. She wasn't sure if she could take another one like that. Wasn't he ready for the real deal?

He shoved himself off the bed and stood, shrugging his shoulders, pulling them back as he rotated his head. She heard joints popping. He stretched as if he'd finished a job and wanted to get the kinks out. Then he wiped her off his chin and looked her way with glittering eyes.

She groaned. Oh, shit, he was so damn hot.

He turned away from her.

Shock sent a shiver through her. Was he finished? She admitted his technique was different and a little constraining for her taste, but she wanted more. She'd gotten a glimpse of his groin. Hell, yeah, she hadn't been the only one wanting more. The impressive bulge against his trousers promised he had the right equipment needed to do the job. But first things first, he needed to let her go.

"Okay. You've had your fun. Uncuff me." She jingled the handcuffs.

He picked up his tie and slipped it into his jacket as he sat next to her on the bed.

"No. I don't think so. Not yet," he said in his usual soft soul-sucking voice.

Heat traveled down her torso and centered on the area now tender from his enthusiastic treatment. She liked how he didn't raise his voice. She'd liked it on the plane, though she'd thought it was from wanting to keep their polite conversation private. But she now realized it was normal for him, if she could call him normal in any sense of the word. What man didn't take what was freely offered?

"What do you want?" She narrowed her eyes at him.

When he kept quiet and lifted his chin, she kicked out. In a lightning quick move, he caught her ankles and then threw his torso across her knees. In seconds, he had her feet fastened together with his tie. A snap of his wrist brought a sheet off the other bed, and he wrapped it around her feet. If she'd planned to kick him again, the cushion would make it no more than a nudge.

"Enough already," she protested. "Who are you?"

He continued to ignore her. Her stomach tightened, and she swallowed to keep the fear down. Was he an operative out for revenge? Had she killed a friend or a brother of his? Which organization was he with? Blinded by lust, what had she missed?

"Who do you work for? Who are you?" she asked once again.

Those eerie amber eyes caught hers. "I'm your worst nightmare, Ms. Olivia St. Vincent."

A chill swept her body. He'd called her by her real name.

An Excerpt from

CIRCLE OF DANGER

ARTHUR RYKER SPRANG out of bed and immediately stood at attention, feet apart, his scarred hands in the "ready" position at waist level. One hand cupped by the other, restrained but prepared to kill. He shook his head and sighed. Just once he wanted to leave his bed like a regular person and not like a trained monkey.

"A bad dream?" a deep voice asked from the bedroom entrance. With one pierced black eyebrow lifted, Jack Drago leaned against the doorjamb.

Ignoring the question, Ryker walked naked into the bathroom. When he returned to grab some clothes out of the closet, Jack hadn't moved but his gaze had most likely inspected every inch of the room. There wasn't much to see. A king-sized bed sat in a corner while a mirror-less dresser was centered against one wall—no pictures or the usual bric-a-brac to give away the occupant's personality. Then again, maybe it did. Rather stark for a man who owned enough properties and businesses to keep his organization in the best covert weapons money could buy. He didn't care what Jack thought about his bedroom. Except for a few hours of sleep and a shower and shave, Ryker rarely spent time in the room.

"What do you want?" he asked, glaring at his second-in-command.

With cold blue eyes, Jack studied him, and then his gaze shifted away.

Ryker grunted. Not many people could deal with looking at the thick scars down the side of his body, but it was his blind eye that bothered most. White from the scar tissue damaged in a fire so many years ago, he normally hid it beneath a patch. But he'd be damned before he slept with one on. So if Jack decided to make a habit of waking him in the morning, he could fucking well get use to the sight. Considering the man had four visible piercings—and who knew how many hidden—along with tattoos covering one arm, he shouldn't have a problem with his scars. The man understood pain.

With sure, quick movements, he thrust his legs into jeans and yanked on a black T-shirt. After tugging on his boots, he strapped a small pistol at his ankle. With his patch in place, using his fingers he combed hair over the strap securing its position. Hell, he needed a haircut again. Maybe he'd shave his head like Jack. A simple enough solution. If only the rest of his problems could be so easily solved.

"She's in trouble," Jack said in an even tone as if his voice could defuse a bad situation.

Ryker's stomach and chest tightened as if he'd been hit. He knew who Jack referred to without adding a name. She happened to be part of why his life was so complicated.

"Did you hear me?" Jack straightened his stance.

"Yeah." Desire to break someone's neck raced through his body. "Where is she? What happened?"

With a sharp snap, he inserted a snub-nose into the shoulder holster hanging at his side and jerked on his leather jacket. He gritted his teeth for a few seconds to regain his composure. Then he took a deep breath, squared his shoulders, and exhaled.

"Last time Bryan heard from her, she'd entered the target's house in Chattanooga and was downloading information off a laptop. He lost communication with her." Jack quickly stepped out of the way for Ryker to move into the dark hallway. "They believe she's still in the house. If the Wizard sticks to his MO, we'll have about three hours before he takes her away or kills her."

Ryker wasted no time in reaching a massive room with mirrors from ceiling to floor. When the mansion was built in the eighteen hundreds, the room was used as a ballroom. It was empty now, except for a Steinway covered with a white sheet, and the high-sheen hardwood floor sounded hollow as he tramped across it. He used the room for one purpose only—to reach the stairwell hidden behind one of the mirrors.

"Took you long enough to spit it out." Ryker glanced at his second-in-command.

Jack remained quiet, staring straight ahead. Ryker didn't really expect an excuse. The man knew how he felt about that. No excuse for failure, especially when it came to protecting Marie.

Four months earlier, Ryker had moved The Circle

compound from the suburbs of Atlanta to an area near the Smoky Mountains. The mansion was situated in the middle of almost ten thousand acres, which included a large mountain filled with a network of tunnels and bunkers perfect to house the facility he needed. Last year, the final phase of the project was completed and now they were training new recruits in the underground Sector. The nearly fifteen square miles provided the privacy he needed. In a world filled with evil people, his covert organization of assassins came in handy.

Their footsteps echoed in the long, well-lit tunnel. A semi could pass through the passageway without scraping the side mirrors or the tips of muffler stacks.

"Who was her backup?" Ryker asked.

When a few seconds passed without an answer, Ryker stopped and faced Jack.

"They're handling it."

Ryker continued to stare.

His second-in-command sighed. "She went in without a backup."

Jaw clenched, Ryker strode to the iris scan next to a large metal door. A buzz sounded and he slammed the door against the inner wall.

The gripping pain in his belly grew and reminded him of the fear he lived with for years before he took over control of The Circle. She could not keep doing this to him. He refused to allow anything more to happen to her. She knew this and still didn't listen.

The noise level in the basketball court–sized room almost broke the sound barrier with printers running and people shouting or talking to those sitting next to them—or to others on the Internet or satellite phones—along with the clicking of keyboards. Each wall covered with large screens captured a different scene of people living their lives in various parts of the world. In the center of the room, faces bleached white by the monitors in front of them, the supervisors and handlers communicated with their operatives.

Ryker stopped in the middle of the bullpen, searching for his prey.

The balding, whipcord-thin Bryan Tilton stood over a handler shouting instructions and pointing at the screen. Maybe a sixth sense alerted Bryan. He looked up and his eyes widened.

Ryker charged toward him, ignoring the people ducking for cover behind partitions and beneath desks.

"You son of a bitch!"

His fist clipped Bryan on the chin, sending the man sliding across the floor. Desire to flatten the asshole's pointy nose almost overrode all of Ryker's control. Good thing Bryan remained sprawled out on the linoleum.

Standing over the man, Ryker opened and closed his fists. The temptation to punish him further for his stupidity warred with the fear of jabbing the cartilage of the idiot's nose into his brain.

"I swear, sir, I told her to wait until I could get backup in place, but she wouldn't listen." Bryan cupped his jaw and shifted it from side to side. "Two of our operatives are held up in a traffic accident about twenty-five miles from her last location."

"Last location?" Ryker gritted his teeth.

"The target's house, off Riverview Road." Bryan scooted back when Ryker took a step. The man's head bobbled on his skinny neck. "As soon as Phil and Harry reach it, they'll extract her."

Afraid he would crack the man's chicken neck, Ryker turned away and pointed at the nearest handler.

"You! Sal?" Mohawk trembling, the pale man nodded. Ryker said, "Tell Phil and Harry to call me on my cell as soon as they reach the house. Do not go inside! Jack and I will be there in twenty minutes. Have them wait for us." He turned back to Bryan. "Have the *Spirit* ready in five minutes." His helicopter could cover the miles quickly and land almost anywhere.

MARIE BELTANE STRUGGLED against the chains restraining her on a cot that reeked of sex and urine. She stifled a groan. No, no, no. Nausea travelled up her throat.

All the beams and pipes overhead felt like they were squeezing the air out of the room. Basements were never among her favorite rooms. The dampness and creepy-crawly things always gave her the willies.

She still couldn't believe she'd been caught. Bryan had sworn it would be an easy gig. Prior surveillance had revealed the man worked each evening at a massive bank of computers. Go in and download a flash drive–load of info and get out. The target always left his house at nine in the morning and didn't return until nine that evening. Breaking into the house when most people ate dinner in the surrounding homes had sounded so easy. Few would look out their windows as they settled down in front of their plates or televisions or both. Hours would pass before he returned home. But he came back early.

Oh, God, she'd screwed up big time!

He looked like a fourteen-year-old with his cartoon-themed T-shirt and his mop of hair, but she knew from his file he was between twenty-six and twenty-eight. During their surveillance, they never got a clear photograph of him. Whenever he entered or exited his house, he did so through his garage. His SUV had tinted windows, preventing anyone from seeing inside.

The man standing with his back to her had outmaneuvered every defensive tactic she'd been taught. He didn't fight like a kid. Jack was right. She needed to work harder on her moves. If she had, she wouldn't be in this predicament. The nerd had surprised her, taking her down with unexpected ease.

She refused to cry even though she couldn't stop the trembling in her body. Every inch ached from his battery of hits and kicks. For a scrawny man, he'd moved fast and hit hard.

Her head hurt from holding back tears. She'd hoped to never be in this position again, to be under someone's control. No matter how many times she reminded herself this was different from before, the horror of repeating history pushed her to keep her eyes open. Staying aware of her enemy helped to keep her calm.

"You're not very smart. I'm efficient in seven different types of martial arts." His stiff words failed to impress her. He moved, revealing what he held in his hand. The huge syringe with a shiny green substance in the barrel had a needle longer than her forefinger. "Just because I'm a geek doesn't mean I'm unacquainted with ways to defend myself."

Marie stared at the needle. The duct tape covering her mouth muffled her scream. Ever since he jumped her, she'd tried to see a way to escape, while keeping calm.

She tried to be brave. She kept telling herself, screaming would only be a waste of energy. Stifling the panic engulfing her would keep her alive.

"Wait until this stuff hits your bloodstream. I'm told the sensation is similar to that last second before reaching an orgasm. In other words, you'll do anything to get off." He chuckled and lifted her shirt. He tugged at the waistband of her jeans.

She flinched when the needle slid into the soft skin near her hip.

"Perfect for where I'm sending you." He jerked on the jeans until the tips of his fingers brushed her pubic hair. "White American women—especially petite, natural blondes like you—are quite popular in parts of the Middle East and Asia. Virgins are preferred but rare here unless we go much younger." He shrugged. "Then you get into AMBER Alerts and they're too much trouble. Anyway, bitches like you are plentiful and disposable."

He pulled harder at her jeans, taking her panties down. She froze. Her stomached churned with the thought of what he might do next. Then he pushed the needle deeper. The liquid burned, becoming hotter as he eased the plunger down. The pain took her mind off her fear for only a second. When she tried to move away, the rattling chains reminded her she wasn't going anywhere. Tears pooled at the corner of her eyes and she turned her head, refusing to let him see her cry.

"A formula created by . . . a fucking genius! Especially created to use on sneaky sluts like you. The Wizard is a god!" He laughed. The back of his hand grazed her cheek. "I know it stings, baby. Sorry . . . no. I'm not sorry. You have the look of an ice princess. I love seeing an uptight cunt like you suffer. You have no idea what you've gotten yourself into. This wonder drug is highly addictive and from what I'm told, it has long-lasting effects. You'll grow to love it."

The grin on his smooth face terrified her more than anything else he'd done. Her vision blurred. The man leaned over her, his brown eyes dark and merciless. She whimpered. Every cell of her body tingled.

"Do you feel it? It takes a little while to set in. The Wizard said it tingles all over and next, for a small time, you'll feel like you're floating on water. Then you'll get sleepy and then—*bam!*—you'll be like a bitch in heat." He cackled and thrust his groin several times against her leg and the side of the cot. He punched the air with his fist and did a little dance. When he turned his back, he reached for something on a table nearby. "Now let's see what all of you looks like."

Light glinted off the scalpel. He swiped at the air above

her as if he wielded a sword. No matter how brave she tried to be earlier, she couldn't stop her limbs from shaking harder and her stomach from twisting. She squealed behind the tape.

The sound of slicing material had her arching away from his touch. *Please don't cut me. Oh, please, God, help.* In seconds, he peeled away her clothes. He rubbed his groin and a lascivious grin marred his youthful face.

"Not bad, though I find the scars a shame, yet rather interesting. It looks like someone used a belt or whip on you. Have you been a bad girl?" He slid his hand down her bare thigh and over a long, thin white scar. "There are clients who would love to add to them."

She turned her head. Swallowing several times to keep from choking on vomit, she concentrated on the number of blocks in the basement wall. She could get through this. It wouldn't be the first time her body had been used. Eventually, she'd find a way out.

Just as she heard his zipper go down, a loud blast shook the walls. Dust sprinkled onto her face. She blinked her eyes. The room looked smoky, choked with plaster powder.

"What the hell?" The man ran toward the stairs as he struggled to pull up his pants. One foot on the bottom step, he stopped, staring at the door.

A smaller blast was followed by shouting and heavy footsteps running across the floor above. Whoever had come a-knocking were making their way through the house.

"Well, babe, you're on your own. I hope they appreciate the gift I'm leaving them." He laughed and disappeared beneath the stairs into a black void.

Her eyelids felt so heavy. Tingling travelling across her torso rushed down her legs and arms, and then a feeling of lightness and floating followed. A strong breeze brushed her naked body. Someone had found the basement. A wave of dizziness pushed her under and she closed her eyes, unable to lift them even when she felt someone fighting with the chains holding her down.

"Damn it, Marie. You better be alive," a deep voice growled.

She smiled. Deep inside, she knew he'd come for her.

About the Author

CARLA SWAFFORD lives in Alabama and is married to her high school sweetheart. A third-generation storyteller, she loves every shade of romance and the many paths taken to find that happily ever after.

Visit www.AuthorTracker.com for exclusive information on your favorite HarperCollins authors.

Give in to your impulses . . .
Read on for a sneak peek at five brand-new
e-book original tales of romance
from Avon Books.
Available now wherever e-books are sold.

NIGHTS OF STEEL
The Ether Chronicles
By Nico Rosso

ALICE'S WONDERLAND
By Allison Dobell

ONE FINE FIREMAN
A Bachelor Firemen Novella
By Jennifer Bernard

**THERE'S SOMETHING
ABOUT LADY MARY**

A SUMMERSBY TALE

By Sophie Barnes

THE SECRET LIFE OF LADY LUCINDA

A SUMMERSBY TALE

By Sophie Barnes

An Excerpt from

NIGHTS OF STEEL
The Ether Chronicles
by Nico Rosso

**Return to The Ether Chronicles, where
rival bounty hunters Anna Blue and Jack
Hawkins join forces to find a mysterious
fugitive, only to get so much more than they
bargained for. The skies above the American
West are about to get wilder than ever . . .**

Take his hand? Or walk down the broken stairs to chase a
cold trail. Anna's body was still buffeted by waves of sensation. The meal was an adventure she shared with Jack. Nearly
falling from the stairs, only to be brought close to his body,
had been a rush. The hissing of the lodge was the last bit of
danger, but it had passed.

The wet heat of that simple room was inviting. Her joints

and bones ached for comfort. Deeper down, she yearned for Jack. They'd been circling each other for years. The closer she got—hearing his voice, touching his skin, learning his history—the more the hunger increased. She didn't know where it would lead her, but she had to find out. All she had to do was take his hand.

Anna slid her palm against his. Curled her fingers around him. He held her hand, staring into her eyes. She'd thought she knew the man behind the legend and the metal and the guns, yet now she understood there were miles of territory within him she had yet to discover.

Their grips tightened. They drew closer. He leaned down to her. She pressed against his chest. In the sunlight, they kissed. Neither hid their hunger. She understood his need. His lips on hers were strong, devouring. And she understood her yearning. Probing forward with her tongue, she led him into her.

And it wasn't enough. Their first kiss could've taken them too far and she'd had to stop. Now, with Jack pressed against her, his arm wrapped around her shoulders and his lips against hers, too far seemed like the perfect place to go.

They pulled apart and, each still gripping the other's hand, walked back into the lodge room. Sheets of steam curled up the walls and filled the space, bringing out the scent of the redwood paneling. The room seemed alive, breathing with her.

Jack cracked a small smile. "This guy, Song, I like his style. Lot of inventors are drunk on tetrol. Half-baked ideas that don't work right." He held up his half-mechanical hand. "People wind up getting hurt."

"Song knows his business," she agreed. "So why the bounty?"

He leveled his gaze at her. It seemed the steam came from him, his intensity. "You want a cold trail or a hot bath?"

She took off her hat, holding his look and not backing down. "Hot. Bath."

Burbling invitingly like a secluded brook, the tub waited in the corner. The steam softened its edges and obscured the walls around it. As if the room went on forever.

With the toe of his boot, Jack swung the front door closed. Only the small lights in the ceiling glowed. Warm night clouds now surrounded her. A gentle storm. And Jack was the lightning. Still gripping her hand, he walked her toward the tub, chuckling a little to himself.

"My last bath was at a lonely little stage stop hotel in Camarillo."

The buckle on her gun belt was hot from the steam. "I'm overdue." She undid it and held the rig in her hand.

"I'm guessing you picked up Malone's trail sometime after the Sierras, so it's been a few hundred miles for you, too."

It took her a second to track her path backward. "Beatty, Nevada."

"Rough town." He let go of her hand so he could undo the straps and belts that held his own weapons.

She hung her gun belt on a wooden peg on the wall next to the tub. Easy to reach if she had to. "A little less rough after I left."

His pistols and quad shotgun took their place next to her weapons. He was unarmed. But still deadly. Broad shoulders, muscled arms and legs. Dark, blazing eyes. And the smallest smile.

They came together again, this time without the clang of gunmetal. The heat of the room had soaked through her clothes, bringing a light sweat across her skin. She felt every fold of fabric, and every ridge of his muscles. Her hands ran over the cords of his neck, pulling him to her mouth for another kiss.

Nerves yearned for sensation. Dust storms had chafed her flesh. Ice-cold rivers had woken her up, and she'd slept in the rain while waiting out a fugitive. She needed pleasure. And Jack was the only man strong enough to bring it to her.

An Excerpt from

ALICE'S WONDERLAND
by Allison Dobell

**When journalist and notorious womanizer
Flynn O'Grady publicly mocks Alice Mitchell's
erotic luxury goods website, the game is on. They
soon find themselves locked in a sensual battle
where Alice must step up the spice night after
night as, one by one, Flynn's defenses crumble.**

AN AVON RED NOVELLA

Flynn O'Grady had gone too far this time. It was bad enough
that Sydney Daily's resident male blogger continued to push
his low opinions about women into the community (he
seemed to have an ongoing problem with shoes and shopping), but this time he'd mentioned her business by name.

How dare he suggest she was a charlatan, promising the

world and delivering nothing! The women who came to Alice's Wonderland were discerning, educated, and thoroughly in charge of their sexuality. They loved to play and knew the value in paying for quality. They knew the difference between her beautiful artisan-made, hand-carved, silver-handled spanking paddle (of which she'd moved over 500 units this past financial year, she might add) and a $79.95 mass-produced Taiwanese purple plastic dildo from hihosilver.com.

Still, while Alice didn't agree with the raunch culture that prevailed at hihosilver, she'd defend (with one of their cheap dildos raised high) the right of any woman to take on a Tickler, Rabbit, or Climax Gem in the privacy of her own home. Where was it written that men had cornered the market for liking sex? O'Grady had clearly been under a rock for at least three decades.

Alice reached for the old-fashioned cream-and-gold telephone on her glass-topped desk and dialed. She knew what she needed to do to make a man like Flynn O'Grady understand where she was coming from. As the phone rang, she re-read the blog entry for the third time. Anger rose within her, but she pushed it down. She'd need her wits about her for this conversation.

"O'Grady."

Alice took a deep breath before she began. "Mr. O'Grady, we haven't met, but you seem to know all about me."

A brief silence on the other end.

"I see," came the answer. "Would you care to elaborate?" His voice was deep and husky around the edges. He should have been in radio, rather than in print.

"Alice Mitchell here. Purveyor of broken promises."

Another pause.

"Ms. Mitchell, how . . . delightful." His tone made it clear that it was anything but.

"I'm sure," said Alice, raising one eyebrow slightly, allowing her smile to warm her words. "You've had quite a lot to say about my business today. I was wondering if we could meet. I think I deserve the right of reply."

"I'm not sure what good that would do, Ms. Mitchell," he replied, smoothly. "You're more than welcome to respond via the comments section on my blog."

She'd had the feeling he'd try that.

"I think this is more . . . personal than that," Alice purred down the line. "I'd like to try to convince you of my . . . position." She stifled a laugh, enjoying every second of this. She could easily imagine him squirming in his chair right now.

The silence that followed inched toward uncomfortable.

"Er, right. Well, I don't have any time today, but I could see you on Wednesday," he said.

It was Monday. Give him all day Tuesday to plan his defenses? Not likely.

"It would be great if you could make it today," she said, a hint of steel entering her tone. "I'd hate to have to take this to your boss. I suspect there may be grounds for a defamation complaint, but I'm sure the two of us can work it out . . ." She left the idea dangling. The media was no place for job insecurity in the current climate, and she knew he was too smart not to know that. He needed to keep his boss happy.

"I could fit you in tonight, but it would need to be after 7.30," he said, his voice carefully controlled.

'"Perfect," she said, "I'll come to your office."

She put down the phone, allowing him no time to answer, then sat back in her chair. Now all she needed to do was select an item or two that would help her to convince Flynn he should change his mind.

Standing quickly, she prowled over to the open glass shelving that took up one wall of her domain. Although it might be of use in getting her point across, it was probably too soon for the geisha gag. She didn't know him well enough to bring out the tooled leather slave-style handcuffs. Wait a minute! She almost spanked herself with the paddle that Flynn O'Grady had derided for overlooking the obvious.

Moving to a small glass cabinet in the corner, she opened the top drawer and inspected the silken blindfolds. She picked up a scarlet one and held it, delicate and cool to the touch, in her hand.

Perfect.

An Excerpt from

ONE FINE FIREMAN

A BACHELOR FIREMEN NOVELLA

by Jennifer Bernard

**What happens when you mix together an
absolutely gorgeous fireman, a beautiful but
shy woman, her precocious kid, and
a very mischievous little dog? Find out in
Jennifer Bernard's sizzling hot *One Fine Fireman*.**

The door opened, and three firemen walked in. Maribel
nearly dropped the Lazy Morning Specials in table six's lap.
Goodness, they were like hand grenades of testosterone rolling in the door, sucking all the air out of the room. They wore
dark blue t-shirts tucked into their yellow firemen's pants, thick
suspenders holding up the trousers. They walked with rolling
strides, probably because of their big boots. Individually they
were handsome, but collectively they were devastating.

Maribel knew most of the San Gabriel firemen by name. The brown-haired one with eyes the color of a summer day was Ryan Blake. The big, bulky guy with the intimidating muscles was called Vader. She had no idea what his real name was, but apparently the nickname came from the way he loved to make spooky voices with his breathing apparatus. The third one trailed behind the others, and she couldn't make out his identity. Then Ryan took a step forward, revealing the man behind him. She sucked in a breath.

Kirk was back. For months she'd been wondering where he was and been too shy to ask. She'd worried that he'd transferred to another town, or decided to chuck it all and sail around the world. She'd been half afraid she'd never see him again. But here he was, in the flesh, just as mouthwatering as ever. Her face heated as she darted glance after glance at him, like a starving person just presented with prime rib. It was wrong, so wrong; she was engaged. But she couldn't help it. She had to see if everything about him was as she remembered.

His silvery gray-green eyes, the exact color of the sagebrush that grew in the hills around San Gabriel, hadn't changed, though he looked more tired than she remembered. His blond hair, which he'd cut drastically since she'd last seen him, picked up glints of sunshine through the plate glass window. His face looked thinner, maybe older, a little pale. But his mouth still had that secret humorous quirk. The rest of his face usually held a serious expression, but his mouth told a different story. It was as if he hid behind a quiet mask, but his mouth had chosen to rebel. Not especially tall, he had a powerful, quiet presence and a spectacular physique under his firefighter gear. She noticed that, unlike the others, he wore a long-sleeved shirt.

His fellow firefighters called him Thor. She could certainly see why. He looked like her idea of a Viking god, though she would imagine the God of Thunder would be more of a loudmouth. Kirk was not a big talker. He didn't say much, but when he spoke, people seemed to listen.

She certainly did, even though all he'd said to her was, "Black, no sugar," and "How much are those little Christmas ornaments?" referring to the beaded angels she made for sale during the holidays. It was embarrassing how much she relived those little moments afterward.

Tossing friendly smiles to the other customers, the three men strolled to the counter where she took the orders. They gathered around the menu board, though why they bothered, she didn't know. They always ordered the same thing. Firemen seemed to be creatures of habit. Or at least her firemen were.

An Excerpt from

THERE'S SOMETHING ABOUT LADY MARY

A SUMMERSBY TALE

by Sophie Barnes

When Mary Croyden inherits a title and a
large sum of money, she must rely on the help
of one man—Ryan Summersby. But Mary's
hobbies are not exactly proper, and Ryan is
starting to realize that this simple miss is
not at all what he expected . . . in the second
Summersby Tale from Sophie Barnes.

Mary stepped back. Had she really forgotten to introduce
herself? Was it possible that Ryan Summersby didn't know
who she really was? She suddenly dreaded having to tell him.
She'd enjoyed spending time with him, had even considered
the possibility of seeing him again, but once he knew her true

identity, he'd probably treat her no differently than all the other gentlemen had done—like a grand pile of treasure with which to pay off his debts and house his mistresses.

Squaring her shoulders and straightening her spine, she mustered all her courage and turned a serious gaze upon him. "My name is Mary Croyden, and I am the Marchioness of Steepleton."

Ryan's response was instantaneous. His mouth dropped open while his eyes widened in complete and utter disbelief. He stared at the slender woman who stood before him, doing her best to play the part of a peeress. Was it really possible that she was the very marchioness he'd been looking for when he'd stepped outside for some fresh air only half an hour earlier? The very same one that Percy had asked him to protect? She seemed much too young for such a title, too unpolished. It wasn't that he found her unattractive in any way, though he had thought her plain at first glance.

"What?" she asked, as she crossed her arms and cocked an eyebrow. "Not what you expected the infamous Marchioness of Steepleton to look like?"

"Not exactly, no," he admitted. "You are just not—"

"Not what? Not pretty enough? Not sophisticated enough? Or is it perhaps that the way in which I speak fails to equate with your ill-conceived notion of what a marchioness ought to sound like?" He had no chance to reply before she said, "Well, you do not exactly strike me as a stereotypical medical student either."

"And just what exactly would you know about that?" he asked, a little put out by her sudden verbal attack.

"Enough," she remarked in a rather clipped tone. "My

father was a skilled physician. I know the sort of man it takes to fill such a position, and you, my lord, do not fit the bill."

For the first time in his life, Ryan Summersby found himself at a complete loss for words. Not only could he not comprehend that this slip of a woman before him, appearing to be barely out of the schoolroom, was a peeress in her own right—not to mention a woman of extreme wealth. But that she was actually standing there, fearlessly scolding him . . . he knew that a sane person would be quite offended, and yet he couldn't help but be enthralled.

In addition, he'd also managed to glimpse a side of her that he very much doubted many people had ever seen. "You do not think too highly of yourself, do you?" He suddenly asked.

That brought her up short. "I have no idea what you could possibly mean by that," she told him defensively.

"Well, you assume that I do not believe you to be who you say you are. You think the reasoning behind my not believing you might have something to do with the way you look. Finally, you feel the need to assert yourself by finding fault with me—for which I must commend you, since I do not have very many faults at all."

"You arrogant . . ." The marchioness wisely clamped her mouth shut before uttering something that she would be bound to regret. Instead, she turned away and walked toward the French doors that led toward the ballroom. "Thank you for the dance, Mr. Summersby. I hope you enjoy the rest of your evening," she called over her shoulder in an obvious attempt at sounding dignified.

"May I call on you sometime?" he asked, ignoring her

abrupt dismissal of him as he thought of the task that Percy had given him. It really wouldn't do for him to muck things up so early in the game. And besides, he wasn't sure he'd ever met a woman who interested him more than Lady Steepleton did at that very moment. He had to admit that the woman had character.

She paused in the middle of her exit, turned slightly, and looked him dead in the eye. "You most certainly may not, Mr. Summersby." And before Ryan had a chance to dispute the matter, she had vanished back inside, the white cotton of her gown twirling about her feet.

An Excerpt from

THE SECRET LIFE OF LADY LUCINDA

A SUMMERSBY TALE

by Sophie Barnes

Lucy Blackwell throws caution to the wind when she tricks Lord William Summersby into a marriage of convenience. But she never counted on falling in love . . .

"Do you love her?" Miss Blackwell suddenly asked, her head tilted upward at a slight angle.

Lord, even her voice was delightful to listen to. And those imploring eyes of hers . . . No, he'd be damned if he'd allow her to ensnare him with her womanly charms. She'd practically made fools of both his sister and his father—she'd get no sympathy from him. Not now, not ever. "You and I are hardly well enough acquainted with one another for you to take such liberties in your questions, Miss Blackwell. My